INVISIBLE
MONSTERS

H. L. MACFARLANE

COPYRIGHT

To Kirsty, for all the shades of grey.

THE OUTDOOR SPORTS SOCIETY

POPPY

It was just three weeks until the Outdoor Sports Society's annual retreat and Poppy, the president, was screwed.

The retreat was always in mid-May. Any later and it interfered with final year student graduations; any earlier and, of course, most of the members would have to miss the trip for exams.

Poppy King had booked somewhere two months ago, thrilled that she had actually organised something well ahead of time. But, to her disbelief, the booking had fallen through just one week later due to a financial mishap that Poppy could do nothing about. Poppy hadn't told anyone about it, convinced that she could find a replacement retreat in plenty of time.

She *should* have confirmed a new location at least a month ago. She'd had all semester to look. And yet here Poppy was, desperately trying to find a place that could take in all thirty club members for two weeks that was close enough to mountains and rivers and caves for the club to explore to its heart's content. Within budget.

She was screwed.

Fred will have a fit when he finds out, Poppy thought ruefully. *Well, he'll be over the moon that I've messed up and then he'll have a fit.*

Frederick Sampson, vice-president of the Outdoor Sports Society, was everything that Poppy was not. Where she was reckless he was endlessly careful; where she was impulsive he had everything planned; where she was lazy he had been up since six in the morning getting ready for the day. Between the two of them they had headed up a fantastic year for their beloved club...but that didn't mean they hated each other any less.

"He's going to kill me..." Poppy muttered, laying her head on her arms in dismay. She was beginning to think that, finally, she would have to accept failure. This wasn't something she could half-ass and yet that was exactly what she'd tried to do. It seemed only fitting that her laziness took all year to come back around and punish her.

The problem with this was that Poppy King never failed. She knew this was what infuriated Fred about her most of all: she would put in the minimal amount of effort possible, or take the least amount of responsibility for her actions, and yet everything always turned out okay for Poppy. This extended into their shared love of high-adrenaline outdoor sports. Poppy was obsessed with free-climbing, free-diving, open water swimming...anything that didn't restrict her with ropes and wires and life jackets. This made her very popular with many members of the club, who revelled in her recklessness.

She never fell. She never hurt herself. Not once in her six years in the club had she so much as bruised an arm.

Fred, on the other hand, was the pinnacle of 'do it by the books'. He knew every safety protocol, every knot that could be tied, every way to get out of a hazardous situation. This in turn made *him* popular with many members of the club – particularly those who were just starting out – who liked how safe Fred made them feel.

Ultimately when the two of them had run for president last year the vote had been tight. But Poppy's enthusiastic and lively attitude had won over the majority and so, here she was, the president.

How she wished now that Fred had won.

Cassandra O'Donnell, the social convenor, would step in to help once a location had been chosen. She'd organise the schedule, come up with wickedly fun group events, purchase all the food and drink required for the two week trip as well as sort out any heath and safety issues that might eventually arise. And then there was Andrew Forbes, the treasurer, who was responsible for making sure Poppy didn't go over-budget.

Which won't be a problem if I never find a place.

Normally in situations like this Poppy would call her best friend Rachelle for help. But Rachelle Cole was the secretary for the society and had been friends with Fred almost as long as she'd been friends with Poppy. She'd feel obliged to rope Fred in to help.

Poppy would be damned before she let that happen.

For a moment she thought about asking Andrew to come to her aid but she knew something like this would overwhelm him. Though he had come on in leaps and bounds since Poppy had convinced the quiet, awkward boy he'd been four years ago into joining the society, Poppy knew that a last-minute attempt to find a retreat location would send him into a frenzied panic. She couldn't do that to him.

She considered Nate, too, another member of the club

whom Poppy was close to, but he was just as irresponsible as she was. He would never be able to help her out in time; he would only serve to distract her.

A happy distraction, though, Poppy thought longingly as she blew hair out of her face. Nate Richards and Poppy had been flirting all year, occasionally ending up in bed together after alcohol-fuelled club socials. The two of them had bleached their hair and then dyed it silver to win a bet, which ended up looking great against Nate's dark skin but Poppy had been certain washed her out. She had since dyed her hair back to its original ash-brown colour, though she had kept a streak of silver at the front. Just for Nate. He joked that she looked like a superhero now, which suited Poppy just fine.

She sighed. It seemed ridiculous to her but Poppy almost wished she had coursework to distract her from her fruitless, desperate quest for an appropriately-priced retreat. But she had reached the end of her environmental ecology Masters degree a few months prior; all that was left now was to graduate.

With Fred. Ugh.

For Fred and Poppy had known each other ever since they started their undergraduate degrees as fresh-faced eighteen-year-olds. When they ended up studying the exact same subjects – and then the same Masters course – Poppy decided that Fred had been placed on Earth as some kind of desperate measure by the universe to keep her in check. He was in all her classes. Her tutorials. Her club. Her social circles.

And yet they could not stand each other. Not once over the past five and a half years had they reached any kind of friendly compromise, aside from the front they put up to run the society together. Though Poppy didn't want to say goodbye to her time at the club she was more than eager to move on to the next section of her life, which she was determined to ensure Frederick Sampson would not be a part of.

But even that thought caused Poppy to wince. She had no

idea what she wanted to do after she graduated, after all. It wasn't as if she was especially keen to use her degree for anything useful: she was more than tempted to jet off to Australia or New Zealand and learn how to scuba-dive. But right now her life plans extended only as far as summer, when Poppy would move back to her parents' house for a few months whilst she worked out what to do next.

For what felt like the hundredth time in the past fifteen minutes she refreshed her emails for want of anything productive to do. Poppy perked up in interest when a new email appeared, with the heading 'Outdoor Sports Facility – Opening Month Deals'. She checked the email address it had been sent from; it didn't look like spam. Curiosity (and panic at her dire situation) having overcome her, Poppy opened the email.

It read:

Dear Poppy King,

The Highlands Adrenaline Sports Facility is due to open next month. Due to some unfortunate setbacks the group we had booked in for the first two weeks have had to cancel, leaving the centre available for hire during the middle-to-end of May. We are keen to replace the cancellation with another group in order to get the word out about the state-of-the-art facility that my team has worked so hard to create.

To that end, I would be willing to offer a marked discount on the cost of hiring the facility if your university society would be open to the possibility of making use of the centre and, if all goes well, help to spread the word to similar societies about us. The facility is fully catered and residential; all expenses are included in the price of hiring the centre.

If this is something you would be interested in then I would love to hear from you!

Kind Regards,

Dorian Kapros

Facility Manager

Poppy had to read the email through several times before the words finally sank in. She got plenty of emails about outdoor centres to her presidential email, of course, but most of them were far too expensive or hopelessly far away or run down beyond repair. As a result, the offer this Dorian Kapros had put on the table seemed too good to be true.

And yet...

Pulling out her phone, Poppy typed in the contact number the centre manager had provided with his email. No doubt the centre – if it was brand new – would be far too expensive to hire even *with* a discount, but Poppy would never know if she didn't ask.

Poppy's heart was beating far too quickly as she waited for the call to go through, making her weirdly aware of her blood pumping around her entire body. It was an uncomfortable, alien feeling; she didn't like it at all.

When the other end of the line clicked – signalling the call had been accepted – Poppy jumped in shock and just barely managed to avoid knocking over the tepid coffee by her right hand that she'd completely forgotten existed. It surprised the students all around her who were studying for exams. They collectively glared at her, so Poppy fled from her desk to take the call in the corridor.

"Hello, this is Poppy King!" she said, slightly too quickly and too loudly. Her voice reverberated in the empty corridor, causing her to cringe. "I just got an email through about your centre and I had a few—"

A low, musical laugh cut right through Poppy's rushed sentence and she stopped talking, entranced by the sound. "I never expected to hear from you within five minutes of sending that email, Miss King," the laughing voice said. "I'm glad you called."

"Is this – is this Mr Kapros?" Poppy asked, stammering a little despite herself. The man's voice was potentially one of the most enticing things she had ever heard, which only caused her heart to beat faster.

"Call me Dorian. Now, Poppy – can I call you Poppy?"

It took Poppy a beat too long to reply. "Of course!" she eventually let out, feeling entirely like a fifteen-year-old idiot instead of a twenty-four-year-old woman who should know better than to crush on a literal disembodied voice.

Dorian laughed again. "I'm assuming you're calling because you think my offer must come with some kind of catch?"

Poppy nodded for nobody but herself to see. "I've never heard of your centre before, Mr – Dorian – but since it's so new I'm going to guess that even with a discount it's likely too expensive for my club."

"On the contrary," he said, "I'd much prefer to have a group in for our opening weeks even at a greatly reduced price than have nobody at all. I'm happy to work with whatever budget you have."

"Are you...serious?"

"Absolutely. I've sent you through a full brochure of the centre for you to peruse. My apologies; I should have attached it to my original email. Everything has just been a bit chaotic up here, what with the cancellation and all."

Poppy held a hand to her mouth for a moment, heart hammering in excitement at Dorian's offer. "You definitely have space for thirty overly-loud, excitable university students?" she asked, just in case the man needed some sense knocked into him about Glasgow's most manic sports society. *Could this beautiful-sounding stranger really be the solution to all my problems?* she thought, desperate to believe that he was.

It sounded too good to be true.

"Of course, Poppy," Dorian reassured her. "We're trying to target ourselves towards larger groups so your club is a perfect fit. I'll be on hand for the entirety of your stay – along with some instructors who know the surrounding terrain really well – but other than that your group is free to do whatever they wish."

"Um...is alcohol permitted?" Poppy asked, feeling as if she was looking a gift horse in the mouth. But she knew more than a few members of the club who would kill her if she chose a dry retreat venue.

A snort of amusement. Poppy's face reddened at the sound. "Just so long as you don't try and use the indoor climbing equipment whilst inebriated," Dorian said, "then I encourage it."

Her eyes widened. "You have indoor climbing stuff? So you're not just an outdoor centre?"

"See, this was why I should have sent you the brochure first," he replied, entirely apologetic. "We have a fully-equipped indoor climbing suite, along with both indoor and outdoor pools, a gym and a sauna. And a couple of hot tubs."

"And you're *sure* you want my club anywhere near this place?"

Dorian laughed once more; Poppy melted a little. She was past caring about how stupid she felt. "Honestly, I'm the one who asked you to hire the place. I'm not going to suddenly change my mind."

"So this would be the two weeks beginning the thirteenth of May?"

"Yes."

Poppy grinned. "Then I guess we have a deal."

"Excellent!" Dorian exclaimed, sounding so genuine in his excitement that Poppy found herself liking the man more and more with every word his voice uttered. "I'll send through a contract and we can get the paperwork sorted as soon as possible. Thank you for responding so quickly, Poppy; I can't tell you how happy I am that a club with as many promising athletes as yours has will be using my facility."

Poppy frowned at her phone, taking a second or two to process what Dorian had said. "You...know about us?"

"I saw a few articles about you guys in a magazine I read," Dorian admitted. "I'd been meaning to email your club for a while, if I'm honest. Secretly I'm rather pleased the other group cancelled."

Oh, this guy is smooth, Poppy thought. *Every word out of his mouth is pure flattery. I could get used to this.*

"I guess we have a reputation to uphold, then," she said, struggling to keep her voice even in the face of her rapid heartbeat.

"No pressure whatsoever!" Dorian chuckled. There was the smallest of pauses before he added, "I look forward to meeting you, Poppy King."

She mouthed along to his words as he said them, her body positively buzzing with anticipation. "The same to you, Dorian," she replied, hopelessly and effortlessly sincere, before hanging up the call with a twinge of regret that it had barely lasted five minutes.

Looking through the brochure Dorian had dutifully sent her Poppy couldn't believe her eyes at how beautiful the Highlands sports facility was. When he'd said state of the art he'd meant it. And Casey would go *wild* when she saw the hot tubs. Furthermore, now that Poppy had been saved by some kind of divine intervention she wouldn't have to admit defeat to Fred and ask him to save her ass.

Poppy couldn't *wait* to rub it in.

Just as soon as she Internet-stalked the man with the sexiest voice she'd ever heard in her entire life, of course.

Dorian Kapros

POPPY

There was nothing like a tipsy group of university students trapped on a four-hour-long bus ride to make even Poppy wish they'd miraculously arrive at the sports centre within the next five minutes. Too many students needed a bathroom break: they were loud and raucous and restless. Though she was tipsy, too, Poppy longed for nothing more than to look out the window and see that they'd arrived at their destination.

She couldn't wait to meet Dorian Kapros.

Poppy's Internet search had brought up surprisingly little about him, having only unearthed Dorian's name in relation to the upcoming opening of his facility and some other – seemingly unrelated – articles which mentioned him. Something about him screamed *secretly very wealthy,* though Poppy wasn't sure what. Perhaps it was her over-active imagination.

When the bus finally parked in a little town nestled deep in the Highlands Poppy sighed in relief. But when she hopped off the bus she looked around, confused. "Where the hell is the sports centre?" she wondered aloud, for nobody to hear in particular.

"Hey there!" a voice called out. A man appeared in front of them, smiling amiably. "The name's Patrick," he said as he shook Poppy's hand. "Are you the university club heading up to Kapros' new centre?"

Poppy nodded as Rachelle got off the bus and landed on the gravelled pavement beside her. "I'm Poppy, the president of the Glasgow Outdoor Sports Society. Do you know where we go from here?"

"If you unload the bus and follow me that would be great. You still have a final leg of the journey, you see."

Poppy raised a curious, suspicious eyebrow when Rachelle caught her eye. Her best friend laughed; of course a retreat that Poppy herself had organised wasn't going to be straightforward.

"If you insist, Patrick," Poppy said. "Lead the way."

"This Patrick guy's pretty hot," Casey murmured a few seconds later when she caught up with them, an appraising expression on her face as she watched Patrick direct them towards their final mode of transport. "In a Highlands and Islands kind of way, but hot nonetheless."

"What does that even mean?" Rachelle asked, dubious but amused.

Cassandra hailed from a tiny village in Northern Ireland of which Poppy couldn't even remember the name. For some reason, though, she understood exactly what Casey meant. Patrick was dark-haired and rugged, as if the violent winds that battered the north of Scotland had shaped him themselves. He looked as if he could easily hoist any of the young women in the society up and over his shoulders without so much as breaking a sweat.

"He's...charming," Casey said, waving a hand about meaninglessly. "You wouldn't get it, Rachelle. You're a city girl through-and-through."

"Coming from the girl who shed all but her accent when she moved to said city!"

Casey pouted her perfectly painted lips. "Boys like my accent; what can I say?"

"If we're staying around here for two weeks then I'm sure you can try it on with him, Casey," Poppy said, rolling her eyes, "but let's get ourselves settled in first. I'm pretty certain some of the altogether drunker members of the club are desperate to get to a bathroom."

Rachelle frowned. "There was a toilet on the coach."

"Which was blocked about an hour into the journey."

"Oh, ew. I didn't need that mental image."

The three of them laughed away the comment when Fred joined them. Poppy resisted the very strong urge to punch him in the face.

"King, what's going on?" he asked, frowning. He was always frowning at Poppy. "Seems like this guy is leading us to a river."

"A loch."

"And that somehow makes this better?"

Poppy shrugged. "May as well know the country you live in, Sampson."

"Can you guys just stop arguing for one minute?" Rachelle sighed.

But Casey seemed to agree with Fred. "There wasn't any mention of us needing more than the bus to get to this place, Poppy. If they're expecting us to hire a boat or something...I think Andrew might have a breakdown."

"Relax, guys," Patrick called over to the group, simultaneously making them aware of the fact that he'd listened in to their entire discussion. "The final leg of the journey is included in the price of hiring the centre...alcohol and all."

Casey perked up immediately. "Alcohol?"

Patrick grinned as he brought them over to a small ferry – or large boat, depending on how one looked at it. "This is my baby, the *Cassandra*."

"Fuck off, no it's not."

Poppy burst out laughing at Casey's remark – in particular at Patrick's obvious confusion. "Her name's Cassandra," she explained for his benefit, pointing at the young woman in question with a thumb.

He chuckled; it was a pleasant sound. "Well let's pretend I named it after you, then. Though such a beautiful lass deserves to have a ship named after her, not my tiny old boat."

Casey seemed to glow at the compliment. She gave the man her most radiant smile. "Maybe you can show me about the *Cassandra* when everyone's on board?"

"It'd be my pleasure."

Fred and Rachelle watched the exchange with blank faces that entirely hid their bemusement. Casey enjoyed flirting more than anyone they knew: the ease with which she fell into the lap of a handsome man was ridiculous.

Poppy kept up a responsible presidential act until everyone was on board the boat, most of whom immediately entered the glass-fronted passenger cabin. Poppy followed suit, whistling in admiration when she spied a long, varnished, wooden bar. Patrick leapt over it and pulled out a few miscellaneous bottles of spirits, then motioned Poppy over.

"Feel free to help yourselves to anything from the bar – Dorian's treat," he said when Poppy reached his side. Then he winked at her.

Poppy blushed furiously despite herself. "H-how long will

the journey take to the centre?" she asked, stammering slightly as she thought of the mysterious Dorian she was so close to finally meeting. "We didn't know you could only get there by boat."

"About thirty minutes. Technically you can drive there but the road's far too narrow and winding to get a bus along. A boat is much safer. And way more fun."

Poppy smiled. "I think most of us would agree with that sentiment."

"If you can keep watch over your group I'll get the engine started and we can head off. Oh, and" – he raised his voice so the whole group could hear – "there are a couple of toilets just off the corridor to your right. I'm sure a few of you need them."

There was an immediate rush of about six or seven students who bolted in the direction Patrick had pointed to, causing a smattering of laughter to fill the room.

Casey all but ran up to the bar after Patrick left to start up the boat. "Quick, Poppy," she urged, "make me a drink so I can chase after him."

"Why don't you make it yourself?"

"But you're the barman."

"Do I look like a man?"

"Okay, the bar *lady*."

"Move over, Morph, I'll do it."

They both turned; it was Nate, his silver hair shining brilliantly under the lights of the cabin.

Poppy grimaced at the nickname. "You really couldn't think of a better superhero name for me, Nate?"

"I've legitimately never seen you in pain. And morphine comes from poppies. What else would you expect me to call you?"

"My real name, maybe?"

"Never, Morph," he said, resolute, ruffling the silver streak in Poppy's hair before taking her place behind the bar. "Vodka cranberry for you, Casey?"

"Oh, I do enjoy that you know my drink order."

Poppy left Nate to play barman whilst she searched the cabin for Andrew, who had stayed characteristically quiet and, therefore, unseen for most of the journey. It was his first time away from home for longer than two consecutive days; Poppy wanted to keep an eye on him to make sure everything was okay.

She eventually located him sitting with Fred at a small, circular table, so she hung back for a minute or two knowing that Fred was doing exactly what she herself had planned on doing. Though Poppy couldn't stand the guy he was just as dutiful as she was in making sure Andrew felt safe and comfortable.

When Fred caught her eye he took the hint and left, allowing Poppy to take his place.

"Howdy, partner," she joked, looking around the room before settling her eyes on Andrew. "Kinda looks like a cowboy tavern in here, don't you think? What with all the wood and the little tables and the deer heads on the wall."

Andrew's eyes shifted to take in the animal heads mounted above the bar. "I don't like them."

"Do you want to go stand out on deck, then? I'll go with you."

Andrew was visibly relieved by the prospect. "Please."

And so the two of them vacated the busy cabin, making their way to the prow of the boat just as the engine came to life and they began to leave the jetty. Poppy saw a few of the townspeople watching the boat leave from shop windows, their faces warped by the glass. She wasn't sure if she was imagining it but it very much seemed as if they were happy the boat was gone.

I suppose they don't want a bunch of rowdy university students around to make a load of noise, she concluded. *If I lived here I wouldn't want a club like this one around to bother me, either.* Poppy resisted the urge to shudder at the very thought of living in a town so small. She would die of boredom if she was forced to live somewhere this quiet and unassuming.

Although the location isn't too bad...

This was an understatement. With the hills and mountains surrounding the remote town – as well as the loch and rivers and streams that ran into it – the place was a haven for an overly-energetic, outdoor-loving person like Poppy. She always found it funny that she could be so active and so lazy at the same time...as had her parents, who'd spent much of her teenage years struggling to get Poppy out of bed for school in the morning. That task had fallen to Rachelle once they'd become flat mates at university, though Rachelle quickly learned that there was little joy to be had from forcing Poppy King to get up in the morning.

Realising that her mind had already wandered instead of paying attention to what was going on in front of her Poppy glanced at Andrew and asked, "Feel any better?"

He nodded.

"I can't believe your parents actually let you come on the retreat, Andrew," she said, encouraging him to talk about the tricky subject. "They almost lost their heads when you wanted to do that overnight kayaking trip last year!"

Andrew shrugged. "They're not happy about it. But I told them: I'm an adult and I have to move away from home eventually. If I can't last a two week trip away from them then I'll never be able to live alone."

Poppy smiled gently. Andrew's parents only wanted to protect him, she knew, but lately he'd been doing so well that people meeting him for the first time generally didn't catch on to the fact he wasn't neurotypical. Poppy was deeply, fiercely proud of Andrew for coming out of his shell: when he'd come along to a taster session for the Outdoor Sports Society four years ago he'd barely been able to speak three words strung together to her.

"I'm glad they trusted you enough to go," she said. "And you're right; it's something you need to do to be independent. And besides that – this trip is going to be *fun*. So have fun and don't worry about anything except the next fourteen days."

Andrew sighed at this. "I don't want to graduate. I don't know what to do after summer."

"You and me both," Poppy replied, patting him on the shoulder for a brief second as a gesture of solidarity. "I'm still tempted to fly off to New Zealand and spend my life snorkeling and bouldering and ignoring any and all adult responsibilities. Wanna join?"

Andrew's soft brown eyes lit up with genuine excitement at the prospect. "Can I?"

"If you promise I won't be your babysitter then sure."

He nodded gravely. "I'll work hard so that you don't have to be one."

"The point of the whole thing is to *not* work hard, Andrew," she said, rolling her eyes. "The point is to have fun, instead."

But Andrew seemed confused by this. "Don't we have to work hard so that we can then have fun? If we have fun all the time then won't it all seem less fun?"

"That's annoyingly logical. I don't like it. Do you want a drink?"

He shook his head. "I prefer it out here. I think I might ask

Patrick what kind of engine he's running. I hope it's a Kelvin."

"Aren't those the super old-school ones? The rare ones?"

"Yes!" Andrew seemed delighted that Poppy remembered. He was obsessed with engines. She didn't get it, of course, but he talked about them so enthusiastically that Poppy had learned far more about them than she probably ever needed to know.

At least if engines happen to come up in a pub quiz I'll sail through the questions, she thought, amused.

"It doesn't seem likely that Patrick'll have one of those Kelvin engines if they're rare, Andrew," Poppy told him in order to school his expectations.

"I know. But I'd be happy if he showed me whatever one he uses, anyway."

"Then why don't you go ask him right now?"

He grimaced. "Casey is with him. Won't it be socially unacceptable if I interrupt them?"

"Ah, I suppose so."

When Andrew first joined the club Poppy had taken him under her wing and taught him exactly what was 'socially acceptable' and what was not. Though her intentions had been pure, Fred was furious that Poppy taught Andrew *her* version of what he should and shouldn't do...because some of it was wildly off the mark. But Andrew had taken her lessons to heart, flawed as they were. And at the very least what Poppy taught him about interrupting two people having a private conversation was generally correct.

"I'll leave you here, then, if that's okay," she said. "I think I might wrangle a vodka or two out of the free bar we have."

Andrew gave her a small, genuine smile. "Okay. See you later, Poppy."

"You'll see me in literally fifteen minutes when we dock the boat."

"I know. That's what I meant by *later*."

Shaking her head at Andrew's infallible logic, Poppy re-entered the cabin only to see Nate showing off his barman skills to the rest of the club. He was throwing bottles into the air only to catch them behind his back or between his legs; Poppy couldn't help but laugh.

"Tell me, Nate," she called out over the ruckus, "how many drinks have you actually managed to make serving people like that?"

He flashed a grin her way. "Two, probably. People are just serving themselves."

It was true – little groups of three or four had simply taken bottles from behind the bar to share amongst themselves. Poppy had to wonder whether they'd taken the 'drinks on Dorian' a little too far.

Thinking about the man with the beautiful voice again caused Poppy's stomach to lurch. She didn't understand why she'd found it so appealing. *It's just a bloody voice,* she reasoned, grabbing the bottle of vodka out of Nate's hand and pouring herself a shot. *Grow up, Poppy.* She poured another.

The final ten minutes of the journey were over before Poppy knew it, and when her stomach reeled again it wasn't because of nerves but due to the boat stopping.

"Alright, guys," she called out, just as Fred did the same. They glared at each other, neither one wishing to relent to the other. But then Poppy decided to let Fred have this one simply so she could leave the boat first. There was someone she was dying to meet, after all.

And so Poppy ran out of the cabin despite the fact Fred's narrowed eyes followed her the entire way. Even Rachelle and Nate watched her bolt out of the door in surprise. When she got outside she saw Andrew very passionately talking to Patrick about engines, Casey trudging along looking thoroughly put out by his interruption.

Clearly he couldn't wait until it was 'socially acceptable' anymore, Poppy mused, entirely ignoring Patrick's warnings to wait until the boat was properly tied up and the gangway put down before leaping over the side of the boat. She nimbly landed on the wooden planks of the jetty without so much as a glance back at the people leaving the cabin.

Because Poppy had spotted him.

The man with the beautiful voice.

The man who had completely and utterly saved her skin with a single email.

Dorian.

POPPY KING

POPPY

DORIAN KAPROS SOMEHOW, INEXPLICABLY, LOOKED EXACTLY the way Poppy had imagined he'd look. He had a lean-muscled frame that was typical of rock climbers and swimmers, obvious even under the long-sleeved T-shirt and dark trousers he was wearing. His face and forearms were tanned, suggesting he spent many long hours in the sun.

Walnut-brown, wavy hair was swept back from Dorian's face in a perfectly haphazard fashion that looked effortless. It was the kind of hairstyling she'd seen guys at university desperately try and fail to emulate with bottles and bottles of product.

Dorian's blue eyes were framed by dark eyelashes and thick brows, and sparse stubble lay along his jawline. It looked like his nose may have been broken once or twice in the past.

Oh fuck, Poppy thought as she stared unabashedly at the man. *I'm staring. I'm staring. Stop staring.*

He gave her a dazzling smile. "Nice landing, Poppy King." Poppy thought his voice sounded even more musical in person; her ears began to itch, and she took an instinctive step closer to the man. His smile widened. "Though you might let Patrick tie up the boat next time."

"You – how do you know I'm me?" Poppy asked, feeling like she wanted to punch herself at how stupidly she'd worded the question.

"I had a hunch. I'm not wrong, am I?"

She shook her head. "Not wrong. I'm Poppy. And you're Dorian."

It wasn't a question. Poppy hadn't even needed to hear Dorian speak to confirm that it was him.

He chuckled at the statement. "Yes, I'm me. Did you have a pleasant journey?"

"The bus not so much," she admitted. "The boat, absolutely. Um...thanks for all the alcohol."

He quirked an eyebrow. "Are you drunk?"

"Not at all," Poppy lied smoothly. In truth she was somewhere past tipsy, thanks to her bus drinking and the shots of vodka on the boat. But she didn't want Dorian's first impression of the president of the Outdoor Sports Society to be that she couldn't even last a four-hour-long journey sober.

Dorian smiled as if he knew Poppy might be lying but didn't care. "I guess we should wait for everyone to get off the boat before I show you around the facility. Where are your bags?"

Poppy stared at him blankly then down at herself. She'd been in such a rush to meet him that she'd left all of her belongings in the cabin with Rachelle. Blushing furiously she tried to laugh it off. "I may have left them with a friend. I'll be right back."

"You can't just leave all your shit with Rachelle, King!" Fred hollered. Poppy turned; Fred was walking towards her with

Rachelle, who was struggling with her own bags as well as Poppy's.

She rushed forward to take her belongings from her, smiling apologetically. "Sorry, Rachelle. I never meant to leave you with them."

"How many times have we heard that before?" Fred muttered, glowering at Poppy. Then he looked past her, saw Dorian, and straightened up immediately. "You must be Mr Kapros," he said, voice formal as he moved forward to shake the man's hand. "I'm Fred Sampson, the vice-president of the Glasgow Outdoor Sports Society."

Dorian smiled politely. "Pleasure to meet you. Is that everyone off the boat now?"

Poppy glanced behind her. Patrick was leading up the rear, Andrew and Casey still in tow.

"Just about, yeah," she said, shuffling her bags onto her shoulder as she moved to stand even closer to Dorian's side. When Casey and Andrew reached them Poppy saw Casey's eyes light up at the sight of Dorian.

Jesus Christ, she thought, suppressing an urge to sigh. *Haven't you just spent the last half an hour flirting with the guy beside you? Leave Dorian alone.*

In truth Poppy had no right to be so possessive of the man. She wasn't even sure she *wanted* to try and charm Dorian into bed with her, thinking that perhaps admiring him from a distance would make for a decidedly less complicated two weeks staying at his facility. But that didn't mean she would allow Casey to throw herself at him, either.

Dorian scanned over the entire group as Patrick walked over to join him. "There were thirty of you in total, right? I'm counting thirty."

Fred nodded. "That's correct."

"Great. Let's head inside, then. Are you staying awhile

before taking the boat back, Patrick?"

He shook his head. "I still have a couple supply runs to do. I'll be back tomorrow." He grinned at Casey, who tore her eyes away from Dorian for long enough to give Patrick her attention once more. "I guess I'll be seeing you around, Cassandra."

She blushed prettily at the comment. "I look forward to it."

Playing him for a fool, Poppy couldn't help but think as Patrick made his way back to his boat, glowering despite herself. But then she remembered that she should be looking at her new surroundings rather than berating Casey – especially considering Dorian was beginning his tour of the facility. Cursing her lack of an attention span, Poppy focused on what the man was beginning to say.

"I'm sure you're all excited to try out the equipment we have here—"

"You mean the hot tubs," Casey interrupted, flipping her shiny auburn hair over her shoulder as she did so. "Where are they?"

Dorian laughed softly. "We'll get to them. The facility is made up of the central building we're entering just now," he said as everyone made their way through the front doors. He motioned to a set of doors on his left and then on his right. "And two wings to the east and west. The west houses staff quarters and the infirmary so you won't find yourself in there often – hopefully. The east wing is where you'll all be staying, whilst the centre building houses the gym, pool, sauna, indoor climbing equipment and social spaces."

"And the hot tubs?" Casey pressed as the group walked past one of the aforementioned social spaces, the northern wall of which was made up of climbing walls. It was large, airy and entirely glass-fronted to the south. "The outdoor pool?"

But they all saw it simultaneously through the glass wall. The pool overlooked the loch itself, the purple, heather-covered mountains making for an impressive backdrop. "Through here," Dorian said, smiling, taking the group through a set of doors that led back outside. To the left of the pool was a raised wooden decking area which the hot tubs were sunk into.

Casey squealed with delight. "You never told us it was a God damn *infinity pool*, Poppy!" She turned to gawk at Dorian. "You sure you want us anywhere near this place?"

"That was one of your president's first concerns."

"Glad to know you have such faith in the club, guys," Rachelle joked. "But seriously, Mr Kapros, this place is gorgeous."

He smiled beautifully for her. "Call me Dorian, Miss...?"

"Rachelle," she replied as her face flushed. "Call me Rachelle."

Behind her Poppy saw Fred stiffen at the interaction.

Serves you bloody right for breaking up with her, Sampson.

Though Poppy didn't want Rachelle flirting with Dorian any more than she wanted Casey to, it was about time her best friend became interested in someone who wasn't Fred. Rachelle and Fred dated for the better part of two years when Rachelle first joined the club; the overarching animosity between Poppy and Fred had inevitably caused a strain on the relationship. Fred ended up breaking up with her, though Poppy was sure he was still in love with her – and blamed Poppy for the break-up.

"How about I show you all to the living quarters?" Dorian suggested. "Then those of you who are sober enough can try out the climbing walls, if you want."

There was a smattering of laughter throughout the group, though the majority of people were still covetously looking at the hot tubs. Casey cast a longing glance over her shoulder towards the outdoor pool that promised she'd go swimming before she went climbing, which didn't surprise Poppy at all. Swimming was what her friend was best at: she was the strongest swimmer in the club by far.

But, despite their hot tub and swimming pool desires, all thirty club members dutifully made their way to the east wing when Dorian led them towards it. "Most of the rooms are twins," the facility manager said when they reached the living quarters.

"Ooh, wanna room with me, Poppy?" Rachelle suggested.

"As if you had to ask."

"Poppy actually has a room to herself, if that's okay," Dorian cut in apologetically. "As do the rest of the executive board. I figured that was the fairest way to split up the single rooms."

"At least you get your own room too, then," Poppy said to her best friend. In reality she was glad for the single room; she didn't think she could cope with sharing a room with anybody for two weeks. Though she and Rachelle lived in a flat together that was as close quarters as Poppy could deal with. She was a classic only child who needed her own space.

And if something were to happen between me and Dorian...

Poppy shook her head out of the gutter. She was *not* here to do something like that. She was here to climb and swim and hike and completely forget about having to decide what to do with the rest of her adult life.

Suddenly remembering Andrew, Poppy pulled Dorian to the side when the group passed through a set of double doors. "Andrew Forbes is our treasurer," Poppy said in an undertone, "so he'll be in a single room, too, but is there one close to where I'll be sleeping?"

"Why, are you two going out?" Dorian asked, amused. "I could always put you in a twin room if you—"

"Oh god, no!" Poppy exclaimed, a little too loudly. People walking close by looked at them curiously, so Dorian bent his head so Poppy could murmur into his ear. She appreciated the gesture, though being in such close proximity to the man inevitably sent indecent thoughts racing through her mind.

Poppy forced her brain to focus on the subject at hand. "Andrew is autistic," she explained to Dorian. "It's his first time away from home for longer than a night. I'd rather I was close by if anything happens or he needs me."

Dorian smiled in understanding as he stretched back up to his full height. "Got it. Which one of you is Andrew?" he called out.

Andrew looked over in surprise when he heard his name. "That's me."

Dorian waved him over and the younger man obediently walked over to join him. "Everyone who isn't on the board – go wild choosing your rooms," Dorian said, pointing down the main branch of the corridor. "Andrew, Poppy, Fred and Rachelle, follow me."

"And me!" Casey bit out, indignant.

"But of course. You must be the social convenor?"

"Casey, yes."

And so the five of them followed Dorian down a corridor on their left. "I said these were single rooms but in reality they're more like doubles," he admitted. "They're meant to be more expensive." At the end of the corridor was a much smaller social area made up of two sofas and a couple of arm chairs surrounding a glass coffee table.

Dorian stopped in front of two doors on his left. "Poppy, Andrew – take these two. They're the closest together."

Andrew looked at Dorian and then Poppy in understanding. The hint of a smile lit up his face as he sidled up to her. "Thank you, Poppy."

She waved a dismissive hand. "Don't mention it."

Dorian turned to the group with an air that signalled the end of the tour had been reached. "Well then, I'll let you lot get settled. Come find me when you want to try out any of the climbing equipment just so I can run through the safety talk; I'll be in my office in the west wing." He looked at Poppy as he said this, and she took it as a hint that *she* should be the one to go and find him. Her stomach flipped happily at the implication...though her head reasoned it was likely because she was the only one Dorian really knew.

Poppy didn't spend long dumping her stuff in what would be her bedroom for the next two weeks. She did, however, pause long enough to appreciate the room itself. The bed was smaller than a standard double bed – which was the size she was used to – but it gave her more room than a single bed so she wasn't going to complain. A quick test of the mattress confirmed that it was comfortable and new.

Then Poppy spotted that the room had an en suite bathroom and her heart soared. Knowing that she wouldn't have to traipse sleepily down a corridor in the middle of the night looking for a toilet left her feeling very happy about the room arrangements indeed.

Then Poppy quickly changed into a sports bra and leggings, flinging her hair up into potentially the messiest ponytail ever and lacing up her trainers, eager to try out the climbing walls as soon as possible. She laughed when she saw her reflection in the mirror, taking a few seconds to fix her hair before bolting out of her room to find Dorian's office.

She passed by the climbing walls in question on her way over, spying several members of the club already happily snacking on food in the social area Dorian had shown them before.

"You not even going to take tonight off from climbing, Morph?" Nate asked from his position lounging on a grey leather corner sofa, a bottle of half-drunk beer in hand.

She shook her head and grinned. "Absolutely not."

Poppy swiftly made her way to the west wing, where Dorian's office was, though curiosity got the better of her and she wandered down the corridor first instead of dutifully knocking on his door. The infirmary was on her left as well as two other very clinical-looking rooms. She tried the doors on her right but each and every one of them was locked.

I suppose if they're staff quarters they wouldn't want people like me snooping about, Poppy reasoned.

The corridor ended with a stairway up to another floor. Wondering what could be up there, Poppy made it halfway up the stairs before she heard the sound of footsteps behind her.

"What are you doing, Miss King?" Dorian asked. He didn't sound annoyed; rather, Poppy thought he might have been amused.

She turned and smiled apologetically. "I'm sorry. I'm really nosey. I came through to get you for that climbing wall safety talk."

"I gathered. Incidentally, my office is the first door on the left when you enter the corridor. I'm fairly certain my name's on the door."

Poppy laughed nervously before following Dorian back through to the central building, unwittingly admiring the way his hips moved as he walked. "I know. I was just...exploring."

Dorian eyed her curiously over his shoulder. "There's plenty of exploring to be done outside. I doubt you'd find anything interesting in the west wing...aside from my bedroom."

Poppy gawked at the obviously outrageous comment. She didn't know how to reply so she decided not to say anything at all, which seemed to be precisely the reaction Dorian had hoped for. The two of them waited in patient (Dorian) and awkward (Poppy) silence by the climbing walls until another four or five people who were interested in scaling them joined, including Fred and Andrew.

Poppy saw Casey and a few other people make a beeline for the outdoor pool, which was glittering beneath the late afternoon sun. Poppy knew she'd probably try out the pool when the sun set; there was something about swimming at twilight that she'd always loved.

Dorian's safety talk was short and sweet. He went over how to use the equipment – all stuff that the group was familiar with – before Poppy promptly ignored it all and began nimbly climbing up the wall without any equipment whatsoever.

"King!" Fred exclaimed furiously. "What the hell are you doing?"

"Free-climbing," Poppy called back simply. "I won't go all the way to the top." She was lying, of course. Poppy loved free-climbing more than anything else in the world. She never, ever fell.

Except that, this time, she did.

Poppy King had almost made it to the top of the climbing wall, expertly navigating the hand and foot holds like it was second nature, because it was. But then she glanced at Dorian, curious to know if the handsome man with the beautiful voice was watching her.

He was.

Like a hawk analysing a rabbit two hundred feet away Dorian was watching her. Even from this high up she could see the blue of his irises peering, observing, calculating. They were too bright. They were a distraction Poppy had not prepared for.

And she fell.

A whoosh of air rushed past her ears before Poppy landed heavily on her right side, crushing her arm beneath her with a sickening crunch. For a few seconds she lost consciousness. For a few seconds nobody spoke. For a few seconds not a soul in the room seemed to breathe. A fall like that meant several broken bones at the very least, but the way Poppy had landed...

When she sat up, cringing in pain and barely able to see or hear or think, most everyone cried out in shock and relief.

"How the hell is she—"

"Oh my God I thought she was dead—"

"I've never seen Poppy fall!"

"Poppy, your arm..."

Poppy couldn't focus enough to look at her injury, though she didn't need the full function of her eyes to know that it was red and hot with blood. Before she had the chance to react, however, someone swept her into their arms and carried her away.

"I'll deal with this!" Dorian exclaimed as he clutched her to his chest, voice hazy and faraway in Poppy's ears even though she could hear his heart battering against his ribcage clear as day. "I'll call an ambulance if I have to. Fred, Andrew – can I leave it to the two of you to clean up here? There's some bleach in the kitchen!"

"What happened?" Poppy groaned in Dorian's arms as they left the cacophony of the central building behind them. Her eyes flickered beneath their lids until she forced them open. "I don't – I don't fall."

Dorian laughed humourlessly. "Seems like you do, Poppy King." He kicked open the door to the infirmary and placed Poppy on a bed before hurriedly grabbing everything he needed to clean and dress her arm.

There was so much blood. As her vision returned to her it was all she could see. Poppy had never considered herself queasy before but the sight of her *own* blood made her head spin painfully. And was that – bone?

Dorian made quick work of cleaning up the blood, brows knitted together in worry as he worked. Poppy could tell what he was thinking: if she'd bled this much then she must have hurt herself very, very badly.

But then Dorian's frown melted into confusion. "I don't understand."

Poppy risked looking down at her arm. Now that Dorian had cleaned up the worst of the mess she could see her arm was hardly even bleeding anymore. The exposed and broken bone Poppy had been so sure she'd seen had disappeared. Even as she stared the long slash that rent open her skin began to seal itself.

She didn't want to say anything. She didn't want *Dorian* to say anything.

Because Poppy knew this would happen.

There was a reason she never fell – that she climbed so recklessly. Because, as a child, when she *had* fallen, she'd never gotten hurt the way she should. When she realised that cuts and scrapes healed inordinately quickly Poppy learned to hide that she had ever been hurt at all in front of people. She knew it wasn't normal to heal this rapidly.

"You don't have any broken bones."

Not a question: a statement.

Poppy shook her head.

"Did you hurt yourself anywhere else?" Dorian asked. He began dressing and bandaging Poppy's arm, for all the good that it would do.

She shook her head again.

Dorian's frown returned, growing deeper and deeper as he continued working in silence. Poppy didn't dare say anything. She didn't know *what* to say, anyway. Then he rubbed a hand against his face, unwittingly smearing some of Poppy's blood across his mouth.

The man froze, a blank and unsettling expression plastered across his face as he stared at Poppy. She wanted to look away from his eyes; they pierced through her like knives. In that moment she knew that *he* knew something, somehow.

"Um, Dorian...?" Poppy asked uncertainly. Any normal person would have cleaned the blood from their face immediately. Dorian didn't. He continued staring at Poppy as if he couldn't believe what he was seeing. Considering how quickly she'd healed he probably couldn't.

Finally, after several interminably long seconds, Dorian averted his eyes and took a step back from her. "Go clean the rest of yourself up, Poppy," he murmured. "Maybe don't tell anyone about your...arm."

Poppy got up wordlessly – wobbling dangerously on her feet before regaining her balance – and when Dorian didn't say anything more she walked away. But when she reached the door to the central building, she paused.

What do *I say to everyone?* she worried. *Though only a handful of people actually saw the fall everyone will know about it by now. And I'm barely hurt.*

She glanced back at the door to the infirmary. She couldn't understand Dorian's reaction whatsoever. It wasn't how anyone normal would have responded to what he saw happen with his own eyes. Poppy was hopelessly, confusingly curious.

Looking upwards she saw that the ceiling tiles of the facility were akin to those found in offices and schools – the kind one could lift easily. Judging the height she'd need to get through the ceiling, Poppy kicked off the wall to gain enough momentum to grab one of the metal rails that supported the tiles. She swung in place for a few seconds then hauled herself up, head bumping the tile out of the way as she did so. Poppy winced at the pain in her arm when she put her weight on it.

With some effort she pulled the rest of her body through the ceiling before her arm finally gave way, taking a deep, shuddering breath after she put the tile back in place. "What the hell am I doing?" Poppy murmured, shaking as she crawled through the ceiling until she was certain she was above Dorian in the infirmary. She just barely lifted the edge of a tile to confirm this: the man was pacing back and forth as he muttered to himself. Something about him seemed different.

Poppy wasn't sure what.

"...fucking blood. Immortal blood!" he hissed, running a hand through his hair with an anguished expression on his face. "I can't bid her off. God no. *I want her.* They can't know, otherwise—"

Dorian abruptly paused in his nonsensical rambling. With unnaturally keen eyes he located Poppy's position in the ceiling just as she replaced the tile. Her breathing came in loud, sharp, painful gasps that she could hardly control; everything about the situation she was in screamed *danger.*

Somehow finding the strength to turn around Poppy made to escape back the way she came. But then the tile behind her came crashing down and she felt an excruciatingly tight, cold grasp around her ankle.

With a scream Poppy was wrenched from the ceiling, landing heavily on the linoleum floor at Dorian's feet. She stared up at him in shock that quickly curdled into fear. Dorian didn't look like himself at all. He loomed over her, much taller than he'd been before. *Impossibly* tall.

The arm that hauled her from the ceiling ended with dark, gleaming, wickedly sharp claws. They were all she could focus on; one swipe of those claws across her throat and Poppy thought that even she might die before she could heal herself. Whereas before Poppy couldn't get air into her lungs fast enough, now she found she couldn't breathe at all.

Dorian's grin was feral as he continued to somehow change

form in front of her very eyes.

"You really are too curious for your own good, Poppy King."

ANDREW MARTIN FORBES

DORIAN

SHE WAS NEVER SUPPOSED TO FIND OUT. None of them were. And yet Poppy King, president of the club Dorian had sought so hard to pin down, had found out anyway.

Poppy wouldn't stop screaming. Dorian stared at her for a moment or two before bending down to pick her up, forcing her to stand on her own two feet with the wall behind her for support. Then he covered Poppy's mouth to suffocate the scream out of her even as she struggled and writhed in a futile attempt to escape him. But, eventually, Poppy got the idea that Dorian wasn't going to let go if she didn't keep quiet.

She grew silent.

"Good," Dorian muttered, finally letting go of her mouth. Poppy trembled in front of him, a shadow of the confident young woman who had leapt from Patrick's boat to greet him. "You must know what will happen now."

"I – I don't," she stammered. "What did you mean, bid me off? What's going—"

"Be quiet. Just be quiet," he ordered, moving away from Poppy to resume his frantic pacing whilst his human guise fell away entirely. Out of the corner of his eye he saw Poppy gaping at him in horror.

I suppose it's not every day you watch a human transform into a monster, he mused. *Or, rather, a monster pretending to be human turn back into a monster.*

In truth Dorian didn't look all that terrifyingly 'monstrous', going by his kind's standards. He had clients who looked far worse. For Dorian was a satyr, if a human was going to describe what he was. His powerful, dark-furred, hooved legs could kill a man with a single kick, and his clawed hands were capable of ripping out a person's throat. In this form Dorian brushed an inhuman eight feet tall – though the intricate network of horns that wove around his head added several additional delicate-pointed inches to his height.

"I can't believe this," he said, too shocked to keep his thoughts to himself. "After all that planning – finding the *perfect* humans to sell off – you waltz right in and change everything." He walked purposefully towards Poppy, who backed herself against the wall as if she hoped it might swallow her up so she didn't have to face him.

She let out a yelp when Dorian grabbed her arm and held it up, ripping open the bandages he'd so carefully wrapped just ten minutes ago. He laughed in disbelief at what he saw, eyes widening as he took in the unmarred skin where once there had been blood and bone. Poppy's arm had almost completely healed.

"How long have you known you were like this?" Dorian demanded. Poppy stared at him in blind, silent terror. "Answer me, Poppy," he crooned, his voice a beautiful mockery of the one he'd known from the very beginning she would fall for. The one she would obsess over from the moment she heard him speak on the phone.

Poppy kept her grey eyes on his, though it was clear she wished to look at literally anyone or anything else. "I..." she mumbled, finally finding her voice, "as long as I can remember."

Dorian barked out a laugh. "And then you fall right into my lap. How fortuitous. You have to die now, of course. I thought I'd have more time with your club to show off their strengths and weaknesses to my clients but they'll know something's up if you disappear. Guess I'll have to expedite the entire process."

"The entire process of what?" Poppy asked. It seemed as if she had entirely glossed over Dorian telling her she was doomed to die in favour of finding out what was going on.

Curious to the end. At least she's consistent.

Dorian let go of her arm; Poppy immediately clutched it to her chest. "Humans don't eat sick pigs or fatty cows or diseased sheep, do they?" he asked, knowing what her answer would be. Poppy shook her head. Something about her expression told Dorian that she didn't like where this was going. *Of course she doesn't,* he thought maliciously. *No human would.* "We don't like eating sub-par humans," Dorian continued. "We want you to be as fit as physically possible. But your club is...on a whole other level."

"I don't know what you mean by that."

Dorian waved a clawed hand. "Sure you do. You are what you eat." He cocked his head to the side as he considered his explanation. "Well, it's not so literal for humans as it is for us, I suppose. If we consume human flesh from some unhealthy, lazy, unskilled sack of nothing then that's exactly what we get out of it: nothing. Empty calories, as it were. We need to eat again so quickly...which isn't good when we don't want you to know we're around."

His eyes swept up and down Poppy's frame, and he smirked. "But if we eat someone who is, say, a daredevil climber, who never falls and has the stamina and dexterity to climb through ceilings...well. That would keep us going for a long, long time. We'd likely not have to eat another human for years if we ate someone from your club. And it makes us better at whatever it is you were good at, too. Better climbers, better swimmers, better talkers, better senses...my kind would pay handsomely just for your *legs,* Miss President of the Outdoor Sports Society. However..."

Dorian closed the gap between himself and Poppy until she had no space left to move. He crouched down to her eye level; he could see minuscule flecks of blue in her pale irises. "Your worth isn't in your flesh and bones, Poppy King."

What little colour that had returned to Poppy's face over the past couple of minutes immediately drained away.

"I have clients who would pay *millions* for your blood," Dorian said, voice hushed as if he were telling her a secret. He supposed he was. "I'd never have to bid off another high-quality human again for the rest of my life."

"B-but you said you couldn't bid me off," Poppy stammered. "Y-you said—"

"That I'd have to eat you myself. It's true, of course." Dorian trailed a clawed finger across her cheek, pressing against her skin hard enough to cut through it if she had been an average human. But Poppy's skin remained unbroken, though she flinched at the pain he caused. "Why should anyone else have you? I'm the one who found you. I did all the god damn research to locate the perfect group of humans for the monsters in these parts to gorge on. They can have the rest of your group. You're *mine.*"

Dorian stretched his hooved legs back up to their full height and grasped Poppy's chin to turn her head upwards, forcing her eyes to follow him. He marvelled at the throbbing artery in her neck.

"I didn't think I'd ever witness someone like you in my

lifetime..."

It was clear that curiosity was currently overriding Poppy's fear. There was a flash of longing that crossed her face – a yearning to know what she actually was. "What do you...what's in my blood?" she asked, though Dorian could tell it pained her to desire such answers from *him*.

Dorian delighted in the power he held over her, and laughed incredulously at Poppy's lack of understanding. "To think humans don't even know what their own bodies can do. That you haven't yet found an explanation for why you heal so quickly or hardly ever hurt yourself is beyond ridiculous."

"I'd rather say believing monsters exist that want to drink my blood because I heal too quickly is fucking ridiculous," Poppy muttered despite herself.

Dorian only laughed harder at the comment. "I guess that's true, Poppy. Nobody would ever believe you, anyway. They'd think you were crazy. People would think anyone who garbled on and on about a monster stalking them in the night was insane."

Poppy understood Dorian's point immediately. "But I'm not getting out of here alive to tell the tale so what does it matter if anyone believes me, right?"

"Bingo."

She struggled to comprehend her own rapidly-approaching demise. "My blood...my blood will make you heal faster?"

Dorian shook his head in disbelief. "You really just...don't get it, do you? That stuff pouring through your veins isn't just healing and protecting you. It *doesn't die*. And with it in my body I won't die, either. Not for a long, long, long time; longer than any of my kin could fathom, let alone a human. It's as close to immortal as a being could get. As close to a god, even."

"And that power is in my body?"

"Not for long," Dorian said viciously. He grabbed onto Poppy's neck, wrenching her face up to his own as he bared his sharp, pointed teeth and—

"Wait, wait!" she cried, the whites of her eyes bright and shining with fear. "You have to wait!"

Somewhat amused – and curious to see what Poppy would say to no doubt plead for her life – Dorian waited. He raised an eyebrow expectantly.

Poppy took a deep, rattling breath. "I-if drinking my blood extends your life," she began, "then doesn't it make sense to drink as much of it as possible so you can live even *longer*?"

"Your point being?"

Poppy clawed at Dorian's hand clenched around her throat; he loosened it very slightly.

"Blood regenerates," she spluttered. "But if you drink it all in one go, I'll die. You could have eight pints now or eight thousand over time, if you don't kill me."

Dorian dropped Poppy in surprise, barely noticing her huff of shock as she clattered to the floor. She was right; Dorian had simply been too on-edge and excited to think things through. He narrowed his eyes at her. "Why in the world would you prefer that to dying outright? You're signing your entire life over to me. I won't let you go."

"I know."

"So then...what?"

Poppy's eyes hardened as she stared up at Dorian, resolute and determined even as she knelt, insignificantly small and shaking, on the floor. "Let the rest of my club go."

His answer was immediate. "Absolutely fucking not."

"Then I'll kill myself right now!"

A low growl formed in the back of his throat. "You dare threaten me?"

Poppy remained expressionless. "Let them go."

"If I let them go how will I know you won't later kill yourself or try to escape?"

"If you let them go I'll *happily* stay."

He roared out a laugh at Poppy's audacity. But then Dorian thought of a cruel, twisted compromise that he would thoroughly enjoy watching unravel. "Half of them," he said. "I'll release half of them. But only one a week. And one person a week also has to be given up for auction. You'll pick them both."

Though Dorian's hand was no longer curled around Poppy's throat, she choked. "I-I'm not doing that!"

"It's either that or they all die, Poppy. It's your choice."

"I...then what happens every week after I p-pick these people?"

"They stay here until half of your group has been given up," he explained, making the rules up as he went along. "Just to keep you from saying anything to anyone and to ensure you don't try to run off. After that I'll let them go."

Poppy's eyes widened. "What am I supposed to say to keep them here for fifteen weeks?!"

"I'll leave that up to you." Dorian grinned wickedly. "I guess you'd be sacrifice number one. So who's the first to be saved?" He realised he was genuinely curious about who Poppy would choose. Her best friend, perhaps. Or that silver-haired boy Dorian had noticed kept looking at her. He wondered if they were together. Or—

"Andrew," Poppy breathed, completely and utterly defeated but also sure of her choice. "Andrew. It has to be Andrew."

He smiled. "Of course. I suppose that one was obvious. I'm interested to see who you'll decide to give *up* next week. But for now..."

Poppy stared at Dorian as he turned and walked away, returning to Poppy's side with a scalpel. "I guess I'll cut that arm of yours back open. Everyone thinks it's injured, anyway."

He motioned for Poppy to stand up; numb and frightened beyond belief she obeyed. She held out her arm without a word, though she was shaking from the very tips of her fingers down to her toes. She closed her eyes when Dorian placed the scalpel against her skin.

But the blade didn't cut through. It was as if the metal was blunt. Old. It was only by using far more pressure than should have been necessary that the blade finally cut open Poppy's arm. Then it healed within seconds, leaving no trace that she had ever been hurt.

Frowning, Dorian tried again and again and again. Poppy winced with every attempt. But the small, slender cuts Dorian had been carving into her flesh simply weren't sticking.

He stared at Poppy for a few seconds. "I guess you can blame yourself for this," he said, before plunging the scalpel straight through her arm and ripping downward.

Poppy howled in pain but Dorian, anticipating the noise, held a hand against her mouth. Then he brought her mess of an arm to his lips and began eagerly lapping up her blood. He kept his eyes on Poppy's the entire time, watching her watching him drain the life out of her.

There were tears streaming down her face, and she bit into his hand to keep from making more noise. But no longer did Poppy King look scared. She looked resolute. Resigned to her fate.

Good girl, Dorian thought as Poppy's blood began to course through him. It was exhilarating – as if he could literally feel years being added onto his life. He felt powerful. He felt lucky. He felt invincible. He felt—

He felt like he was taking too much blood.

Poppy had stopped biting his hand. Her eyes were turning glassy. Dorian forced his mouth away from her glorious blood, catching Poppy and holding her to his chest just as her legs gave way. He carried her over to the infirmary bed and gently sat her down, watching with continued amazement as the mess he'd left of her arm began to fix itself.

It was healing far more slowly that before.

"Less blood next time, then," he muttered, as much to himself as to Poppy, who was barely conscious. With adrenaline-shaking hands he cleaned and re-dressed her arm, as if the past half an hour hadn't happened at all.

It took a few minutes for Poppy to properly regain consciousness and, in that time, Dorian's human form gradually began to return. When she focused on him once more Dorian looked exactly as he had done when she'd first arrived on Patrick's boat.

Poppy didn't seem surprised by the reversion. She was expressionless, which Dorian supposed was the least he should have expected given that he'd just drained part of her life away.

But she'll get it back, and then I'll *get it, until the end of time.*

"Fifteen people," Poppy said quietly, her eyes downcast. "Fifteen people. Fifty percent. Fifteen—"

"I think you get it," Dorian chuckled. Then his laugh grew louder and brighter in genuine elation, his brain overloaded with more dopamine and adrenaline than he'd ever experienced before. "One a week to live, and one a week to die!"

"Let Andrew leave in two weeks," Poppy demanded through Dorian's laughter, a little of her previous spark finally returning.

"And why should I do that?"

"That's when everyone would expect the trip to end. When

I have to think of a reason for them to stay. Let Andrew go. He can't – the only reason he's here is because of me."

Dorian was tempted to say no. If Andrew suspected something had gone awry then he could blow the entire operation. And keeping Andrew here would torture Poppy, which Dorian discovered he loved doing.

But what she was giving Dorian was worth one allowance. Her blood now coursing through his body was priceless, after all. Granting her this one, measly request was nothing.

"Fine," he said. "He can go. Everyone else waits. And if you even *think* to try and tell people that something's wrong – if it seems like you might be planning some kind of escape – I'll slaughter them all."

The two of them said nothing for a while, Dorian's threat hanging heavy in the air between them. Poppy wasn't looking at him, choosing instead to stare at her hands. He'd never seen a person so pale; it made the blood splattered on her clothes and skin all the more unsettling. She looked half a corpse. A ghost.

"I'm going to go," Poppy eventually murmured, struggling off the bed to wobble towards the door. Dorian had to hand it to her: Poppy was strong. He had taken so much from her he'd expected her to fall unconscious and sleep for days.

"At least you can make it believable that you fell now," Dorian called out after her when she opened the door and disappeared down the corridor, chuckling at his own comment once he was well and truly on his own again.

It seemed as if the next fifteen weeks with the Outdoor Sports Society were going to be very fun indeed. Pulling out his phone, Dorian called Patrick.

"Change of plans," he informed his friend the moment he picked up.

An inhale of concern. "The good kind or the bad kind?"

Dorian grinned. "The excellent kind."

ROSS BRIDGES

POPPY

POPPY DIDN'T KNOW HOW SHE HAD the strength to escape from the infirmary. Not that she was technically escaping, given that she had just signed her life over – as well as the lives of fifteen of her club members – to a monstrous sociopath. Emphasis on monstrous.

For that's what Dorian Kapros truly was, both figuratively and literally: a monster. He wasn't something Poppy could have ever dreamed existed.

What was *he?* she thought blearily as she staggered down the hallway. But the vision in her brain of Dorian-the-monster was currently hazy and indistinct due to all the blood she'd lost. Poppy would tackle the question later, when she had more life running through her body and a functioning nervous system.

Poppy wished she could go straight to her room but in order to get there she had to make her way through the central building. And everyone would be there, waiting to find out how she was.

She looked down at her arm. It was viciously painful beneath the bandages: the mess Dorian had left it in after draining her life away was arguably even worse than the original fracture that had caused Poppy to bleed in the first place.

And now she had to somehow, impossibly, convince everyone that she had broken not one single bone in her body when she fell. For even though Poppy's arm was currently horribly injured – and would take longer to heal now that Dorian had drained her of so much blood – any serious damage would disappear in a matter of days. When that time came she wouldn't be able to explain away her advanced healing. People had to believe that it wasn't serious *now*, not later.

Hard to do that when I look like I almost died, Poppy mused when she caught her appearance in a window. She laughed somewhat bitterly. "I *did* almost die," she told her reflection. "Twice."

Never before had Poppy King been so painfully aware of her own mortality.

And yet...though she was still to fully comprehend and process everything Dorian had said to her, one thing stuck in Poppy's head more than any other: her blood was 'immortal'. Dorian had explained what that meant for one of *his kind* if they consumed her blood. What he hadn't explained, however, was what that meant for Poppy.

Does this mean I'll live an absurdly long life, too? she wondered, horrified at the prospect. If she was going to have to spend the rest of her life enslaved to a monster then she'd rather that life were a short one.

But she didn't want to ask Dorian about it. She never wanted to speak to him again if she could help it, though she knew that was an impossibility.

Forcing away further thoughts of Dorian and monsters and her own strange blood, Poppy struggled with the door to the social area whilst trying her best to take several deep breaths and control her heart rate. But she failed miserably, stumbling gracelessly into the crowd of people who stood to attention the moment they spotted her.

"Oh my god Poppy, are you okay—"

"What the hell happened?!"

"How are you still alive?"

"Hey, hey, give her some space!" Nate called out, pushing his way through the throng to reach Poppy. Throwing her uninjured arm over his shoulders he guided her to one of the grey corner sofas, ordering someone to get her a glass of water once they both sat down. Rachelle and Casey huddled around Poppy a second later, their eyes equal parts upset and concerned as they took in her condition, whilst Fred sat on a coffee table opposite them all.

He stared impassively at Poppy. It was beyond disconcerting.

Behind Fred stood a horrified and anxious Andrew who clearly didn't know what to do. Poppy smiled wanly at him. *At least he's safe,* she thought. *At least I've saved him from everything.*

When one of the youngest members of the club, Jenny, handed Poppy a glass of water, she took it with the meekest thanks she had ever uttered in her entire life. Then Nate turned her to face him, pausing long enough before speaking to cast a critical gaze over Poppy's arm.

"Morph, honestly..." he muttered, dark eyes narrowed in confused disbelief. "How are you *this* okay? That was such a huge fall."

Poppy forced a smile to her face before spewing out a lie. "It wasn't that bad, not really. It wasn't as high a drop as it seemed. My legs are gonna be bruised, probably, but the worst of the damage is to my arm. Can't believe I fell on my *arm,*" she added on with a self-deprecating laugh. "I didn't even try to roll out of the fall. It's not like me at all."

"You're damn right it's not like you."

Poppy shivered despite herself. Fred had spoken with absolutely no sympathy in his voice. She glanced at him out of the corner of her eye, not daring to meet his stare directly. There was something about his inscrutable expression as he watched her that made her realise he was onto...something.

Dorian's threat reverberating inside her agonised brain, Poppy tried to fumble for an excuse that would placate her rival. She couldn't have him work something out, after all. Despite Frederick Sampson being, well, Frederick Sampson, Poppy would never willingly wish a fate of being devoured by monsters on him.

She didn't wish it for anyone at all.

And yet Poppy herself had to sentence half of the people currently in this very room to their deaths. Her own club. Her friends.

Then what seemed like a throwaway comment on Dorian's behalf finally hit her, and Poppy froze.

'My kind would pay handsomely just for your legs,' he'd said. *Did he mean that literally?* she worried, deeply disturbed. *Am I condemning the people in this room not only to death but to a slow, torturous one? Will they be conscious when monsters rip off their limbs? Will they—*

"Poppy?"

Poppy looked at Rachelle with blind eyes, and she realised she hadn't responded to Fred's statement. She'd simply gotten lost in her own horrified thoughts and grown colder and colder, though the inside of her skull was burning and her heart was circulating what little blood she had left around her body so quickly Poppy was sure she was moments away from passing out.

"I'm sorry," she just barely choked out. "I-I'm in a lot of pain right now. I'm...going to bed. Can I explain everything in the morning?"

"Of course, Poppy!" Casey and Rachelle said in unison. "We'll help you to—"

"I'll help her," Nate interrupted, sliding a shoulder beneath Poppy's arm as he spoke and helping her to her feet. "Come on, guys, give us some space. Go have fun. Morph's okay; just leave her alone."

Poppy turned her head to see Casey and Rachelle watch her leave with worried expressions on their faces. And then there was Andrew, who looked like he was at a complete and utter loss for what to do. She had no doubt that was precisely the case, and not for the first time in the last hour Poppy distinctly regretted ever convincing him to come along on the trip.

Lastly there was Fred, frowning at Poppy as she walked away – like he always did.

Except it wasn't the same frown. Something had changed.

Everything had changed.

"Looks like you could actually do with your namesake, Morph," Nate joked when they reached the executive board bedrooms. "Speaking of – did that Kapros guy give you any painkillers? You sure you don't need to go to a hospital? You look really pale."

"That's more from the shock of falling," she said. "I don't fall, remember? My pride has been well and truly torn to shreds." *As well as my body and soul.*

But Nate didn't look convinced. "Is your arm broken?"

Poppy shook her head. "I thought it was, but it wasn't. I think I must have ripped it open on a karabiner lying on the floor or something. Under that I'm not even sure I have a sprain. It's a miracle, really."

"You sure you're not a real superhero, Morph? *Indestructible Girl* – the girl who never dies!" She winced at how accurate Nate's comment was but he assumed it was due to the pain she was in. "Okay, I get it, time for bed," he murmured, hurrying Poppy into her bedroom. He let out a low whistle when he saw the interior. "And here was me thinking the twin room I'm sharing with Rich was pretty nice. This is *hotel* nice. And you have an en suite?! Lucky."

"Nice choice of words, Nate," Poppy joked as she surveyed the white linen of the bed and then her bloodied clothes. She decided against sitting on it.

Nate glanced at the bed, too, but with a completely different intent. "When you feel better remember to invite me round for a sleepover," he flirted. It was an outrageous comment – as outrageous as Dorian's bedroom comment had been not even two hours prior.

The mere thought of Dorian made Poppy feel disgusting. How could she have entertained the idea of sleeping with him whilst the club was staying in his slaughterhouse?

She gave Nate a small smile that belied her current train of thought. "When I'm better for sure," she said, knowing that she never would be, and that she could never be with Nate in that capacity again. She couldn't have *any* proper relationships with the people in the club again. Not when she was sending half of them to their doom.

But in order to save the other half Poppy would have to continue acting as if nothing was wrong. Which meant she had to brush off today's incident like she always did – like it hadn't phased her. So she walked over to Nate and hugged him, allowing him to ruffle her dishevelled hair even though Poppy was fairly certain it had blood in it.

"Take care, Morph," Nate said as he left her room, wearing an expression that very much suggested he wanted to stay to make sure she really was fine.

When he was gone Poppy struggled out of her clothes and flung both them and herself in the shower, scrubbing at the fabric, her skin and her hair with a furious intent. She wanted all traces of her blood gone. It was difficult, since she had to keep her injured, wrapped-up arm dry, and the steam was making her dizzy, but Poppy – being stubborn as usual – persevered.

Discovering upon leaving the shower that there was a large, white, fluffy bathrobe neatly folded on a shelf below the sink, Poppy dried herself off and buried herself in the garment before collapsing onto the bed. She spied her phone where she had abandoned it on the bedside cabinet; grabbing it she discovered that it was barely seven in the evening.

And that she had no phone signal.

Which means I can't contact anyone for help even if I was willing to risk it, Poppy thought ruefully. Something told her that nobody else's phone was likely to be working, either, and that Dorian probably had the only operational one in the entire facility. It wouldn't be surprising to Poppy at all if that was a deliberate move on Dorian's part rather than an unfortunate coincidence.

What if he was the one responsible for our first booking getting completely fucked up? she realised in sudden horror. *We'd have never come here, otherwise.* It wasn't pleasant at all to think of how much Dorian may have manipulated Poppy even before she heard his painfully beautiful voice over the phone.

"I don't want to think," Poppy mumbled into her pillow. "No thoughts. An empty head. Just go to sleep..."

She repeated the words like some kind of mantra until she eventually realised she *was* falling asleep. Poppy was vaguely aware of Rachelle opening the door and peeking her head in some time later, then Casey doing the same thing. An hour after that Andrew knocked on her door and called out her name in question. It was the only thing that nearly got her out of bed.

But Poppy sunk deeper into the duvet and ignored Andrew, too.

When Poppy woke up properly it was close to two in the morning. She was exhausted; wondering what had woken her she realised she could hear someone shuffling about in the corridor. Terrified that it was, for whatever dreadful reason, Dorian, Poppy crept out of bed and inched her bedroom door open, wondering what was going on.

But it wasn't Dorian. At first Poppy wasn't even sure *who* it was. But then she heard the person begin to mutter.

"Bitch thinks she can ignore me just like that, huh? Boat guy is *so* much better. Slut. We'll see who she thinks is better..."

Poppy recognised the voice as belonging to one of the third year club members, Ross Bridges. After Casey admitted to both her and Rachelle that Ross had been creeping her out Poppy had taken to watching him closely during socials. And, sure enough, he was constantly leering at her younger friend. Poppy hadn't wanted to let him come on the trip. She really hadn't. But since Ross *technically* hadn't done anything wrong she couldn't stop him.

I should have prevented him from coming, anyway, Poppy thought regretfully as she watched Ross stalk down the corridor towards what she could only assume was Casey's room. She wondered if he was drunk or high to have spoken out loud about his misguided, irate opinion.

When he reached for Casey's door handle Poppy inched out of her room to confront him. "Stay away from her, Ross," she said, her voice infuriatingly weak and insubstantial. Poppy didn't like feeling this vulnerable in front of a man who clearly had ill intentions.

Ross looked shocked to see her – surprised to be caught out, clearly – but then he smiled as if everything was fine. He held up his phone. "Sorry, King," he said doggedly. "Didn't mean to wake you. Casey messaged me asking me to come to her room, so, um..."

"The hell she did. Get back to your own room, Ross."

His face darkened. For a moment it looked as though he was going to speak to Poppy the way she'd heard him talk about Casey, but then he schooled his expression.

"You know what? You're right. Even though she asked me to it's really late, and I shouldn't have disturbed you especially after that fall. Are you okay?"

Poppy resisted the urge to call him out on his false concern. "I will be when I get some sleep. Night, Ross."

"Night, Poppy."

And then he skulked back the way he came. Poppy didn't leave the corridor until she was sure he'd gone; when he reappeared and saw she was still there he flinched and backed away, probably hoping Poppy hadn't seen him in the dark.

He's going to try again if he's sure he won't get caught, Poppy realised with absolute certainty. *He's been planning to corner her on this trip for weeks.*

As Poppy crawled back into bed she was struck by a gut-wrenching, twisted, disgusting conclusion. She bolted for the toilet, violently retching the second her knees banged against the cold, tiled floor.

Ross Bridges had to be the first person she sacrificed. Poppy knew it down to her very core. He had planned to do something vicious and pre-meditated towards another person. He had to go.

The fact that the decision had been so easy only made Poppy feel even sicker. Just like that she had condemned a person to death...or worse.

When Poppy dragged herself into bed a second time she wished more than anything that when she fell asleep she could simply stop existing, or be lulled into believing everything that had occurred today was some kind of bizarre fantasy and had never really happened.

It stood to reason, therefore, that Poppy King did not fall asleep again that night.

RACHELLE COLE

DORIAN

A FULL WEEK HAD PASSED SINCE Dorian discovered what Poppy was and consumed her blood. Since then she had managed to avoid speaking to him altogether – a feat Dorian was more than a little impressed with.

Through careful observation he discerned that Poppy's arm had almost completely healed seven days after he'd torn it apart, though she still had it tightly bandaged and acted as if it hurt. But Dorian saw that, when she was alone, Poppy moved around freely and easily, like her arm had never been harmed in the first place.

Currently Dorian was sitting in the surveillance room watching the entire club eat dinner; cameras were set up to watch almost everything in the facility. This was both for security purposes and to provide his clients with a twenty-four-hour media cycle of the people they were interested in purchasing. Dorian was expecting several of those clients to visit by the end of the following week to finalise their purchases based entirely on the information they garnered from the cameras.

A few 'middle men' acquaintances had also been posing as instructors from day one. Dorian was patiently waiting on them providing a list of the members of the Outdoor Sports Society they wished to procure on behalf of other members of their kind. Dorian had always intended to be rid of the entire group once their two week 'trip' was over, after all. In a few scant days he was supposed to be enjoying a fat bank account and an empty facility to abandon, all the better for him to plan the next auction in three years' time.

How things had changed, all because of Poppy King and her immortal blood.

Dorian wondered what kind of excuse Poppy was going to come up with to encourage her club to stay for an additional thirteen weeks. It would have to be an inordinately compelling lie to convince twenty-eight people to hang around of their own free will for so long. To that end he knew he'd have to ask her what she was going to say before the two weeks were up, since ultimately if Poppy came up with nothing substantial then Dorian himself would have to think of a reason *for* her.

He'd said he wouldn't help her, of course, but if the only other option was for pandemonium to ensue as the club tried to leave the facility then of course Dorian would come to Poppy's rescue.

Not that she was the kind of human who needed rescued. Rather, considering how near-invincible Poppy was, Dorian gathered she was the kind of person who preferred to *do* the rescuing. He realised with amusement that in a cruel and twisted way she was doing exactly that.

But she couldn't save everyone.

Dorian had gleefully watched Poppy over the surveillance cameras for the past week, face visibly tortured by the decisions she had to make as she lay on her bed, exhausted yet unable to sleep. She'd quickly distanced herself from her friends – using her injury as an excuse for her out-of-character behaviour. In particular Poppy was resolutely not reciprocating the silver-haired Nate's flirtations, which occurred so often that Dorian was sure the two of them had previously engaged in some kind of casual arrangement.

He had a sneaking suspicion that Andrew – the quiet, awkward young man whom Poppy had immediately chosen to save – also had a crush on Poppy, but she was woefully oblivious to his feelings. Dorian almost felt sorry for him.

Almost.

A few attempts at conversation with Andrew had been made since then, Dorian trying to work out for the life of him why Poppy felt the need to save him before her evident best friend, Rachelle. Andrew had an obsessive nature and was highly focused on his interests, and he was clearly one of the most talented members of the Outdoor Sports Society going by what Dorian had seen of him thus far. *A shame not to sell him,* Dorian thought on more than one occasion, when Andrew scaled the climbing walls faster than almost everybody else or completed forty lengths of the pool at six in the morning when not a single soul was awake.

But Andrew was generally detached when it came to anything he didn't enjoy, and he only spoke to a few people in the club – namely Poppy, Fred, Rachelle and Casey. Especially Poppy. It became apparent very quickly that she treated him calmly and gently as if he were her baby brother, which only made the crush Andrew had on her even funnier for Dorian to witness. He wondered if Andrew was aware of how Poppy saw him.

And then there was the third man in Poppy's life, who was perhaps the one Dorian was most interested in: Fred. Frederick Sampson did not like Poppy at all, and Dorian was quick to see why. The two were complete opposites: even when Poppy was acting morose and quiet she still found it in her to snap and snarl back at her nemesis when he bothered her, and he always responded in kind. Dorian realised he'd have to be careful of Fred. He struck him as the kind of person who'd immediately become suspicious of anything which resulted in a change in Poppy's behaviour.

Nobody knows you better than the person who truly, viscerally hates you, Dorian thought with a smirk. He pushed his chair away from the surveillance area and stood up, brushing down his clothes before making his way through the corridors towards the central building. He looked outside when he passed the glass doors out of the facility. It was a glorious evening, with the low-hanging sun turning the loch to molten, glittering gold.

The weather had been fair all week so the club had spent most of their time so far outside; they'd gone swimming in the loch several times as well as hiking up one of the nearby mountains the day before. Poppy, of course, hadn't joined any of these outdoor activities due to her 'injury'. But there were far more rigorous outdoor activities planned for the following week – bouldering, gorge-walking, rock climbing and abseiling – which Dorian highly suspected Poppy would insist on joining out of sheer boredom and impatience.

Even though she absolutely couldn't.

Every time Poppy was left behind at the facility Dorian had planned on speaking to her. To his fury Rachelle and Casey had hung back twice, then Andrew, then Nate, respectively. It was clear that many members of the club were willing to give up exploring in order to keep Poppy company, though aside from her closest friends she had refused all their offers with a soft smile and sad eyes.

Nobody in the club liked seeing her so shaken up and out of sorts; her fall had surprised them all.

Except for Fred.

Fred seemed to take some kind of sadistic pleasure from seeing his club's president finally fall from grace. Half of

Dorian completely agreed with Fred feeling this way; the other half of him wanted Poppy to shove it in the man's face and get right back into her reckless free-climbing like nothing ever happened.

But Poppy was yet to revert back to the happy, confident, free-spirited person Dorian had first met a week ago. He supposed she never would. But, at the very least, she had to *pretend* to be that person, in order to convince the rest of her club that nothing was wrong.

Dorian very much wanted that version of Poppy King to reappear: it would make it all the more satisfying when he crushed her spirit again and again, every week that she had to give up the name of a friend to die.

Thinking about the fact he was mere minutes away from draining her blood sent shivers down his spine. The blood Dorian had taken from Poppy before was still roaring through his body; the feeling of invincibility it created hadn't diminished in the slightest over the past week. It only made him want more. And, going by Poppy's complexion, her body had regenerated every last drop Dorian had taken.

So her body itself produces blood faster than the average human, he concluded with a satisfied smile, stopping by the kitchen on his way to the social area to grab a bottle of water. As he drank from it he wondered if he could drain Poppy more frequently than once a week once the initial fifteen weeks had passed and her friends were either dead or gone.

She wouldn't have the choice to refuse him, after all. She'd agreed to stay with Dorian for the rest of her life. With sickening glee he considered the fact that Poppy didn't know her lifespan would be far, far longer than that of an average human. He couldn't wait to eventually break it to her – that she was stuck with Dorian for more lifetimes than she could fathom.

It was with genuine interest that Dorian wondered what

would have happened if Poppy and her group hadn't been 'scouted' by him. Poppy wouldn't have gotten old. *When would she have noticed?* he thought. *And what would she have done once she did?*

That was how the last human with immortal blood had been found, Dorian was sure. His kind followed rumours of humans who never seemed to age religiously. Of humans who moved about more frequently than was necessary. Of humans who would reappear as a 'new' person decades later. But most rumours turned out to be exactly that: rumours. The people tracked down were merely on the run from someone or in witness protection or, in some cases, simply aged well.

It was why Dorian was so amazed by the fact that he – who was very young by his kind's standards – had discovered one of the very humans they all dreamed of finding. The form he maintained around people was of a man approaching thirty years old, which was in fact his true age. Dorian only had to live thirty measly years before finding Poppy King.

The last monster to procure a human with immortal blood had been well over one hundred when they'd found them. Dorian was pretty sure the human had also been alive for a similar number of years.

How fortuitous that he should find the next one so young.

Dorian finally reached the social area and stood on the very edge of it, watching a small group who had finished their dinner play cards for a minute or two. Then he cast his gaze over the expansive hall, frowning when he couldn't locate Poppy anywhere. When he saw that two of the people playing cards were Casey and Nate he walked towards them, intending to ask them where their elusive friend was.

Casey brightened immediately at the sight of Dorian, smoothing her hair over one shoulder and smiling radiantly. Cassandra O'Donnell was a very attractive, charming young woman, which was no doubt why Patrick had told Dorian he wanted her. He still wasn't sure if Patrick wanted to eat her or sleep with her but Dorian didn't have it in him to care right now.

He only had eyes for Poppy.

"Hey, Dorian," Casey said when he came to a stop by the sofas. The group was playing poker, and going by the pile of chips by her side Casey was winning. "You hungry? We just ate dinner but there's plenty left."

Dorian shook his head. "I'm actually just about to have my own. It's different from what you guys had, though."

"You too good for the food you serve us, Kapros?" Nate threw over at him from his position on the opposite side of the coffee table. He didn't take his eyes off the cards in his hands, scrutinising his next move with an unnecessary amount of concentration. Nate didn't seem to view Dorian as a threat, probably because Poppy had neither spoken to nor looked at Dorian since the day they'd arrived.

He laughed. "Definitely not. I just didn't want spaghetti bolognese."

"Then what *do* you want?"

"Poppy," Dorian replied, which both answered the question of what he wanted to eat and why he had joined the group in the first place. Nate flinched at his answer; Casey looked put out. In the far corner of the social area Andrew looked up from the chess game he was playing with another club member Dorian was fairly certain was called Rich. "Where is she?"

Casey motioned over to the infinity pool reluctantly. "She's standing out there. Watching the sunset. Though she could do that in here given the fact the entire wall is made of glass."

"Thanks, guys," Dorian replied when he shielded his eyes from the setting sun and finally spied where Poppy stood, promptly walking away from the group and exiting the building without another word.

Poppy was languishing over the barrier that surrounded the decking and the hot tubs, a motionless silhouette against the brilliance of the sun dipping beneath the mountains. Her shoulders flinched when she heard footsteps behind her. "Go away," she muttered, still staring out at the sunset.

Dorian promptly joined her, leaning over the barrier as if he meant to watch the scenery, too, but he only had eyes for her face. Poppy's expression suggested she was witnessing someone getting mauled to death rather than the blindingly beautiful colours of the sky as the sun slowly bowed below the horizon.

"Gladly, if you come with me," Dorian said, smirking at the way Poppy's hands curled into fists as if she meant to punch him. He almost hoped she would. "I hardly think you want me to cut you open in front of everyone."

A flash of horror crossed Poppy's eyes. "Why does that have to be *now*? Why not later?"

"After you've eaten is probably the best time to do it, don't you think? When your blood sugar is highest. It'll make you less likely to faint."

Poppy stared blankly at the sky once more, entirely deflated. "That is stupidly logical. Sounds like something Andrew would say. *Drink someone's blood after they've eaten so they recover faster.* Hilarious."

"You get on very well with Andrew," Dorian noted. "I figured you had to, since you chose to save him first, but I admit I still don't quite get it. Is it because he's—"

"Don't talk to me about Andrew," she cut in, fired up once more.

"Then let's talk about who you're saving and putting up to slaughter this week, then."

She looked at him like he had...asked her to choose

someone to die. Dorian almost laughed at the thought.

"How can you ask me that so casually?" Poppy whispered, looking behind her as if to ensure nobody was around to hear their morbid discussion.

He shrugged. "Because I care little and less about who you save and who you give up."

"You're a—"

Poppy paused mid-sentence. It was obvious what she was going to say.

Dorian's lips curled into a smile. "Go on; say it. You know you want to."

Instead Poppy walked away, making for the door without another word. But she glanced back at Dorian as she did so as if to say, 'Fine, let's do this in private'.

Dorian paused for a moment simply to appreciate the way Poppy looked in the bleeding sunset. The solitary silver streak in her long hair flashed like a dagger whenever the wind caught it. Her irises, so pale they were usually almost colourless, contained every hue currently dancing in the sky above them.

Perhaps it was because of the twisted, tortured expression on her face. Perhaps it was because he was the one responsible for it. Either way, Dorian thought Poppy looked astonishingly beautiful in the twilight.

He followed her wordlessly back through the doors and straight to the left, ignoring the looks of her curious friends sitting in the social area as they watched them head to the west wing. When they reached the infirmary he locked the door behind them.

Poppy turned around immediately, panic-stricken by the click of the lock. "Why did you do that?!"

"So nobody comes in and sees what we're doing, clearly." She let out a large gust of air when she saw the sense in

Dorian's comment, then collapsed onto the pristinely white medical bed. "There's no need to be so on-edge, Poppy," he continued breezily as he got to work setting up an IV drip. "It's not like I'm going to kill you."

She glanced at the IV warily. "What's that for?"

"You really think I'd be so vicious as to rip open your arm again if I could avoid it?"

"Yes." Her answer was flat with dead certainty. Dorian couldn't help chuckling as he motioned for her to sit up on the bed.

"If all my kind were really that violent then, trust me, humans would know of our existence," he said. "No, our eating habits are rather...refined, nowadays."

"Yes, because human trafficking is *so* refined."

"Humans do that too."

"Humans who are monsters." Dorian stared at Poppy pointedly. She seemed to work out what she'd said a second too late and, though it was obvious he would likely disagree with her, said, "Humans who are monsters and *literal* monsters are two different things."

"Are they really?" Dorian mused, gently and carefully removing the bandages from Poppy's arm even though he doubted she was hurt beneath them at all. As expected, when he fully uncovered her arm he saw it was entirely healed, the skin unblemished. There wasn't even a scar. "Does anywhere still hurt?"

She shook her head. "Not since Tuesday."

"Four days ago?" He raised an eyebrow. "Interesting."

"What is?"

"Working out how quickly you can make fresh blood and heal like before. Even you must see how that's a curious topic."

"Not if you're using the information to work out how

frequently you can drain me, it isn't," she scowled, removing her arm from Dorian's grasp in protest. He was quick to take hold of her wrist again to expose the length of her forearm.

"So you're not stupid, after all," he joked, enjoying the way Poppy's mouth formed the words *fuck off* in response to his jibe. But then Dorian schooled his expression and forced his amusement away. "Right, keep your arm out. I don't know how easy it'll be to get a needle through. You've had immunisations before, right?"

Poppy paused. "Yes, but that was when I was younger. Like before thirteen. I didn't heal quite as quickly back then."

Dorian hadn't thought about puberty being linked to the full onset of a human's innate nutritional value before. He supposed it made sense when he considered that none of his kind ever ate children because of their underdeveloped muscles and organs. Poppy's blood was clearly no different.

Frowning slightly in concentration, Dorian located a vein in Poppy's arm and tried to push the needle through. But, just like with the scalpel, Poppy's skin resisted the metal. He tried again with more pressure, glancing up at Poppy when she let out a huff of discomfort at the sensation.

"It's not going through," he said simply. "I'm going to have to push deeper. It's going to hurt. Talk to distract yourself."

"Talk about—*ow!*—what?"

"Tell me who you're saving and giving up."

"Rachelle," Poppy replied immediately. She flinched away from Dorian's increasingly rougher attempts to break her skin; whenever he managed to just barely push through the wound healed immediately.

"That one was obvious," Dorian replied, eyes firmly on the needle. "What about the tougher choice?"

There was a moment's hesitation this time. Poppy sighed heavily. "Ross Bridges."

"Huh."

"What does that mean?"

"I didn't expect you to actually give me a name so easily," he admitted. "You didn't even try and reason with me to spare your club again."

Poppy let out another sigh. Her shoulders slumped. "What's the point? You wouldn't."

When Dorian looked up at her again he saw something rather dead and defeatist in her eyes, as if Poppy had done nothing but mull over the deal Dorian had forced on her every second of every day this week. It satisfied him to no end that, though Poppy hadn't spoken a word to him since he'd first drained her blood, he'd clearly been the only thing on her mind.

"No," Dorian said, digging the needle so harshly into Poppy's arm that it broke in two, "but it would be highly enjoyable for me to listen to you beg."

"You're sick."

"Maybe a little. This isn't working, Poppy."

"Evidently!"

"Why Ross?"

"Does it matter?"

"I suppose it does." Dorian tossed the broken needle expertly into the bin. "What does someone have to do for a decent human being to sacrifice them? I somehow doubt anyone in your group is guilty of murder. It's a fascinating question."

It was clear Poppy didn't want to give Dorian the satisfaction of an answer. But then: "I caught him trying to creep into Casey's room," she admitted quietly. "He wasn't planning anything nice. And he clearly intends to try again when he's sure he won't get caught. I want him the hell away from her."

"And that's enough for you to sacrifice his life?"

"Who else can I choose?!" Poppy exclaimed, growing rapidly more emotional.

Dorian chuckled, for he felt the answer was obvious. "Fred, for starters."

"I hate him because he's Fred," she said, clucking her tongue in distaste, "not because he's a bad person."

"But you saved Rachelle and Andrew because they're your friends. Seems like nepotism if you ask me."

"They also happen to be two of the most honest, hard-working, lovely people in the club. That I'm friends with them is a coincidence."

Dorian's mouth opened in surprise. "You're going to be unbiased with your choices?"

"...maybe," Poppy muttered, averting her eyes from his. She rubbed at her arm in discomfort. "I don't know. I'm working it out. Either way, Ross goes first."

"Fine by me. I'll take him next week when your two week 'trip' is officially up – when you have to tell the group why they absolutely have to stay."

Poppy stared at him in horror. "No. He has to go *now.*"

"So quick to throw his life away. I'm appalled."

"I'm tired of staying up all night just in case he tries to sneak into Casey's room," Poppy said, entirely ignoring Dorian's false disappointment.

He considered this for a few seconds. The weight of his deal with her as well as worrying about Ross Bridges was clearly affecting Poppy's sleep and, by extension, her health. Dorian had to keep her in the best shape possible. "Is he the one with the crazy upper-arm strength?" he asked, thinking about an arm wrestling competition the club had indulged in the night before.

Poppy nodded.

"Will your club believe it if I say I kicked him out and called the police after I found him trying to get into Casey's room?"

"It's not like anyone has phone signal to find out otherwise," Poppy replied, her voice strangely calm considering the topic of conversation. "And that's what I caught him doing, anyway. If I say you caught him at it a second time then people will understand why you did what you did. It'll work."

"Then consider your problem taken care of."

She made a face. "Don't talk about it like that."

"I like you much better like this, by the way. When you're not ignoring me and looking like someone just died."

"Hell if I care if you like me!" she spat, raising her arm as if she wanted to hit him. Dorian grabbed it.

"Getting physical is never the answer, Poppy King," he murmured, all smirks and false seriousness. "Well, not in an infirmary, anyway. In a bedroom—"

"Don't touch me," Poppy bit out, disgusted.

Dorian laughed before calming back down. "I still have to cut you open."

"I know. I was procrastinating."

"I'm going to have to do something similar to last time."

"I know. Hence the procrastination."

He loosened the grip on her arm. "I'll try and keep it cleaner this time."

Poppy's face grew uncertain when Dorian retrieved a knife. It was much larger than the scalpel he had used before. "Please don't take as much blood this time," she said, her voice small and quiet. It took Dorian aback – both her tone of voice and the fact she said *please.*

"That was by accident," Dorian explained in lieu of saying sorry. He positioned the blade above Poppy's arm with careful precision. "I don't make the same mistake twice."

And so Poppy clenched her eyes shut as she prepared for the knife to go through her skin, but after a few seconds she peeked through her lashes to see that Dorian had paused. "What are you doing?" she asked, thoroughly disconcerted.

"I could give you a painkiller, you know," he said. It had never crossed his mind before; then again, Dorian had never anticipated being in this situation in the first place.

But Poppy shook her head. "Just fucking do it, Dorian."

It was the first time Poppy had uttered his name since her discovery of his true nature. For some reason it unnerved him. So he plunged the blade into Poppy's arm, holding her down in order to prevent her from squirming away. She let out a wordless cry of pain as Dorian quickly brought the heavily bleeding limb to his mouth, once more revelling in the sensation of literally drinking in life. It filled up every crevice of his body, making Dorian feel fuller and stronger than ever before.

There was an unbearable, tingling sensation behind his ears that told him his human form was mere moments away from crumbling down around him. But Dorian didn't want to transform in front of Poppy again. He didn't think she'd be able to handle it; part of him knew she hadn't even begun to process the way he really looked.

A minute later Dorian had to force himself to pull away from Poppy's arm before he got carried away. He stared at her, knowing his face likely looked plenty monstrous even without transforming given the blood that was dripping from his teeth and tongue and lips.

"Thanks for dinner," he said, risking a smile simply to see

what Poppy would do. But Poppy didn't respond even when Dorian first cleaned himself up and then her arm, wrapping it in fresh bandages with adrenaline-shaky hands. So he added on: "It was far less messy this time."

Poppy wasn't looking at him, much less listening to him. It made Dorian wildly frustrated; he felt tempted to forcibly *make* her look at him – to push her down on the bed and—

And then what? Dorian shoved the feeling to the side. He was deliriously high on Poppy's blood. No doubt that had something to do with his thoughts.

He stepped away to let Poppy get back to her feet and cast a critical eye over her. *Less pale than last time,* Dorian concluded, relieved. There was barely a stagger to her gait as she walked towards the door and unlocked it.

"Don't forget about Ross," she muttered, and with a slam of the door she was gone.

"I won't!" he called out after her, though he knew she likely couldn't hear him. Dorian was already keenly aware of how much he wanted more of Poppy's blood as he stood there, staring at the bed the young woman had only just been sitting on.

He licked his lips in longing, wondering if there would ever come a point when he took enough to satisfy him.

Dorian couldn't believe it when he literally caught the doomed man, Ross Bridges, in the act of skulking outside Casey's bedroom door hours later when everyone was asleep.

"Well aren't you a worthless son of a bitch," Dorian laughed, immediately injecting a sedative into the startled man before hefting him over a shoulder and dumping him in a locked room in the west wing.

One of his clients was going to be very, very happy indeed.

INTERLUDE I

When Ross Bridges woke up his first instinct was to take a swing at the fucker who had crept up on him.

But he couldn't.

It wasn't because he was strapped to a bed, though that was the circumstance in which he now found himself.

His right arm was gone.

Ross began to scream in horror, the sound louder and more guttural than anything to have come out of his throat in his entire life leading up to now.

Nobody heard him.

ANGELICA FISHER

ANDREW

POPPY WAS ACTING WEIRD. WHICH WAS odd, because Andrew Martin Forbes was used to being the weird one. Not that he thought any of his own behaviour was weird, of course, but other people thought he was so he supposed he must be.

The Outdoors Sports Society was halfway through its second week at the Highlands Adrenaline Sports Facility. Andrew had, on the grand scheme of things, thoroughly enjoyed his time there. Most people wouldn't think this was immediately apparent given his demeanour, but those who counted knew.

Andrew didn't want the trip to end, all things considered. Ever since Poppy asked him if he wanted to join her on her 'escape adulthood' trip to New Zealand he had decided to use the two week club getaway as a test to see if he truly would be able to go. So that Poppy wouldn't have to babysit him, as she'd put it.

For though Andrew wanted nothing more than to be seen as an adult by those around him – especially his parents –

Poppy's plan of simply never having to care about being one was even better. And Andrew felt most comfortable when he was outdoors, surrounded by water and rocks and boats and trees and as few people as possible.

Well, that wasn't strictly true. Andrew very much enjoyed being part of the club, even though there were many people he did not like within it. But he liked finally being part of something and making genuine friends on his own for the first time in his life. It was his biggest achievement.

He thought back to his first week at university four years ago when a hyper-active, keen-to-help Poppy King had somehow convinced Andrew to come along to a freshers' course on climbing at a nearby sports centre. Gangly, soft Andrew thought there was no way he could do something that required so much coordination, let alone the fact that he'd have to talk to lots of loud, obnoxious people.

But Poppy had been so eager to get him involved and was somehow even happier when Andrew actually showed up for the course. She'd taught him first-hand how to climb. Andrew discovered that, to his shock and delight, he loved it.

Four years later he was no longer soft and uncoordinated. Andrew knew he probably had one of the physically fittest bodies in the club, since he didn't drink or smoke and he made sure to only eat exactly what he should. Andrew enjoyed how good being healthy actually felt; gone were his days spent trapped inside eating junk food with nobody to go out exploring with him as he had done as a child and teenager. His parents didn't like the outdoors, after all.

Now he spent all the time he possibly could outside. The next natural step for him was to move out of his parents' house and become truly independent, but Andrew knew this was the most difficult step of all.

Though perhaps not as hard as he'd originally thought, given that Andrew had finally stood up for himself and managed to argue vehemently with his parents about the very trip he was wishing wouldn't end.

He hadn't told Poppy or Fred about the argument; they'd only worry. But Andrew's parents had been completely against him going on the trip. They didn't even know he'd woken up at five in the morning and sneaked out of the house in order to go on said trip without their permission.

Well I suppose my parents have probably worked that out by now, Andrew thought, laughing a little despite himself.

Fred looked at him in surprise. The two of them were currently tackling the indoor climbing wall using only the blue hand- and foot-holds – the most difficult course on the wall.

"Did you just laugh, Andrew?" Fred asked.

"Maybe."

"What's so funny?"

"Nothing."

"You're a terrible liar."

"That doesn't mean I have to tell you why I was laughing."

Fred paused as he considered this. "True."

They completed the rest of the course in silence, dropping back down to the floor once they were done. Andrew had beaten him to the top, of course, for it had been precisely three months since Fred had last managed to best him. Andrew was proud of that. Though Poppy had gotten him into the club it had been Fred who truly stuck with Andrew when it came to learning the ins and outs of climbing. That was because Poppy's style of climbing was ultimately far too haphazard for Andrew, who preferred the rules and safety of Fred's method.

He only wished both Fred and Poppy would get on together. They were Andrew's two closest friends; he didn't understand why they disliked each other so much. Poppy had tried to explain it to him, once, but that ultimately resulted in her saying that Fred 'just fucking pissed her off'.

Andrew didn't get it.

He avoided the spot on the floor where Poppy had fallen ten days prior, for he could still see her accident in his head. The way her arm had sickeningly crunched as she collapsed on top of it. The way her face was ashen and lifeless for a few horrifying seconds. The way Andrew couldn't even see what exactly was wrong with her from all the blood soaking her clothes and skin.

And yet Poppy was fine. Somehow, against all odds, she was okay. Andrew didn't know how it was possible. In any other circumstance he'd have argued and reasoned through what happened until he understood it. But for this one solitary case, he didn't.

Poppy was alive, and that was all he cared about.

She was bickering at a table with the owner of the facility, Dorian Kapros. Though Poppy seemed to have actively avoided the man after her accident, over the past few days Andrew had noticed them spending more and more time together. He didn't like it at all.

Neither did Nate or Casey. Andrew was usually pretty oblivious about what Poppy affectionately referred to as 'non-PG social interactions'. For his benefit, naturally. But Casey had made it very clear that she liked the look of Dorian Kapros, which confused Andrew because she also liked the look of Patrick, the nice man with the old boat whose surname he later found out was Jones. He didn't have a Kelvin engine in his boat, it had turned out, but the fact he owned a boat at all automatically made him a person Andrew liked.

The reason he was confused by this was that Andrew couldn't fathom ever liking more than one person in a 'non-PG' way. For him that person was, of course, Poppy, which was also why he knew Nate didn't like Poppy talking with Dorian so much, because Nate also liked Poppy.

Nate was nice. He didn't speak too loudly or too quickly to Andrew, and he and his best friend Rich played chess and other games with Andrew when he was being especially quiet at club socials. This was why he was okay with the fact Nate liked Poppy, and that the two of them were kind-of dating.

Except now it seemed like they weren't anymore, though Nate clearly still liked Poppy a lot.

But Poppy was distant with everyone now – not just Nate. By comparison she spent more time talking to Andrew than anyone else, even Rachelle, which Andrew considered odd. It wasn't like her to be so quiet. At first he figured it was a result of Poppy's fall, since she never fell, but now he was beginning to believe that something else was going on.

He thought it might have to do with Dorian. He was a new variable to factor in, after all. But Andrew didn't understand if Poppy actually *liked* Dorian or not. It always seemed as if she was arguing with him, and she never looked happy when she walked away from their conversations. Andrew hadn't asked her about it because he didn't want to find out that she actually *did* like Dorian and all of their arguing was just another social interaction he didn't understand.

"Andrew? Hey, Forbes, get out of your harness before walking over to the social area!" Fred called out. Andrew was surprised; he'd totally forgotten about the harness. Feeling thoroughly embarrassed he shook himself out of it before heading over to sit on the sofa nearest Poppy.

She glanced at him, smiling briefly before tucking an errant strand of hair behind her ear and returning to her hushed, angry conversation with Dorian.

"You know what you're saying?" Dorian asked her.

Poppy rolled her eyes. "Of course I do."

"Yes, but do you actually? Your friends would have me believe you make most of your speeches up on the fly."

Poppy flinched. "Maybe before. But not today."

"Then go give your speech."

Dorian flashed a grin at Andrew when he turned and saw him sitting so close by. Andrew gave him the briefest of uncertain smiles back – he *thinked* he liked Dorian as a person, even if he wasn't supposed to like him if the man liked Poppy – before turning his attention back to Poppy herself.

With a sigh she stood up from the sofa and stalked towards the large glass wall overlooking the mountains, her face like thunder for a moment or two. Then she shook her head, ran a hand through her hair, and when she looked out over the social area her expression was bright and happy and very typically *Poppy.*

"Come sit down, guys!" she shouted out for everyone to hear. "I have some really exciting news for you all!"

Of course everyone rushed over to listen. It wasn't just that Poppy had news; it was that she actually sounded like herself for the first time in two weeks. Of course Andrew wasn't the only one pleased about this.

When everyone in the club had gathered to listen Poppy continued, "I know it's been a bit weird the past few days. After Ross...left—"

"Good riddance!" Casey called out.

When everyone found out about Ross stalking Casey and how both Poppy and Dorian had caught him in the act on separate occasions, most of the group had been shocked. But when it transpired that Casey had been worried about him for a while, and that Rachelle and Poppy had been observing Ross' behaviour on her behalf, the club completely supported the decision to kick Ross out of the facility. It was clearly for the best. Andrew couldn't imagine being in Casey's position, knowing that someone was creeping about her bedroom at night.

He was glad Ross was gone.

"And I know I haven't been myself since my fall," Poppy said, "but things are about to change for us! I'm sure all of you still can't believe how great Dorian's sports facility is." She beamed at the man. Andrew didn't like it. "And I know I speak for many of us when I say we definitely don't deserve getting to use it."

Several people laughed. This was the Poppy that Andrew knew and felt so strongly for. He smiled to himself as Poppy spoke in her easy-going, enthusiastic voice. "But it turns out that maybe we deserve to use it, after all. Dorian is actually a scout looking for the best of the best adrenaline sports enthusiasts in the country."

The air became abuzz with excitement. Even Andrew was interested, temporarily forgetting that he had decided he wasn't allowed to like Dorian.

"That's right, folks," Dorian said, standing up and taking over from Poppy. He was almost a foot taller than her – taller than Andrew and Nate and even Fred. Andrew thought they looked good together despite himself. "I've been watching all of you for the past few days and you have thoroughly impressed me. I have several people very interested in meeting you. The thing is—"

"Ugh, there's always a catch," Casey said in a stage whisper. Rachelle shushed her with a sharp elbow to her stomach.

Dorian laughed. "I think you might like the catch. The problem is that these people can't all come and see you at the same time, and some of them want to put you through altogether more rigorous testing. Overall we anticipate that it might take up to the end of August."

"But that's three months away!" someone called out, stating the obvious.

"Thanks for that, John," Poppy said. "Dorian and the

people he's in contact with are aware of that. So to compensate us – and to convince us into staying in the facility over summer – they're willing to pay each of us up to two thousand pounds, depending on how long we stay."

There was a murmur of approval at the figure.

"What do you mean, depending on how long we stay?"

"Thanks for the obvious question, John," Poppy said, rolling her eyes. "I was getting to that bit. Dorian's contacts are going to pull out anyone they like from the program to discuss further work with them and put them through individual training. Now I know a couple of you are actually set to graduate in a few weeks—"

"Screw that," John said, "I was gonna graduate *in absentia* anyway."

"I'll do the same for two grand."

"Same!"

Andrew nodded along with the people who spoke, thoroughly agreeing with them. He could use the money to help him move out of his parents' house – or travel with Poppy. But if one of Dorian's friends wanted to take him on as an athlete...Andrew couldn't imagine it. Excitement bubbled beneath the surface of his skin. Could he really turn his passion into his career?

Poppy smiled when she saw Andrew nodding, though she didn't meet his eyes. "Well if John, Mateusz, Chloe and Andrew are all okay with graduating *in absentia*, and I know I certainly am, then that leaves...Fred?"

She stared at him. Fred's face was blank; Andrew had no idea whether he was happy or worried about the prospect. But, eventually, he nodded.

The room only grew more excited now that the graduands had agreed to stay.

"Count me in!" someone yelled.

"That's way better money than my crappy waitress gig, anyway," said another.

"I don't even care that there's no Wi-Fi here."

"Think my girlfriend will get the idea that I want to break up with her if she doesn't hear from me for two months?"

That was John again. Lily, who was sitting beside him and had a fiancé, punched him in the arm. "Don't be such a dick, John! Jesus Christ."

"Well it's true," he protested. "How am I supposed to contact her?"

"Just give me the contact details of everyone you wish to be notified," Dorian said. "The centre will blanket contact them all. What you'll be doing over summer involves a Non-Disclosure Agreement for the privacy and protection of the people coming to see you, so your family and partners can only be told that you're taking part in a paid study. Now is there anyone who doesn't want to participate?"

Nobody said anything. Of course they wanted to stay; they were getting paid to do something they loved with a group full of their best friends. Andrew couldn't believe his luck; he had only just been wishing that the trip wouldn't end. Now it was going to last for another three months. Three months!

When it was clear the announcement was over the club began to dissipate in order to get together the contact information they needed to give Dorian. Poppy sidled up to Andrew, so quietly he jumped in fright. He expected her to laugh at his reaction. Instead, she was pale and serious and... sad. Andrew didn't like the look on her face at all.

"I need to speak to you in private, Andrew," she said quietly. Andrew liked the sound of that even less than the look on her face but he followed Poppy outside nonetheless. Out of the corner of his eye he saw Fred was watching them, until

Rachelle distracted him with a question. Rachelle could always distract Fred, even though they were no longer dating. Andrew wondered why they didn't just get back together.

"What is it, Poppy?" he asked when he forced his attention back on her.

Poppy sighed. The wind whipped her hair around her face; a strand of it got caught on her lip. Andrew wanted her to fix it, but she didn't. "Go home, Andrew," was all Poppy said.

He froze. "...what?"

"In four days when the original trip ends," she elaborated. "Go home. There's no way in hell your parents will let you stay out here for three months."

"No."

Poppy seemed shocked by Andrew's immediate rejection. She looked at him with a face full of genuine concern, and chewed on the strand of hair that had flown into her mouth. "Please," she begged. "Think about this seriously. Can you handle being here for potentially fifteen weeks?"

Andrew bristled at the question. "You were the one who encouraged me to come on the trip in the first place, Poppy."

"Two weeks and three months are completely different, Andrew!"

"I know that," he said. He straightened his posture and drew back his shoulders – Poppy always told him that if he had to convince someone of something then he had to say it properly. "But you know I'm enjoying being here. It's relaxing. I don't have to worry about what to do after graduating or about my parents or anything."

She frowned. "Why would you worry about your parents?"

"Because they didn't want me to come so I left home without telling them."

Poppy stared at Andrew, taking a step back in horror. She

grabbed the wooden barrier separating the outdoor terrace from the loch; her hand was shaking. "Please tell me that's not true. Oh, Andrew, please tell me that's not true."

But Andrew stood his ground, though he was confused about why Poppy was overreacting so badly. "It was my choice to come here. And it's my choice to stay. I'm an adult, Poppy. And so are you, whether you like the fact you are or not. So let me make my own decisions."

Andrew didn't wait for Poppy's response. He walked away before she had a chance to convince him that he was, in fact, deadly wrong about being prepared for three months away from home, all but running through the central building and into the east wing.

"Andrew, wait!" Poppy called out a few moments later, clearly following him. He turned to say something to her but, in the time it took him to do so, her attention was already elsewhere. Poppy had paused in front of the communal shower room, her expression grave as she peered inside.

Andrew frowned, confused, as Poppy continued to watch whatever she was watching for a few seconds. Then she shook her head and stalked towards Andrew.

"Angelica is bullying the younger girls again," she muttered. "I think it was Jenny this time. I warned her – I fucking warned her. This isn't high school, for fuck's sake."

Andrew was taken aback. Poppy only swore when she was truly upset. Not just angry; upset. She wasn't close to Jenny Adams – the youngest member of the club – nor was she close to Angelica. But instead of stopping what was going on in the shower room as he'd expected her to, Poppy pulled out her phone and stormed past Andrew towards her own bedroom, clearly having forgotten about why she'd run after him in the first place.

He peered over Poppy's shoulder to see what she was looking at on her phone: it was the club's register of members.

Rachelle and Andrew's names were highlighted. Poppy's name was scored out.

As was Ross Bridges.

Poppy scored out Angelica's name as Andrew looked on just before she entered her bedroom and slammed the door shut. He was thoroughly confused. What did it mean, to have his and Rachelle's names highlighted whilst others were crossed out? There was no connection between the crossed-off names. Andrew had no clue what it meant.

Frustrated that he couldn't work it out he was also aware, somehow, that it wasn't something he could ask Poppy about. If he did then she would lie, even though she never lied. Andrew was certain of it.

Which meant he could only come to one conclusion – the same one he had been fighting with ever since she fell.

Something was wrong with Poppy King.

Andrew was going to work out what it was.

POPPY

"*Ahahahahaha!*"

"Shut up, Dorian."

He didn't stop laughing, the sound infuriatingly full of mirth and lovely to hear. But Dorian was laughing *at* Poppy, not with her. She couldn't stand it.

"I can't believe you fought so hard for Andrew to go and *he didn't want to,*" Dorian heaved, rubbing at his eyes as if he had literally been brought to tears. "You couldn't convince him to leave even though he hangs on your every word! I—"

"Stop it. It's not funny."

"Not to you it isn't. To me, on the other hand..."

Poppy made a noise of disgust and turned from him. She'd never wanted to engage in conversation with Dorian in the first place but after waiting for his 'instructors' to arrive without saying a word for fifteen minutes the silence had grown unbearable. Now Poppy wished she'd been born with enough patience to deal with quiet, for the sound of Dorian laughing at her was far worse.

They were sitting in a small staff room attached to the infirmary awaiting his late-arriving friends. The entire club was going on a white-water rafting trip; the route they'd be taking was littered with targets for those in the group who wanted to try their hand at archery from the back of the rafts. On the face of it this sounded impossible for most people to attempt – even Poppy – but she knew of three club members who would actually be good at it. Mateusz Kowalski, a final year politics student who got on well with Nate and his best friend Rich; Paul Tobin, a third year student whom Poppy got on reasonably well with...and Angelica Fisher.

After Poppy discovered Angelica bullying one of the first year students, Jenny, the day before, she knew she'd have to be the next sacrifice. This wasn't the first time Angelica had bullied the younger students, after all. Poppy had thought she'd stopped for good after both she and Fred caught Angelica in the act and told her they'd kick her out of the club if she kept it up.

Clearly Angelica hadn't listened.

And yet Poppy didn't want to sacrifice her for something so...ordinary. It was callous and wrong, yes, but Angelica could well see the error of her ways, given time. Except Poppy didn't *have* time – she only had three days. Nevertheless, she knew she had to at least speak to Jenny privately to scope out how severe Angelica's bullying was before she condemned her to the same fate that had befallen Ross Bridges.

Poppy glanced at Dorian through a haphazard curtain of hair. She wasn't sure if she wanted to know if Ross was still alive or not...or what state he might be in if he *was* alive.

Dorian, of course, caught her looking. His blue eyes lit up with interest. "What's on your mind?" he asked, a small smile curling his lips which Poppy would never admit that she liked the look of.

"Nothing."

"Doesn't look like nothing to me."

"As if I'd tell you, anyway," she scowled, pushing her hair away from her face before tearing an elastic band off her wrist with her teeth to tie it up. Dorian watched every minuscule movement she made like a ravenous bird of prey. It made Poppy either want to punch him or run off. "And stop pulling me away from my club *to talk*," she added on, flicking her ponytail over her shoulder as she did so. "I hate it. I keep having to fob off stupid questions."

Dorian leaned towards her, immediately intrigued, just as Poppy equally as immediately regretted bringing up the subject in the first place. "Stupid questions? Like what?"

"...never mind."

"See, now I want to know even more. Don't leave me hanging."

Poppy splayed her fingertips across her forehead, feeling a headache coming on that Dorian was solely responsible for. "You do realise that only makes me want to tell you even less, right?" she muttered. "And like I said: I don't want to talk to you. At. All."

Dorian feigned hurt as he countered, "But you're going to spend the rest of your life with me. Aren't you the least bit interested in getting to know one another?"

Poppy stood up to leave – what little patience she possessed well and truly used up – when the door to the staff room opened and four people walked in. One of them was Patrick, which wasn't surprising. He always helped with the water-based activities. It was clear enough to Poppy that he was friends with Dorian, though she still wasn't sure if he knew what was *really* going on. She liked to think he was human, but...

That almost makes it worse, Poppy thought. *A human unknowingly helping Dorian out with his meat farm is all kinds of fucked up.*

The other three Poppy only recognised in passing since she was yet to actually participate in any strenuous outdoor activity. One of them was a very attractive woman with dark brown hair pulled back into a bouncing ponytail much tidier than Poppy's own, who looked to be the same age as Dorian. She barely glanced at Poppy as she swept into the room.

The two who followed her were both men, though they were complete opposites to each other. One of them was raven-haired, broad-shouldered and so tall he towered several inches over Dorian and Patrick. The other man was much smaller, with a lithe frame, white-blonde hair and eyes that Poppy could almost believe were yellow but were, upon second glance, hazel. They both smiled at Poppy when they caught her watching them; she promptly looked away.

"The club are all ready to go," Patrick said. "Except... Poppy?" He narrowed his eyes at her arm, gaze equal parts critical and concerned. "How's your injury? I don't imagine you can take part in something like white-water rafting. Which is a shame," he grinned, "because the course is one hell of a ride."

Poppy didn't know how to respond. She was dying to get out of the facility and she *loved* white-water rafting, but she knew she shouldn't be getting her bandages wet in order to keep up the façade that she was still injured. Then she caught the look on Dorian's face. Something about his expression very much warned her to absolutely not go.

Which meant, of course, she would.

Poppy matched Patrick's grin as she swung her arm around. "The wound has fully closed up, actually," she said cheerily. "It's just a little sore. I don't see why I can't join in today so long as I don't take the lead in the raft."

To her satisfaction Dorian looked furious. Enraged, stormy, murderous. *Good,* she thought, thoroughly satisfied that his good mood had been destroyed.

"Poppy," Dorian began in a tone that belied his anger, taking a step towards her in the process. He touched her shoulder to make her face him; Poppy resisted backing away and giving him the finger. "Do you honestly think that's a good —"

"Come on, Dorian, we haven't seen the president in action at all," the behemoth of a man cut in. He smiled at Poppy once more and held out his hand, though given that she knew he was a monster shaking his hand was the last thing she wanted to do. But she had to, so she did.

If he's this tall as a human then how big is he in his real form? Poppy wondered, uncomfortably aware of the strength of the man's handshake. *He could probably crush my fingers without dropping his human guise even though I'm almost indestructible.*

Poppy desperately pushed such musings to the side. She had long since made the decision that the best thing for her was to learn as little as possible of Dorian's world – including knowing more about her own immortal blood. That way, Dorian would never get the impression that Poppy was at all interested in his kind, his way of life, or him.

"The name's Nick," the man continued, pulling her out of her own head. "I don't think any of us have had the pleasure of meeting you yet, Poppy." He released Poppy from his crushing handshake to gesture towards the thinner man. "This is Steven, and the lovely lady to my right is Aisling."

Aisling still didn't look at Poppy; clearly she didn't think she was worth her interest. For some reason this annoyed Poppy despite the fact it was, in reality, a very good thing.

"It's so nice to finally meet you all like this," Poppy said to the three of them, even though it wasn't. "I look forward to working together now I'm finally on the mend." Another lie.

"Well if you really insist on trying to kill yourself *again*," Dorian said, having schooled his expression to something more like resignation even though his eyes remained tight with irritation, "then you better go get ready. We'll meet the club down by the loch in fifteen minutes."

Poppy swept her gaze over the group of people in front of her. It was clear they wanted to talk without her present, which suggested that Patrick probably *was* a monster. Feeling sick at the thought, she nodded her head in goodbye and quickly vacated the room. But something stopped Poppy from leaving the west wing as instructed.

She glanced back at the door.

I want to know what they're talking about, she realised, hating herself for knowing what she planned to do next. Looking upwards, she wondered if she could get away with creeping through the ceiling as she had done in order to eavesdrop on Dorian almost two weeks ago. The only reason she'd been caught back then was because she'd been so panicked by what Dorian had said.

Now Poppy was numb to words. There was nothing she could hear that would cause her to react like she had done before. It was the only way she could avoid breaking down entirely, after all. Poppy knew it was a flawed coping mechanism – it was only a matter of time before the horror of her situation came crashing down around her – but for now it was working. Smiling grimly she pulled herself up into the ceiling, the action much easier now that her arm was completely healed.

A hand immediately wrapped around her ankle and yanked her back down. For one horrible second Poppy thought it was sharp and clawed, but when she turned her head and saw Dorian she was relieved to discover he was still human.

His face was mutinous.

Dorian wasted no time in dragging Poppy down the corridor until they were out of sight and earshot of the staff room, slamming her against the wall when he was satisfied they were alone.

"Might I suggest *not* eavesdropping on a group of monsters who could rip you apart in a matter of seconds, Poppy?" he whispered into her ear. Poppy struggled against his arms but Dorian held onto her so tightly she could barely breathe let alone escape. So she glowered at him, instead, resisting the urge to spit in his face mere inches from her own.

"Is it so wrong for me to want to know what they're saying?" she demanded.

"I'll *tell* you what they're saying if you'll just stop being so damn nosey!"

"Oh, and I'm supposed to believe you?"

"If it'll stop you wilfully and carelessly putting your life on the line then of course I'll tell you what they're saying," Dorian growled. "Or have you forgotten that in order for our deal to stand that you need to be *alive*?"

Poppy said nothing. She supposed Dorian was right.

"That doesn't change the fact I don't trust you," she muttered after a few tense seconds, turning her gaze to the floor to avoid Dorian's predatory eyes.

"And I don't trust you, yet here we are."

"Let go of me."

Dorian only tightened his grip as he whispered into Poppy's ear once more. "Not until you promise to behave."

She took a few moments simply to listen to the beating of her own heart. It was thumping too hard and too fast in her ribcage; Poppy had no doubt Dorian could feel it against his chest.

"Fine," she eventually said, though it pained her to promise Dorian anything. "Fine. Let me go. I need to get ready."

"Don't stand out today."

Poppy looked up at him. His face was far too close to hers, which only caused her heart to beat faster and push adrenaline around her body, urging her to fight or flee. But Poppy knew she could do neither, so she asked, "What do you mean?"

Dorian sighed a sigh full of impatience. "If anyone sees how talented you are then they'll want you. The fewer clients who have cause to pay you any attention the better."

It made sense, of course, but Poppy didn't like it anyway. It only reiterated that her entire club was being judged in the same manner; if Poppy underperformed then someone else looked better by comparison.

"You have to give excuses for half the group, anyway," Poppy reasoned, "since I'm saving half of them. Surely you can make an excuse for me."

"Are you serious?" Dorian scoffed. "You and I both know that *your* level of talent is not so easily ignored. They'll want to know why I won't let them bid on you, since I shouldn't be taking my best stock for myself. For the others it's fine, but you – they'll ask questions about you. They'll be suspicious. And they can't be suspicious about you."

It was infuriatingly infallible. And yet even still, Poppy felt rebellious. She didn't want to do what Dorian told her. "Okay," she lied smoothly. "No showing off. I'm supposed to have an injury, anyway. Now let me go."

Poppy flinched when Dorian's lips brushed against her neck. He just barely licked her skin with the tip of his tongue. "The fuck are you doing?" she whispered, resisting the urge to scream or possibly cry.

"You're fully healed again?" Dorian murmured softly. "All blood regenerated?"

"I – yes."

"In four days, like before."

"Three," Poppy corrected before she had the sense to stop herself. "I've been fine since yesterday. You took less blood this time, remember?" She hated that she was telling Dorian the truth, though Poppy reasoned it was fear that was making her do so.

"Mhm."

She had no clue what 'mhm' was supposed to mean, but then Dorian's canines bit down into the muscle of her shoulder and Poppy stopped caring about translating it. She didn't dare move; with every tense second that passed Dorian's teeth got sharper and sharper. When his nails began digging into her waist Poppy realised they were turning into claws.

"Dorian, stop," Poppy whimpered, terrified. She could hardly see. Hardly breathe. It felt as if her heart would burst. "I think you're – *stop, please, you're transforming!*"

Dorian froze immediately. For a moment his hold on Poppy tightened, and she bit her lip to stop from screaming, but then he staggered backwards as if drunk. There was something distinctly inhuman about his eyes – the blue was *too* blue, and his pupils were more bar-shaped than circular – yet in the space of a blink they were back to normal.

"Saturday can't come quickly enough," Dorian said, gazing at Poppy longingly. It disturbed her to no end to see him looking at her like that.

A second passed between them. Two. Three.

When it became clear Dorian would say or do no more Poppy pushed past him and all but fled down the corridor, through the central building and into the east wing, not stopping to talk to anyone until she reached her bedroom.

As she changed her clothes with fumbling, nervous fingers, it became clear to Poppy that, if Dorian wasn't careful, he wouldn't have to worry about any of his clients wishing to consume her.

He'd do it himself.

JENNY ADAMS

POPPY

"HEY, MORPH, WATCH THAT ROCK!"

"Way ahead of you, Nate."

Poppy, Nate, Fred, Jenny, Angelica, Casey and the 'instructor' Aisling had ended up in a raft together. Poppy of course hadn't wanted to be in the same boat as Fred but, given her injury, the vice-president had insisted upon it. She was highly aware of Dorian sulking in another raft, watching her like a hawk as much as the intensive course allowed him to. Patrick, in a raft with Rachelle and Andrew, also seemed put out that he wasn't in the same boat as Poppy – because of Casey, she presumed.

Poppy had been careful not to show off *too* much during the course so far. She was still supposed to be hurt, after all, and Dorian's warning echoed sinister and spine-tingling in her head. But with every rock avoided and waterfall ridden and spray of foam in her face Poppy grew bolder. She found herself laughing, high on adrenaline and glee as her raft drew ahead of the rest of the group.

Nate's eyes shone with enthusiasm when they battered around a particularly tough bend in the river. "You seem much better, Morph!" he called out over the crashing waves.

She grinned. "Clearly I just needed some fresh air!"

"Keep your eyes on the damn water, not each other!" Fred yelled at them.

Poppy was sitting beside Jenny, making sure she was as far away from Angelica as possible. Jenny kept glancing at her tormentor with furtive eyes, as if expecting the other girl to sneer at her. But Angelica was too busy hitting her targets to notice the younger girl, whooping in delight when she hit her third bullseye in a row.

Despite how much she didn't like her Poppy had to concede that Angelica was truly an excellent archer. The best in their club, probably, which wasn't surprising given that she was also the star of their university's archery club. And yet it made no matter how talented Angelica Fisher was in the grand scheme of things. Poppy had a decision to make, and it had nothing at all to do with being able to hit the centre of a target.

"I saw you and Angelica in the shower room yesterday," Poppy risked saying as their raft soared over a low waterfall. There was so much noise that her words only carried over to Jenny, which was what Poppy had intended.

The girl's nervous eyes widened. "...what did you see?"

"Enough," Poppy replied, keeping a grin on her face that belied the seriousness of the conversation she'd struck up – she couldn't risk having anyone notice what she was saying. "Why haven't you told me or Fred about it?"

"I – I don't know. I was hoping I could handle it myself."

"What has Angelica done to you? How bad has it gotten?"

Jenny and Poppy both grimaced when the raft glanced against a rock and jolted their spines. "I can handle it," Jenny told her, after they had recovered.

But Poppy couldn't leave the conversation there. Even though it meant condemning a person to death she had to push forward. "That's not what I asked, Jen. As president of the society it's my responsibility to deal with any members acting out of order."

Jenny sighed and cast another glance at Angelica. For a long moment she said nothing at all, and Poppy became convinced she wasn't going to get anything useful out of the girl. But then: "She's hidden my bags and destroyed my coursework before," Jenny let out, speaking so quickly Poppy barely managed to understand what she said. "She once forced me to drink so much at a social that I couldn't stop throwing up, then she took photos and threatened to pass them about if I didn't buy all *her* drinks on future nights out. She pushed me down the stairs once just to see if my balance was good enough to not get injured."

Poppy stared at her, horrified. This wasn't 'ordinary' bullying; Angelica's actions were malicious. Her decision in three days had been made whether she liked it or not. She forced a smile to her face for Jenny's sake and in that instant another, far happier decision was made: Poppy would save Jenny this week. It seemed only fair.

And yet I'm sacrificing a life to monsters, Poppy thought, stomach lurching as she caught Dorian's eye in a raft on her right. He was too busy glowering at her to notice how false her expression was. *How is that fair?*

"Everything will be fine," she told Jenny, which was at least the truth for Jenny specifically. "I'll take care of it."

"You won't – you won't tell her I told you, will you?" the girl asked, face paling at the prospect.

"Of course not, Jen. Just trust me, okay? I'll sort it out."

Jenny looked visibly relieved, which somehow made Poppy feel worse. "Thank you, Poppy. And I'm glad your arm's doing much better; we've missed you out here."

"I've missed all of you, too!" Poppy called out, voice wavering when the raft just barely avoided being toppled over. She refocused her attention on what was left of the course, pushing the boat further and faster until all thoughts of monsters and Angelica Fisher's fate were washed out of her mind.

When they turned the final bend both Poppy and Casey spied a tall waterfall crashing down into the large pool that signalled the end of the course.

Casey quirked an eyebrow at her. "Sure you can handle that with your arm, King?"

"Who do you think I am, O'Donnell?" Poppy replied, flippant and defiant in the face of the inevitable consequences of her next action. But the waterfall was there, and Poppy was Poppy, and all she wanted to do was be herself for a few precious minutes.

It didn't matter that Dorian would scream at her for jumping off a waterfall; right now Poppy simply didn't care.

When finally the raft drifted to a stop in the pool, the two of them ripped off their life-jackets and swiftly jumped out of the raft, unsurprisingly to the sounds of several people shouting at them to come back. But Casey and Poppy paid them no mind, Casey quickly taking the lead with her lightning front crawl.

"Oi, girls, wait for me!" Nate exclaimed as he swam to catch up with them. Of course Nate was going to join them; the trio were well-known to be the biggest daredevils in the society.

Once they reached the other side it was easy to climb up to the top of the waterfall, for much of the journey was walkable. There were only a few places here and there that required the three of them to use their hands to clamber upwards.

"*King!*" Fred screamed up at them when they reached the top. His voice was barely audible over the roaring of the waterfall. "Don't you dare jump with your arm like that!"

But Poppy wasn't listening, and neither Nate nor Casey suggested she back out of the jump. They were all three giddy with adrenaline and the excitement of their impending leap.

Poppy looked at the two of them as she toed towards the edge of the water. "We better make this worth the climb."

"Fred's gonna be fuming that everyone's followed suit," Casey giggled, pointing to a trail of five or six people making their way up to the top of the waterfall.

"Good," Nate said. "He's grown too used to everyone doing what he says over the past few days. Just as well you're healing up to disrupt his influence, Morph."

Poppy rolled her eyes. "Debatable, but okay. You guys ready?"

Nate and Casey nodded as the three of them stood atop the waterfall and looked down, down, down. Poppy's stomach squirmed in terrified delight; it was the kind of feeling she lived for. Yearned for.

Far below she spotted the tiny figure of Andrew as the raft he was on settled against the banks of the pool. He was looking up at Poppy with a smile on his face that suggested he was happy to see her back to her outrageous self once more. She hadn't spoken to him since he'd refused to leave the facility, though Poppy knew she had to make it up to him for that. It wasn't as if Andrew *knew* what was going on, after all. Of course he wanted to stay in the facility with his friends.

Just as Poppy prepared to jump her eyes scanned over Dorian. Irate, disbelieving Dorian.

Serves you fucking right, Poppy thought, giving him the middle finger in a fit of reckless – suicidal – courage. He bared his teeth at her; even from up here Poppy could tell his shoulders were shaking.

She shared one last look with Casey and Nate.

And then she jumped.

For a few blessed moments, there was nothing but the air roaring past Poppy's ears, the lurching of her stomach and the sound of Nate and Casey screaming in frenzied excitement. Poppy had no horrible decisions to make. She didn't need to condemn anyone to death. She didn't have to let a monster drain her blood or give up her freedom. She didn't have to battle with the fact that her life may be a whole lot longer than she ever wanted it to be.

She was merely Poppy King, jumping off a waterfall.

Poppy knew how to dive properly, of course. Halfway through the fall she adjusted her posture, just as Casey and Nate did the same, and by the time they reached the bottom Poppy slid gracefully beneath the surface of the water. She was almost tempted not to resurface – to stay within the safety of the water until she took her final breath and left her doomed life behind – but a hand on the back of her swimming costume hauled her up.

It was Nate, grinning foolishly as he pulled Poppy into his arms and kissed her. For a few moments Poppy was so overcome with adrenaline that she eagerly reciprocated. Her hands slid over his shoulders to the nape of his neck, and she pushed her body against his even as Nate did the same. If Poppy could simply live in the moment – *this* moment – she could be happy.

Eventually Nate broke the kiss to let in a heaving breath of air, and the magic was broken.

"That was fucking brilliant, Morph," he exclaimed, just as Casey broke through the water's surface. She looked at both Nate and Poppy as if she knew exactly what the two of them had been doing, but said nothing about it.

Patrick waded to their side an instant later. He eyed Casey appraisingly. "I knew you were an excellent swimmer, Cass, but that was quite some dive," the dark-haired, possibly-a-monster-possibly-a-man said.

"Casey's the best in our club," Nate replied proudly. Casey beamed at the compliment. "She'd be the best in the swimming club, too, if she hadn't quit."

Patrick looked confused. "Why would you do that?"

"Because they're all self-centred pricks," she explained simply. "And I prefer swimming outside, anyway."

Behind them all, the sounds of several more people leaping from the waterfall interrupted their conversation. Patrick laughed. "Something tells me Frederick won't be happy about the club doing something so reckless under his watchful eye. And you, Poppy!" He turned to face her. "I can't believe you did all that with an injured arm."

"It's mighty impressive," Nick hollered, joining the group when they made their way onto dry land. "We're excited to see what you tackle next, Poppy."

She grinned despite herself. There were still too many happy chemicals in her brain to let her think about what Nick's comment really meant. "Let's just hope I don't hurt myself again."

"Yes, let's," Dorian muttered. "We wouldn't want that at *all.*"

Poppy turned at the sound of his voice; Fred stood beside him, and the two of them very much seemed to be holding a competition to see who could look at Poppy with more white-hot fury. Poppy ignored their expressions, though a sick feeling that had nothing to do with jumping off a waterfall began to creep into her stomach.

"King, what the hell were you thinking?" Fred demanded, pushing in front of Dorian to face Poppy directly. She forced herself to match his stare. "You shouldn't be doing anything like that when you're injured! Just how stupid are you? And now half the club's following your lead!"

"It was as much Casey and Nate's idea as it was mine," she countered, in absolutely no mood to deal with Fred's complaints.

"Don't be so hard on Morph, Fred," Nate cut in, slinging an around Poppy's waist. "She's allowed to have fun, you know. And she didn't hurt herself so no harm, no foul, right?"

Fred looked like he was half a second away from trying to slap some sense into the pair of them. Instead, he turned around and stormed up the long path back to the facility.

"We should start heading back before it gets cold," Poppy murmured, gently extricating herself from Nate's arm in order to run after her sulking vice-president in an impulsive moment of regret. She and Fred might hate each other but he was only mad in this instance because he genuinely hadn't wanted Poppy to hurt herself; she was not so obtuse as to be unable to see that.

"I'm sorry, Fred," she said when she caught up to him. "I didn't intend for anyone to follow my lead. I just wanted to do something reckless."

He stared at her, green eyes incredulous at her admission. "Oh, so you're actually owning up to how stupid you were? Now there's a first."

"Hey. I'm trying to apologise here."

"Don't bother," he said, scowling. Fred was always scowling. "You're lucky you didn't hurt your arm any further. And all that water can't be good for the bandages. You'll need new ones."

"As if you needed to tell me that. I'll sort it when we get back."

When it became clear Fred didn't want to continue the conversation in favour of stewing in his own bad mood, Poppy slowed her pace to allow him to march on alone. She was well aware that Rachelle would probably catch up to him soon and calm him down, as she always did when Fred and Poppy antagonised each other.

Now that Poppy was walking back solo all she wanted was to be able to enjoy the next few minutes in blissful, false ignorance, even though she dreaded where the path she was walking would lead her. *Just a few minutes,* she begged her brain. She hadn't felt so much like herself as she did right now in almost two weeks, and likely never would. *A few minutes to pretend like I'm having the time of my life.*

"The vice-president and that silver-haired boy were *very* impressive in the raft," Poppy heard a sultry female voice behind her say, starkly ruining her solace. "What were their names? Fred and...?"

"Nate, I think. The one who kissed Poppy after they jumped off the waterfall."

"Yes, that's the one. He clearly has no fear of heights, which is great. I wonder how the two of them would fare bouldering in the caves."

"I guess we'll find out next week."

The final remnants of Poppy's good mood disappeared. She was listening to Aisling, Nick and Steven discuss Fred and Nate.

As food.

The sick feeling in her stomach grew, and Poppy found herself tensing her entire body to stop herself from vomiting. She forced one foot in front of the other, continuing towards the facility as if she could not hear the dreadful conversation occurring behind her.

"It's Poppy I want to see more of," Nick commented. He let out a huff of approval. "Girl has no fear. Can't believe she did all that after such a bad fall."

"What about the other girl – Casey?"

"She's mine," Patrick's voice said, once and for all confirming to Poppy that he was one of *them*. "Sorry, guys. Keep your hands off."

"And how the hell did you manage that already?" Steven demanded, clearly irked. "I liked her."

"It's the benefit of being Dorian's best friend; I get first pick."

Poppy held a hand to her mouth to keep back a scream. She shivered violently, barely able to stop herself from staggering to her knees. *Just one more step, Poppy,* she told herself. *Don't let them know you know. One more step. Then another. You can do it.*

It was in this way that Poppy finally reached the sports centre and threw herself into her shower and, after scorching herself dizzy with hot water, crawled into bed. As she lay there grasping at sleep she thought of how flippantly she had acted towards Dorian all afternoon despite what he had said – and done – that very morning.

"I'm so stupid," Poppy uttered, knowing down to her very core that it was true. "A complete fool."

There were three days until she had to give Dorian blood.

Poppy was going to have to do everything in her power to avoid the monster who owned her blood until she had no choice but to face him.

Three days had never passed so quickly. By throwing herself into every activity possible despite her supposed injury, Poppy had successfully spoken to Dorian precisely zero times. She knew she was going to pay for it – and dearly.

She continued doing it anyway.

But now it was time to give Dorian blood. It was therefore to Poppy's confusion that she couldn't actually *find* Dorian. He wasn't anywhere in the central building, nor the east wing or the ground floor of the west wing. Poppy supposed he could be in one of the locked rooms, but what use was that to her? She couldn't get into any of them unless she clambered blindly through the ceiling. She never wanted to risk doing that again.

None of Dorian's clients were at the facility, which meant Dorian wasn't in a meeting or even outdoors with them. It didn't matter who she spoke to - nobody had seen him. Which meant there was only one other place Poppy could check, though she sincerely didn't want to.

The first floor of the west wing.

She suppressed a shudder as she reached the base of the stairs up to the unknown floor. Poppy assumed Dorian's bedroom was up there – he had said as such on her first day at the facility – but it couldn't be the only thing. It meant the staircase leading up to it gave off an even eerier aura to Poppy than the locked rooms did.

And yet Poppy found herself climbing up the stairs anyway, at a loss for what else to do. She didn't want to wait around with her heart thumping in her chest all day for Dorian to find her; she just wanted the whole ordeal over and done with.

"Stupid son of a bitch," Poppy muttered when she reached the top of the stairs. Hadn't Dorian been the one who couldn't wait for Saturday? That's what he'd said when he terrified her before white-water rafting. She'd been sure Dorian was going to pull her into the infirmary as soon as he was able to.

Something didn't add up.

As she wandered along the first floor corridor Poppy grew no further insight into what the rooms lining the hall contained. The doors were all unmarked, windowless and locked. It reminded her of the mental asylums often featured in Nate's favourite horror films, which he had often forced her to watch with him during their many not-quite-dates.

Oh, great, she grimaced. *Horror films. What a lovely thing to think about right now.*

When Poppy reached the end of the corridor she had to admit that she didn't know what else to do. But instead of returning downstairs she sat down on the floor and closed her eyes, slowing her breathing as she took in the lack of noise surrounding her. It was quiet up here in a way that the central building and east wing never were. It was almost peaceful. Almost pleasant.

Almost.

That was how Dorian found her.

"You really put *so* much effort into looking for me, Miss King," he said as he walked down the corridor towards her.

Poppy opened her eyes immediately, frowning when she saw the impassive look on Dorian's face. "What do you mean?"

"Ah, so you're speaking to me again?"

"Only because I have to. What did you mean?" Poppy repeated.

Dorian reached down and easily hauled Poppy up to her feet; she yelped in surprise.

"I was watching you on the CCTV cameras," he said, dragging her down the corridor with what seemed like little-to-no effort on his part. Poppy didn't even have it in her to fight back. "I'm surprised you didn't use the ceiling to look for me, since you love it up there so much."

"You were *watching* me?"

Dorian glanced over his shoulder to give her a level stare. "Are you really that surprised?"

"...I guess not." she admitted. And then: "Where are you taking me?"

"My bedroom."

Poppy stuck her heels into the floor immediately, desperately trying to pull out of Dorian's grip to no avail. "No bloody way!" she exclaimed. "I'm not going in there."

"You will, and you are. Don't make me carry you."

Torn between trying to resist further and knowing she would invariably lose to Dorian's monstrous strength, Poppy began following him again as slowly as possible. She wished her heart would stop beating so quickly, for she wanted to remain level and calm and not in the least bit frightened. After all, that was exactly what Dorian wanted.

Poppy would be damned if she ever gave him that.

"Why your bedroom this time?" she muttered after a few seconds of silence.

"So I can cut you open in the shower," Dorian replied simply, entirely numb to the horror of his own sentence. "I'm tired of having to wipe down the infirmary. It'll be much cleaner this way."

Poppy blinked a few times. She realised that *she* was also numb to the horror of what Dorian had said, for it actually made sense. But it disquieted her nonetheless that she was beginning to think this way, even though Poppy knew fine well it was a coping mechanism to stop her from breaking down.

Dorian pulled her through the first door on the left closest to the stairwell, letting go of Poppy to close the door behind them. One of the walls was entirely made of glass; it overlooked the jagged cliff-faces that hugged the back of the facility. At the very top of the cliff, some ways off, was a grove of trees. The morning light filtered through its canopy, making the grove feel altogether ethereal. As if the trees were an illusion, and if Poppy blinked they would disappear.

Poppy took a step towards the view, curious despite herself about whether she could climb up to explore the grove at some point.

"What are you thinking about?" Dorian wondered aloud as he inclined his head towards another door – his bathroom. "We're going in here."

Reluctantly leaving the view Poppy followed him through. The sheer size of the grey ceramic-tiled shower impressed her, for it could easily fit three or four people. But all such thoughts left her when Dorian slid open the glass door and moved aside to allow Poppy to enter the shower first. Though she didn't want to take another step she forced herself into the unit, leaning against the tiles as she watched Dorian retrieve the same knife he had used to cut her open last time from a cabinet by the sink.

"That thing better be sterile," Poppy remarked, trying to keep her voice upbeat even as her stomach twisted nervously and her arm twitched in phantom pain. Now that she was here she found that she wasn't ready to have Dorian cut her open, after all. *Maybe I should have waited until this evening,* she thought, gulping down a panicked breath. *Maybe I —*

"Of course it is," Dorian replied, cutting through Poppy's thoughts as he moved into the shower and closed the door behind him. "Not that an infection would do all that much to you."

"I'd rather not risk it, all the same."

"Who are you sacrificing and saving this week?"

Dorian sidled up towards Poppy and unwrapped the bandages on her arm. She didn't like how close he was even though it was exactly as close as the last time he'd drank her blood, and the time before that. Perhaps it was because they were in the enclosed space of the shower.

"Angelica Fisher," Poppy breathed out. Dorian traced a line

down the perfect skin of her arm with the edge of his knife. His eyes were transfixed on the motion, shining with inhuman excitement as he imagined exactly where he would cut her. She gulped again. "I'm sacrificing Angelica. And saving Jenny Adams."

"Steven will be happy about that," Dorian murmured, continuing to slide the knife across Poppy's arm. She twitched beneath the blade once, twice, three times, but Dorian did not hold her wrist to steady her. "He had someone interested in Angelica after she impressed them all with her archery skills. Keen eyes are a valuable asset."

Poppy's stomach lurched. "I didn't need to know that."

He raised an eyebrow without tearing his eyes away from her arm. "I thought you wanted to know everything they said? Which would be much easier to do if you stopped avoiding me."

"I—"

Poppy's sentence was interrupted when Dorian violently wrenched his knife through her arm. She screamed; Dorian covered her mouth and slammed her against the tiled wall of the shower, eyes finally on hers to give her reaction his undivided attention.

"W-what happened to *your kind* not being so violent?!" she cried out in agony when she pulled his hand away from her mouth with trembling fingers. Her blood spattered most every surface of the shower, as well as Dorian's face and clothes. "What happened to everything you said last time?"

Dorian chuckled darkly. He licked at a drop of blood that had landed on his upper lip. "What happened to you promising not to show off? Do you realise how many of *my kind* are interested in you now?"

"I was pissed off at you."

"Well, this is me pissed off at you," Dorian spat out, his

expression twisted and angry and far too close to transforming for Poppy's comfort. "What were you thinking? Racing your damn raft into first place, jumping off that stupid waterfall, making a scene with your daredevil boyfriend..."

Something about the last comment irked Poppy out of her terror.

"He's not my boyfriend," she told Dorian.

"Oh, so he just kissed you and wouldn't let you go for no reason?"

"Why do you even care?!"

Dorian responded by sinking his teeth into the gaping wound he had created, bringing Poppy's arm up to her ear so that she could hear every last drop of her blood being drained by him.

There were tears in Poppy's eyes that she was desperate not to shed, and a cry of pain she was determined not to let loose. But it hurt – more than it had before. Much more. Poppy could feel Dorian draining her blood as slowly as possible, dragging out the process for as long as he was physically able to.

"S-stop," she eventually stammered, gaze turning hazy as she tried and failed to focus on the pattern her blood made on the glass door to her left instead of Dorian's fervent, frenzied face inches from her own. "Dorian, stop it!"

He pulled his mouth away from Poppy's arm. It was dripping crimson. "Why should I," he growled, "when you don't know when to listen to me?"

"If I don't act like myself people will get suspicious! You can't get angry at me for being myself!" It was only in saying it that Poppy realised she meant it, and not simply for the purpose of avoiding suspicion. She didn't want to have to *not* be herself for the rest of her life simply for Dorian's sake. If she was going to be by his side whether she liked it or not then he could damn well put up with her being Poppy King.

Dorian stared at her for a few agonisingly long moments before returning to draining her blood. But he quickened his pace, finishing up in a manner of seconds before finally releasing Poppy from his hold. She had to fight not to drop down to the floor of the shower in shock.

"I guess you're right," he muttered, wiping a hand across his mouth to clear it of blood before licking his fingers. "But keep this in mind, Poppy: in three months you won't see Nate or Andrew or Rachelle or *anyone else* again. Perhaps consider stopping Nate constantly trying to get into your bed before you disappear from his life forever."

Poppy wanted to argue with him. She wanted to call Dorian out for overly caring about what she did or didn't do with Nate. But his reasoning was solid, and caused the tears she'd firmly kept back to finally fall.

How had she come this far without actually acknowledging that she'd never see her friends again? Her family? Poppy had known it would happen, of course, but she hadn't let the reality of that knowledge truly sink in. In keeping numb to the horror of her situation Poppy had prevented herself from thinking about it in anything more than hypothetical terms.

Now Dorian was *forcing* her to think about it.

"You can't go downstairs looking like that," Dorian eventually murmured, touching Poppy's arm in order to check if it had stopped bleeding. "Clean up and I'll dress your arm."

"...I hate you."

He stared at Poppy, who stared right back through red-rimmed, tearful eyes. She wanted so badly for him to say he hated her right back.

Instead Dorian smiled bitterly. His teeth were still fanged and red. "I know," he murmured, voice far too soft and gentle for Poppy's liking. "I don't know what else I was expecting from you."

Then he exited the bathroom, leaving Poppy to clean up and wonder what in the world he'd meant.

INTERLUDE II

ANGELICA WAS PULLED ASIDE FROM HER friends on the day the club's initial two week trip was over. Smiling smugly when Dorian informed her that one of his clients was so impressed by her archery that they wanted to offer her a contract, she thought of nothing else but how much better she was than the rest of the group to have been picked first as she followed Dorian up to the first floor of the west wing.

She had never been up there before; to the best of her knowledge Angelica didn't think anyone from the club had. But when she asked Dorian what exactly it was she had to do next she was unceremoniously pushed into a room with an unmarked, windowless door. The door slammed shut behind her with a resounding click.

When she turned to survey the room she saw Ross Bridges, who was missing an arm.

"What the hell..." she uttered, an overwhelming feeling of dread crawling up her spine. Ross stared at her with wild, panicked eyes.

Then she felt a prick in her neck, and then there was nothing.

When she woke up Angelica could not see.

CRAIG HUNT

FRED

FREDERICK SAMPSON HATED POPPY KING WITH every fibre of his being.

He could admit that, in the beginning, his dislike had been a little unfair, since Poppy hadn't actually said or done anything bad directed at him, but as time wore on Fred realised he was perfectly justified in hating her. The two of them were simply too different to ever get on – and Poppy knew it. It was as if she revelled in it, using every aspect of her brash personality to grate on Fred's nerves whenever and wherever she could.

And yet somehow, inexplicably, Fred and Poppy were interested in the same things. The same subjects at university; the same circle of friends; the same extra-curricular activities. That the two of them managed to successfully operate the Outdoor Sports Society as vice-president and president respectively was still something Fred couldn't quite fathom.

He wasn't sure how Poppy had found Dorian Kapros' outdoor facility in her search for a retreat. It certainly wasn't one that anyone else had heard of before, though the fact that it was brand new went a long way in explaining its obscurity. But it served to fuel Fred's suspicion that Poppy had naturally messed up her original booking and that Dorian's centre had landed in her lap as a last-minute solution to her problems completely independently of her actually doing her job. It only made him hate her more for winning the role of president whilst he was relegated to her right hand.

Rachelle always thought he was being ridiculous and paranoid about Poppy. Looking back Fred realised it should not have come as a surprise that his dislike of her best friend had ultimately broken up their romantic relationship. Fred had tried to reign in his negative feelings for Poppy since then for Rachelle's sake – he wanted to get back together with her, after all – and he liked to think he'd had *some* success on that front in recent months.

But Poppy was really trying his patience now. After falling – *falling* – from the climbing wall, her behaviour had been all over the place. In all honesty Fred didn't understand how Poppy wasn't dead or at least severely injured. He'd been sure she'd crushed her right arm into oblivion when she landed on it.

And yet Poppy was fine. Well, as close to fine as Fred imagined she could be. She'd been severely shaken by the fall, though Fred wasn't sure if this was due to her brush with death or the fact Poppy had simply never fallen before. Despite his disdain for her lackadaisical attitude towards safety, perhaps the person most in shock about Poppy having fallen in the first place had been Fred himself. Whether he wanted to admit it out loud or not, Poppy was a superb free-climber. She was the best Fred had ever seen with his own two eyes. For her to fall from a *climbing wall?* It seemed ridiculous.

Once upon a time he might have wished for her to fall just once to pop her over-inflated ego, but things had changed now. Witnessing the way Poppy's arm had been crushed first-hand

and the blood – so much blood – that poured from the gaping wound meant Fred was quite certain he would never wish such a thing to happen again, even to Poppy.

But even so...though Poppy acted as though her arm was injured, which of course it had to be given what happened to it, Fred was becoming increasingly certain that it wasn't hurt the way it should be. For sometimes Poppy seemed completely fine. When she thought someone wasn't looking, or had for all intents and purposes 'forgotten' about it, she used her right arm like it didn't hurt at all.

Fred had thought Poppy's arm was simply getting better – or that she was ignoring her injury – after she enthusiastically joined in with the white-water rafting course and flung herself off the waterfall with Casey and Nate. In the days following it seemed like she'd gone back to her normal, stupid, infuriating self. But then, three days later, Poppy was once more as pale as the day she fell, and she held her arm to her chest as if, beneath the bandages, her flesh had been torn anew. Fred had never been so confused about her erratic behaviour before, and this was *Poppy* he was talking about. The most reckless, headstrong, impulsive and, above all else, unreliable person he knew.

He tried to think back to the fall, once more picking apart the incident to try and make sense of it. Poppy had been distracted whilst she was climbing – by Dorian. Fred supposed that even Poppy could make a mistake in front of a man she liked the look of.

Except she spent the next week avoiding him completely, Fred mused, not for the first time, *and even when she started speaking to him again it seemed as if she'd rather be anywhere else but by his side.*

In truth Poppy had been distant with almost everyone for the first two weeks of the trip, though after the white-water rafting course she seemed far more inclined to be outgoing and sociable once more. But something was still off.

It was as if Poppy King was merely acting the part of Poppy King.

Fred knew Rachelle was worried about her, as were Andrew, Casey and Nate. And though he most definitely *hadn't* wanted to know about it, Nate informed Fred that Poppy kept rebuffing his advances no matter what he did, which was unlike her. Fred considered this odd given she'd reciprocated Nate's idiotic kiss at the bottom of the waterfall but, then again, everything was odd about Poppy right now.

"...how does a retard like you beat my dive time?" Fred heard someone mutter, breaking him out of his thoughts. He was sitting in the small social area outside the board members' bedrooms, whilst the voice came from the direction of the door into the main dormitory corridor. Frowning, Fred put down the book he had been trying – and failing – to read for the best part of an hour and crept towards the door to eavesdrop.

"Is it because you barely speak?" the voice continued. With some difficulty Fred recognised it as belonging to Craig Hunt, a third year student who tended to take his insults of people too far.

Such as right now, Fred mused. He didn't like Craig much.

"You just stand around practising holding your breath so you can beat everyone's time in the water, huh?" Craig continued, his voice unpleasantly slimy. "Is that how it is, huh, Forbes?"

Andrew, Fred realised. *He's speaking to Andrew.* Furious on his friend's behalf, Fred was hell-bent on bashing down the door when an arm cut in front of him, forcing him to stop. Turning around he realised the arm belonged to Poppy, of all people.

She held a finger to her mouth to tell him to keep quiet.

"I've been – I've been practising diving every week," Fred

heard Andrew mumble through the door. "At first I was scared to stay under the water but then—"

"I don't give a shit about your training schedule," Craig interrupted nastily. "But you keep beating all my best times. You don't even care about being first, so why are you doing it, huh?"

Andrew stayed silent.

"Oh, I see. You doing it for Poppy?" Craig suggested, tone even more disgusting than before. "You want her to be so impressed she finally bangs you? I'm sorry to tell you, freak, but you have no chance. You think she'd go for someone like you? Don't make me laugh!"

Poppy stared at the door, incandescent at what she was hearing, yet still she kept Fred back from interrupting the cruel conversation when he made to open the door again.

"Let me stop him," Fred muttered, frowning at her.

Poppy shook her head. "Think how horrified Andrew will be if he knows we heard the whole thing. We can sort Craig out later."

Fred didn't like standing there and doing nothing. He never had. But he had to admit that, at least this time, Poppy had a point. Andrew had been working so hard to become independent. For the two of them to jump out and intervene right now would diminish all his progress.

"You know, I bet I could get Poppy to screw me," Craig said. Poppy bristled by Fred's side. Her cheeks were crimson, and there was a sheen of sweat covering her brow. For a moment Fred genuinely believed she would pass out. "Just to fuck you up, Forbes," the horrible young man continued. "She seems pretty easy, what with her not wanting to leave the club or grow up and all. And she's absolutely mental! I bet she's great in—"

"Shut up about her!" Andrew bit out, so loudly that both

Fred and Poppy took a step away from the door. "Leave her alone!"

Craig only laughed harder. "Man, you're so pathetic. We'll see who she prefers – me or you. Though I doubt you even have the balls to make an actual pass at her."

When it became obvious that Craig had walked away, Fred and Poppy retreated down the corridor and into Fred's bedroom just as Andrew pushed the door open.

"Why'd you follow me in here?" Fred hissed when he realised Poppy had followed him. "Fuck off."

She scowled. "I panicked. I'll leave when I'm sure Andrew won't hear me."

"So what are we doing about Hunt?"

"Just leave that to me."

"Oh, really? Leave it to *you*? What will you do?"

"I have an idea," she said, clearly not intending to elaborate. "It's fine. Let me handle it, Fred."

He frowned down at her bandaged arm, realising quite suddenly that she'd used it to keep him from opening the door. "Your arm seems much better than it was a few days ago," he observed.

She flinched for half a second before schooling her expression, which made Fred immediately suspicious. "What do you mean?" Poppy asked innocently, though she crossed her left arm in front of her right as if protecting it from Fred's gaze. "Of course it's getting better. The accident was close to three weeks ago."

"No, I mean it's specifically better today than it was four days ago. It got worse over the weekend."

"No it didn't."

"Yes it did."

"Fred, I think I'd know how my own limb is doing."

"And I'm calling bullshit. What's up with you?"

Poppy rolled her eyes. "And here was me thinking we had somewhat dialled down the animosity for the sake of the trip. Can't you just give me a break this summer? We literally never have to see each other again come September."

Fred knew she was trying to deflect which only solidified his suspicions that something was going on. That she was lying about something – hiding something. But he also knew there was no way Poppy would actually tell him what was happening.

"Just get out, Poppy," he sighed. He'd have to work out what was wrong in his own time.

Poppy stared at him for a few seconds with an impassive, guarded expression on her face, before quietly opening Fred's bedroom door and creeping over to her own.

Fred had no doubt that Poppy *would* take care of Craig Hunt, though he didn't know why. Maybe she was finally growing up and becoming more responsible, though even as Fred thought it he almost laughed at how unlikely it was.

But Fred had other, more pressing things to think about that were decidedly not pertaining to Poppy, nor Craig, nor anyone else in the club for that matter. Dorian's scout friends would be back in a couple of days to go bouldering with the club and he was determined to impress them. Though he'd never admit it to Poppy, he had just as little clue about what he wanted to do after summer as she did. If he could funnel his love of outdoor sports into a career then Fred was happy to explore that route.

With a resigned shake of his head he left his room to retrieve the book he'd abandoned in the board room social area. He no longer had any desire to read it, of course, but Rachelle had lent it to him. Fred didn't want to lose it.

When he passed by Poppy's door, which lay ajar,

something told Fred to pause. After a few seconds of tense silence he just barely heard Poppy mutter, "Well that was an easy one..."

He froze. What the hell did she mean? Fred stalked back to his room and lay on the bed, pondering just what exactly had been an *easy one* for Poppy.

But, no matter how long he spent trying to make sense of her words, nothing came to mind. The sentence was just as infuriatingly nonsensical and mysterious as Poppy King herself.

NATE RICHARDS

DORIAN

DORIAN WAS GROWING CONCERNED FOR POPPY.

With every day that she showed off her physical prowess and fearless attitude more and more of his clients grew interested in her. In particular, Nick Richardson - who filmed every activity for the benefit of his sprawling, extended family - seemed set on buying her for himself. Dorian didn't want to imagine Poppy getting torn apart limb by limb by his bullish, atrociously strong arms.

He was quite certain his clients wanted *all* of Poppy, not just part of her. She was the best 'Jack of all trades' his kind could hope for, after all. A good swimmer, diver and sprinter. Reasonably intelligent. Perceptive eyes. A smart mouth. And, above all else, a truly daredevil climber who knew no fear. He wondered what his clients would do when they discovered Poppy's blood was infinitely more valuable than her muscles, bones and organs.

I have to make sure that never happens, Dorian thought, sullen. He was almost always in a frantic, glowering mood nowadays, for Poppy was making his job of keeping her under the radar incredibly difficult. Nothing he said or did seemed to make an ounce of difference anymore, as if Poppy had forgotten all of his previous threats and warnings – or simply didn't care. Not for the first time Dorian wondered if it was an inevitability of Poppy's nature to oppose any kind of rule inflicted upon her, or if even a single scenario existed in which Dorian could make her do as he wished.

All things considered Dorian knew he was lucky that, other than the one time Poppy *did* fall, her reputation for being indestructible seemed to hold true. She hadn't scraped or cut or bruised herself in any way that would allow one of his kind to work out just how special her blood truly was.

Fred, Nate and Andrew had cleaned up Poppy's blood after her first fall before Dorian's sparse roster of staff reached it, too, which in retrospect he realised was a stroke of luck he'd have been damned without. Though Dorian's employees had all worked for his father and he considered them loyal to the Kapros family, the discovery of immortal blood would be more than enough to turn them all against him for the promise of a considerably longer life and a fat bank account.

It was in his best interests – and Poppy's, too – that nobody other than him ever found out about her.

Dorian couldn't think about Poppy's fall without invariably remembering what had *caused* her to fall in the first place. She had caught Dorian staring at her, and it had thrown her off-balance. Of course Poppy hadn't known Dorian was revelling in how much money he'd make from selling her off as he watched her; she'd more than likely thought he was interested in her personally, especially after he'd propositioned her earlier that very evening.

A part of him that was growing larger with every passing day wished Poppy would once more look at him the way she'd done before she fell. That their relationship could return to the flirtatious one they'd superficially enjoyed for the smallest fragment of time before Dorian's true nature – and Poppy's blood – got in the way. That his partner for the rest of his now very long life would *want* to be with him, rather than being a prisoner.

Dorian hated the fact he felt that way.

"Hey, Dorian, can you help us with this?" Rachelle asked politely when she walked past him, arms laden with blankets. Most of the club was bouldering in the caves below the cliffs that sheltered the south side of the facility. It followed, though, that even in an outdoor society there would be some people who were claustrophobic and couldn't think of anything worse than willingly entering a hole sunk well below the earth's surface.

Rachelle was one of those people, as was Andrew and three other club members whose names Dorian was fairly certain were Lily, Ciaran and Grace. Patrick had also hung back – since his forte was water-based activities – though he was pretty fond of exploring caves. Dorian was reasonably sure he'd stayed behind simply to keep him company.

He smiled at Rachelle. "Of course. Do you want me to get the barbecues going?"

"Please!"

It was a glorious day. Those that had stayed behind were preparing the small meadow that lay between the facility and the cliffs for a surprise picnic. It had been Patrick's idea; he'd brought along the supplies on his boat, anticipating that the club would readily agree with the plan. The non-bouldering club members had eagerly latched onto the idea. Who didn't love a barbecue on a hot, sunny afternoon, after all?

Only Andrew seemed less than enthused, so Dorian sidled up to him once Rachelle left to busy herself with organising blankets across the meadow for people to lie on. "Want to help me with the barbecues, Andrew?" he asked the young man, not unkindly. Perhaps it was because Poppy had already saved him and so Dorian knew Andrew wasn't doomed to die. Perhaps it was because Dorian actually found him easy to co-exist with. Whatever the reason, Dorian had taken a liking to Andrew, and always made sure to talk to him whenever he saw him.

But Andrew shook his head. "No, thank you. I don't like the smoke. Or eating outside. Do you think I could go back in and read?"

"I mean, you *could,*" Dorian replied, lighting a twist of paper and throwing it amongst the coals of the first barbecue as he spoke, "but then how would you be able to socialise with all your friends? Or help me to keep an eye on Poppy?"

"Why would you need my help to do that?"

He smiled grimly. "Because you're one of her best friends. She might tell you what's up."

"And why do you think something's up?"

Dorian narrowed his eyes at Andrew, wondering if he was playing dumb or was simply oblivious. For it wasn't just that Poppy was putting herself at risk by being, well, Poppy. There was more to it than that, Dorian was sure. He had noticed her becoming altogether increasingly frail as the week went on. He was certain it had nothing to do with her arm given that it had fully healed a few days ago.

No, something else was wrong.

"Do you not think she looks a bit...sick?" Dorian wondered aloud, deciding to be blunt for Andrew's sake. "And she seems rather preoccupied by something."

"Maybe she's just nervous about impressing all your clients?"

"Maybe."

"But she's also not eating, if that's what you meant by looking a bit sick."

Dorian resisted the urge to slide a hand over his face. "You could have led with that, you know," he told Andrew, who merely frowned.

"You asked if something was up with Poppy or if she was sick. Her choosing not to eat isn't either of those things. Unless she's choosing not to eat *because*—"

"I get the picture. Thanks for the information, Andrew."

"Can I go back inside now?" Andrew asked. He was squinting up at Dorian through the bright afternoon sun, clearly eager to get permission to escape it in order to read his book unimpeded. But then he glanced at the mouth of the caves and added, "Until everyone returns, at least."

Dorian waved him off to the sound of Rachelle laughing at him.

"Nice try, Dorian," she called over, eyes hidden behind overly large sunglasses but amusement plain as day on the rest of her face. "You must know by now how literal you have to be with Andrew to get him to answer a question properly. How long do you think the club will be in the caves?" Rachelle fussed around him, placing neatly organised piles of burgers, chicken, sausages and peppers by the barbecues. "Why were you asking about Poppy, anyway?" she added on, when Dorian didn't immediately respond.

"Probably no longer than half an hour," he eventually replied, answering her first question. And then, after a long pause, "I just wanted to know what was wrong with her. She seems...off."

Rachelle slid her sunglasses up, both eyebrows raised. "So you noticed too, huh?"

"Andrew said she isn't eating."

"Yeah. She barely touches her food. But she doesn't seem like she's caught a cold or anything, and she's acting normally otherwise, so hell if I know what's wrong with her. To be honest she's been pretty distant with me lately. Wish I knew why."

Dorian almost felt bad for Rachelle; she'd never know that Poppy was avoiding her for her own good. He supposed he should assuage Poppy's best friend but he had no idea how to. *Should I tell her not to worry even though it's a lie?* Dorian wondered. *Poppy would hate me if she knew I'd spoken to Rachelle about her. Then again, she hates me anyway.*

"Is that Nate?" one of the other girls called out from where they lay on a blanket, propping themselves up on an elbow to take a closer look at the mouth of the caves. They glanced back at Dorian. "I thought they weren't due back yet?"

"Yeah, you're right, Lily," the other girl – Grace, Dorian was sure – concurred. "Is he...holding someone?"

"*Poppy!*"

Rachelle wasted no time in running towards Nate, who had a barely-conscious Poppy leaning heavily against his shoulder as they staggered across the meadow. Dorian felt his insides go cold. He took one slow step forward, then another and another. *What has she done, what has she done, what has she done?* he thought, trying to work out exactly what happened to Poppy by sight alone.

But Nate held up a hand when Rachelle reached his side. "She just fainted, nothing too serious," he said, in a tone that belied how pallid and sickly his dark skin had gone. "Gave us a scare, though; one moment she was climbing up behind me and the next she was hanging off the rope like she was dead."

It was clear Nate was underplaying how much of a fright Poppy had given him – Dorian could see his shoulders shaking. He felt a flash of irritation as he watched the young man grasp onto Poppy protectively when she tried to hold her weight on her own two feet. But then Dorian exhaled deeply and forced his thoughts into order. At least Poppy was conscious.

And not bleeding, he added on after giving her dust-covered skin the once-over. *Things could have been much worse.* But now Dorian's initial panic was being overridden by hot, dangerous anger. Things could have been much worse, yes, but Poppy never should have been in a position to faint in the first place.

"Nate, I'm fine, honestly," Poppy coughed. "You're making a way bigger deal out of this that you need to."

But still he didn't let go of her.

Dorian was just about to storm forwards to take Poppy away from Nate – her opinion of his manhandling be damned – when his senior member of staff came out of the facility and signalled him over. Giving Poppy one hard, final stare which she blatantly avoided, Dorian turned and walked towards the woman.

"What is it, Jane?"

"Mr Richardson – Nick's father – is here," Jane replied softly, as if Dorian had asked her nicely instead of shouting at her in his impatience to deal with Poppy. "For bid number one."

"Ross?"

She nodded. "He says he wants to consume him the old-fashioned way. I set him up in room three on the first floor."

Dorian couldn't think of a worse time for this to happen. He glanced back at Poppy, whom Nate was still refusing to let go of, and felt his anger rise.

Then he had an idea.

"Take Mr Bridges through to room three, Jane. Tell Mr Richardson I'll be with him presently."

Jane turned and left without another word. Then Dorian marched back over to Nate and wasted no time in sweeping Poppy up into his arms.

Nate's eyes widened in alarm. "What are you doing, Dorian?"

"Taking her to the infirmary. You guys just relax out here and watch the barbecues for me."

"I'm *fine!*" Poppy exclaimed weakly, though the lack of strength in her fists as they pounded his chest suggested otherwise. "Put me down. I'm probably just anaemic."

Dorian stared at her incredulously. "Is that supposed to be a joke?" he muttered, for nobody else to hear but her.

She squirmed uncomfortably in his arms without looking at him. "Shut up, Dorian."

"We won't be long," he said to Nate, Rachelle and Patrick, who was watching Poppy in interest and concern from his spot on the grass. Then Dorian left the meadow, returning to the facility with a uselessly-struggling Poppy in tow. When they passed Andrew on their way through the central building he jumped from the sofa he was curled up on, dropping his book in fright.

"Poppy, what happened—"

"I have it under control, Andrew," Dorian cut in, giving him an easy, practised smile. "Just go back to your book." He didn't give Andrew an opportunity to say anything more as he made his way through to the west wing.

But Dorian didn't enter the infirmary. He took Poppy upstairs.

She stiffened in his arms. "Where are we going, Dorian?"

He didn't look at her as he said, "It's Saturday. And I'm hungry. Who are you putting up to sacrifice and save this week?"

"You're really going to – right now? Really?"

"Yes, really. Give me some names."

Poppy didn't say anything for a few moments – her gaze

drifting in and out of focus – before murmuring against his shirt, "Saving Nate. Giving up Craig Hunt. Should you really take blood from me when I just fainted?"

"I thought that wasn't a *big deal*?"

Poppy fought against Dorian's hold on her once more, though his grip only grew tighter. There was no way Poppy King was getting out of what Dorian had in store for her. Eventually she gave up and her body became soft and easy to carry.

"It wasn't," she complained. "But it still happened."

"Then start eating again. Why are you starving yourself, anyway?"

She made a face that, in another situation, Dorian might have found adorable. "I've not had much of an appetite. I wonder why?"

"That's no excuse. You can't put yourself in a position where you might hurt yourself in front of my clients the way you did in front of me."

"But ultimately you can just refuse to take any of their bids on me, can't you? So it shouldn't matter."

"Are you that *stupid*?" Dorian spat out when they reached room number three, throwing Poppy over his shoulder to free up a hand so he could open the door. The room was split in two by a one-way, soundproofed mirror that took up the entire wall. On the other side of the glass stood Franco Richardson, Nick's hundred-year-old father, and a terrified, one-armed Ross Bridges, finally free of all restraints. He backed himself into one corner of the room as the intimidating figure of Franco stared at him.

He put Poppy down on her feet, facing the glass, then leaned against her to prevent her from moving away or falling over – both of which seemed likely given what Dorian was about to show her.

Poppy's bloodless face grew even paler as her vision finally came back into focus and she took in the sight in front of her. "Dorian, what is – what are you showing me?"

"It's about time you saw the full strength of another member of my kind," he said, watching Franco analyse his prey with a sick sense of satisfaction. He should have shown Poppy the worst of his kind from the very beginning to keep her in check. To keep her appropriately petrified, sickened and obedient. That he'd waited so long was a grave error on his part. "Not actually acknowledging what they all are – what *I* am – has made you complacent."

"That's not true!" she protested, wriggling against Dorian in a vain attempt to break free. "I know fine well what you are!"

"No, you don't," he growled, holding Poppy's chin in place with his left hand so that she couldn't look away from what was happening through the glass. "I told you most of my kind aren't violent. Well, that's mostly true – there's not really any other way for us to live if we want to blend in with our prey. But some of us...well, we still relish in our real natures. Our basest instincts. And I think you're the kind of person who needs to *see* something in order to properly understand it. So it's time you saw one of us in action."

Poppy darted her eyes up to stare at Dorian, horror plain as day on her face. "No...you don't mean it. You don't—"

"I do."

"Please don't do this to me."

"You brought this on yourself, Poppy."

Before their very eyes, Franco Richardson's silhouette began to ripple and warp and change until, in the blink of an eye, the tall, broad man was replaced by something monstrous.

Close to twelve feet tall, the creature that took his place had to stoop in order not to hit the ceiling. His bulging muscles and heavy tail took up much of the available space in the room.

Though the golden scales covering his body were reptilian, Franco's head was more akin to an ox; curling, vicious horns framed his inhuman face, eyes gone white with the excitement of blood in the air. A forked tongue darted in-between serrated teeth.

Poppy tried to back away as much as she could from the glass, yelping in fright when it only pressed her closer to Dorian. He smiled grimly, then pushed an intercom button and announced, "You're all set to go, Franco. I hope you enjoy your meal."

Ross, who up to this point was struck silent in blind terror at the look of the nightmarish predator edging closer to him, breathed out a whimper that became a wail.

"This – this isn't funny," he cried. "Let me out! *Let me out!*"

Franco let out a garbled laugh. "The only way you're getting out of here is in pieces, in my stomach."

And then he pinned Ross against the wall, his claws digging into the man's flesh as he let out an agonised scream.

Poppy's heart was beating so hard and fast that Dorian could hear it, with his own heart rate almost matching it from sheer excitement and anticipation. Blood rushed through his ears, informing him that his human guise was slipping.

"Dorian, please."

Poppy's voice was so quiet that Dorian barely heard her. He looked down as his body changed and grew, eyes pinned on the exposed nape of Poppy's neck, then slung an arm around her waist to pick her up. When his reversion to his true self was complete her legs were flailing almost three feet off the ground, and she tried with all her might to kick herself free. But it was to no avail; Poppy was weak where Dorian was inhumanly strong.

"Why Nate?" he asked as he pinned Poppy against the glass

once more, forcing her to watch Franco tear Ross' remaining arm from his body and begin to chew on it like a drumstick from the barbecue Dorian had left just ten minutes prior. Ross' yowl was blood-curdling as he watched Franco's teeth crush through his bones right in front of his very eyes.

"Dorian, let me go!" Poppy screamed, frantically pushing against the mirror. "Just let me out of here!"

He merely smoothed her ponytail away from her neck and ran his teeth along her shoulder. "Why Nate?" he urged once more. "You said you were being unbiased. Why him over anyone else?"

"Let me—"

"Answer me."

"Because I don't want him to die!" Poppy wailed, chest heaving as she closed her eyes to the bloodbath that a mere layer of glass was protecting her from.

Dorian sunk his teeth into the back of her neck; Poppy's eyes went wide in shock and pain.

"*St-stop!*"

But of course Dorian didn't. He was excited, and infuriated, and jealous beyond words. He didn't want to admit it, especially because a human had caused it, but he was. Poppy was *his*. Nate was nothing.

But Nate wasn't nothing to Poppy.

As her blood rushed down his throat Dorian bit into her neck a little deeper, even though he knew he was taking too much.

"Dorian, please..." Poppy breathed out, almost choking on the words. She clawed at his arms. Smashed her fists against the glass. Kicked at his legs. Dorian didn't budge.

Ross' screams grew louder and all the more sickening as Franco ripped into his stomach, spilling his intestines all over the floor. And then he fainted – or died. Dorian wasn't sure which. Regardless, death was inevitable for the unfortunate young man who had thought it clever to stalk Cassandra O'Donnell.

Poppy raised one of her hands to try and grab at Dorian's hair but met the twisted, intricate pattern of horns that encircled his head instead. Her fingers brushed against a pointed ear and grabbed it with what little strength she had left.

She couldn't have known how sensitive Dorian's ears were. But it was more than enough sensation for him to break away in surprise from the bleeding mess of her neck in order to pull her hand away. Poppy turned her head just enough to stare at him with colourless eyes that were rapidly slipping into unconsciousness.

"Stop," was all she said. It came out as barely a whisper through her lips; Dorian had to fight an insatiable urge to kiss the word away. Instead, he bent back down to Poppy's neck and gently licked clean the wound he'd made, sucking away any blood that continued to trickle out.

Just as Franco began to devour what was left of Ross from the feet-up, Poppy passed out.

Dorian smiled in satisfaction, tucking her in against his chest with a tenderness he had never shown her whilst she was conscious, his adrenaline-taut body slowly returning to its human form as he left room number three for his own bedroom. He placed Poppy on top of the duvet, settling her head against a pillow with the utmost care. With the wound on her neck concealed, one could almost believe she had merely fallen into an exhausted sleep.

"Time to take you out of commission for a few days," he muttered, lying beside the unconscious woman in order to examine her closely. Poppy's chest barely rose and fell with the laboured breaths she was taking. Her lashes fluttered, eyes roving beneath their lids against the terror Dorian had forced upon her. He took notice of the dust and dirt that covered her clothes from the caves, thinking somewhat excitedly about changing Poppy into something clean. He pushed a few stray strands of silver hair away from her deathly pale face and then simply...watched her.

Dorian didn't understand the overwhelming possessiveness that he felt for Poppy King – part of him thought it might be because of her blood coursing through his veins – but he didn't need to.

Poppy was his until the end of time. Everyone else could die for all he cared.

MEGAN LO

POPPY

Poppy had no idea for how long she'd been asleep. When she regained consciousness, however, it was immediate, full of panic and so dizzying that she almost fainted from the mere action of sitting up.

Spots of red and white attacked her vision; it took a few seconds of blinking them away before Poppy adjusted to the golden light in the room. At first she didn't recognise where she was. The large bed with its dark blue sheets was unfamiliar, as were the well-made oak wardrobe, table and chest of drawers. It was only because one of the walls in the room was entirely made of glass that Poppy finally realised where she was.

Dorian.

Her last lucid memories washed over her so brutally that Poppy was almost sick. She clenched at the gnawing, painful feeling in her stomach, wishing to either vomit away the feeling or for the nausea to pass. Poppy was in too much shock to realise she only felt this way because she was starving.

Swinging shaking legs over the side of the bed, Poppy located the door and made an attempt to escape. But something gave her pause. *Where are my clothes?* she worried, picking at the fabric of the sinfully soft, over-sized grey T-shirt that she was now wearing. She was still wearing her underwear, which settled Poppy's heart rate somewhat, but other than that her clothes were nowhere to be seen.

The smell of tea tree wafted into her nose. Poppy frowned, pulling her hair over her shoulder in order to sniff it. She glanced in the direction of Dorian's en suite bathroom.

Did he wash *me?* she wondered, thoroughly affronted by the notion. But Poppy didn't want to waste any more time trying to work out what the hell was going on or what Dorian may or may not have done to her whilst she was unconscious. She simply wanted to get the hell out of his bedroom.

A single step towards the door was all Poppy managed before she collapsed face-first onto the carpet, for she lacked the strength to support her own weight. "For fuck's sake," she muttered, her voice hoarse and dry from disuse. "How long was I out?"

As if on cue the door opened, revealing a – human – Dorian holding a tray laden with food. Upon spying Poppy lying in a crumpled heap on the floor he quirked an eyebrow in her direction, then swept into his room and placed the tray down on the bedside table.

An amused smile stretched across his face. "Get back in bed, Poppy."

She didn't respond. Seeing him as a smiling, gentle human once more was deeply unsettling, so Poppy turned her gaze to the carpet but otherwise didn't move. But when Dorian knelt down beside her she recoiled immediately. "Don't touch me!" Poppy snarled, baring her teeth and holding a hand to her chest as if it could keep her heart from bursting out of her ribcage. "Don't come near me."

"Then get back in bed," he said mildly. "You need to eat. And rest."

"Hell if I'm spending even *one more second* unconscious with you around."

"Oh, so now you're going to wear yourself out through lack of sleep instead of lack of food? Sounds like a great plan."

Poppy glared at him, taking note of the fact Dorian looked as if he should take heed of his own advice and rest: there were shadows beneath his eyes, and his usually artfully dishevelled hair was an unforgivable mess. *Has he been staying awake to watch me sleep?* Poppy thought with disgust. *Or is there another reason he looks so tired?*

Eventually Poppy came to the conclusion that sitting on the floor and staring at Dorian Kapros was far worse than lying in bed and eating, so with an immense effort she struggled to her feet and collapsed back onto the bed, slamming her head against the pillows in resignation.

When Dorian placed a tray in her lap with soup, a sandwich and orange juice upon it she resisted the urge to flinch once more. "How did you know I was awake?" she muttered, picking up the sandwich and investigating it with dutiful suspicion before taking a tiny bite of it.

"I didn't," Dorian admitted, perching on the edge of the bed as if he had somehow gained a respect for Poppy's personal space that never existed before now. "I was going to wake you up. You've been asleep for three days."

"Three – three *days?*"

He nodded. "Clearly you needed it."

"You *made* me need it!"

"That was deliberate. Now eat, unless you really don't care about the welfare of the rest of your club anymore."

Poppy flinched at the comment – particularly the off-hand

way in which Dorian relayed it – before begrudgingly eating everything on the tray. With every mouthful she realised just how ravenous she truly was, though still Poppy left the crusts of her sandwich behind. She'd never eaten them before; she wasn't about to start now.

She ate in silence, decidedly not looking at Dorian as she did so. But he didn't seem to mind, content to steal Poppy's crusts and dip them into her soup before chewing on them slowly, as if deep in thought.

"You eat human food no problem," Poppy observed aloud, when curiosity inevitably got the better of her.

Dorian swallowed the bread in his mouth and shrugged. "What of it?"

"If you – if your kind can eat what we eat then why eat humans?"

He considered his answer for a moment or two. "A cat can eat plant-based food as part of its diet, but if you don't feed it meat then it'll die. It's an obligate carnivore."

"So humans are cat food, and other animals are plants?"

"I guess so," Dorian chuckled. "But 'human food' doesn't give us any physical or mental advantages, either. If I were to consume a good-quality human I wouldn't have to eat for five or six years...longer if they're particularly exceptional."

"That was more information than I wanted."

"Liar. You can't pretend like you're not interested."

Poppy glowered at him. "Stop telling me what I do or don't want, Dorian. All I want is to get as many people away from your god damn slaughterhouse as possible. I don't care about the biology of a monster."

Dorian sobered. He took the now-empty tray away and placed it on the bedside table, before sitting back upon the bed to stare at Poppy. She noted that he'd inched just a little closer to her.

"How are you feeling?"

"How do you think?" she snarled, running a hand across the back of her neck to feel the slightly raised indentations that were the only remains of Dorian's attack. "What you put me through was...sick. Psychotic."

"I know. You had to see it, though."

"No I didn't! Never in a million years did I have to—"

"They'll do far worse to you if they ever realise you have immortal blood, Poppy," Dorian cut in, deathly serious. "You have to understand that. And if literally watching one of your club members get eaten alive is enough to force some sense into you then so be it."

A shiver ran down Poppy's spine at the reminder of what she'd seen. She glanced at Dorian through a curtain of hair; with his appearance broken up by strands of brown and silver, she could almost see his other form shimmering in the air around him.

His *true* form.

Poppy had always been a fan of Greek mythology growing up. She was an only child, and with no siblings to play with she had thrown herself into the story books and encyclopaedias her parents bought to entertain her. In his true form Dorian reminded her of the god Pan, Poppy supposed, though she never remembered Pan's teeth and nails being so sharp and sinister. And Dorian didn't have two horns, like a goat – rather, he seemed to have what could only be described as a complicated, delicate crown of bone woven around his hair.

His ears were what Poppy expected from a satyr or a faun based on her childhood books. Pointed, elongated, inhuman ears. And the legs. Furred and bandied, raising Dorian far higher off the ground than any human, with hooves which would likely crumple a person's skull with barely a kick.

Dorian was a monster through and through, yet once Poppy had gotten over her horror at his true appearance she realised he was starkly, inhumanly beautiful. Even more so than his human form in a twisted fairy tale kind of way, though Poppy was loathe to acknowledge either form being anything but repulsive to her. The angles of Dorian's face – previously broken nose and all – looked *right* when he was his true self. And his blue eyes took on an edge Poppy simply couldn't describe. They were haunting.

They forced you to look at them and pay no heed to the fangs angled right at your flesh with the intent to destroy you.

And that damn voice. Poppy didn't know if Dorian looked and sounded the way he did because honest-to-goodness, real-life monster versions of satyrs were naturally as appealing as he was, or whether he moulded himself to the image humans had created of the lustful, mischievous Pan.

Either way, Poppy couldn't help but concede, *at least he doesn't look like the thing that killed Ross.*

"Do you seriously think I can't see you looking at me if you hide behind your hair?" Dorian asked as he reached out to tuck several strands of it behind Poppy's ear.

She pulled away immediately. "I told you not to touch me."

"That'll be pretty difficult to abide by, considering I have to touch you to take your blood. Speaking of..." Dorian tilted his head and locked his eyes on Poppy's neck. She wasted no time in reorganising her hair around her face to throughly cover it. "Biting the back of your neck is probably a much better way of taking your blood than cutting your arm open again and again. Certain people are beginning to get suspicious."

By 'certain people' he meant Fred, Poppy knew. She made a face at the suggestion and collapsed against the pillows. "It hurt like hell. I don't want you to do it that way again."

To Poppy's surprise Dorian's expression turned apologetic.

"It only hurt because I made it hurt. I could have been much... gentler."

"And that's supposed to make me feel better? Having me watch another human being get dismembered before my very eyes wasn't enough – you had to put me through physical agony, too?"

He looked away. "I was...in a mood."

"Are you a child?!" Poppy fired back, skin prickling in righteous anger. "You put me through all that because you were *in a mood?* How am I supposed to put up with you for the rest of my life?" She buried her face into the pillow, scrunching her eyes closed as she willed the very world around her to disappear. "You're an overgrown, monstrous *child...*"

Dorian laughed humourlessly at her comment, then shifted position on the bed until he was lying beside Poppy as if it was the most natural thing in the world. *So much for his apparent new respect for boundaries,* she thought, though Poppy didn't have it in her to push him away.

"I'm sorry, Poppy," he murmured softly. "I won't do it again."

"Like hell you won't."

"Okay, I'll endeavour to try my *best* not to do it again."

Poppy didn't say anything. Of course she wanted to know why Dorian had been upset and angry, but part of her knew it was somehow to do with Nate. She wanted to avoid talking to Dorian about her friends as much as possible – *especially* Nate, of all people – so she decided to keep silent on the matter. But then she remembered something else she wanted to ask him, and turned her head to frown at Dorian.

"What did you do to me whilst I was unconscious?"

He had the sense to look abashed, though Poppy didn't believe it to be genuine in the slightest. "Well, it's not like I could leave you in a dusty, bloody mess on my bed, could I?"

"Dorian—"

"Hey, I left your underwear on," Dorian cut in, his false shame dissolving into a smirk as if he could hide his amusement no longer.

"You *washed my hair.*"

"You say that like it's a terrible thing."

"It's creepy as hell!"

"I wasn't aware. Guess I know for next time."

Poppy felt like screaming. She dragged a hand over her face. "I can't believe you. I honestly can't believe you. You're a shitty monster *and* a shitty human. Fucking great."

Dorian seemed genuinely affronted by this, sitting up in order to cross his arms over his chest. "How am I a shitty monster?" he complained. "I'd rather say I'm an excellent one."

"You're a capitalistic son of a bitch. You make a fortune from what's basically slave-trading. You're scum."

He burst out laughing. Poppy suppressed the urge to slap him, if only because she didn't want to get any closer to Dorian than she already was.

"God, you're something else, aren't you?" he said, incredulous. "Tell me, Poppy, which situation is better: allowing my kind to roam through your streets picking off people as and when they want to, or controlling the situation by only making excellent-quality humans available that diminish the requirement for my kind to eat as frequently?"

Poppy didn't reply. Dorian's logic was infuriatingly solid.

"Look, Poppy," Dorian continued when she stayed silent, "you eat cattle and pigs and chickens and fruits and vegetables because they're your food source. Ours is humans. There's nothing inherently wrong with that."

She knew this, of course. It didn't make it any easier to

swallow. Discovering that humans weren't the apex predator they'd always prided themselves on being was difficult to comprehend, even though the proof of it was staring Poppy far too closely in the face.

"Making money off something essential for living still makes you a shitty monster," she eventually muttered, more to herself than to Dorian.

When Dorian grabbed her arm and pulled her onto his lap Poppy let out a yelp. She struggled against his grasp but his lean, well-muscled arms kept her in place. He rested his chin on top of her head.

"What are you *doing?*" Poppy seethed, digging her nails into Dorian's arms in the vain hope that he would let go.

He didn't.

"I won't take blood from you this week," he said simply, ignoring Poppy's question entirely.

"Is that supposed to be some kind of half-assed apology for what you did to me?"

"Sort of. Maybe. I guess I just think you deserve a break. You still have to sacrifice and save a person, though."

Poppy let out a noise of disgust. "Of course I do. Let me go, you over-sized fucking goat."

"Low blow, King."

"Now you sound like Fred."

Dorian squeezed her. "Are you ever going to sacrifice him?"

"Why should I tell you?"

"Because I'm curious. And I won't let you go if you don't."

She sighed heavily, turning her gaze to the glass wall of Dorian's room as she thought about how to answer. It was a beautiful day outside – late afternoon, going by the angle of the sun. Something about the golden light gilding the trees of the grove nestling on top of the cliff made her heart hurt with an odd mix of longing and nostalgia, though of course Poppy had never set eyes on the place prior to last week.

"Poppy?"

"No," she said, answering Dorian's question with a voice that sounded faraway even to her own ears. "He's too good a person."

A shift in the way Dorian held her broke Poppy's dreamlike state. She glanced down at his arms, noting the way his muscles had tensed as he replied, "Oh, so we're back to being unbiased after saving Nate, are we?"

"Will you just *shut up* about Nate?" Poppy bit out testily. "He's a good guy. Even you have to admit that. He should get to live."

"If you say so."

Poppy struggled against Dorian's iron arms once more but to no avail. Eventually she gave up completely, turning soft against his chest with a huff of defeat. When she tilted her head up a few seconds later she saw that Dorian was looking down at her, so Poppy kept her eyes on his and resolutely did not break his stare.

"What is it?" Dorian asked curiously. Poppy watched as his gaze lowered to take in her very much indecent state of undress, so she self-consciously tugged at the hem of the over-sized T-shirt to try and cover more of her thighs to absolutely no avail.

"Do you like me?" she mumbled, feeling her heart hammer sickeningly against her ribcage. She didn't know which answer would be worse.

"Of course I like you. You're an attractive idiot."

Poppy narrowed her eyes. "That wasn't the answer I was expecting."

"And why is that?"

"Typically one doesn't show a person they like a live demonstration of a person getting eaten."

"I suppose not," Dorian mused. "But that was for your own good."

A brush of a hand down her arm to her waist caused Poppy to shiver. She was acutely aware of how easily Dorian could break any number of bones in her body with the fingers he now so gently trailed across her, though she much preferred that train of thought to the other, far more shameful, idea her brain was currently concocting.

"You're so twisted," Poppy said, if only to force her attention back on what really mattered.

"Why, thank you."

She bashed the back of her head against Dorian's chest, thoroughly resigned by his carefree attitude towards permanently traumatising her. "Sometimes I think it would have been easier if I just let you lock me up in an abandoned room somewhere," Poppy bit out, "so I never had to interact with you until the end of time. You would come in and drain my blood whenever you wanted but otherwise leave me alone to go insane within my own head. Sounds preferable to me than what *this* is." She motioned around her with her supposed-to-be-injured arm.

Dorian dug his nails into Poppy's waist just enough to make her wince. "Now who's the twisted one? That's completely fucked up."

"Nothing about my situation *isn't* fucked up."

"...I guess so."

A pause. And then: "What did you tell the rest of the club about what happened to me?" Poppy asked. "I don't imagine my friends would accept 'Poppy's sleeping in my bed' as an excuse."

Dorian chuckled into Poppy's hair; the sound tickled her scalp. "That's exactly what I told them, actually. Rachelle and Casey even came up to see you whilst you were sleeping. I told them I was staying in another room, of course."

"...but you weren't, were you?"

"Of course not."

"That's even creepier than washing my hair."

"Debatable. I *do* need to sleep, you know," Dorian pointed out. "It's not like I lay there and watched you constantly for three days."

"No, only sometimes, which is a million percent creepier than not doing it at all."

Dorian sighed in an exaggerated fashion. "Must everything you say be a curse, a sarcastic quip or an insult?"

"To you?" Poppy nodded. "Absolutely."

"I suppose I deserve that. Do you think you can stand now?"

"If you let go of me."

He loosened his grip on Poppy somewhat reluctantly, then she moved off the bed and smoothed out the T-shirt she was wearing. It barely hit her thighs with her standing completely upright.

"Where are my clothes, Dorian?" she murmured, turning from his gaze when a flush of embarrassment reddened her cheeks.

He waved a hand dismissively. "I gave them to Rachelle. I think she washed them and put them back in your room."

"So...what am I supposed to wear back to the east wing?"

"Just wear what you have on."

Poppy rounded on him, embarrassment turned to indignation in the space of a second. "You can't be serious.

I'm assuming this T-shirt's...yours?"

He merely smiled.

"People are going to think we're – that we're—"

"That we're fucking? Probably not a bad cover, you know. Certainly would explain why you sneak off to see me all the time."

"I do *not* sneak off to see you!" she protested, appalled. "*You* pull me away from my friends, not the other way around!"

"Whatever helps you sleep at night," he grinned, knowing Poppy was seconds away from punching him in the face. Then he said, "There's a pair of denim shorts in the top drawer over there that'll fit you."

"Why would you have a pair of shorts that fit me?"

He shrugged. "After we made our deal I ordered some stuff online. Patrick brought it over a week or so ago. It's not like I can expect you to wear the same two weeks' worth of clothing for the rest of your life."

It was somehow both a horrendous and a thoughtful gesture. Ignoring the disgusted shiver that ran down her spine, Poppy moved over to riffle through the drawer. She scanned across the other clothes inside that Dorian clearly intended for her – woollen jumpers, a few T-shirts, a waterproof jacket and a couple of pairs of dark leggings – until she found the denim shorts in question, pulling them on as quickly as possible before making a beeline for the door.

Dorian rushed off his bed and reached the door just as Poppy opened it. "Wait, you're heading out now?" he complained, looking thoroughly put out.

"You really think I want to hang around here any longer?"

"...probably not," he admitted, seeming genuinely sad by this inevitable truth. Poppy struggled not to call him pathetic.

"Are you going to behave yourself?"

"If by that you're asking if I'll eat and be more careful around your *friends* then yes, I suppose I have to," she said, because the last thing Poppy wanted was for Dorian to decide she needed to watch another of her club members getting eaten alive.

Dorian seemed visibly relieved by her answer. "Good. And don't flirt with Nate too much. You'll only break his heart."

Poppy slammed the door in his face.

GREGORY FRASER

ANDREW

NOBODY WAS HAPPIER THAN ANDREW WHEN Poppy finally awoke three days after she'd fainted. He supposed that Nate or Rachelle or Casey could have given him a proverbial run for his money, but Andrew still liked to think he was the happiest.

Or perhaps *relieved* was more appropriate.

When Poppy came through to the central building from the west wing she was wearing a very large, grey T-shirt Andrew didn't recognise. He wondered if it was Dorian's, and whether it was part of a social interaction he shouldn't ask about. But he wanted to know; he wanted to know so badly it hurt.

Just what was going on with Poppy and Dorian?

Why had the facility manager put her into his own bedroom to rest? If sleep was all she needed then her own room would have been just fine. Better, even. Poppy would've had her friends around to look after her. But Dorian had said it was too loud in the east wing and what Poppy needed was peace and quiet. Andrew *did* agree with this, and had almost asked if he could move over to the west wing, too, for the same reason.

But something told him Dorian would deny his request.

"Afternoon, sleeping beauty!" Nate called out happily as soon as he spied Poppy. He was playing Monopoly with Andrew, Rich, and Robin Fraser, whom Andrew didn't know all that well. To be honest he didn't know why they were playing Monopoly in the first place – nobody seemed to like it very much – and their game was quickly abandoned once Poppy came and sat down beside them.

"Hey, guys," she said bashfully, picking up the tiny silver dog from the Monopoly board and twiddling it between her thumbs. "Miss me?"

"Tonnes."

Andrew nodded sagely in agreement.

Poppy laughed at the expression on his face. "Andrew, I'm fine. I just needed to sleep."

Nate scoffed at the comment. "That was *a lot* of sleep, Morph."

"How's your arm, Poppy?" Robin asked politely. Poppy held up her bandaged arm and stared at it as if she only just remembered it existed. She wiggled her fingers enthusiastically.

"Much better. It was probably a bad idea to use it so soon after hurting myself; clearly my body didn't like me very much for putting so much strain on it."

"You've seriously had the worst bout of luck, King," Rich laughed. "It's almost like karma's come round to bite you in the ass for not following a single safety protocol your entire life."

"Hilarious."

Nate looked put out when Poppy chose not to sit down. He tried to grab hold of her wrist but Poppy pulled her arm to her chest before he could. He frowned. "You sure you're okay, Morph? I'm not gonna lie, you scared the shit out of me in the cave."

"I'm fine, trust me. I just hadn't had much of an appetite for a few days. I shouldn't have gone bouldering on an empty stomach. It's my own fault." Poppy plastered a smile to her face that Andrew thought *almost* looked genuine. Almost, but not quite. "I swear I'll take better care of myself," she continued. "Starting by throwing myself in the shower. I feel disgusting having slept for so long."

Nate looked surprised. "But you smell like...eucalyptus?"

"Tea tree," Andrew corrected just as he stood up to follow Poppy back to the east wing. He sniffed the air by Poppy's head. "Definitely tea tree. My mum buys tea tree shampoo for me. She says it smells so much better than all those..."

The other men chuckled as Andrew embarked on an overly long explanation about why he knew Poppy smelled like tea tree, though Poppy herself seemed to have flinched at Andrew's observation. She walked away without another word, which confused Nate, but when he made to get up and follow her Rich pulled him back down.

"Give her some space," he muttered. "Come on, she just woke up."

Though Rich's comment could also have applied to Andrew he followed Poppy through to the east wing regardless. Something told him that Poppy would not turn away his company, though he didn't know why he knew that. "Craig Hunt was scouted when you were asleep," he told her once he reached her side.

Poppy's face seemed to grow white, though it was hard to tell considering how pale she was these days. "Is that so?" she murmured, not looking at Andrew as she spoke.

"Yes. I don't like that he got picked but I'm glad he's

gone."

"You didn't like him?"

"No."

"And why is that?"

Andrew didn't want to tell Poppy about what Craig had said to him. To do so would involve him telling her how he felt about her, and Andrew didn't know if he could do that. "He wasn't very nice," he ended up saying, which wasn't a lie.

Poppy laughed bitterly. "I guess he wasn't. At least he's out of your hair then, Andrew."

"Out of my hair?"

"You know, he's gone. He can't bother you." She picked a loose thread from Andrew's shirt, put it on her head and then ran a hand through her hair until it fell out. "He's out of your hair."

He snorted at Poppy's demonstration. She always explained phrases Andrew didn't understand as literally as possible. "I get it now. Thanks. Have *you* been scouted, Poppy?"

"Oh god no. I've been an uneven mess for weeks! Who'd want *me* working for them?"

Andrew didn't understand. He'd been stealing looks at the class register Poppy kept on her phone whenever he could. He felt guilty about it, since it involved him unlocking her phone when she wasn't around. He hadn't *meant* to find out the password on the device but now that he knew it he couldn't help but check out her list every few days.

Everyone she had crossed off, except herself, was now gone. Andrew had thought it was to do with who got scouted but that didn't explain why Ross Bridges' name was crossed off. It also didn't explain the names that were highlighted – including his own. But the other names that were highlighted were good people. Nice people.

Other than Poppy, the names who were crossed off were *not* good people. Andrew would know: Ross, Angelica and especially Craig were particularly nasty to him. If Poppy's name wasn't also crossed off, Andrew would have easily concluded that she was marking off who she wanted gone from the club whilst highlighting who she wanted to stay.

And if that were the case...Andrew had some suggestions for her.

"Do you know Megan Lo, the third year economics student?"

Poppy stared at him just as she opened her bedroom door. She waved Andrew in with her; he sat on the chair in the corner and watched as she rummaged through her luggage for new clothes.

"Bit of a subject change," she finally replied. "Of course I know Megan."

"Did you know she scammed a website into giving her loads of free clothes?"

"How do you know that, Andrew?"

"I heard her talking to Angelica about it on the bus."

"She got away with it? Ah, I could *so* do with going for a swim. Wanna join, Andrew?"

He nodded. "I'll go get changed. She got away with it. She's planning on doing it again."

Poppy said nothing. She was staring at the T-shirt she was wearing with a blank expression. Then she peeled the garment off right in front of Andrew.

He spluttered in shock. "Um, I'm going to – I'll go get changed!"

She giggled. "Andrew, there's barely a difference between a bra and a bikini. No need to get so embarrassed."

Even though what Poppy said was logical, Andrew didn't

agree with it. Or, at least, his *body* didn't agree with it. He rushed out of Poppy's bedroom and into his own, getting changed into his swimming trunks whilst desperately trying not to think of the girl he was crazy about wearing only a bra and a tiny pair of denim shorts.

He beat her to the pool by several minutes, so Andrew swam a couple of lengths before taking a deep breath and sinking to the bottom, holding his knees to his chest in order to calm his racing heart. A few seconds later a splash at the other end of the pool alerted him to the fact Poppy had joined him.

Once she located Andrew she swam over and sat on the bottom of the pool with him, holding her hands out until he took them. Andrew had no idea what was going on, but when he looked at Poppy's eyes through the chlorinated water it almost looked like she was crying.

He wanted to comfort her.

He didn't know how.

After about a minute of wide-eyed staring and squeezing each others' hands the two of them resurfaced, though Andrew could have stayed underwater for much longer than that – he could hold his breath longer than anyone else in the club, after all. He followed Poppy over to the edge of the pool where it overlooked the loch, watching as she closed her eyes and raised her head to the sun. A contented sigh slipped from her lips as if she hadn't felt its rays on her face in days.

Andrew supposed she hadn't.

"Did you really just faint in the caves because of hunger?" he asked quietly, after glancing around to make sure nobody was within earshot. But most of the club was on a hike; Nate, Rich and Robin had only hung back to keep Andrew company, since he hadn't wanted to leave in case Poppy woke up.

Poppy smiled at him. Andrew thought it was perhaps the

saddest smile he'd ever seen. "That's exactly what happened, Andrew," she said. "Don't worry about me. It's like you said two weeks ago – I'm an adult. It's time I acted like one...starting with making sure I actually feed myself."

"Did you know Greg's sister has leukaemia?"

"Andrew, I swear, what the hell is all this about?" Poppy demanded, evidently suspicious. "I never had you pegged for a gossip. First Megan, now Greg Fraser..."

"I'm not a gossip," he protested. "I just listen."

"I didn't know about his sister, if that answers your question."

"I think it's why he's working so hard to get scouted," Andrew explained. "So he can get together some money for her. His family want to go overseas for some experimental treatment."

A pause. A faint trembling in the air caused goosebumps to rise on Poppy's arms, though Andrew wondered if it was their conversation that was causing them instead. "Why are you telling me this?" she asked, very quietly.

"I just think it would be nice if people who actually deserved to get a break got it. Instead of Angelica or Ross or Craig, I mean."

Poppy's eyes narrowed. "Ross wasn't scouted. Dorian kicked him out."

He flinched. "Oh yeah. I...forgot."

"You never forget anything."

"I do so."

"Only when you want to avoid an awkward topic of conversation."

For a long moment it looked like Poppy was going to press the matter further. But then she dunked her head beneath the surface of the pool and shot back up, flipping her long hair back in a graceful arc. It reminded Andrew of the mermaid in *The Little Mermaid.* He liked that film.

"I guess I can relate to wanting to avoid awkward topics of conversation," Poppy eventually replied, wringing excess water out of her hair as she did so. Glancing at Andrew, she added, "I always have your back, you know. You can talk to me about anything."

"Am I allowed to have *your* back?"

Poppy pretended to think for far too long, then grinned. "You *better* have my back, Andrew. You saying you haven't until now?"

She made a wave in the water with her arm, sending it splashing into Andrew as punishment. Though he held up his hands with the intention of blocking it, before Andrew knew it he had splashed Poppy back and was laughing louder than he had in weeks.

"Oh my – *Poppy!* When did you wake up?!"

Rachelle ran up to the edge of the infinity pool with Casey close behind her, having just returned from the hike most of the club was on.

Casey squealed in delight when she saw Poppy, then expertly dived into the pool – clothes and all. "Just what I wanted after all that walking!" she cried out once she resurfaced. "It's *roasting* today. Oh hi there, Poppy. Didn't know you were still alive."

"Bitch."

Casey stuck out her tongue as she pulled off her top and shorts, leaving her in her underwear and nothing else. When Rachelle started pulling off her clothes to join them, too, Nate, Rich and Robin came out of the social area and watched the scene in disbelief.

"No fair, Andrew," Nate pouted, making quick work of removing his T-shirt just as the other two followed suit. "You abandon us and end up in the pool with three lovely, barely-dressed ladies?"

"I call a conspiracy," Rich laughed before bombing into the pool.

What's in the air today that's making everyone take their clothes off? Andrew thought in confusion. Under normal circumstances he would have been completely overwhelmed by this turn of events, not least because he had been frozen to the spot the moment Casey started stripping off her top. But now that Poppy was awake and well and back with the group Andrew found that he could tolerate the noisy crowd – at least for a while.

The group continued to splash and dive and wrestle with each other beneath the surface of the water, the air filled with the sounds of laughter and screams and incessant chatter until long after the sun set.

Everyone was having fun together like they had done before the retreat. Easy, escapist, meaningless fun with nothing sinister whatsoever behind it.

And Dorian was nowhere in sight.

INTERLUDE III

WHEN MEGAN WAS INFORMED BY Dorian Kapros that she had been scouted she couldn't hide her surprise. Sure, she was a pretty decent rock climber, and she'd performed better than usual in the caves, but there were many people in the club she'd have thought would be picked over her. Still, she wasn't going to complain.

Like most people in the club Megan had never been to the first floor of the west wing, so she had no reason to suspect that the room she was brought into was anything but normal.

Then the door was locked behind her and she took in the sight of the people already inside.

"An-Angelica?" she whispered, her brain struggling to register the sight of her friend lying despondent on a bed. More than that: Angelica was missing her eyes.

Megan spared a glance for the young man sitting on the floor in the corner of the room, who was doing nothing but slowly rocking back and forth without saying a word. He didn't seem to notice her presence. "Craig?"

"Megan?" Angelica babbled uncertainly as she tried to sightlessly find her friend. "Megan, is that you?"

"Yes! What's going—"

Angelica choked on a sob. "Not you, too!"

Craig opened his mouth as if he was going to say something, but nothing came out. He had lost his tongue and all his perfect white teeth.

Megan felt a prick on the side of her neck and a hazy cloud of unconsciousness took over.

The scream she held in her throat was never released.

FRANCIS GREENE

FRED

"CASEY, ARE YOU *READING?*"

"Even I enjoy a book now and again, Rachelle."

"No, it's impossible. I refuse to believe it. What're you reading?"

Casey's cheeks reddened slightly. "I'm not telling you. Go back to talking about whatever you were talking about."

Rachelle looked at Casey protectively clutching her Kindle with an expression that very much suggested she'd find out what the book was sooner rather than later. She had a way of worming information out of people, after all.

"Worst date, Rachelle," Nate urged. "Come on, spit it out." He grinned at Fred. "Just because your ex is currently in the room with us doesn't mean you can't tell us."

"Oh, I have no doubt her worst date was with *Frederick*," Poppy drawled, nimbly avoiding the magazine Rachelle threw at her.

Now that Poppy was awake everything finally seemed to be getting back to normal again, with the club feeling very much like it had done for the past year despite some of the members having left its numbers already. But that's what struck Fred as unusual and unsettling.

It was *too* normal.

He gave Poppy the finger. "The only bad dates Rachelle and I had were ones you interrupted, King."

She held a hand to her heart in mock horror. "Me? Mess up your dates? Never."

To Fred's left Andrew choked on a laugh. It somehow pissed Fred off more to know that Andrew found Poppy's interfering funny, rather than disapproving of it. He kicked him gently. "Never had you down as a co-conspirator, Forbes."

Andrew inched away to prevent Fred from kicking him again. "I was *not.*"

"What, so Poppy merely regaled you with her exploits, instead?"

"Yes."

"Of fucking course."

"We're getting off-topic!" Nate cut in, eager for Rachelle to answer his question. He was the worst gossip in their friend group by far.

"Oh, what's the topic?"

The entire group turned at the sound of the voice; it was Patrick. Casey looked up from her Kindle, a dazzling smile playing across her lips as she allowed the man to sidle up beside her on the sofa. "Hey there, Patrick."

"Hey there, beautiful. What're you reading?"

"That's what *I* want to know!"

"Shush, Rachelle," Nate scolded. "Patrick, we're talking

about worst dates. Rachelle's dodging the question because hers was probably with Fred."

Patrick raised his eyebrows. "The two of you went out?"

"For nearly two years!" Casey exclaimed, seemingly shocked that Patrick did not know this despite the fact he was a stranger to them all but a month ago. "Poppy got in the way, of course."

"I didn't really."

Fred scowled at her. Of course Poppy would never take responsibility for the strain she'd put on her best friend's relationship. It would be so very *un-Poppy* of her to do so.

"Uh-oh, King, what did you do?" Patrick asked, curious.

"I mean it, I didn't do—"

"Let's not get into this," Rachelle said over the top of her best friend. "It's all in the past. And *you* were just as bad as Poppy, Fred."

"I was not!"

She let out an exaggerated sigh, reclining back against the sofa with the air of a long-suffering old woman. "Children, the both of you."

"So your worst date was with Fred, then?" Nate pressed on, determined to get an answer out of Rachelle despite her efforts to avoid doing so.

To everyone's surprise, however, she shook her head. "Not with Fred. With Robin."

Fred stilled. *Robin Fraser? She went on a date with—*

"Robin in the club Robin?" Andrew asked, leaning forward with an obvious interest in the topic at hand that had been decidedly lacking mere moments before. "*That* Robin?"

Rachelle giggled. "Yes, Andrew, *that* Robin."

Poppy's eyes shone with interest, reaching over the armchair she was lounging on to prod Rachelle's head before complaining, "You never told me about this, you bitch! When was it?"

"Um, a couple weeks before we left for this trip," Rachelle explained, glancing at Fred somewhat bashfully. That she'd gone on a date with Robin was most definitely news to him, since they weren't at the stage of discussing potential love interests with each other yet. Of course they weren't – Fred still hoped they'd get back together. "It ended with Robin throwing up all over me. Don't really need to say more than that."

Casey wrinkled her nose "Oh, *ew.*"

"Take it you didn't go on a second date, then?" Patrick asked. Fred watched as Casey flipped her hair over her shoulder so that the man could play with it, and he wondered – not for the first time – if the two of them had finally moved past shameless flirting to actually sleeping together.

Rachelle blushed. "Well, no, but that's because of the trip."

Nate looked incredulous. "Wait, so you *want* a date number two? With *my* Robin?"

"I wasn't aware your friends were your property, Nate," Poppy teased. He shrugged the comment off.

"I didn't want to go out again at first," Rachelle explained. The blush across her cheeks grew more crimson with every passing second. "But...I don't know. Maybe it's because we've all been in such close proximity over the past few weeks. Either way, we're gonna wait until after summer before trying again, I think."

Fred didn't say anything. He liked Robin Fraser. If he didn't still have feelings for Rachelle then he'd be all for the two of them dating. But he *did* have feelings for her, which meant he didn't like this at all.

Casey snuggled in against Patrick when he finished playing with her hair, which he'd braided, her reading all but abandoned. "I say you just go for it now, Rachelle," she told her friend. "What've you got to lose? You're both here for summer so just screw away and enjoy yourself."

"Eloquently put as usual, Casey," Nate laughed, though it was clear he agreed with her. He was sitting squashed up on the same armchair as Poppy, arms wrapped around her as she all but sat in his lap. Patrick watched them with a curious look on his face that both Andrew and Fred caught.

"I don't know," Rachelle said doubtfully, pulling Fred's attention back to her once more. "I think a summer without any boy trouble would be good for me."

"That's fifty shades of fucked up."

Rachelle swung around to stare at Casey immediately. "Please don't tell me you're reading that shite. *Please.*"

Casey blinked innocently. "I don't know what you mean."

"Aw come on, O'Donnell," Nate chided as Poppy giggled. "We all know that's from *Fifty Shades of Grey.* Is that why you didn't want us to know what you were reading?"

"Wait, you *all* know the line? Doesn't that mean you've all read the book, too?"

"I haven't," Andrew chimed in.

Poppy rolled her eyes. "Of course you haven't, Andrew. Casey, there's this thing called a cinema, you know. It shows films, one of which was *Fifty Shades.*"

"Poppy and I got black-out drunk and went to see it on Valentine's Day when it came out," Nate said, snorting at the memory.

Rachelle giggled. "Ah, that was a date you *definitely* ruined, Poppy. Fred and I went to see the same screening."

"Ew, unironically?"

"Shut up. Casey, how is it that you're only reading the book now? It came out ages ago."

"Because I'm horny, that's why. I haven't gotten with anybody since—"

"Let's chill out on the sex chat before we give Andrew a heart attack," Poppy cut in, throwing a look at Andrew that was somewhere between concern and amusement. But Andrew bristled at the notion.

"I *am* an adult, remember. I can handle it."

"Is that so, Forbes?" Fred teased, making to kick him once more.

Andrew kicked him back. "It's not like I don't know that Casey sleeps around."

"*Andrew!*"

He narrowed his eyes in confusion as both Patrick and Nate roared with laughter. "But she does. What's wrong with saying so?"

Casey giggled very prettily for Patrick's benefit. "I mean, he's not entirely wrong. But even so: Andrew, that's not something you should say out loud."

"But why not?"

"I thought you'd helped Andrew out with stuff like this, Poppy."

"You honestly expected her to help him out *properly*?" Fred barked, incredulous. He looked at Andrew. "Forbes, generally speaking you shouldn't talk in such open terms about whether someone sleeps with a lot of people or not."

Andrew only looked more confused. "But...you guys do it all the time."

"Yeah, behind the person's back..."

"Poppy!"

"But it's true!" she protested. "Andrew, just do you. Say whatever you want. If someone doesn't like what you're saying then fuck 'em."

Fred stood up, abruptly fed up of the conversation and the way it pertained to his ex-girlfriend sleeping with someone else. Rachelle glanced at him as if she knew exactly why he was leaving. "I'm going to grab some food from the kitchen," he said, fabricating an excuse to leave without arousing suspicion. "Anyone want anything?"

"Oh, I'll have—"

"Except King."

Everyone shook their heads, so Fred made his way towards the kitchen with no plans to actually eat anything. He ran into Dorian on the way; they didn't speak often so Fred assumed the facility manager would stay silent as they crossed paths. He was subsequently surprised when Dorian actually *did* speak to him.

"Have you seen Patrick, Fred?" Dorian asked politely. "I was expecting him in my office about half an hour ago."

"He's in the social area flirting with Casey," Fred replied blandly. Dorian looked over his shoulder at the group, his face darkening almost immediately. "What's wrong, Dorian?"

"...nothing," the other man muttered, stalking away before Fred could press him for a better answer.

But all Fred had to do was watch Dorian join the group to understand what had caused his bad mood. The scowl on his face when he saw Poppy practically sitting on top of Nate spoke volumes.

Of course he's into Poppy bloody King, Fred thought, thoroughly pissed off by the notion. *Of fucking course.*

When Fred reached the kitchen he was surprised to see his friend, Francis. The two of them had been closer in previous years – they shared several classes in their undergraduate degrees – but for whatever reason they had been distant over the past year or two.

"Hey, Fred," Francis smiled when Fred wandered over to the fridge on the hunt for sandwich-fillers. He was as well making something to eat now that he was here, after all.

"Hey," he replied to Francis. He was halfway through making a ham and cheese sandwich when he realised his friend was alone, so Fred asked, "What're you doing in here by yourself?"

"Just needed to think, I guess?"

"What about?" he pressed, fishing around the cutlery drawer for a knife. "The scouting?"

Francis shook his head. "No." A long pause. "I...I don't really know if I should talk about it."

That piqued Fred's interest. He put down the knife he'd found and leaned against the counter top. "Fire away. It's not as if I'll tell anyone."

Francis looked uncomfortable. "I don't – it's not something that I'm all that proud of. You honestly won't tell anyone?"

"I already said I wouldn't. And clearly you want to talk about it, otherwise you wouldn't have even said this much."

Francis still looked uncomfortable, but then he sighed and relented to tell Fred what was on his mind. "You know how Dorian and Poppy found Ross creeping on Casey?" he began. Fred nodded, not liking at all where this was going. "And then we found out that Casey had complained about him already, but since he hadn't *technically* done anything wrong that anyone else had witnessed, Poppy couldn't prevent him from going on the trip?"

Oh, yes, I definitely don't like where this is going. Yet Fred merely nodded again, already in too deep to turn away from whatever Francis was going to say next.

"Well, the thing is," Francis continued, "I knew Ross had done something pretty shady before. There was this girl in the theatre club – I think Rachelle might know her, actually – who he'd been seeing, but the girl brushed him off. He was pretty obsessed with her for a while. He followed her home one night but her flat mate called the police."

Fred closed his eyes for a moment and pinched the bridge of his nose, wishing that he had chosen not to come into the kitchen at all to save himself from learning about Ross' previous track record. "Why didn't you tell me or Poppy about this before the trip, Francis?"

"But I didn't know he was creeping on Casey! I didn't think it mattered!"

"Yeah, but even so he might have done it again to *any* of the girls in the club. It's something we should have known about." After a pause, Fred asked, "How did you know about this, anyway?"

Francis shifted his feet uncomfortably. "I may have...I might have encouraged him to not take no for an answer with the girl he was seeing. I know I was wrong!" he added on quickly when Fred opened his mouth to express his outrage. "It's just...at the time, you know, nobody really said anything about these things. It's only recently that everyone kicks up a fuss—"

"This kind of behaviour is *never* okay, regardless of whether people are talking about it or not! And Ross didn't act like this bloody decades ago, Francis. It was literally this year. Jesus Christ."

"Ooh, am I interrupting?"

Fred glared at Poppy as soon as he spied her by the door, which she was knocking upon in an exaggerated fashion. "The hell do you want?" he demanded.

"You ignored me when I said I wanted a drink from the kitchen," she said, heading over to the fridge and browsing through it until she found a carton of orange juice. She grinned at the object as if it was the best thing she'd seen all day. "Oh, amazing, unopened. Just my luck."

Behind her, Francis looked aghast at the possibility that Poppy had overheard the entire conversation about Ross. Fred had to admit he couldn't tell whether she had or not; Poppy was being annoyingly jovial as she swigged orange juice straight from the carton before deciding to take the entire thing back with her to the social area.

"I'll be right back," Fred muttered to Francis, wasting no time in hurrying out after Poppy to stop her in her tracks before she reached the rest of their friends. When he grabbed hold of her sleeve Poppy looked down at his hand in disgust.

"The hell do you want, Sampson?"

"Did you hear what Francis and I were talking about?"

"What, you mean where he admitted to egging Ross on and allowing him to stalk girls?" Poppy replied off-handedly. "No, not at all. Didn't hear a *thing*."

"Poppy—"

"Using my first name, Frederick? This must be serious."

"Don't tell anyone."

Poppy pushed him away. "And why shouldn't I? He was complicit. But there's no point now, anyway. Ross is gone."

"Exactly."

"Just so long as you're aware that Casey could have avoided so much stress and fear if Francis had opened his bloody mouth and told us about his scumbag friend ages ago."

"I know, I know." Fred rubbed his temple; it was beyond infuriating for Poppy to have the moral high ground when that was usually *his* place. "Thanks, I guess."

She raised an eyebrow. "Don't thank me. I'm not doing this for you – I'm doing this for Casey. She'd be horrified if she knew about this."

And then Poppy walked away, though the air about her seemed to have changed. When she wandered into the kitchen she'd seemed – possibly superficially – happy and directionless. Now it seemed as if she had a purpose.

Fred didn't like that at all, not least because he didn't know what that purpose was.

I need to work out what's going on with Poppy King, he thought, for the hundredth time.

RUBY MACMILLAN

DORIAN

AFTER TWO WEEKS OF HAVING RESTRAINED himself from drinking Poppy's blood Dorian felt like he was dying. Okay, he knew that was an exaggeration – not least because he had consumed several pints of Poppy's life-prolonging blood already – but he'd gotten so used to the weekly routine that going fourteen days without the stuff felt like torture.

He hadn't yet tested the effects of the blood currently in his system. Dorian kept telling himself that he'd cut himself open the next time he had the opportunity to do so and yet, six weeks later, he still hadn't attempted anything of the sort.

"Your turn, Kapros," Patrick said, gesturing towards the table. They were playing poker with Aisling, Nick and Steven before the three of them departed from the facility on Patrick's boat. Dorian was losing, but he didn't care.

"Fold," he replied immediately, dropping his cards onto the table in order to stand up and look through the glass wall towards the loch. Most of Poppy's club was outside sunbathing on the shore or swimming in the loch – it was a very hot day.

He had to wonder why the five of them were inside playing cards on such a day.

"You didn't even look at your cards," Aisling complained, before picking up a new one and raising the bet Patrick had placed on the table.

"I know. I don't care."

"Charming. What's on your mind?"

"Nothing."

"You're a terrible liar."

Dorian glanced at her, determined to keep his expression as blank as possible. Aisling was very wealthy, very influential and very, very intent on buying both Nate and Fred. She preferred her prey to be male and particularly good with both heights and the deepest, darkest depths of the earth. Heights to enhance her natural talents, and depths to make up for what she lacked.

For Aisling was a harpy – in more ways than one. Dorian didn't like her very much, though he'd never made his dislike obvious. He'd only been in the human trafficking business for twelve years, after all. Twelve years and five rounds of bidding across Europe, learning under his father's tutelage for the first three trips. Aisling had been a loyal client of his father and, after his passing, had decided to stick with the Kapros business even though Dorian was still 'wet behind the ears', as she put it.

Nick was in a similar boat insomuch as his father had been good friends with Dorian's and wished to continue supporting the business. Steven and Patrick were the only contacts in the room Dorian had made himself, though he had many more spread across the world. He knew that, in just a few more years, he would be just as respected and well-established a trafficker as his father had been.

Which was why Dorian's deal with Poppy was killing him,

though she didn't know it. For he had promised thirty top-quality humans in the prime of their life to his clientele. *Thirty.* But now Dorian only had fifteen.

Well, fourteen, he corrected. *Poppy's mine.*

So far his clients had been content with Dorian's dramatic change in schedule, believing that his fifteen week analysis of their potential food was to their benefit. It wheedled out those who weren't truly top-quality, he had told them. And it's not like they were paying for him to do this. *Dorian* was. If anything, most of his clients only respected Dorian more for putting so much care and attention into his business.

But there were some who were growing impatient – like Aisling. She knew who she wanted and yet here she was, empty-handed. Dorian had no idea how to tell her that she'd never get her hands on Nate Richards.

And possibly not Frederick Sampson, either. Dorian was still on the fence about that, though; he wasn't convinced Poppy could be as unbiased as she thought she could be. The day would come where she would slip up and sacrifice Fred before she could stop herself. And then—

And then she'll feel horrific.

Dorian got a sick sense of pleasure from knowing this even as part of him felt sorry for Poppy. Though he had made up the rules of their agreement on the spot – setting things up to be as innately cruel and monstrous as possible – the pain on Poppy's face when she came to terms with every blow he dealt her was becoming harder and harder for Dorian to watch, and he began to regret the rules he had imposed.

On more than one occasion Dorian wondered whether it would have been better to sell off the entire Outdoor Sports Society and whisk Poppy away against her will in the very beginning instead of playing their bloody, twisted game. It certainly would have saved Dorian many a headache.

But Poppy would never be able to forgive me. Not that she's likely to ever forgive me for what I've done, anyway.

Dorian knew he only had himself to blame.

"If you're going to sulk off into the distance then we'll be off," Nick joked, though both Steven and Aisling stood up as if they were happy he suggested it.

"Want to check out the club in the loch before we head back?" Steven suggested. "I think they were having some diving competitions."

"Casey'll win them no problem," Patrick said assuredly. The man was well and truly enchanted with the girl, though Dorian knew Casey's attraction in return wasn't exclusive. She still flirted with *him,* for one.

"Can't believe Dorian let you have her before opening the market," Steven muttered. "Nepotism through and through."

Patrick merely shrugged his shoulders. "I'm not gonna complain when I benefit from it. I'll catch you all down by the loch; I just need to talk to Dorian first."

Aisling, Nick and Steven dutifully exited the facility, though Aisling cast the pair of them a curious, suspicious glance before leaving.

"Your bad mood wouldn't have something to do with a certain Poppy King, would it, Dorian?" his friend asked the moment they were out of earshot.

Dorian scowled. "When you put it like that I sound pathetic."

"That's because you *are*...though in all fairness I guess I can't criticise you. I wanted Casey as soon as I saw her. And Poppy is ridiculously talented. Why don't you just tell everyone she's off the market?"

Dorian was quiet for a few moments. He hadn't told Patrick about the blood pouring through Poppy's veins. He may have been his best friend but something that valuable simply wasn't worth risking for anything, even friendship.

"I considered that," Dorian admitted, because of course he had, "but then my clients will only grow *more* interested in her because I'm keeping her back. And she's the best of the best in the club; there will be those willing to pay a stupid amount of money for her. It's hard enough for me to justify not selling Casey and she's middling at best at anything not water-based."

"She's also gorgeous, and charming, and hilarious," Patrick said, listing the girl's qualities on his fingers as he spoke. "There's a lot to be said for those. It's not just physical capabilities that are passed on through our food, remember. Not to mention when they're used as a *breeding partner.*"

Dorian raised an eyebrow. "I was wondering which route you were going to follow with Casey. I suppose the latter is rather appealing...though I didn't know you were wanting to start a family, Patrick."

When Patrick joined him to gaze out at the loch his eyes immediately found Casey, who was bombing into the water alongside Nate. "The earlier I start the earlier I can be done with it," he said, and though he sounded impassive the smile on his face suggested to Dorian that his friend wished to have children far more than he was letting on. "What are you wanting Poppy for?"

"I...don't want any offspring," Dorian replied. And then, to avoid actually answering the question: "You should get back to your boat, Patrick. I have some paperwork to sort through."

"You should probably work out what you want sooner rather than later, you know," Patrick said, giving him a pat on the shoulder. "Though I'd suggest keeping her around. You can't rely on my friendship as your only source of company forever."

Dorian focused on that singular word as Patrick bid him goodbye and left the facility: forever. Could he and Poppy really cope with being by each others' side *forever?* Dorian had royally messed things up with Poppy from the very beginning, after all, and now it was all but certain he had caused so much damage that there was no repairing their relationship.

"Ha! What relationship?" Dorian muttered as he moved through to the west wing. There was no circumstance in which he could have had any semblance of a normal relationship with the young woman. The only reason they had met at all was because Dorian had earnestly sought out her club for monsters to gorge upon. He had always intended for a client to pay him handsomely for Poppy.

He'd never wanted her for himself until the moment that he did...in more ways than one.

Dorian hated himself for that.

When he saw the woman he was currently obsessing over loitering outside his office Dorian halted in his tracks, beyond surprised. "Poppy?" he wondered aloud. "I thought you were outside with everyone else."

Poppy's sodden hair was plaited down her back, dripping loch water onto the floor even as she stared Dorian down. He'd never get over how fearless those pale eyes could look, especially when they were aimed at him.

"I wanted to talk to you whilst everyone was still outside."

"What about?"

She breathed in deeply. *Not a good sign,* Dorian thought. *A deep breath always precedes a difficult request or question.*

"Let me see the other club members," Poppy said. "The ones who aren't dead."

And there it is.

Dorian pinched the bridge of his nose. "What purpose would that serve?" he asked, exasperated. "You didn't want me to show you what happened to Ross. Why should this be any different?" In truth he'd expected Poppy would ask to see her fallen club mates eventually but that didn't make her request any less annoying.

"Are you honestly asking me what the difference is between you *forcing* me to watch a man get dismembered and me *asking* you to let me see the current state of those still alive?"

"But there's no point. They're all doomed to die sooner rather than later."

Poppy grew a little paler but resolutely stood her ground. "Just show me," she said. "I can handle it. It's my responsibility to shoulder the knowledge of what's happening to them. It's my fault, after all."

Dorian sighed then, with some reluctance, waved for Poppy to follow him along the corridor and up the stairs to the first floor. He stopped in front of one of the locked doors, throwing a key card in the air before catching it and using it to open the door.

"It's not your fault, though," he said almost as an aside when the door clicked open. "It's mine. You're saving people. Remember that."

"Yes, at the expense of others."

"I was going to kill them all until you suggested a compromise."

Confusion and suspicion were apparent across every inch of Poppy's face, and she crossed her arms. "Why are you trying to make me feel better? *You're* the one who's revelled in my misery up to now."

"Maybe I'm getting sick of it all," Dorian replied, so quietly that Poppy likely didn't hear him.

When they entered the room and Dorian closed the door behind them Poppy did a short circuit of the long, narrow room. "There's nothing in here," she said, waving at the empty space around her.

"That's because it's an observation room. The wall over there is—"

"Let me guess: a one-way mirror?"

Dorian nodded as he made to pull up the blind that covered the wall. He glanced at Poppy uncertainly. "Are you *sure* you want to see this?"

"No. But I need to."

So he pulled on the blind. Dorian knew what Poppy was going to see and how she would likely react; even so, he kept his eyes on her face to observe her change in state nonetheless.

Ross Bridges was long gone, of course. Angelica Fisher was missing her eyes, whilst Craig Hunt's teeth and tongue were gone. Megan Lo was missing both of her legs. She lay sobbing uncontrollably on a bed.

But Poppy's face stayed impassive as she took in the sight before her. Dorian couldn't read her expression at all, though when he looked down and observed her shaking, white-knuckled fists he realised she was fighting to keep from visibly reacting as much as possible.

"Francis Greene," she whispered without once taking her eyes away from the tortured, half-mad people in front of her. "I'm giving up Francis Greene."

"And saving?"

"Ruby MacMillan."

"Which one is that?"

"A first year," she replied, not looking at Dorian. "Dad's a policeman. If she went missing the investigation would never stop. And she's a good person...as good as anyone in the club could be, really."

Dorian was impressed with Poppy's answer. He hadn't known she was taking the *reaction* to members of her club going missing into consideration and yet, here she was, doing exactly that. He found himself moving over to stand behind Poppy before he could stop himself, gently twisting her wet, braided hair over a shoulder when he reached her. "Can I—"

"Later," she interrupted, turning him down immediately. "Later. And I said I didn't like it there. It hurt too much."

"I told you that was because I meant for it to—"

"Which means you could do that again. Stick to my arm. I want to leave now."

Numbly he fulfilled her request, leading Poppy out of the room without another word. She left the west wing at a speed that suggested she most definitely didn't want Dorian to follow. "But when's *later?*" he mumbled to himself, thoroughly put out by Poppy's rejection. Poppy would be surrounded by her friends for the rest of the day – it was so warm they'd likely stay outside until late at night. Which left—

When Poppy goes to bed.

Dorian grinned wickedly at the thought, knowing that it was entirely inappropriate to corner Poppy when she was literally in bed. It was what she'd sacrificed Ross Bridges for, after all. *Well, Ross never intended to consume Casey's blood, but the creeping into a woman's room part is the same.*

But he was desperate for her blood and, perhaps more than that, Dorian was desperate to prove to Poppy that using her neck instead of her arm needn't be painful at all. Feeling a twitching below his stomach, Dorian forced himself to return to his office and the mountain of paperwork he had to content himself with until Poppy retired for the night.

And then his fun would begin.

POPPY

Poppy's day had been long and exhausting. Most of it had been distractingly great; one part of it glaringly not. But she knew she needed to be aware of the current state of those she'd sacrificed. Dorian had been right, before, when he said Poppy had to *see* things in order to acknowledge they were real. That they were happening.

Now she had literally seen what her choices had done. To Megan. To Craig. To Angelica.

And to Ross, Poppy thought with a shiver, turning restlessly in bed for the tenth time in as many minutes. But even through the shiver she was uncomfortably hot. The weather had been so balmy over the last week that Poppy had taken to wearing the over-sized grey T-shirt Dorian had given her to bed, because it was the coolest and most comfortable item of clothing she possessed for sleeping in. She hated it with every fibre of her being, of course, but it was the only thing she didn't want to claw off her body in the heat.

A few quiet minutes passed by during which time Poppy's mind was blank of all thoughts but one. For there was one conclusion Poppy had definitely reached when she'd seen what had befallen the people she'd sacrificed: she needed to find a way for everyone to escape.

Not just those who still had all their limbs. *Everyone.*

Nobody deserved the fate Poppy had forced upon them – even if Dorian was now insisting it wasn't her fault nor her responsibility to feel guilty on their behalf. She resolved to try and scope out a possible exit plan over the next few days without arousing suspicion from anyone, wondering if she could rope Andrew into the exercise under the guise of mapping out the area. It was a pastime he was very enthusiastic about, so Poppy was reasonably certain he'd jump at the opportunity to help her.

Satisfied with having finally made a concrete – if not detailed – decision Poppy closed her eyes, sank into her pillow and finally allowed herself to drift off to sleep. *Save everyone, save everyone,* her brain repeated as a kind of twisted lullaby. *Find a way out and save everyone.*

What felt like barely a minute later but could have, in reality, been hours, Poppy thought she could hear the sound of a door opening and closing. But when she turned to see if anybody had entered her room and prepared to shout at them a hand swiftly clamped across her mouth.

Someone slid beneath the duvet, wasting no time in pressing their body against Poppy's back despite her protests. She knew it could only be Dorian, even before she recognised his scent and the height difference of his body to hers.

Poppy looked over her shoulder as best she could to see the detestable monster disguised as a man behind her, half a smirk dancing across his lips at her outrage. In defiance she bit into the meat of his hand, though Dorian didn't so much as flinch.

"Keep your voice down and I'll let go of your mouth," he murmured, his lips brushing against her ear. Poppy's face grew hot at the sound, for he was using his tantalising voice meant solely for seduction and entrapment. It only caused her to bite down harder on Dorian's hand before, finally, forcing herself to let go. "That's better," he said, pulling his hand away and shaking his wrist in the process. "You sure you don't have fangs? That hurt like a bitch."

"What are you doing in my bed?!"

When he snaked an arm around her waist Poppy flinched. "You said *later,*" Dorian breathed against her skin, as if that explained anything at all. "This is about as later as it can get. I'm hungry."

Poppy couldn't believe what she was hearing; she almost wished Dorian's hand was across her mouth just so she could bite it again. "You honestly couldn't wait until the morning this *one time?*"

"Not when I've waited two weeks I can't. Are you wearing my T-shirt?" Dorian asked, picking at the fabric where it slid against the top of Poppy's thigh.

"You gave it to me," she insisted, trying to ignore his fingertips on her leg. "It's mine."

"I'm not complaining. I rather like seeing you in a T-shirt and little else."

When he slid a hand beneath the hem of the garment she reached down and slapped him away. "What are you doing, you perverted prick?"

Dorian nuzzled his face into her hair and chuckled; it was disgustingly affectionate. "Choice words. I'm hungry and I'm horny. At this point they feel like the same thing."

"Go fuck a goat, then!"

He only laughed harder into her hair before smoothing it away from the nape of her neck. When his teeth grazed against the skin there Poppy tried to move away. Dorian, of course, held her firmly in place.

"I'm not letting you drink from me in a situation like this," she protested, wriggling against Dorian despite how fruitless her protests were. "You've somehow made it *even weirder* than it was before."

"It won't hurt, I swear."

"You're breaking through my near-unbreakable flesh with your teeth; of course it'll hurt."

Poppy tried to kick Dorian away but he trapped her leg between his own, only further locking her in place. *He wasn't joking when he said he was horny,* Poppy thought despite herself as something distinctively hard prodded against her hip. Her face grew warmer and then warmer still because of it. *No way am I getting turned on by this,* she chastised, thinking that perhaps she shouldn't have turned down Nate's many offers of a sleepover over the past several weeks. *It's just been too long since I—*

"Of course that part will hurt," Dorian said, tracing his lips along the line of Poppy's shoulder and back to her neck again. "But cutting your arm to ribbons hurts more. And it'll feel much, much better once I've bitten through...I promise."

"What are you, a vampire?"

"No. They don't exist."

"I find that hard to believe coming from someone literally wanting to suck my blood."

"None of my kind would willingly drink blood over eating your flesh, normally. It's the equivalent of eating stale bread over a steak. You're the exception."

Dorian's hand found its way under Poppy's T-shirt during her distraction, tracing his fingers across the skin from her navel to the top of her stomach. She sucked in a breath. "S-stop doing that," she stuttered, her body growing hotter and tenser with every passing moment. Poppy didn't like how Dorian was making her feel in the slightest, yet he didn't seem to be listening to anything she said to push him off. "Fine!" she finally relented. *The sooner this starts the sooner it can be over.* "Drink your stupid blood however you like. Then get out of here."

"As you wish." The words tickled Poppy's neck and then, before she had an opportunity to suck in a preparatory breath, Dorian sunk his teeth into her flesh. The pain was sharp and immediate, but by this point Poppy had grown used to it enough to keep her senses as Dorian began drinking from her.

Going by the concurrent change in sharpness of his fingernails against her stomach, Poppy concluded that Dorian must only be able to break through her skin by dropping his human form slightly to use his 'real' teeth, which unnerved her to no end.

Just how much of him changes in order to do this?

But when she twisted around to try and see how much of him had changed, Dorian weaved a hand through Poppy's hair and held her head in place. "If you move it'll hurt more," he explained in a soft yet excited voice. "I don't want that. Just... trust me."

Though Poppy didn't trust Dorian about anything she wasn't exactly in a position to dispute him. So she stopped trying to turn her head, her body stiff as a board as he returned his attention to the job of tearing open her flesh.

When he finally opened her up the second wave of pain was even sharper and more intense than the first. Poppy couldn't contain the gasp that escaped her lips.

"Shh," Dorian whispered against her neck as blood began to well up where he'd bit her and run down her skin. With a deft tongue he cleaned the escaped blood before returning to the wound itself, sucking and nibbling and licking at it until the initial pain Poppy felt had well and truly subsided.

It was replaced by...something else.

She didn't know how to describe it. What Dorian was doing didn't feel bad but it didn't feel particularly good, either. Poppy supposed the closest comparison she had was receiving a really deep love bite. *But they only feel good in the moment, and you have to actually want them,* she found herself thinking as Dorian continued his slow yet assured assault on her neck. The hand in her hair fell down to her arm, then her thigh, whilst his other hand continued to creep higher and higher up Poppy's stomach. The prodding behind her hip grew even harder and more insistent.

Poppy didn't know what to do.

What Dorian was doing was somehow, inexplicably, more

sexual than any sexual encounter Poppy had ever actually had. And she wasn't exactly vanilla when it came to the bedroom, either.

"Dorian, stop," she bit out when she finally came to some semblance of her senses, which was becoming almost impossible to do. What was going on had to stop. It had to—

When Dorian's fingers swept below the lace of her underwear Poppy bit her lip. She couldn't cry out. Couldn't make a sound. Otherwise Andrew or Rachelle or Casey or – lord help her – Fred would discover what was going on.

It took Poppy a moment to realise Dorian's breathing had become more accelerated than hers. He squeezed her leg between his own; it filled Poppy with a longing she was loathe to admit to. She knew Dorian hadn't taken enough blood yet – that he was deliberately taking his time. When the hand on her stomach had finally crawled up high enough to brush against her breasts Poppy wondered if Dorian would dare to touch them deliberately.

Part of her wanted, more than anything, for him to do so.

But then Dorian broke from her neck. "I feel so much better now," he sighed, contentedly cleaning the last of Poppy's spilled blood in lazy circles with the tip of his tongue.

"...I'm pretty sure you're still horny," Poppy bit out before she could stop herself, nudging against Dorian's erection to prove her point. But what was she hoping for – for Dorian to push things further than he already had? Ten minutes ago Poppy would have staunchly refused such a suggestion.

"Mhm," was all Dorian said. He shifted his body weight slightly, dropping his hand from Poppy's stomach to rest beside her.

"Dorian?"

"Here..." he mumbled, in a manner that very much implied he was drifting off somewhere else entirely.

Poppy's face flushed with anger, embarrassment and a frustration she didn't want to own up to. "Dorian, don't you dare—"

But it was too late.

He'd fallen asleep.

INTERLUDE IV

FRANCIS' REACTION TO THE GROUP OF 'scouted' club members had been much the same as everyone else before him. But he hadn't been sedated and taken away for surgery yet. No, he sat by mute Craig Hunt with absolute terror in his eyes at whatever fate was going to befall him.

When three unfamiliar people were brought into the room by the woman who 'looked after' them, Francis backed away into a corner in panic. This is it, he thought. This is where I die.

But they didn't want him.

They wanted Angelica.

"Shame someone already got her eyes," a woman with greying hair and a wrinkled face said, "though her performances across the board for the first two weeks was very impressive indeed. Yes, Jane, tell Dorian I'll take her."

Jane turned and left the room without another word, leaving the older woman with her two companions. When they moved forwards to take hold of Angelica she bolted back in a literal blind panic, kicking the bed over that she'd been sitting on in the process.

"Come now," the woman scolded, "don't be like that. If you struggle this will only be worse for you."

Angelica wasn't listening. She thrashed against the people grabbing hold of her, kicking and clawing away at their arms and legs.

The woman's expression grew dark. Everyone else in the room – save for Megan, who couldn't move due to the absence of her legs – receded as far back as they could, knowing in their very souls that something terrible was about to happen.

None of them could have expected the woman's body to wriggle and stretch and transform into what could only be described as some kind of snake. A massive, coiling, silver snake, whose scales and teeth flashed beneath the artificial lights set in the ceiling overhead.

Someone screamed; Francis didn't know who. It might have been him. But nobody could look away as the snake – unseen by Angelica – darted towards her, unhinged its jaw and swallowed her whole.

For half a second Angelica cried out in shock, but with a sickening crunch she fell silent.

Nobody else dared to even breathe.

The snake swallowed a few more times, pushing Angelica down its throat and along to its stomach. And then, as if it was nothing, it turned back into a mild-looking, grey-haired woman. She glanced at her companions as she dabbed at her mouth.

"That was far less refined than I wanted it to be. I'll have to have words with Dorian about keeping his humans separated for clients in future. But no worries, what's done is done. Come now." She motioned to the other two, one of whom opened the door for her.

When all three of them were gone nobody dared look at each other. They couldn't comprehend what they'd seen. But it had happened nonetheless...and was most likely going to happen to them, too.

I should never have told Fred about Ross Bridges, *Francis thought numbly, somehow certain to his very core that his confession had something to do with his current position.*

I should have kept my mouth shut.

Thomas Pope

FRED

"Watch your feet, Fred!"

"Huh? Oh—"

Fred narrowly avoided stepping into a narrow crevasse in the earth that would have resulted in a seriously painful twisted ankle, if not a full-on broken leg.

Rich laughed at his rare fumble. "Not like you to be so clumsy. Better pay more attention to where you're walking. This hill is full of holes and shit under the heather."

Fred murmured his thanks, though he knew fine well why he hadn't been paying attention and had no intention of changing that any time soon. For his mind – and eyes – were elsewhere.

Namely on Poppy and Andrew.

They were up to something, Fred was sure, and something told him it wasn't simply innocent fun. The two of them had been exploring in and around the facility as of late, setting up scavenger hunts in the process that most of the club invariably joined in on. They also went for early morning jogs together.

This kind of behaviour wouldn't have been so strange if Poppy and Andrew had acted like this in the past. But Poppy was *never* known to get up in the morning willingly – let alone for exercise – and Andrew was the last person Fred expected to organise complicated games that involved working with other people if he could avoid them.

The entire club was currently out on a leisurely hill climb, the recent bout of hot weather making full-on hiking almost impossible without risking an extreme case of sun stroke. And so everyone was content with taking their time picking a path up one of the gentler slopes dressed in as little as could still be considered decent. For Casey this meant a bikini bizarrely paired with proper hiking boots, as she was determined to get a full-body tan. Patrick, who was joining in on more and more of the club's activities that he wasn't required to be an instructor for, very much appreciated her choice of attire.

Fred scanned the hillside as he and Rich caught up with Nate. Robin had just left the darker-skinned man to walk on ahead with Rachelle – something which irked Fred no matter how much he tried not to think about the two of them. Casey was several metres ahead of them, Patrick in tow, though Fred spotted at least three or four male club members eyeing up her golden, glowing skin with desperate and obvious sexual frustration.

Given that we've all been living together for a month and a half I suppose their reaction isn't all that surprising, Fred thought, comfortable enough to admit that even *he'd* be eyeing up Casey if he wasn't still pining for Rachelle.

Lastly, several paces behind him, Poppy was encouraging Andrew to climb a tree just off the path they were supposed to be following, laughing and swinging from branches like they were four years old. Dorian watched them from a careful distance though Poppy was, as usual, ignoring him. After a few more seconds he shook his head and sighed.

Fred almost thought it looked as if Dorian was annoyed at himself for watching Poppy at all.

So far four people had been scouted by Dorian's clients. Along with Ross, who'd been kicked out, twenty-five members of the club remained with eight and a half weeks left of their residence at the facility. Although they had lost just a sixth of the club's total members Fred was feeling their absence fairly keenly, and he wasn't the only one. Cliques and best friends had been split apart, leaving some club members feeling a little out of place and awkward.

Fred was determined to fix this...somehow. He didn't want to have to rely on Poppy all the time for spontaneous ideas like her silly scavenger hunts to make people feel included. He was sure he could be just as imaginative as she was if he tried.

He just needed an idea.

And then he stood in one.

"Good thing it's so fucking hot out, otherwise walking with one foot like that would be disgusting," Nate joked when Fred shook out his now-sodden shoe. He'd stood in a shallow stream but, upon closer inspection, Fred realised that much of the stone beneath the water was smooth and unbroken, beginning at some point further up from where they stood and ending a few metres behind them.

Without giving himself the time to doubt himself, as he usually did, Fred took off his shoes and tested the rock. It was slippery, and there was just enough current in the stream that the water tugged at his ankles to insistently move him back down the hillside.

Nate and Rich looked at him, suspicious. "The hell are you doing, Sampson?"

But Fred didn't respond, merely grinning as he threw off his T-shirt and abandoned it by his shoes before running further up the hill, following the stream. When he passed

Rachelle she broke away from Robin and followed him.

"What's going on, Fred?"

"The stream," he said when he reached what seemed like the best place to start. Several club members were watching him curiously, pausing in their tracks to see what he'd do next. "It kind of looks like a—"

"Water slide?" Rachelle finished for him, grinning as foolishly as Fred the moment she worked out what he was thinking.

"Exactly. Want to try it out?"

"As if you had to ask."

To Fred's surprise Rachelle took all of her clothes off, but she was wearing a bikini underneath. She raised an eyebrow at him blatantly staring at her.

"You really thought I was gonna get naked?"

"I'd bloody well hope not."

She laughed. "You first, or me?"

"Together?"

"I'm sure that won't fail at all."

And so the two of them took a deep breath, gathered up the courage to run, and deftly slid into the stream. With a squeal from Rachelle and a somewhat bumpy start, the stream easily carried them down the hillside so quickly that Fred worried for a moment they'd end up crashing into a rock. But when they reached a bend he grabbed hold of Rachelle's waist and rolled the two of them out of the stream, sliding along on the grass for a few metres until they eventually petered out to a stop.

Covered in blades of grass and dandelion fluff, the two of them stared at each other in momentary, stunned disbelief that Fred's plan had actually worked, then burst out laughing.

"Again?" Fred suggested, wiping himself down after he stood up.

"I think there might be a line now."

He glanced back to where they'd started and saw several people ridding themselves of shoes and clothes in order to emulate Fred and Rachelle, the air abuzz with excitement. A wave of satisfaction washed over him. *See, King? You're not the only one who can—*

"What made you think about doing this?" Rachelle asked, clearly reading something in Fred's expression that she didn't understand.

"You really think King is the only one capable of thinking up fun shit to do?" he countered, immediately defensive.

"That's not what I meant and you know it."

Fred calmed down just as quickly as his temper had flared. Of course Rachelle wasn't trying to antagonise him. She wasn't *Poppy,* after all. "The group's been a bit...off-kilter," he explained. "Since people started getting scouted, I mean. I just wanted to get everyone to socialise more with the club members whose friends are now gone."

A warm and affectionate smile spread across Rachelle's face. She squeezed Fred's hand a little; it made his heart hurt. "That's really kind of you, Fred. I'm glad you're looking out for everyone."

Fred didn't want to read more into Rachelle holding his hand than he already was, so he forced his thoughts somewhere else. "Speaking of," he murmured, shielding his eyes with a hand as he scanned the hillside. "Where'd Andrew go?"

"Wasn't he with Poppy?"

"That's King racing down the stream with Nate and Casey."

Rachelle chuckled. "Of course. You want me to see where he's run off to?"

"Nah, let me do it," Fred replied, regretfully pulling his hand away from Rachelle's. "He can't have gone far."

And so Fred wandered away in the direction of the trees he'd seen Andrew and Poppy climbing before. But Andrew wasn't anywhere to be seen, even when Fred checked behind every trunk and craned his neck to investigate the branches above him. Frowning, he continued looking around until he saw the tell-tale signs of trodden grass and followed the path it made away from the rest of the club. As the sun's rays beat down upon Fred's skin and dried him off he picked his way over shrubbery and heather and rocks, all the while cursing aloud for not having put his shoes back on before venturing out.

When eventually he spied Andrew, Fred was surprised to see him crouching behind a reasonably-sized boulder. "Andrew?" he wondered aloud, though Fred had the sense to keep his voice hushed. Andrew's shoulders jolted in surprise at the sound of Fred's voice, but then he gestured for him to crouch down beside him. "What's wrong?"

"Over there," was all Andrew said, pointing over to his left. Fred peered around the boulder, the stone almost painfully hot against his splayed fingertips.

"Andrew, I don't see – oh, is that Tom and Nic? What are they..."

But then a garbled, inhuman noise permeated the air that caused Andrew to hide behind his hands and the tiny hairs on Fred's spine to stand on end despite the heat. As the sickening noise continued Andrew began to rock on the spot.

Fred didn't like this one bit.

"Get Poppy, get Poppy, get Poppy," Andrew stuttered out, repeating the demand over and over and over again.

"Why her?" Fred bit out, frustrated despite himself. "Can't I help, Andrew? What are they doing over there? What's making that noise?"

Andrew peeked out from behind his hands; his eyes were overly bright, his pupils contracted to tiny pins. "Mountain goat. They're hurting it."

"They're – Andrew, how do you know? You can't see anything from over here."

He nodded in the direction of a couple of trees closer to Tom and Nic. "I was over there, before. I couldn't take the – the noise. I don't know what to do. Please get Poppy."

"Andrew, I can deal with—"

"Please get Poppy."

Fighting the urge to scowl and scream and generally give in to a tantrum not befitting his age, Fred stood up and stalked back the way he had come. When he reached Poppy's side he grabbed her arm and pulled her away from the rest of the group without so much as an explanation. The club, having become accustomed to this sort of behaviour between their president and vice-president, left the two of them to it.

Poppy, however, was not happy with Fred having pulled her away. She tried to wrench her arm out of Fred's hand and failed; he was sickeningly gratified to see a flash of concern cross Poppy's face when she realised she wasn't strong enough to break away from him.

"The hell do you want, Sampson?" she growled.

"Andrew needs you."

Poppy lowered her proverbial hackles immediately and stopped struggling, her expression now sober and serious as she followed Fred along the path that would lead them to Andrew. It still shocked Fred to see how quickly Poppy's attitude changed when it came to Andrew, though she'd been like this from the very first moment she'd convinced him to join the club. Only for Andrew was Poppy ever consistently and faithfully responsible.

It was just about her only saving grace in Fred's books.

As soon as they reached Andrew's side the goat in the distance let out another pained, horrific scream. Poppy's gaze darted in the direction of the sound before looking back at Andrew, whose rocking had only grown more severe in Fred's absence. She bent down and squeezed his hand tightly, rubbing his back until Andrew finally seemed to realise she was there.

"What's going on, Andrew?" she asked, voice very soft and gentle.

"It's Tom and Nic," Fred answered for him. "Andrew says they're hurting a goat or something."

Poppy broke from Andrew and ran over to the source of the noise without another word, leaving Fred to chase after her in shock at the abruptness of her exit. It didn't take them long to reach Tom and Nic, who jumped in alarm once they realised they weren't alone.

"...the fuck is this?"

It had been Poppy who spoke, but Fred shared the sentiment. For there on the grass lay a wounded goat, an ugly, bloody gash rending its stomach open. Fred had dissected animals in university before, but the shining, pulsating organs visible through the wound combined with the animal's wild and terrified eyes had him retching in seconds.

It took him a few *more* seconds to realise both Nic and Tom were holding bloodied sticks, which they dropped as soon as Fred stared at them in disbelief.

"It was already hurt when we got here," Tom explained quickly. "We were just—"

"What?" Poppy demanded. "Just torturing the poor thing?"

Nic looked at the ground uncomfortably, not daring to match Poppy's furious eyes. "It's gonna die anyway..."

"How would you like it if someone cut you open and poked at your guts instead of helping you out?!" she screamed, surprising even Fred with the sheer volume and fury of her voice. She took a step towards the pair of them; they both took a step back. "Is that what we should do, huh? Kick you to the ground and tear you open, then laugh as you howl in pain?"

Fred frowned at her. "King, that's a bit—"

"What kind of a person needlessly tortures another living creature for the sheer hell of it? Fucking psychopaths, that's who!"

Tom didn't like that at all. "Hey, watch your tongue. What we did was wrong; I get it. But we didn't mean anything by it."

"Oh, so as long as you *didn't mean anything by it* then it's okay?" The goat continued to cry out for help. Its voice grew gradually feebler with every passing second, which only further served to upset Poppy. "So if I picked up a rock and flung it at your face it doesn't count so long as I *don't mean anything—*"

"King, stop it."

"Or what, Fred?" Poppy fired back. "Are you honestly siding with them?"

"Of course I'm not, but—"

The conversation was abruptly interrupted by the sickening sound of bone snapping. The group turned to face the goat.

Dorian was kneeling beside it. He'd broken its neck.

Fred blinked at him, speechless. He hadn't even heard the man approach – and neither, by the looks of things, had anybody else. It was thoroughly disconcerting.

More alarming was that Poppy seemed happy Dorian had appeared. Dorian, whom she actively avoided with obvious dislike.

"I think everyone needs to calm down," Dorian said, his voice gentle, expression bland. He barely spared Nic and Tom a glance before he told them, "Both of you, get back to the centre and clean the hell up. You're covered in blood."

The two of them hadn't seemed to have realised this yet but, upon looking down at themselves, saw that Dorian was correct. Tom glowered at Poppy one final time then turned and left with Nic in swift silence before they could be berated any further.

Fred didn't know what to do. He altogether felt like he shouldn't be watching Dorian turn his soft gaze to Poppy whilst Poppy stared at the dead goat, the beginnings of tears in her eyes. He didn't think he'd seen her look so vulnerable since she fell.

But when Dorian made to take a step towards her, Poppy took a step back. "I-I'm going to tell Andrew everything's fine," she mumbled, before sprinting off.

Which left Fred standing awkwardly with Dorian, at a loss for what to say. "How much did you hear of King's...outburst?" he eventually asked.

Dorian smiled grimly. "All of it. I followed you and Poppy over here."

"You're scarily quiet."

"I know." More awkward silence, and then: "You should go help with Andrew, Fred. I'll take care of the goat. I can't leave it out in the open."

Fred watched as the man bent down to the goat's side, running a hand over its curved, glossy, horns with surprising tenderness. *Must be an animal person,* Fred thought somewhat numbly as he headed to where Andrew had been crouching, but Poppy had already taken him back into the fold of the club. He'd calmed down a lot by the looks of things now that Poppy had assured him everything was fine.

But something struck Fred as blatantly *off* about the events of the last twenty minutes; if he'd been suspicious of Poppy and Andrew before it was nothing compared to how he felt now. He wondered why Andrew had been so adamant that Poppy see Nic and Tom torturing the goat. *It's not as if she could actually do anything about it, just...shout at them.*

Fred had to admit that the pure vitriol Poppy spat in their faces had taken him aback. Never had he known her to be so angry in all the six years he'd known her. Scathing at times, yes. Brutal in her criticism, absolutely. But violently, intimidatingly furious?

It was a side Fred hadn't known existed.

It was a side that scared him.

But, more than that, her reaction only added more fuel to Fred's mounting fire of suspicion that something was going on – something he was fairly certain wasn't anything good. For the first time in his life Fred felt a pang of regret that he wasn't friends with Poppy. He was sure she knew *exactly* what was going on, and given how much they hated each other Fred doubted she'd ever tell him what that was.

Which meant Fred would have to get much, much sneakier and far more suspicious of Poppy's every action if he was to have any chance of discovering what she was hiding.

JOHN CAMPBELL

DORIAN

Poppy's reaction to the tortured mountain goat kept resurfacing in Dorian's mind all week, even as he went about his general day-to-day life. Even now, having only just woken up to the early morning sunshine slanting into his bedroom, it was the very first thing he thought about.

Perhaps it was because it had been a *goat*. Perhaps it was because he'd never seen her react so viscerally to anything else before. Perhaps it was because the creature being tortured wasn't human.

Regardless of the reason, it only served to increase Dorian's regard for Poppy. Not that Poppy would know this, of course, given that she was ignoring him as usual. But there was something about the *way* she was ignoring him that meant Dorian wasn't annoyed by her doing so. He wasn't sure what it was, but it felt distinctly different from when she'd ignored him out of sheer terror and hatred when she'd first discovered what Dorian really was.

He missed being in close proximity to her, though, so he

was determined to break through the icy wall she'd thrown up in defence against him. Dorian thought back to the last time he'd taken her blood, wondering if he could get away with pulling the same stunt later that very day.

He somehow, regretfully, doubted it.

Dorian regretted most of all that, when he'd last drained Poppy's blood, he'd fallen asleep. Like a child after consuming a hot drink in the middle of winter, or a blind-drunk university boy who'd found himself tumbling into bed with someone, Dorian had slipped into unconsciousness. Yes, he'd gotten the blood he craved. But he had entered Poppy's room wanting far more than that.

For whatever reason Dorian was certain that – had he stayed conscious – Poppy would have been inclined to go along with his desires. He'd felt her maddeningly quick heart beat when he whispered in her ear, after all. He'd heard her accelerated breathing, and saw the blood that rushed to her face in direct contradiction of the fact he'd been draining it from her.

Whether Poppy would admit to it or not – Dorian assumed not – at least in a physical capacity she clearly liked him. This wasn't news to him, of course, but weeks and weeks of hard work had been put in to rid Poppy of the terror she felt that blindly overwrote her attraction to him. Dorian didn't want to destroy all that effort by messing up *now*. Ultimately, Poppy was going to be spending the rest of her long life with him. Though it had appealed to Dorian at first in a sick, twisted way, the last thing he wanted was for her to hate and fear him for the entire duration of that life.

To that end Dorian knew he needed some kind of impetus to encourage Poppy to lose her inhibitions around him and forget that he was an eight-foot monster responsible for her club mates being devoured alive.

Crawling into her bed at night was out. Dorian needed something new.

And then it hit him: the solution to his problem was so human and basic in nature that it had completely escaped him until now.

Alcohol.

But he knew Poppy would never willingly get drunk with only him. No, Dorian had to rope in her entire club, a thought which caused him to laugh out loud. Something told him it wouldn't be hard to convince them to get drunk at all.

Stifling a yawn, Dorian threw on a grey button-down top and a pair of jogging pants, running a hand through his dishevelled hair before making his way down the stairs and through to the kitchen in the central building for a cup of coffee. He didn't much care for the taste but even monsters appreciated caffeine.

He stopped in his tracks when he spied Nate and Poppy by the fridge. Nate was hugging her from behind, his arms slung over her shoulders whilst Poppy browsed through the fridge with the energy of a lethargic zombie.

"Rather early for you, Poppy," Dorian said with false brightness, making his presence known. "Morning, Nate."

The other man nodded in polite hello, then glanced behind Dorian when Casey, Fred and Rachelle swung open the door to the kitchen.

"Poppy?" Rachelle yawned. "What are you doing up so early?"

"Dying," she muttered, eyes barely open. After giving up her half-hearted search of the fridge she finally found the energy to shrug Nate off before continuing, "Who wants to jog on a *Saturday morning*? Weekends are days off."

"Somehow I don't think Andrew understands that."

Poppy made a face; Nate ruffled her hair. "C'mon, Morph, don't be like that," he crooned. "No point going back to bed now you're up. Unless..."

He gave her a filthy look that Poppy was far too tired to acknowledge. Dorian saw it, though. The muscles along his jaw tensed up at the knowledge of exactly what Nate had been trying to do before he'd walked in and fortuitously interrupted him. Then, knowing that Poppy was in no way, shape or form capable of any kind of decision-making when she was this tired, Dorian silently went about making her a cup of tea whilst he made himself some coffee.

"What's everyone getting up to today, anyway?" Fred asked the room at large. "Other than King falling asleep on the spot."

Poppy mustered enough strength to give him the finger.

"It's nice out again," Casey said, "so Rachelle and I thought we'd see if anyone was up for a picnic by the loch and then just generally kicking about doing nothing in the sun." She turned to Dorian. "Nobody's coming up today to observe us, are they?"

Dorian shook his head. "Play away to your heart's content."

Casey sighed dramatically. "I *wish*. We'd need booze for that."

He perked up immediately. Only Cassandra O'Donnell could provide Dorian with the most natural segue into his *get Poppy drunk* plan. He flashed her his most brilliant smile; Casey blushed. "That's an excellent idea, Casey. So you guys didn't have the sense to bring *any* alcohol with you? I did wonder why you'd all stayed sober."

"Nah, people brought booze," Nate chimed in, "but most of it was demolished after two weeks. Folk were just drinking in their friend groups. None of us thought we'd be here for so long. Or so far away from, you know, a shop."

Dorian ignored the jibe. "I could get Patrick to bring through some alcohol next Saturday, I'm sure."

Casey's face was bright with enthusiasm. "Really? Oh my god, you'd really do that for us?"

"Of course. You've been here for weeks now; lord knows you all deserve to get drunk."

"Absolutely trashed, you mean."

He chuckled. "I would never endorse such a thing." But Dorian glanced almost imperceptibly at Poppy, who was still in no mood to respond to anything being said even as she frowned in suspicion. Her frown only deepened when Dorian handed her the cup of tea he'd been making.

"The hell is this?" she demanded.

"Caffeine loaded with sugar, just the way you like it."

Poppy looked at the liquid as if Dorian had roofied it, then shrugged somewhat and retreated into a shadowy corner of the kitchen to drink it in peace.

"We better start organising stuff for next Saturday, then," Casey said, looking at Nate. "Wanna help me rally the troops?"

"What needs organising when it comes to drinking?" Fred wondered aloud. Casey merely laughed at the question.

"You're no fun, Fred. There's *tonnes* to organise. We need to get some playlists together, and set up the social area for dancing, and think up some hideous drinking games, and—"

"Okay, okay, I get it," he interrupted, throwing his hands up in protest before making a beeline for the door. "You guys have fun with that. I'm going to see if Andrew wants a jogging partner, since King is catatonic."

Poppy didn't reply, too content with drinking tea and waking up as she was.

Nate looked at her incredulously. "God, you really aren't a morning person, are you? C'mon, Casey, Rachelle – I'm sure Robin will want in on this. John, too; he's been dying to have a social. Probably misses all his ardent followers back at uni."

And so the rest of them left without making any breakfast, which Dorian had assumed they'd come into the kitchen to make in the first place, leaving only himself and Poppy.

When Poppy finished her tea a few minutes later she put her cup down on the nearest table, then splayed her fingertips across her forehead as if she had a migraine. "Save John Campbell this week," she muttered. "Should have thought of him before."

Dorian put down his coffee by Poppy's empty cup and stalked over to join her in the corner. "Is he the overly-loud, brash one who interrupts almost everyone?"

She nodded. "His family's rich as fuck. No way could we spirit him away."

Dorian almost smiled at her use of *we*, though he didn't comment on it lest Poppy scowl at him. "At least he seems like a pretty decent guy."

"Yeah...most of them are. That's the problem." She chuckled darkly. "Never thought I'd say that people being decent was a problem."

"But *some* of them aren't, though. So who's up this week: Nicolas Frey or Thomas Pope?" Dorian had been sure to remember their names after the goat incident.

Poppy's eyes hardened immediately. "Tom first."

A moment of silence, then Dorian closed what little distance there was between the two of them. He grazed his fingertips across Poppy's hips, resisting the urge to pull her in against him. "You're wearing my T-shirt again," he murmured.

Poppy didn't even push him away. "I wear it to bed. Get over yourself. And get your teeth away from my neck. We're in public."

"I'm fairly certain people would misconstrue what I was doing, anyway," Dorian replied, decidedly doing the opposite of what Poppy ordered. He ran his left hand from her hip to her hair, sliding his fingers through it in order to clear away stray strands from the artery pulsing beneath his teeth.

He bit into her before Poppy had a chance to protest further.

"Do-Dorian!" she gasped, though she quickly quietened with a single, furtive glance at the kitchen door. If anybody came in Poppy would have to hope they 'misconstrued' what they were seeing, which Dorian had gleefully gambled on stopping her from stopping *him*.

He pressed her further against the wall as he continued, the familiar surge of adrenaline coursing through his veins once more as he filled up on her blood. Poppy raised her hands to Dorian's chest in a feeble attempt to push him away, but ultimately thought better of it and merely clenched the fabric of his top between her fingers.

Poppy's skin was hot against his mouth. It made Dorian want to take more blood as he licked at the puncture wounds, but he resisted. He'd gotten better at taking less – much better – and Poppy's body had likewise gotten better at healing faster. There was barely a two day lag before she was back to normal between feeds now.

Dorian's mouth lingered on Poppy's pulse for a few seconds, testing how far she would tolerate his close proximity. When she said nothing he brushed his lips up to her earlobe, intending to bite it.

"Don't you *dare*."

He burst out laughing at Poppy's immediate rejection, pulling away from her in the process. "Fine; I get it," Dorian said, wiping his mouth whilst Poppy pulled her hair back around to cover her neck. "You're giving in though – even you must know that."

She scowled. "Fuck off."

"No thanks for the tea?"

"Thanks for the tea, and fuck off. Better?"

"Much."

He turned and left the kitchen before Poppy could say anything else, body thrumming with energy and life and power as he casually raised his hand in goodbye. His carefully lazy, easy-going approach to wearing Poppy down was working. Dorian knew it. Poppy knew it.

Saturday couldn't come quickly enough.

Nicolas Frey

POPPY

"Right, its official: I miss Tinder."

"Only Cassandra O'Donnell could come out with such a line whilst sitting in a luxury hot tub, at sunset, in the Highlands of Scotland, with her two closest female friends," Rachelle said, wrinkling her nose at the mere idea of Tinder. "You can't be serious, Casey!"

Casey shrugged. "There's nothing wrong with wanting to shag a guy I don't know, is there?"

"That's not the point."

"So what *is* the point?"

"What about Patrick?"

Poppy stayed silent through the entire exchange, though she longed to comment on the matter. She still hadn't gotten over the fact that she'd heard Patrick boasting to Aisling, Nick and Steven that Casey was *his*. Poppy knew she was going to save Casey, of course, so in reality she was in no danger, but that didn't mean she wanted her to sleep with the monster posing as a man, either. In fact, Poppy was completely and utterly against it, though she couldn't vocalise her issue with the whole thing without being able to tell Casey *why* she was against it. On the face of it Patrick was a fantastic match for her friend; Poppy had no reason to deter her from exploring anything with the man.

Apart from the fact he isn't actually a man. And wants to eat her. Just the minor stuff.

Casey waved a hand dismissively. "Yeah, I'm into Patrick, but I *know* he's into me. So it's a sure-fire thing, you know? I'd rather try it on with a guy who's a challenge first. Like Dorian."

"But he's Patrick's best friend! And..." Rachelle stared pointedly at Poppy, who had to fight not to grimace. She raised an eyebrow instead.

"Go on: finish that thought, Rachelle."

"Aw come *on,* Poppy," her best friend complained, splashing her with hot, bubbling water in the process, "you can't possibly be so oblivious that you don't know how he keeps looking at you. Almost every word out of his mouth directed at you is a flirt."

Poppy had to wrestle away the image of Dorian in her bed that immediately flooded her brain. If she reacted to it even slightly then Rachelle and Casey would be sure to pick up on it, and then she'd never hear the end of it.

She sighed emphatically. "Just because a guy acts like that doesn't mean I have to accept his advances." It wasn't untrue, not really, but it was altogether too ineffectual a statement to cover the entirety of Dorian's interactions with Poppy.

Though how am I supposed to tell Rachelle and Casey that the guy cuts and bites me open every week and I can do nothing about it, and now he's making me feel weird when he does it? Poppy could almost laugh at the tragic absurdity of it all.

"See?" Casey nodded enthusiastically. "Poppy gets it. They're not entitled to anything. And besides, Poppy has Nate."

"I don't *have* Nate."

"So turn him down properly, then."

Casey's words came out perhaps a little harsher than she'd intended going by the apologetic look on her face the moment after she'd uttered them. Poppy supposed she couldn't blame her for being annoyed – Casey was just as close with Nate as she was. And Poppy *hadn't* turned Nate down properly. Yet. But what was Poppy supposed to say? Somehow she doubted Nate would buy 'Sorry, I've signed my life over to the devil and I don't have it in me to sleep with you so casually anymore'.

She sighed. "You're right, of course. I know I need to turn him down properly. It's just..."

Rachelle splashed her with water again, so Poppy splashed her back. "Poppy, you *do* know that you're actually allowed to like Nate, right?" she said. "You don't have to turn him down just because you're not *in love* with him. Casual is fine. Don't beat yourself up about it."

"You're only saying that because you and Robin are blissfully in the *casual* stage right now."

Her best friend blushed furiously. "How do you – we thought we were being pretty sly about it."

"Don't make me laugh!" Casey burst out, though she already was. "You think I can't hear the two of you when you're in bed? My room's next to yours, remember?"

The comment made Poppy flinch. If Casey could hear Rachelle and Robin when they were trying to keep quiet did that mean *Andrew* had heard Dorian when he came into Poppy's room? He certainly hadn't mentioned anything about it.

For the first time Poppy considered whether it might really

have been the right choice to pretend that she was sleeping with Dorian already simply to dispel any suspicion regarding their behaviour. But even as she thought it she staunchly rejected it; she didn't want to be associated with Dorian like that, whether fake or otherwise.

You're giving in though – even you must know that.

That's what Dorian had said to Poppy. It was maddening that he said it – to be so presumptuous as to come to such a conclusion on his own.

What was even worse was that it wasn't entirely untrue.

"You know what?" Poppy called out over Casey's teasing of Rachelle. "Fuck talking about boys. Casey, go screw whoever you want. Rachelle, just have fun with Robin and don't care what anyone else thinks."

"And you and Dorian? Nate?"

"There *is* no me and Dorian. And I'll sort Nate out myself. So let's talk about something else. *Please.*"

Casey narrowed her eyes. "Are you okay, Poppy? You seem...off."

"I'm just a bit tired, is all."

But neither of Poppy's friends were buying her excuse.

"How's your arm?" Rachelle asked.

Poppy had replaced the bandages previously wrapping her arm with a compression sleeve. It was far less inconvenient for her to work around and didn't need constantly changed after getting wet, which saved her many a secret trip to the infirmary. She wished she could get away with wearing nothing at all, but that would involve faking a scar. Poppy didn't have the skills, nor the tools, to pull that off, and she was certain it would be more hassle than keeping her arm covered for now, anyway.

Besides, in eight weeks I won't have to pretend that I'm hurt anymore, and fourteen members of my club will be dead.

A chill ran down Poppy's spine despite the hot water, which only served to concern her friends even more.

"Poppy?"

"I'm fine," she said quickly, not looking at either of them. "My arm's fine. I just regret having ever fallen in the first place."

"You've been totally different since you fell," Rachelle murmured. Casey nodded in agreement.

Poppy knew she had to tread carefully. "What do you mean?"

"You're way more...serious?" Casey suggested. "I don't know how to put it. Even when you're acting like an idiot you seem more—"

"Responsible," Rachelle cut in. "It feels like you're more responsible. Are you finally growing up now life after university has caught up with you?"

Poppy almost laughed in relief at the very plausible excuse Rachelle handed her on a plate. "I had to grow up eventually, right?"

"I thought you were gonna be the first one they scouted this summer for sure," Casey said. She twisted her sodden auburn hair to squeeze out tiny droplets of water and plaited it with expert fingers, then reclined her head against the edge of the hot tub. She let out a huff of air. "To be honest I thought all three of us would've been picked by now."

"I was kind of thinking that, too," Rachelle admitted, downcast. "Well, definitely the two of you at least."

"I know, right?! How the hell did Craig freaking Hunt get chosen over me on the basis of his diving? It's ridiculous."

Had the two of them been looking towards Poppy at that very moment they'd have noticed how pale she grew at their comments. Her friends were complaining about not being chosen as food. They were complaining about being alive, and they didn't know it.

Poppy hoped they never would.

"Guys, I don't think it really works solely based on how good we are compared to other members of the club," she said. The irony was that it *was*, insomuch as the best members of the club were being saved by Poppy herself. "I think different scouts are looking for different things. Casey, Craig was probably picked because the scout was looking for a guy. And I've been injured *and* I'm unpredictable *and* I'm lazy. Honestly, who'd be stupid enough to want to work with me?"

When Poppy laughed she was relieved to hear it sounded genuine. Both Casey and Rachelle seemed to feel better after Poppy's explanation, which could only be a good thing.

"I guess you're right," Rachelle agreed. "You *are* a lazy shit."

"Mean."

When the sun finally finished setting – which was late, given that it was mid-July – the three of them finally extricated themselves from the hot tub and made their way back to their rooms to change. It was only when Poppy was finally alone once more that she collapsed in a heap on her bed, giving up on changing clothes after throwing on a T-shirt and feeling very much like a disaster of a human being.

"They said I was more *responsible,*" she muttered under her breath. "Responsible for murdering people, maybe."

A knock on the door startled Poppy out of her head far sooner than she was expecting. Wondering whether she could simply ignore it, she stared at the door until the person on the other side announced who they were.

"Poppy?"

"Andrew? Is that you?"

"Yes, it's Andrew Martin Forbes."

Poppy chuckled. "Thanks for the clarification. Come in."

Andrew's eyebrows rose so high when he saw Poppy that she could hardly see them through the tawny hair that fell across his forehead. His face turned scarlet; for a second Poppy though he was choking on something.

"What's wrong, Andrew?" she asked.

He turned away. "You – um, your T-shirt..."

Poppy glanced down and remembered that she hadn't bothered putting shorts on over her underwear yet, and her T-shirt was crumpled around her waist from rolling around on her bed in worry. She didn't have a bra on. From where Andrew was standing, Poppy realised that far too much of her was on show.

She sat up immediately, pulling her T-shirt down to cover as much of her as possible. Laughing sheepishly, she said, "You'd think by now I'd have learned how to conduct myself in front of other people. Apparently not. Sorry, Andrew."

He peeked back around to make sure it was safe to look at Poppy once more, then cautiously sat on the bed a respectable distance away from her. "It's okay," he said. "I've seen more of Casey than that, though I didn't mean to and then she stayed naked just to embarrass me for as long as possible but then Rachelle told her off."

Poppy grinned, feeling an irresistible urge to tease Andrew. "So how do I compare with her? From what you saw, anyway."

Andrew stared at her in horror. "I – I – I don't think I want to—"

"Andrew, I'm kidding. Put your heart back in your ribcage already. What did you want to tell me, anyway?"

He stared down at his chest for a few moments as if wondering how to put his heart back in the right place. "Will

Nic be the next one scouted, do you think?"

Poppy chose her next words very carefully. "What makes you say that?"

Andrew didn't reply. He merely locked eyes with Poppy and stared at her in silence.

How much does he know? she wondered, though she felt oddly calm about the idea that Andrew knew *something*. Otherwise his snippets of information about members of the club, as well as his willingness to help her organise scavenger hunts as a cover for exploring the area, made little to no sense.

She decided to take a massive, dangerous risk.

"...yes," she said, very quietly.

Andrew smiled slightly. "Okay. Thank you, Poppy."

And then he left. Just like that, Andrew got up and left her room, leaving Poppy to stare at her door in numb horror at what she had just done. She'd been expressly forbidden from telling anyone about what was really going on. *Anyone,* including Andrew. She wasn't supposed to hint or even vaguely suggest that things were not as they seemed. She was supposed to *prevent* people from doubting what was going on.

And yet here Poppy was, having willingly confirmed whatever theory Andrew had, which only put him – and the rest of the club – in even more danger from Dorian and his clients.

Poppy burrowed beneath her duvet, feeling wretched beyond belief at her recklessness. This summer, more than anything else, was teaching her that it wasn't a trait she should be proud of. It was literally killing people...and now it might slaughter even more.

"I've made a huge mistake," she mouthed, fighting an insurmountable urge to sob. "A huge, huge mistake."

LILY JOHNSON

FRED

DESPITE THE NUMEROUS SOCIALS FRED HAD taken part in before he had somehow *never* seen the members of the Outdoor Sports Society drink quite as much as they were currently consuming. Perhaps it was the weeks and weeks of sobriety preceding it. Perhaps it was the fact they were away from home and absolved of all their usual responsibilities. Perhaps they merely wanted to get as royally, sickeningly wasted as possible. Fred suspected all three reasons were relevant in various proportions for each and every member of the club.

The one exception was Poppy King. Somehow this didn't surprise Fred at all, though in any other situation her relative sobriety on such an occasion would invariably rouse suspicion from him.

But that was the thing: Fred was *already* suspicious of Poppy. He'd expected her to avoid alcohol.

He was determined to find out why.

POPPY

As the sun set and night fell upon the Highlands Adrenaline Sports Facility there was little and less Poppy could do when people handed her shots and expected her to drink the dubious-coloured liquids right in front of them. She'd tried to stay sober. Really, she had. But Poppy King was still Poppy King, and by eleven in the evening her relative clear-headedness was beginning to cloud over in a happy alcoholic haze that was diminishing her desire to stay responsible and in control of her actions.

I'm in trouble, she thought, though for the first time in eight weeks Poppy was thinking this not in direct relation to any of her club members getting eaten alive. Rather, it was very much to do with the hungry glances an achingly good-looking, dark-clothed Dorian kept throwing her way even as Poppy tried her damnedest to stay as far away from him as possible.

But he was making things difficult, finding excuses to join every conversation Poppy was having just as easily as she was running from him and knocking back shot after shot each time she found herself thinking she'd rather like to rip his clothes off. But Dorian kept a constant eye on Poppy even when he *wasn't* trying to integrate himself into her conversations, making Poppy far too aware of his presence at all times and reminding her he'd set up the entire evening just to get her drunk and suggestible.

It was working far too well.

I shouldn't have worn this damn dress, Poppy thought as she looked down at herself. Casey, Rachelle and Poppy had all gotten ready together; it was only at their behest that Poppy dressed up at all. If she could have gotten away with it she'd have slung on a pair of shorts and a T-shirt and been done with it.

But no. Poppy was in a slinky, silver-grey, button-down shift dress with delicate little straps that showed off her tanned shoulders and her collarbones, which were protruding out more than they used to. Poppy took it as a sign that she really had to eat more, otherwise she'd have no strength left to coordinate an escape from the hellhole that was Dorian's facility.

Casey had covered every edge of her in highlighter, determined to turn Poppy into a shimmering, ethereal disco ball that reflected the blue and pink lights Nate had rigged up to flash inside the social-area-turned-nightclub. It wasn't a bad look paired with bare legs and heeled boots, if Poppy was honest. But that was the problem. Poppy looked really good. Great, even.

And Dorian simply wouldn't stop staring.

In truth Poppy thought Casey and Rachelle looked better than her. Casey was dressed akin to the hugely popular fashion bloggers she followed on social media – backless pink bodysuit and high-waisted, black leather skirt, paired with dark lipstick, perfectly straightened auburn hair, fishnet tights and chunky-heeled black boots.

Rachelle, on the other hand, wore a leopard-print dress that would have looked tacky on Poppy but somehow looked magnificent on her best friend. She had curled her hair and swept it all over one shoulder, her neck and wrists adorned with gold jewellery.

Poppy ran a hand through her own hair, feeling entirely self-conscious. She had left it long and loose, since it was usually in a pony-tail. She felt entirely unlike herself.

Except this *wasn't* unlike herself. Up until eight weeks ago Poppy King had relished nights where she and Casey and Rachelle had fussed over what to wear whilst listening to ridiculous pop music and getting drunk on too much wine and vodka. She even loved the inevitable hangovers, when she'd crawl into Rachelle's bed and they'd watch trashy TV, eat pizza and complain about how bad they felt.

It was something Poppy would never experience again.

She had to make tonight count.

When Poppy saw that Dorian realised she was standing alone and once more made a bee-line for her across the makeshift dance floor she not-so-subtly rushed towards Casey, though her friend was surrounded by a gaggle of male club members all clearly very interested in her and horny as hell. Poppy was surprised that Patrick wasn't one of them, though a sweeping glance of the cavernous room confirmed that Andrew had waylaid the man several feet away. He was talking in an animated fashion, which meant Poppy knew he must be talking to Patrick about engines.

She snorted in laughter.

"What's so funny?" Casey asked when Poppy finally barged through to her side, signalling for everyone to leave them alone.

She shrugged, then pointed over to Andrew and Patrick. "I think someone is cock-blocking Patrick and he isn't even aware he's doing it." Poppy was very happy about this, all things considered. *Things* being that Patrick was a monster that wanted to eat Casey. Or fuck her. Or both. Poppy really wasn't sure.

Casey laughed. "Bless his soul. I suppose I should thank him."

"How so?"

"Because I wanna go for Dorian tonight. Unless that's a problem? You said it wasn't the other night."

Poppy struggled not to flinch. She wanted to scream at the fact she couldn't protest despite having several very valid, very terrifying reasons for why her friend should leave Dorian alone.

But even that wasn't strictly true. She *could* protest. All Poppy had to do was say she was interested in Dorian. That she was sleeping with him. One glance in his direction, however, was all Poppy needed to strengthen her resolve that she would never give him the satisfaction of using such an excuse.

He'd take advantage of the situation – in public and *in private,* Poppy thought, certain. *Hell if I'm giving him that power.*

Casey raised an eyebrow. "Poppy King? Earth to Poppy?"

"Shit, sorry," she sputtered. "I'm just a bit drunk. I suppose you can go after Dorian all you want – if that's what you *do* want. Though I'm fairly certain pretty much any guy in this room would happily get with you."

"Nobody in the club counts. I could shag them back home."

Again, Poppy struggled not to flinch. Some of them would never *make* it back home. She was desperate to talk to someone about this fact, to help her process her feelings and tell her she had no choice but to give up a few people to save the others. But the only one she could share this topic of conversation with was Dorian, and he was the last person – monster – she wanted to talk to about it.

But then Poppy spied Andrew, looking slightly despondent because Patrick had finally managed to escape his clutches, and she had an idea. She couldn't talk to Andrew about everything but she could talk to him about *something.* That it was terrible Andrew had any inkling about what was going on didn't matter to Poppy right now; she was drunk, and liable to spill secrets, and he was the only one she could possibly talk to.

"I'm gonna make Andrew dance," Poppy said to Casey before swiftly leaving her, though she saw her friend use the opportunity to immediately walk over to Dorian. Poppy forced herself to ignore her friend's attempts at seducing him, carefully constructing her expression and taking purposeful strides towards Andrew. When Poppy grabbed hold of his arm and pulled him onto the dance floor Andrew gawked at her.

"W-what are we doing?" he spluttered.

"Dancing, obviously," Poppy replied, slinging her arms around his neck as if they were slow-dancing, though the music playing was loud and frenetic.

"I don't like this song," Andrew complained.

"So why are you still in the room?"

"Because..." Andrew considered his answer; Poppy could practically see the cogs inside his brain turning. "This might be the last time we're all together."

Without warning Poppy pulled him in close, and Andrew cried out in shock. "Who do you think should stay?" she murmured against his ear, aware that people were watching the two of them curiously. It wasn't uncommon for Poppy to drag Andrew along with her to social events, of course, but the way she was dancing with him was far more akin to the way she danced with Nate.

Andrew seemed to hesitate. "Like, from...everyone?"

"From everyone."

"You."

Poppy should have expected such an answer. It still hit her hard to hear it. She hid a grimace. "Apart from me. Apart from the board. Who do you think should be going home?"

When Andrew looked around the dance floor with absolutely no subtlety whatsoever Poppy almost laughed, but then she caught Dorian's eye and saw he was in the process of trying to back away from Casey. He raised an eyebrow Poppy's way, which she dutifully ignored.

He was going to reject her friend, that much was clear.

Poppy was relieved for several reasons, though one of those reasons in particular she refused to acknowledge even as Dorian ran a hand through his perfectly tousled hair and flashed a grin her way.

"Lily Johnson," Andrew said eventually, bringing Poppy out of her own head.

She blinked. "Why Lily?"

"She has a fiancé. She misses him. They're getting married at Christmas. I think everyone would be quite sad if that didn't happen."

"That's...rather astute of you, Andrew."

"She won't get crossed off, then?"

Abruptly Poppy stepped away from Andrew, a frown on her face that she tried and failed to conceal. "You saw my phone, didn't you?"

"I - I didn't mean to," he stuttered, looking wildly uncomfortable. "Well, not at first—"

"Oh, god. Andrew—"

"Mind if I cut in?"

The pair of them swung their heads around to stare at Dorian, who had taken Poppy stepping away from Andrew as an opportunity to finally swoop in and steal her.

Poppy scowled. "I do, actually."

"Good thing I don't. Andrew, you look horrified. What did Poppy do this time?"

"I was teaching him how to dirty dance. I wasn't finished."

"Is that what that was?" Andrew asked, momentarily astounded. "I wouldn't have thought being so close together would allow you to dance, but I suppose it wasn't *not* fun..."

Dorian looked at the two of them rather quizzically as if trying to work out if something suspicious were afoot. But then he smiled, took hold of Poppy's hand like it was the most natural thing in the world, and pulled her away towards the edge of the dance floor by the glass wall overlooking the loch and the mountains.

Given that it was mid-July it wasn't truly dark outside, and it was deathly still, so the loch perfectly recreated a glimmering, glittering version of the mountains upon its surface. It was truly breathtaking scenery. The kind Poppy adored. Outside there were several club members sitting outside to take it all in as they drank and swam in the pool, but Poppy was determined not to get swept up in the scenery right now no matter how pretty it was.

"Can I not have *one* night of fun without you bothering me?" she complained, turning her attention back to Dorian with extreme reluctance. "You're ruining my buzz."

He laughed. "We can't be having that. But I can't be having you ignoring me all night, either."

"I can."

Dorian snaked his arms around her waist and pulled her closer, though Poppy kept her fingertips splayed against his chest to prevent him getting *too* close.

"I know this was all a ploy to get me drunk, you know," Poppy finally said after silently swaying on the spot for a minute or so. "You're not as clever or as cunning as you think you are."

As if to counter her point, Dorian grabbed hold of one of Poppy's hands and spun her around; when he brought her back in she was so surprised that her arms ended up slung over Dorian's shoulders – a reflex reaction she immediately regretted.

Dorian was too close now. Far too close. The blue and pink disco lights flashed in his eyes and for a fleeting moment Poppy was sure they were glowing from within.

He leaned toward her ear. "Is that so?" he murmured, finally answering Poppy's jibe. His hands slowly but assuredly crawled down her back, sending shivers running through her that Poppy couldn't throw away as entirely unpleasant.

To her right Poppy saw Casey firing betrayed glances her way. Poppy could only stare back at her and mouth an apology before Dorian demanded her attention again.

"Does it matter that this entire night was a ploy to get you drunk?" he asked, seemingly genuinely curious about Poppy's answer. "Everyone's having a good time. It was the right thing to do."

"You don't *care* about that, though."

"Why should I?"

Poppy tried to pull out of his arms, disgusted, but Dorian merely tightened his grip on her. "Sorry," he said, for once actually sounding sincere. "I'll be nicer."

"I don't want you to be nicer when it's all bullshit."

He pretended to look offended. "This coming from the girl who looked just about ready to jump into bed with me the moment she saw me? I was all fake niceties back then."

"I did *not*—"

"You did. You absolutely, one hundred percent would have come to my bedroom that very first night if I'd invited you, had *certain circumstances* not gotten in the way."

Poppy weighed her next words carefully. "And you'd have just...gone along with it? Knowing you were sending me to my death two weeks later?"

Her question finally broke through Dorian's arrogant, carefree attitude. The easy smile slid from his face, and the muscles of his arms grew taut around Poppy's waist. There was a look in his eye – a gleam, almost – that suggested he didn't like what she'd said in the slightest.

"Clearly it was a good thing you fell, then," he muttered, so quietly Poppy could barely hear him over the music.

"For *you*," she retorted. "It would have been better for me to have died with the rest of my club, probably. At least I'd be dead by now instead of—"

"Don't say that."

"What, the truth?" Poppy slid a hand from Dorian's shoulder to the back of his neck, twisting her fingers into his curly hair to pull his ear closer to her lips – all the better for him to hear every honest word she spoke to him. "You don't want me to tell you how I actually feel? You want me to stay quiet and let you live out the stupid fantasy in your head where I give in to the insatiable urge to fuck you despite everything you've—"

He kissed her. Without a single moment of warning Dorian turned his face until his lips found Poppy's, kissing her so fervently – so insistently – that Poppy found herself allowing it to happen for several frozen, stupefied seconds.

She hated it.

She longed for it.

She pushed him away the moment she came to her senses.

"How *dare* you—"

Dorian merely kissed her again, harder and more desperately than before. And then he picked her up, hoisting Poppy over his shoulder before rushing away from the dance floor despite her protests. She banged her fists against his back over and over again as Casey and Andrew and a shocked, angry Nate watched Dorian head out the south exit that led to the meadow at the bottom of the cliffs.

He only stopped once they were outside and well out of earshot of anyone who might have been lingering by the doors; when finally he put Poppy down against the stone wall of the west wing she looked as if she might murder him.

"What's wrong with you, you son of a bitch?!" she roared. "I was literally telling you I *don't* want anything to do with you and then you kiss me? What kind of stupid logic is that?"

Dorian's lips twisted into a smirk, though his eyes were disconcertingly serious. "The kind of logic that takes into account you're with me for life. That understands how fast you make my heart beat, and how when you ignore me all I want to do is take you away from all your friends and lock you in my room. The kind of logic that acknowledges the fact I'll always be a monster to you, but that you look so beautiful tonight I can't help but hope you're drunk enough to pretend that, for once, I'm just a man."

Poppy merely stared at him, shocked into speechlessness. She didn't know what to say. For what *could* she say? Everything Dorian had just said was atrocious. It was appalling.

But she *was* drunk enough to let him get away with it.

Almost.

She looked at her feet, rubbing a hand against her arm as a cool breeze blew around them. "You're – Dorian, what am I supposed to do?" Poppy finally asked him. "You can't possibly know what's going on in my head, or how I'm dealing with the nightmare my club is in. You have my blood for life, and that won't change. But anything else...you said it yourself. You're always going to be a monster to me."

"...you're sacrificing Nic this week, right? Who are you saving?"

The sudden change in subject caused Poppy to look straight back at him: Dorian's expression was blank, betraying nothing about whether he was upset with her rejection or not.

"Lily Johnson," Poppy eventually said, very quietly, as if someone was hidden in the shadows listening in on their conversation. She repeated Andrew's explanation from earlier. "She has a fiancé."

Dorian nodded slowly and then, very gently, ran the back of his hand along Poppy's jawline until he reached her ear. When he pushed her long, windswept hair over one shoulder she didn't stop him.

"It's Saturday," he said, which was as close as Dorian had ever gotten to asking for permission to drink from her. He didn't lean in until it was clear Poppy wasn't going to protest.

This is weird, Poppy thought the moment Dorian's breath tickled against her neck, the full length of his body pinning her to the wall. Her heart was hammering against her ribcage so hard it was painful. *Too weird. It's the alcohol. Or because he kissed me. I don't want this. So why do I want this?*

Poppy cocked her head to one side before she could stop herself, exposing more of her neck for Dorian's sake. His eyes grew wide at her clear consent, taking in the sight of her willingly giving herself to him, before grazing his teeth along the line of the artery in her neck. Poppy was aching for him to do it – to bite through and spill her blood before she came to her senses – but Dorian took his time, nibbling her skin and flicking his tongue against it as if working out where to bite.

"Dorian–"

And then he did it. A flash of sharp, deliberate pain and then it was gone, replaced with something Poppy couldn't quite describe. Whatever the feeling was, it was deeper and darker than when Dorian had accosted her in bed. And he was watching her intently out of the corner of his eye, not breaking contact as he slowly – so slowly – drained Poppy of blood.

When his hands started roaming up her thighs and waist and breasts and dared to begin unbuttoning her dress Poppy did not stop him. She knew she needed to; she even brought her hands up to prevent his nimble fingers from unclothing her further. But, instead, Poppy found herself reaching beneath the hem of his shirt to feel Dorian's skin beneath her fingertips. His eyebrows rose in surprise, and for a moment he stopped draining Poppy of blood entirely, before continuing his feed as if fearful Poppy would retreat if he drew too much attention to what she was doing.

Poppy cautiously slid her fingers up Dorian's stomach. His body was hard and lean-muscled. This wasn't a surprise: Poppy fully expected it given how adept he was at rock climbing. And it wasn't as if she hadn't imagined what Dorian felt like, in guilty snippets of hazy consciousness just before she fell asleep. But feeling his skin – and his rapid heartbeat – beneath her fingertips was entirely different from imagining the sensation.

She dug her nails into Dorian just to see what he would do. Poppy thought he'd bite down harder against her neck. Instead, he pulled away from the wound and licked the remaining blood away, moving his mouth up Poppy's neck until he reached her ear. Dorian kissed it, then bit it, his breathing ragged and uneven.

Then he stopped. Dorian pulled away and stared at Poppy, even as a fine line of her blood began to run down from his mouth. With a flick of his tongue he cleaned it away.

And then he watched, and waited. With ragged breath, a tautness in his jaw and blue eyes turned dark beneath the night sky he watched Poppy, looking for a sign to push things further.

Don't give him one, Poppy thought, over and over again. *Don't do it. This is wrong.*

She didn't give him a sign; instead, Poppy King slid her arms around Dorian's shoulders and pulled him to her, reaching up on the tips of her toes to grab at his hair and drag his lips down to meet hers with fierce desperation.

Dorian eagerly complied. Though his tongue had the metallic tang of blood upon it Poppy still let it into her mouth, jumping up to wrap her legs around Dorian's waist when he shoved her against the wall and slid the straps of her dress off her shoulders.

"What happened to what you said earlier?" Dorian asked breathlessly in a minuscule space between kisses. He ran his teeth over her neck and bit down – not to break the skin and eat but as a barely controlled display of longing – until Poppy gasped.

"This is only happening because I'm drunk," she said, the answer a useless lie. "Because I'm – I'm going to hell anyway."

"That's the spirit." He turned his gaze up, in the direction of his bedroom window, though his expression was torn. "How do you feel about fucking outside?"

Poppy indulged a dangerously stupid and filthy impulse to reply, "It wouldn't be the first time."

"Now *that's* what I like to—"

But then a rustling nearby immediately silenced him, and Dorian roved his head from side to side, listening hard. "Someone's watching us," he whispered.

Poppy froze in his arms. Someone was *watching* them. Watching Poppy allow Dorian to undress her, to kiss her and –

Drink my blood.

Slowly, very slowly, Poppy extricated herself from Dorian and pushed him away. She redid the buttons of her dress; Dorian had made it all the way down to her navel. "This was a mistake," she uttered, running off before she could make any more stupid decisions. Not that she could imagine one much stupider than the one she'd just indulged.

"Poppy, wait!" Dorian pleaded, running after her as she headed back into the social area. "Don't go. *Please.*"

But Poppy had, finally, come to her senses. Being drunk or her soul being damned weren't good enough excuses for what she'd been doing. No excuse would ever be good enough.

She shrugged Dorian off when he tried to turn her around and lost herself in the throngs of people dancing to cheesy nineties pop. When Nate handed her a shot she eagerly downed it, though Poppy flinched at the glare he sent over her shoulder, towards Dorian.

Someone had been watching them together. *Watching.* Withholding a shiver Poppy wondered if they'd heard everything she and Dorian had said to each other, or if they'd seen him dig into her neck and drink her blood like the inhuman monster that he was.

Poppy couldn't bear to look at Dorian for the rest of the night. She merely drank, and drank, and drank, until finally she passed out in bed with the hope that, come morning, everything terrible that had happened to her would turn out to be a nightmare.

POPPY

Fred had witnessed Dorian and Poppy's interaction outside. He hadn't heard it, but he'd seen it. Well, as much as he could have seen from his hiding place.

The problem was that Fred didn't understand *what* he'd seen. Poppy seemed desperate to get away from Dorian. She'd been furious. She'd been frightened. And then she'd kissed him. She'd kissed him and the pair of them would have likely gone much farther if Fred hadn't moved.

Why was he biting Poppy's neck so hard? Fred wondered as he lay in bed, struggling to think properly through a drunken haze. His eyes were droopy; he knew sleep would wash over him in minutes, if not seconds. *I'm sure she was—*

Bleeding.

That night he dreamt of monsters.

CASSANDRA O'DONNELL

DORIAN

DESPITE HAVING EVERY INTENTION OF CREEPING into Poppy's bed early the next morning – to beg her to reconsider that what happened between them wasn't a mistake, to continue from where they'd been interrupted, to simply lie there with her as they both dozed – Dorian slept in. He was exhausted and more than a little hungover. He had no doubt *everybody* was.

Especially Poppy.

It was with some effort that Dorian finally dragged himself out of bed, wincing at the sunlight streaming through the glass wall of his room and burning his eyes. When he reached the bathroom he gulped down a glass of water, turned on the shower and immediately sat on the floor of the cubicle the second the water was hot.

Dorian relished in the water pressure on his head and neck and shoulders. Sighing, he rested against the tiled wall of the shower and closed his eyes, content to remain there, unmoving, for fifteen minutes.

He'd been in his human form for so long. Too long, it often seemed. Dorian needed to break free and run on his own two legs at a speed mere humans could only dream of reaching.

He needed to stretch. He needed to be tall. He needed to be himself.

Halfway through, he thought, only somewhat reassured by the notion. *I'm halfway through this mistake of a summer. Just seven more weeks and I can do what I like until my next trafficking stint.*

It was only in thinking this that Dorian realised Poppy would be disgusted and horrified if he continued his day job, as it were. He'd never had to consider the rights or wrongs of his work in the eyes of humans before. He hadn't needed to.

But now Dorian knew with crushing certainty that he could never do it again. To have Poppy beside him for the rest of his days – to try and make her life as good as possible in the process – he couldn't sell humans to monsters. It was something unconscionable to her. Unforgivable, in a way Dorian didn't think he would ever be able to justify.

He got out of the shower.

After sliding into a loose white shirt and jeans before half-heartedly rubbing his hair dry with a towel Dorian made his way to the central building of the facility. He needed to talk to Poppy. About – everything.

We need to have a plan for when summer ends and her friends are either dead or gone.

With every passing day Dorian wanted more and more to stop the bidding on the remaining members of Poppy's club. It would be so much easier if he and Poppy could simply run off now, especially since saving more of her friends might encourage Poppy to soften her stance towards Dorian. But he couldn't do that; to stop the auction now would mean almost certain death. Prominent, disgustingly wealthy clients were putting their trust in Dorian to provide them with high-quality food. If that food were to suddenly disappear Dorian would be hunted down and punished for it.

So why do I still feel tempted to run off, anyway?

It wasn't like Dorian at all to want to stop his work. He had always been proud of it. Even worse was the fact he wanted to quit for someone else – a *human*, no less. It only made him desire all the more to slough off his human skin simply to know what the real Dorian Kapros actually wanted out of life.

He had never felt less like himself.

Dorian was surprised when he ran into Poppy halfway down the stairs of the west wing. She looked like she was suffering from a hangover far worse that Dorian's, and very much not in the mood to discuss what had and hadn't happened between the two of them the night before.

"Where's Casey?" Poppy demanded when she saw him, before Dorian could so much as voice a hello.

He frowned in confusion, stopping in his tracks when it became clear Poppy wasn't going to move from her position on the stairs. "Not with me, if that's what you're asking," he said. "Or have you forgotten already that I rejected her?"

Poppy scowled. "This isn't about you. Or it might be. Where is she?"

"She isn't in her bedroom?"

"Would I have come all the way over here to ask you if she was?"

"If you can't find her then I think you probably know where she is, Poppy."

"I – what?" Poppy seemed taken aback by Dorian's answer. "What do you mean?"

Dorian sighed, running a hand through his still-damp hair

and knowing full well this wasn't a conversation he wanted to have with Poppy on the best of days...and this was *not* the best of days. "She disappeared last night with Patrick. I imagine they're still sleeping on his boat."

Poppy's face grew ashen. "H-how could you let this happen?"

"What do you mean, how could *I* let this happen? I'm not responsible for what Patrick does, just as you're not responsible for what Casey does."

"But he's *like you!*" she spat in his face. "Why would you let him anywhere near—"

"Because Patrick claimed her from the beginning."

There. He'd said it. Dorian should have told Poppy about Patrick's claim weeks ago, but he hadn't. Looking at the way Poppy shook with fear made him feel utterly ashamed of himself for keeping the truth from her.

"But..." Her face twisted in pain and disbelief. "I'm saving Casey. This week – *now*."

"You can't."

Poppy closed the distance between them and banged a fist against Dorian's chest. "What do you mean I can't? You told me I got to save one person a week, and I'm saving her! I was always going to save her!"

Dorian didn't want to tell her why. And even though he cared for Patrick – he was his best friend, after all – he couldn't help but wish that Casey hadn't caught his friend's attention. "They've slept together," he said. "No doubt several times by now. That's why."

"What do you mean *that's why*? Why should it fucking matter that they screwed each other?!"

"Poppy, keep your voice down," Dorian hushed, making to cover her mouth as she swatted him away.

"Don't tell me what to do. Just explain what you mean. Why does it matter that they slept together?"

How could my situation have changed so much that it actually matters to me that Casey has been signed over to Patrick? Dorian wondered, closing his eyes for a moment before finally saying, "Because Patrick never wanted to eat her. He wants Casey as a...breeding partner, for want of a better term."

Poppy grew bug-eyed. "He wanted her for *what?* Can't he just go – fuck another monster? Why would he want his *food* to carry his abominable offspring?"

"Watch your mouth," Dorian bit out, finally beginning to lose his temper despite the fact Poppy had every right to be angry with him. "Patrick's a good guy. Don't insult him."

"I'll do whatever I damn well please!" she countered, outraged at Dorian's admonishment. "And you didn't even answer my question. Why are you avoiding answering it?"

He ran a hand over his face, completely resigned. "It's... complicated. You saw what Nick's father, Mr Richardson, really looks like. I don't imagine you'd forget."

Poppy said nothing, though her pupils contracted and she inched away from Dorian.

"And you've seen what I really look like," Dorian continued. "We're completely different. A lot of monsters look nothing alike, Poppy. It makes us rather...incompatible with each other."

"Can't you just screw in human form to overcome that?" Poppy asked, catching on to what Dorian was insinuating immediately.

"Yes and no. The problem is we don't really know what our *offspring* will end up being. What they'll look like – what they'll be capable of doing. It's a risky business. But if a monster impregnates a human, instead, we can ensure we'll know what the result will be."

"Oh, that's just great," Poppy said, voice dripping with sarcasm. "Except for the poor human woman who has to give birth to some kind of monstrosity that might literally break her open in the process. No, that's not happening to Casey. I'm saving her. That's it."

"I can't do that, Poppy. She might be pregnant already for all we know."

"She can get a fucking abortion, I don't care! She's not staying with Patrick!"

"Yes she is!"

Poppy slapped him. It stung Dorian's cheek, though it was nothing compared to the vicious expression on her face. "Do my decisions mean *nothing* to you, Dorian?" she fired out. "Have I only ever had the semblance of choice here? Were you always going to get your way no matter what I said or did?"

"This is the only thing I can't cha—"

"Like hell you can't! Don't...please don't do this to her," she pleaded, all her previous anger gone in an instant. Tears began to stream down her face. "Don't condemn her to a fate worse than mine. I know you said last night that you don't care for any of my friends, but it can't be true. Even you can't be that heartless. You can't."

Dorian didn't know what to say. He *wanted* to say that he'd tell Patrick to leave Cassandra O'Donnell alone. But this was part of their way of life, and Patrick was the closest thing to family Dorian had left. He couldn't interfere with his friend's happiness.

Poppy could tell from his face that Dorian wasn't going to give her the answer she wanted. When he reached out for her she backed down the stairs, shaking her head in disbelief. "I can't believe I kissed you," she muttered. "I can't believe, even for a moment, I forgot what you were."

"Poppy—"

"Get away from me!"

And then Poppy ran, darting down the rest of the stairs and along the corridor until she disappeared behind the slamming of a door. Dorian sank onto the step she'd left him standing on. He didn't have the energy to move.

"What have I done?" he wondered, for nobody but himself to hear.

Dorian knew that he'd irreparably broken whatever tenuous, carefully-constructed bond he'd managed to form with Poppy.

There was no charming his way out of this one.

KIRSTY WHITE

ANDREW

Something was even more off concerning Poppy than usual.

Now that she knew Andrew had some inkling about what was going on he'd thought Poppy would tell him what was wrong, but she hadn't. Not a single word on the matter had been shared between them, though Andrew was desperate to learn what was *actually* going on regarding the 'scouting' of club members.

Three days had passed since the entire club got drunk. Three days since Dorian kissed Poppy and Casey disappeared with Patrick. Even Andrew could tell that both Poppy and Casey had been acting awkward with each other since then. He wondered if it had something to do with the fact Casey had been talking to Dorian and then Dorian ignored her in favour of dancing with Poppy. But Casey had Patrick, so in reality Andrew didn't understand what was going on.

He didn't like thinking about Dorian kissing Poppy, and what might have happened after he carried her away. But they had gone outside – and hadn't been gone for long – so Andrew clung to the hope that nothing of note had occurred between them. That hope was a lie, though, and Andrew knew it. So did Nate, who had also watched in disbelief when Dorian and Poppy returned to the central building that night looking, for want of a better word, *ruffled.*

Andrew had to conclude that something happened between them, though it hurt his heart to reach such a conclusion. *But since then Poppy has been avoiding Dorian even more than she's been avoiding Casey, though,* he thought, puzzling over the situation. *And Patrick has been spending most of his time at the centre to be with Casey.* He wondered if the two issues were somehow linked.

Most of the club was currently relaxing in the social area or climbing on the indoor walls. After weeks of fair, sunny weather the sky had finally grown dark and heavy with clouds. It was with a collective sigh of relief that it started raining; though Andrew liked being outside the air had grown too dry and oppressive, so he was glad for the downpour. And he liked the noise the raindrops made as they hit the windows, the pool, and the ceiling.

"Poppy, are you sure you're okay? You don't look too good."

Andrew's head darted up from the book he was reading. The person who had spoken was Kirsty White, one of the second year students who was friends with Jenny Adams and Lily Johnson. She was a nice girl but fairly quiet, even by Andrew's standards. He couldn't say he'd ever spoken to her.

Poppy smiled grimly at Kirsty before shaking her head. "It's just a headache. I'm fine, Kirsty. Thanks for asking." When Kirsty retreated to the east wing Poppy glanced over at Casey, who was cuddled up on an armchair with Patrick in much the same way as she and Nate used to sit together. And though Poppy looked away quickly before either Casey or Patrick noticed her staring, Andrew caught it. He caught it the second time, too. And the third. When Poppy sighed heavily Andrew could only conclude she had some kind of problem with her friend being together with the older man.

He knew not to ask about the issue in front of everyone, so he didn't.

Kirsty returned from the east wing bearing a box of codeine and a glass of water which she promptly handed over to a very grateful Poppy. "I figured you needed something a bit stronger than ibuprofen," Kirsty explained, almost apologetically. "And I always travel with codeine in case I get migraines. Sorry if I'm being annoying after you said it was nothing."

Poppy laughed softly with genuine fondness in her eyes. There was a reason the vast majority of the club loved Poppy and had voted her president, after all. Andrew would know. "Don't be ridiculous!" she said before swallowing the painkillers down with a swig of water. "Where would I be without you guys looking out for me all the time? I don't deserve it. Thank you, Kirsty."

Andrew knew, then and there, that Kirsty's genuine, selfless act of kindness was going to ensure she was safe. Though in truth he still had no clue what was happening with everyone who was 'scouted', Poppy's erratic self-decline implied that it wasn't anything good.

He wished she'd tell him.

"Could those hickeys be any bigger, Casey?" Fred commented the moment he sauntered into the social area, raising his eyebrows at her before falling onto the couch beside Andrew. Andrew sidled away an inch or two, since Fred was too close.

However, though Fred's jibe had been aimed at Casey he was now looking at Poppy with a dead-pan stare. She met his gaze with a glower, but seemed to snuggle just a little further into the blanket she had wrapped around herself.

Andrew didn't understand. Poppy *had* no love-bites.

"Very funny, Fred," Casey replied. Patrick pretended to give her another one until she squealed and pushed him away.

"Nothing wrong with a good hickey in the heat of the moment," Patrick joked, kissing Casey's forehead before pulling her back in against his chest. Poppy bristled despite herself, something which Casey noticed.

She frowned. "Something wrong, Poppy?"

"Nothing. Just a headache."

"You're looking a bit anaemic these days, King," Fred drawled. Andrew stared at him; the comment hadn't sounded like he was concerned. Rather, it felt altogether like an accusation, though Andrew wasn't sure why.

"Leave off it, Sampson."

"You sure Kapros didn't go too far giving *you* hick—"

"I said leave it alone."

"Oh, but we're all so curious, Poppy," Casey joined in. Again, Andrew was sure the comment wasn't meant kindly. He had to wonder why everyone was rounding on Poppy when she was clearly feeling miserable.

Poppy didn't look at her. "About what?"

"Don't act coy now! You know fine well we're *dying* to know what happened between you and Dorian."

"Aw, leave her be, Cass," Patrick said. "What happened between them is between them." Andrew was grateful for him saying so, though he wasn't sure if Patrick had spoken on Poppy's behalf or Dorian's.

Casey merely scowled. "What, so Poppy just gets away with it again? Never accountable for her actions, even when she swears just five minutes before being carried away by the guy that she has *absolutely no interest in him whatsoever?* Nah, I'm calling bullshit."

"What are you insinuating, Casey?" Poppy asked, bristling

beneath her blanket.

"You know fine well what I'm insinuating! And this isn't even the first time you've done this to me!"

"...what?"

Casey extricated herself from Patrick to stand up. "Oh, look at me, I'm the perfectly daring, irresponsible Poppy King," she mocked, imitating her friend in a way that made Andrew deeply uncomfortable. To his left Fred choked on a laugh.

Andrew didn't like seeing the two of them making fun of Poppy, so he got up and left as quickly as possible. When he was halfway across the social area he saw Dorian walking towards him and so Andrew stopped, at a loss for what to do.

"Stop being a bitch," Poppy muttered, though there was no malice to her words. She merely sounded resigned.

Casey laughed incredulously. "*I'm* the bitch? Not the girl who, after hearing that her friend is super into a guy, immediately goes after that guy because she *knows* they'll fall for her instead? Even when she claims not to be interested?"

"Just lay off, Casey."

"No, why should I?" She swept her gaze around the social area just as Dorian reached Andrew's side. Poppy couldn't see the two of them standing and watching from where she sat, so Dorian's presence remained unknown to her.

Dorian was silent as a statue as he observed the situation. Andrew didn't want to remain beside him – he wanted to run away before Casey and Poppy ended up having a full-blown shouting match – but he didn't know how to leave Dorian's side without being awkwardly rude.

"I shouldn't keep quiet about it any longer," Casey continued, an ugly snarl curling her mouth, "not when most of the club still fawns over how *great* you are. Well guess what, Poppy: you're not so great. You were a shitty friend to Rachelle when she was going out with Fred, and you were even shittier when I liked Nate and still decided to screw him for fun."

Andrew thought Poppy would surely say something. *Anything.* Instead she merely hung her head in silence and kept to herself.

"See, she won't even defend herself," Casey said. "She knows I'm right! And Nate wasn't even the first guy she did this with. He was just the one who hurt me most, because I liked him so much. But that didn't matter to you, did it, Poppy? Just so long as you had your fun, right?"

Patrick held out a hand to try and pull Casey back onto the armchair but she shirked him off. "Come on," he said, "you've said your piece. Now—"

"Don't try and shut me up, Patrick! This has been a long time coming, and anyone who has ever *mattered* to Poppy knows it."

Finally, Poppy dropped her blanket and stood up. She walked over to Casey with an eerie calm, though Andrew could see her hands were shaking. "You're right," she uttered. "Of course you're right. I'm the worst. And yet still—"

She slapped Casey in the face, the sound reverberating off the walls so viciously Andrew was taken aback by the noise. Then she promptly turned and ran out of the social area towards her bedroom without taking her eyes off the floor.

Beside Andrew, Dorian rubbed his left cheek as if he'd felt the slap himself. He glanced at him. "You know, don't you?"

"No," Andrew replied matter-of-factly. "I don't know anything about girls."

Dorian merely shook his head, leaving for his office as he quietly laughed to himself. It took Andrew a beat too long to realise Dorian may have been referring to something else entirely – something that had nothing to do with the girls fighting each other. *I do know something,* he thought, *but I also don't. And I don't know how to make Poppy trust me enough to tell me everything.*

Fred and Patrick consoled a crying Casey. Part of Andrew wanted to make her feel better, too: he didn't like seeing anyone cry and Casey was, after all, his friend. But she had brought Poppy's anger on herself with her cruel goading, and had clearly also hurt Poppy in the process. Poppy, who was more important to Andrew than anyone else in the world.

And so Andrew retreated to his bedroom, determined to work out what to say and do so that Poppy would, finally, confide in him. He desperately wanted to knock on her door and make her feel better after her argument with Casey, but he knew he'd likely flounder and fail.

He was glad Nate hadn't been around for their argument. Something told Andrew his presence would have only made things worse. But despite Nate not being there, Andrew still knew one thing for certain.

Everything was about to get worse anyway.

INTERLUDE V

Nobody joined them this week. Nicolas had lost both his legs, just like Megan before him. He couldn't stop screaming, especially whenever he looked at his best friend. For Tom hadn't lost anything yet, but there was a fear in his eyes that told Nic he knew it was only a matter of time before something unspeakable befell him.

Going by what Megan was saying and the empty look in Craig's eyes, it was only a matter of time for all of them.

Grace Kang

FRED

After Casey's long-awaited beat-down of Poppy, Fred had been temporarily too gleeful to follow around after her to work out what she was hiding. But now, five days later, he was well and truly back to being suspicious of Poppy King. For there was something deeply wrong with her, which seemed only tangentially related to her falling out with Casey.

Poppy was paler and frailer with every passing day, though she seemed determined to pour all of her energy into besting the entire Outdoor Sports Society at climbing, diving, abseiling, and mountain biking. She was even demolishing Andrew on their morning jogs, insisting they go a little further and a little faster each time. And she was avoiding Dorian like the plague. Everyone else assumed it was because of what Casey had said.

Fred knew better.

When he spied Poppy and Dorian together in the meadow he was sure she'd been bleeding. Dorian had bitten her. *Bitten* her. And yet when Fred had looked for signs of the man's violent onslaught there had been nothing.

Poppy's skin was smooth and unblemished, as if Dorian had never touched it.

It didn't make any sense. And when Fred made a comment about love bites Poppy had shied away from it, as if she knew there was something wrong. Which meant there *was* something wrong. And it didn't just have to do with Poppy but with Dorian, too.

Yet it was Poppy who was the key. Through Poppy Fred would finally understand what the hell was going on.

He just had to work out *how* to go about getting the information he desperately needed.

"What are you thinking about so hard?" Rachelle asked, knocking Fred on the head with her knuckles as she sat down beside him. He was sitting outside, feet swinging in the pool, enjoying the fresh air and relative quiet that allowed him to mull over his fledgling plan properly.

He kept his eyes on his feet. "You don't want to know."

"Jesus Christ, Fred," Rachelle sighed, predicting exactly who Fred was thinking about with terrifying accuracy. She pulled off her shoes to dip her feet in the water beside him. "Will you just give Poppy a break? Do you not think Casey giving her the cold shoulder is enough for her?"

He snorted. "She deserved it and you know it."

"You really asking me if I believe my best friend deserved to be humiliated in front of everyone for something that should have been a private discussion?"

"And there you go, defending her again over everyone else."

"You know," she said, clearly irritated, "you're just as bad as Poppy is. Worse, even. You pride yourself on being sensible and careful and always looking out for people but you absolutely *thrive* on pissing Poppy off and insulting her."

"She does the exact same to me!"

"Yes, but here's the thing: I hate it when you do it." Rachelle stared at him with a serious, stony expression. "You *mean* everything you say. You want every barbed word out of your mouth to do as much damage as possible. Poppy doesn't think about what she's saying at all."

"And that somehow makes her better?"

"Yes, because it isn't premeditated! Even now, you're sitting here obsessing over her acting weird this summer. You wanna know how much time she wastes thinking about you? Precisely none. Why can't you give it a rest?"

"Because something's wrong!" Fred exclaimed, making to touch Rachelle's shoulder before thinking better of it. "She's hiding something. Don't tell me you can't see it."

Rachelle looked like she was about ready to tear her hair out. "She's miserable, Fred, *that's* what's wrong! I genuinely don't think she wanted Dorian to kiss her, and now Casey has fallen out with her, and Poppy's absolutely not speaking to anyone but Andrew because of it and I'm pretty certain she's homesick as hell."

Fred raised an eyebrow. "You finished justifying her actions for her yet?"

"You're such a dick when you want to be, you know that?" Then Rachelle looked down at her hands, which she was twisting nervously in her lap. "And I think..."

"What?"

She sighed. "I think she's – I don't know – *scared* of Dorian. Or something. I can't put my finger on it, but I've never seen her act like this with anyone before. I'm sure she isn't just avoiding him because he kissed her."

Of course Fred thought back to Dorian biting Poppy open.

Right up until that moment she *had* looked scared. And sad, and uncertain, though Fred didn't care too much for those emotions right now.

Poppy being scared of Dorian was a fact he hadn't really taken into consideration yet.

So she's scared of him, but let him hurt her. Only she wasn't hurt at all. She—

"Rachelle."

His ex-girlfriend seemed surprised by Fred only saying her name. "What is it?"

"Have you ever seen Poppy without bandages or that compression sleeve on her arm?"

She frowned. "No. Why would I?"

"She never asked you to help her wrap up her arm? Even though you're her best friend and the first aider for the club?"

"Why would she? Poppy always goes to the infirmary to have them changed. Look, Fred, just leave her alone—"

"I know," he interrupted. He stood up and retrieved his shoes. "I will."

But Rachelle got up too, clearly unconvinced. "Where are you going?"

"To make a sandwich. I'm hungry. You want one?"

"Um, no thanks," she replied, blushing slightly. She ran a hand through her hair somewhat uncomfortably. "Robin and I are going to have a picnic in the meadow soon, so..."

Fred didn't trust himself to say anything that didn't sound false. He made do with smiling before setting off for the kitchen, knowing Rachelle could see right through his faux-sincerity, though it turned into a scowl the moment he was alone again. Rachelle had moved on from him, that much was clear. At this point Fred wasn't sure if he actually wanted to get back together with her or whether he was simply furious that his relationship with Rachelle was another thing Poppy King had ruined for him.

"I can't believe she played around with Nate knowing that Casey liked him. What a bitch," Fred heard a female voice say from further down the corridor. He edged closer and saw that it was Grace Kang, talking to Ciaran Radin-Kirkwood.

Fred didn't particularly like either of them: Grace was a nasty gossip and Ciaran was never very nice to Andrew. Fred hadn't seen the two of them talk much before, but with Grace's best friends – Angelica and Megan – having both been scouted, clearly Grace was desperate for new people to talk and complain to.

He lingered behind them as they all made their way to the kitchen, especially interested in where the conversation was going considering the fact Fred himself had only just been complaining about Poppy.

"You know Craig was gonna try his luck with Poppy?" Ciaran told Grace. "Glad he didn't, all things considered. Although had Casey been into him then no doubt Poppy would have thrown herself at him."

Grace cackled. "Exactly. Casey said it all! God, Poppy is such a low-key slut and we never knew it. At least Casey was *honest* about sleeping around. Poppy lying about doing the same is what makes her so much worse."

The pair of them paused when Poppy herself appeared in the kitchen doorway directly in front of them; her expression suggested she'd heard their entire conversation. "Yes, I'm such an awful person," Poppy said, unapologetically shouldering past Grace in the process.

As soon as she was behind them her face darkened into something akin to spite, only much worse. For some reason it gave Fred pause. Poppy looked *intimidating*, even taking into account the sickly pallor of her face and her generally underfed appearance.

When she spied Fred her mouth twisted into a scowl. "Just...fuck off, Sampson," she muttered before rushing away, though Fred hadn't intended on saying anything whilst Grace and Ciaran were within earshot.

For Fred realised he wanted to do something he had literally never imagined doing in the six years he'd known Poppy King: he wanted to speak to her *alone*. Away from Rachelle and Andrew and Nate and Casey. Away from the club. Away from Dorian.

Fred had questions he wanted answered.

Poppy would give him those answers, even if he had to force them out of her.

RICHARD DEACON

POPPY

IT WAS LATE. SO LATE THAT nobody was awake and therefore nobody bothered Poppy on her way to the kitchen, though she didn't know why she was going there. She had no appetite. She wasn't thirsty. But she couldn't sleep, and she couldn't bear lying wide awake in her room, surrounded by rooms and rooms of people who were no longer speaking to her.

And so Poppy reached the kitchen, turned the tap on for want of background noise and slid down against the fridge to the floor.

Then she wept.

She wept like she'd done on that first night nine weeks ago, when she'd discovered the horrific truth about Dorian and his outdoor sports facility. She wept until she was choking on her sobs, barely able to breathe.

But it wasn't enough. There was no outpouring of emotion that could make Poppy feel better. She and Casey were resolutely not talking to each other. The rest of the club was dutifully keeping its distance until the two girls sorted out their differences, except for Andrew, whom Poppy was spending more and more time with. But their time together was largely silent simply because Andrew had no idea what to say and Poppy didn't have it in her to speak. Even Nate and Rachelle were giving Poppy some space, though she was sure the former was doing it because he was jealous of Dorian and the latter was doing it because she thought space was what Poppy wanted.

It wasn't.

But in five weeks they'd all be gone in one way or another, and Poppy would be left behind. Alone, with the weight of her decisions crushing her. Only she wouldn't be alone.

She would be with Dorian, and that was worse.

Poppy had dutifully allowed him to drink from her the week after she'd found out Casey had belonged to Patrick from day one. All she'd uttered was the name of the person she was saving – Kirsty White, simply because she gave Poppy those painkillers. It was a small gesture, but it was the nicest thing that had happened to Poppy that entire week, and ultimately Kirsty was a good person.

But Poppy was running out of obviously *good* people and *bad* people. Or, more to the point, she was running out of people doing bad things that warranted being singled out for. And she couldn't save Casey. Even though she wanted to. Even though she was desperate to. Dorian wouldn't let Poppy save her, and it was killing her inside.

Dorian hadn't even tried to speak to her since she'd slapped him. Even when he'd drained her of blood he'd kept things as impersonal as possible, and when Poppy wavered and swayed on the spot afterwards he didn't try to help her.

In fact, even as her health obviously deteriorated Dorian continued to say nothing. Poppy was pouring all her resentful, lonely energy into beating absolutely everyone at any task set in front of them, to the point that Nick, Steven and – reluctantly –

Aisling grew more and more impressed with her with every passing day. But, despite her showing off, Dorian didn't once try to break Poppy *or* their silence in retaliation.

It wasn't even as if she was acting out so that he *would* say something to her: Poppy wanted Dorian as far away from her as possible. No. Poppy was hoping, bleakly, that she would continue to weaken and wear herself out until, eventually, she would slip and fall from a ledge that was simply too high for her to recover from.

Poppy King wanted to die, but she didn't have the courage to pick up a knife and put herself out of her own misery.

She felt pathetic.

"...Poppy? Is that you?"

She darted her head up, wincing when the lights flickered on. The fluorescent brightness danced in front of her eyes, only made worse by the heavy tears stuck between her lashes.

"R-Rich?" Poppy stammered when she recognised Nate's best friend.

He looked horrified by the sight of her. Without another word he grabbed a wad of kitchen roll and knelt in front of Poppy, gently wiping at her face as he chewed his lip in concern. "What's wrong, Poppy?" he asked. "...is it Casey?"

Poppy only sobbed harder.

Rich seemed at a loss for what to do. "Poppy, can I...how can I help you?"

"Nobody can help me," she wailed miserably. "This is all my own fault."

"Everyone knows it isn't," he said, trying his best at a reassuring smile. "We know how flighty Casey is. I'd have spoken to you sooner, only..."

"I kn-know. Nate. Nothing changes the fact that I *have* been messing him around."

Rich grimaced. "It's not that – not really. It's more like he's heartbroken, and he doesn't know how to handle it."

That, of course, made Poppy feel worse. A fresh wave of tears hit her and Rich, realising what he'd done, flailed about as if unsure of whether he could hug her or not.

"Poppy, I'm sorry! I shouldn't have said that! I'm so sorry—"

"It's okay. I deserve it."

"You don't. Nobody deserves to be this upset and have someone stupidly make them feel worse."

Poppy let out a garbled laugh. "What's one more blow, right? May as well get it in whilst I already feel wretched, right?"

Neither of them said anything for a while, though eventually Poppy's sobs quietened until she was almost back to normal. She looked at Rich. "Thanks for checking up on me. Why are you in here so late, anyway?"

He glanced at the fridge Poppy was leaning against. "Had a hankering for orange juice. Stupid, I know. It's almost four in the morning."

She giggled despite her awful mood then, with some effort, pushed up off the floor and moved away from the fridge she was blocking. She gestured towards it. "Be my guest."

Rich took the entire carton out with the clear intention of taking it back to his room with him. He regarded Poppy seriously. "Go back to bed, Poppy," he said. "Being up in the middle of the night won't make you feel better, but sleep probably will."

"In a bit," she said, forcing a small smile on her face. "I'm just going to...I don't know. Clean up. Then I'll go to bed, I swear. Thanks for checking up on me, Rich."

He didn't look convinced by Poppy's answer. But when he realised there was likely nothing more he could do to improve her mood, Rich dutifully left.

Poppy shoved her face under the freezing water still pouring from the faucet when she found herself alone once more, then turned the tap off. She rubbed at her eyes and took several deep breaths, willing herself to calm down. Rich was right, of course: she needed to get some sleep.

When Poppy heard the door creak behind her she assumed he was having second thoughts about leaving her alone. "Rich," she said, turning for the door with another forced smile on her face, "I swear I'm going to – oh."

It wasn't Rich; it was Fred.

Poppy narrowed her eyes, annoyed when she had to sniff away tears before demanding, "The hell do you want, Sampson?"

Fred closed the door behind him but didn't answer Poppy's question. The glass panel in the door was a square of pitch blackness, for the corridor was dark, in stark contrast to the ugly lighting of the kitchen.

When Fred stalked towards her Poppy instinctively moved away from him until her back hit the sink. "This isn't funny, Fred," she said. "If you were trying to scare me or catch me crying: congrats. You managed both. Hooray. Now if you'll excuse me—"

"You're not going anywhere."

He held out an arm to prevent Poppy from rushing past.

"Fred, seriously—"

"I have some questions for you, and you're going to answer them. No snide comments or bullshit answers or evading what I'm asking."

Poppy crossed her arms in an attempt to seem merely annoyed with Fred rather than worried or intimidated. "And why should I answer anything you ask of me?"

"Show me your arm."

"What?"

Beneath the compression sleeve Poppy's skin itched wildly. It was all Fred needed to say to confirm to Poppy that he'd worked out something he shouldn't have.

"You heard me," he said. "Show me your arm."

"That's not even a question."

Fred took a step towards her. "I don't care. Show me."

"No."

"And why not?"

"Because you're telling me to." Poppy thought Fred would lose his temper with her speaking back to him the way she was but his face remained eerily calm and expressionless. She frowned, unsure about what Fred's intentions were. "Look, I'm just going to g—"

Fred lunged for Poppy's arm and, in the process, grabbed one of the kitchen knives drying on the dish rack behind her. When he pointed the tip of the blade against Poppy's jugular she had no choice but to stay where she was.

"Fred," she gulped, trying her best to stay level-headed even though she was anything but, "what do you think you're playing at? This isn't funny."

His green eyes flashed beneath the fluorescent lighting. "It isn't meant to be."

Without moving the knife Fred grabbed at the compression sleeve, meaning to rip it away. But Poppy reached for the blade of the knife, wrapping her hand around it before elbowing Fred in the face. He yelled in surprise; Poppy used his momentary distraction to shoulder him out of the way.

She barely made it two feet before Fred yanked her painfully back by her hair. When her eyes found Fred's she saw his nose was bleeding.

"Who the hell grabs a knife by the *blade*, King?" Fred

muttered, almost to himself. He seemed torn between taking off Poppy's compression sleeve once more and forcing open the hand that held the knife. She had no choice but to loosen her grip to prevent the blade biting into her flesh, though it hadn't yet managed to cut her.

That was the opportunity Fred needed. Pulling on Poppy's hair even harder he grabbed her wrist and crushed it with his hand until Poppy was gasping in pain and dropped the knife entirely.

"Fred, let me go!" Poppy yelped. His grip only grew tighter.

And then Fred saw it – Poppy's hand was fine. There was barely a mark that ever indicated she'd grabbed the wrong end of a knife.

There was nothing there at all.

His eyes went wide with disbelief, though Fred must have had an inkling of what would happen given that he'd wanted to see Poppy's arm in the first place. He tossed her to the side and retrieved the fallen knife, grinning maliciously as he turned back to face her.

Poppy tried once more to escape for the door, eyes darting round wildly to try and find something she could use against Fred. But the cutlery drawer and knife block were both behind Fred; Poppy had nothing but her fists, and she was weak from malnutrition and exhaustion.

"Show me your arm, Poppy," Fred repeated. Poppy could only numbly shake her head as she took a step away from him.

When Fred grabbed her again she was starkly reminded of when he'd pulled on her arm and demanded she follow him to help Andrew on the hike, back when Nic and Tom had tortured the mountain goat. Poppy had become uncomfortably aware that Fred was stronger than her. And Poppy didn't know how to fight – not properly. If Fred really wanted to he could easily overpower her.

The knowledge crept up Poppy's spine like an ice-cold spider.

I'm in trouble, she thought, just as he finally ripped away the compression sleeve on her arm.

"...how?" Fred asked after an agonisingly long silence, voice eerily quiet. He stared at the smooth, unmarred skin of Poppy's forearm, which was trembling beneath his fingers. "How come you don't have a scar? How come you're completely fine?"

"Fred, leave me alone—"

"*How do you heal so quickly?!*"

"I don't know!"

"I don't believe you!"

"Why would I lie about this?!"

Poppy frantically tried to pull away from Fred; he viciously pushed her against the fridge and pinned her in place with a hand on her throat.

"Because you lie about *everything,*" he hissed, taking an unreasonable amount of pleasure from seeing Poppy's nails desperately scrabbling at his hand in an attempt to free herself. Fred only squeezed her neck tighter until she choked. "You and Kapros are up to something," he continued, "and I want to know what it is. I want to know why I can do *this* and you heal right back up."

Fred slashed Poppy's arm open with startling power and speed; she cried out, coughing and spluttering, when Fred finally released her neck, then frantically clutched her bleeding arm to her chest. But the proverbial damage had been done – the cut had already healed, and Fred had witnessed it happen.

He shook his head in disbelief. "What *are* you, King?"

"Stop this, Fred!" Poppy made another attempt to push past him, making it within five feet of the door when she felt the cold bite of steel slice into her thigh. She collapsed to her knees and then down to the floor when Fred removed the knife and plunged it into her back, straight through one of her kidneys.

Poppy screamed. She couldn't stop. She had thought it was painful falling from the climbing wall; she'd thought it was bad when Dorian first mutilated her arm and drank from her. But those incidents were nothing compared to the excruciating pain of Fred removing the knife and stabbing Poppy through her liver, then slashing her hamstrings, before jamming the blade into the meat of her shoulder.

"*Fred!*" Poppy begged, coughing up mouthful after mouthful of blood when Fred paused long enough for her to drag herself away a few precious inches. She knew the wounds he was inflicting were healing. She knew he was watching.

She knew if she didn't get away that she would die and Poppy realised, with aching clarity, that she wasn't ready for death after all. She wanted to *live.* There were still people in the club to save. People she wanted to say goodbye to. People she loved.

Poppy had thought her life ended the moment she'd handed it over to Dorian.

She'd been wrong.

Behind her, Fred laughed cruelly as Poppy's body continued healing itself. The floor was slippery with blood. *Her* blood. It covered Poppy's – no, Dorian's – T-shirt and soaked into her skin. When she risked a glance at Fred she saw he'd been splattered with it.

Along with his gleaming eyes, the twisted set of his mouth and the garbled laugh that followed, Poppy concluded that Frederick Sampson had gone completely insane. *When did this happen?* Poppy thought through her blind terror. *When did Fred become so undone? Why didn't I notice?*

But Poppy knew why she hadn't noticed. She'd never spared Fred and his mental state a second thought in her entire life.

"Where do you think you're going?" Fred called out when Poppy tried to haul herself towards the door once more, flipping her onto her back. She mouthed a wordless scream when the action sent jarring waves of pain through her currently-healing organs.

When Fred plunged the knife into Poppy's stomach all she could do was sob. She'd lost so much blood – and she'd been too weak to begin with.

Fred continued laughing as her flesh tried to heal itself around the knife. "You're a monster, King," he murmured. He pulled out the blade and slashed through Poppy's T-shirt, over and over again until she was covered in bleeding, biting wounds. "Completely inhuman."

"You're...the monster," Poppy barely got out. She was losing consciousness; this was simply too much pain for her to bear. As a cut healed Fred merely replaced it with a new one, until there was not a single inch of Poppy's skin left untouched by blood. Even her hair was drenched in it.

Fred barked out a laugh at her comment. "Does it even count when you heal this quickly? In five minutes nobody will know I hurt you at all!"

"*You're killing me!*"

"No I'm not!" he screamed, slamming the knife back into Poppy's stomach with both hands. It was so painful she blacked out for a second, but she regained consciousness when he removed the blade. "You can't die! You can't die, otherwise when you fell from the climbing wall you would have! I'm not doing *anything* to you!"

In desperation Poppy arched her neck back to look at the door, wondering how she could possibly reach it. It was all she could do to withhold a gasp when she realised someone was watching through the glass panel.

Andrew.

A horrified, stricken, shaking Andrew, who clearly had no idea what to do.

Poppy did.

Dorian, she mouthed. *Get Dorian. Get Dorian. Get Dorian.*

When Andrew disappeared Poppy turned her attention back to Fred, who was too engrossed in his violent, psychotic breakdown to have noticed what had just transpired.

"Tell me what's going on, King!" he demanded, though Poppy was growing limp beneath him. "Tell me why you're like this!"

"Don't...know..."

Poppy's eyelids fluttered. She'd lost too much blood. She was going to die. She was going to die and, even then, she was still refusing to tell Fred about Dorian's plan.

Stubborn and stupid to the end, she thought hazily. *To think Frederick Sampson would be the death of me.*

When the door slammed open and Fred was wrenched away from her Poppy instinctively knew who was responsible. "Dorian," she cried weakly, though her vision was too blurry for her to make him out.

Then she closed her eyes and slipped into nothing.

CIARAN RADIN-KIRKWOOD

DORIAN

DORIAN DIDN'T EVEN REVERT TO HIS true form when he threw open the kitchen door and flung Fred off Poppy as if he were weightless. He didn't have to.

With what Andrew had told him Dorian could easily rip a man in half using human hands alone.

When Dorian awoke to the sound of frantic, heavy banging on his door he'd known something was wrong. He hadn't expected, however, to open his door to a hyperventilating Andrew Forbes. But all it took was for Andrew to mouth the word *Poppy* and Dorian was racing out of his room, immediately awake and urging Andrew forward to take him to her.

The sight before him in the kitchen was sickening, in a way that watching members of his kind consume humans never had been. It was a bloodbath. *Poppy's* bloodbath. Dorian could just barely make out her pale, unfocused eyes through the crimson of her skin.

"Dorian," was all Poppy said before her eyes closed. Dorian was stricken, thinking for one awful moment that she was dead. But he could see her chest rising and falling; proof that Poppy was still alive.

But not for long, he thought, bending down and very carefully sweeping Poppy into his arms. She was slick and slippery with blood. The metallic tang of the stuff filled Dorian's nostrils, waking in him a desperate longing to drink it despite the terrible situation Poppy was in.

The realisation that followed caused Dorian to freeze. The kitchen was covered in *Poppy's* blood. His staff couldn't go near it. If they did they'd know what it was. So Dorian turned and stared at Andrew, who grew steadily more ashen as he took in Fred's unconscious body lying in a crumpled heap by the fridge.

Then the young man stared at Poppy and burst into tears. "She's not dead she's not dead she's not—"

"Don't worry, Andrew, she'll be okay," Dorian said, forcing his voice to remain soft and calm.

But Andrew couldn't comprehend this. He merely shook his head and cried harder. "I saw him – I saw Fred with the knife. Over and over again. How is Poppy not d-dead?"

With a hand he realised was shaking, Dorian lifted up one of Poppy's arms. Though it was happening worryingly slowly compared to usual, the multitude of criss-crossed gashes on her skin were healing before Andrew and Dorian's very eyes.

"You can't tell anyone about how special Poppy is, Andrew," Dorian said in answer to the awe and disbelief evident in Andrew's eyes. "Nobody can know. *Nobody.* Do you understand?"

Andrew raised a hand and helplessly gestured towards the state of the kitchen. "People will know when they see this. Or Fred will say—"

"Fred won't say anything or I'll slit his throat," Dorian spat out, meaning every word of it. "Andrew, look at me. Don't look at Poppy. I need you to clean this mess up. Every last drop of blood. And get Fred back to his room unnoticed. Can you do that?"

"No!" was Andrew's immediate reply. The look on his face suggested he might be sick. Dorian couldn't blame him. "What about your staff? Can't they do it?"

"No. Absolutely not."

"Why?"

If Dorian's arms weren't full carrying Poppy he'd have dragged a hand across his face. But if Poppy could be endlessly patient with Andrew then so could he. "I can't explain it right now, Andrew," he said. "I need to help Poppy. But if anyone were to come across the kitchen like this then Poppy would be in trouble. *More* trouble. You don't want that, do you?"

Andrew slowly shook his head.

"Is anyone else awake? Why were *you* awake?"

"Nobody else is awake as far as I know," Andrew mumbled. "And I – um, I couldn't sleep, and I knocked on Poppy's door because I knew she hadn't been sleeping well lately, either. But she wasn't there so...I went looking for her."

Dorian could have hugged the man for loving Poppy so hopelessly. It had, quite literally, saved her life. He settled for smiling at him instead. "You're a good person, Andrew, and an even better friend to Poppy. Do her this one huge favour and clean up the mess in here. I swear you'll get an explanation when I can give you one."

As soon as Andrew, still full of reluctance, nodded, Dorian whisked Poppy away with him to the first floor of the east wing on swift, silent feet. When he closed his bedroom door behind them he grabbed a large blanket and covered the duvet with it before gently placing Poppy down upon his bed.

Beneath the thick layer of blood Dorian saw Fred had torn through Poppy's clothes.

She's wearing my T-shirt, he realised in horror. It gave him an overwhelming urge to vomit – to look at the tattered, bloody material and to know that, had Dorian indulged his urge to keep bothering Poppy rather than dutifully giving her space, he might have prevented what Fred had done.

He was the one watching us in the meadow two weeks ago, Dorian concluded, certain. *He saw me drink from Poppy. He was merely waiting for an opportunity to corner Poppy on her own.*

Even if Poppy had screamed and shouted at him to go away Dorian should never have allowed her to be alone for a single second. Having her hate him was infinitely better than what had just transpired. Now Dorian didn't even know where to start helping her: Poppy was as crimson as her name. A complete and utter mess.

He didn't know what to do, so he did what he did best.

Dorian drank her blood.

With every drop of Poppy's blood on his tongue Dorian hated himself more and more because all he *wanted* was more of it. In places the blood had already begun to dry; he rubbed it away with shaking fingertips.

Poppy's eyes were roving beneath their lids, signalling that she might wake up at any moment. But Dorian didn't want her to wake up – not when her skin was stained red and the cuts on her body were taking an achingly long time to heal.

His stomach lurched when he cleared enough blood away to fully visualise the deep, vicious marks on Poppy's stomach that told him Fred hadn't merely cut her skin-deep. He'd stabbed right through her organs, something only further confirmed when Dorian gingerly rolled Poppy onto her front to see if Fred had done any damage to her back.

He cut her to ribbons, over and over again, Dorian thought, appalled. For below the gashes which were in the process of healing lay even more, already sealed cuts which would have long since disappeared had Fred not continued hacking away at Poppy's body.

"I should have killed him," he spat out as he turned Poppy onto her back once more. "I should have gutted him like the snake he is."

"No..."

Dorian was startled out of his thunderous thoughts by the word. Poppy's eyes fluttered open, so he abandoned his half-finished clean-up job in order to sit by her head and smooth away her blood-sodden hair. The faded silver streak had taken up the colour so well it was scarlet; Dorian wondered if it would remain red forever.

"Don't try to speak," he soothed, stroking Poppy's cheek so gently he just barely brushed it with his hand. Her face had been the one part of Poppy Fred hadn't touched. Dorian didn't have it in him to wonder why.

When Poppy's eyes finally opened all the way she immediately cried out and tried to recoil from Dorian. But he held her in place, though he hated having to do so.

"Poppy, it's me!" he told her, trying very hard not to hurt her as Poppy struggled against his grip. "It's Dorian! Fred isn't here! Please – you have to calm down. Take a breath. You're okay."

Poppy's chest heaved as she struggled to follow Dorian's orders. She slapped her hands against her stomach as if expecting to have to hold all her organs in. When she realised the wound had closed up, however, Poppy's eyes lost some of their panicked glaze and her breathing slowed.

"I'm not dead," she whispered.

"No. Not dead. Only nearly," Dorian replied, smiling

slightly despite how genuinely close he'd been to losing Poppy.

She shivered. "I've never been in so much pain. And the blood – there was so much blood. Dorian—"

He pulled her in against his chest before he could stop himself, rocking back and forth when Poppy's breathing began to grow more erratic. "You don't have to talk about it, Poppy. It's okay. You're okay."

"Is he – is Fred—"

"Dead?" Dorian guessed. His expression darkened. "No. But he should be. Are you still against sacrificing him?"

"No."

Poppy's answer was so immediate and resolute that it took Dorian by surprise. He pulled away from her an inch to watch her expression, but there was no uncertainty to be found there. "...this week?"

She shook her head. "No. Grace Kang is this week. And Ciaran Radin-Kirkwood is next week. I'm done trying to be fucking unbiased. If they're going to talk about me like I'm the worst person on the planet then I'll be that person. They can rot in hell. And Rich stays – Nate's best friend."

"That's...and Fred?" Dorian was thoroughly confused by Poppy's dramatic shift in attitude towards how she picked her sacrifices. Not that he was complaining: he rather enjoyed the malicious look on Poppy's face.

"Last," Poppy muttered. She held up an arm to inspect it – the one she'd originally fallen on – and laughed bitterly. "He can be last, and his suspicions and fears can eat him up inside until there's nothing left, and then he'll know what's been going on all along, and he can regret ever thinking it wise to torture me."

"Poppy, wouldn't it be much safer to get rid of him sooner rather than—"

"I want him to know I could have saved him," she interrupted, sure of herself even though she was shaking. "I want him to *know* he signed his own death warrant. I want him to know that he fucked everything up all on his own. All he had to do was trust me, like I trusted him even though I hated him."

Dorian said nothing. This was an entirely new side to Poppy King – one that nobody else had likely ever seen. A vengeful, almost-broken woman who had been pushed too far. Dorian knew he was largely responsible for that. He didn't regret it one bit. For if it drew Poppy into his arms as she waved goodbye to her remaining ties to humanity how could Dorian be upset about it? He'd simply have to take it upon himself to terrify Fred into silence before he said anything to anyone.

Then Poppy sighed and all her vengeance was gone. She glanced at Dorian. "Where's Andrew? What happened to him?"

He smiled. "Andrew will be fine. Focus on getting better and then you can thank him. I imagine he'll stick to you closer than ever before after what happened."

"I owe him my life."

"And so do I. You really did choose the *best* person in your club to save above everyone else, Poppy."

Poppy's eyes shone too brightly at that. She sniffled back a few tears, gingerly running a hand through her hair before promptly stopping when she realised how disgusting it felt. Her face twisted into a grimace as she looked down at her bloody appearance, and then –

She noticed the blood-drenched, tattered remains of the T-shirt currently clinging to her skin. It wasn't nearly enough fabric to protect Poppy's modesty. Her eyes grew wide with an entirely different kind of horror, and her face flushed with embarrassment.

Dorian could only laugh. "Are you honestly more concerned about how naked you are than the fact you're covered in blood, Poppy? Someone needs to realign your priorities."

She rolled her eyes. "*You're* dressed. I'm allowed to be mortified."

"Easily fixed," he murmured, hoisting his top up and over his head before dropping it on the floor. But when he reached down to remove his trousers Poppy grabbed his wrist to stop him.

"Okay, you're taking it *way* too far, Dorian."

"That's where you're wrong: I never take it far *enough.*"

Dorian pulled what remained of Poppy's T-shirt off before she could properly react to what he'd said, then with the utmost gentleness pushed her back down onto the bed.

"Dorian—"

His mouth traced the line of her collarbone, tongue flicking out to taste the blood on her skin. Much of Poppy's chest was still covered in the stuff. Now that the mood had changed Dorian was intent on enjoying every last drop of it – as well as the body beneath it.

Being very careful not to put any of his weight on her, Dorian climbed on top of Poppy. He slid a hand down her stomach, past her navel, and beneath her underwear. When she gasped he grinned. "Something tells me you're not in a position to push me away this time," he said, before trailing kisses down her neck.

"Something tells me I'm not in a position to be *doing* this."

He chuckled. "Don't worry; I won't do much. Just...explore a little."

When his mouth reached Poppy's breasts he licked and nibbled on them eagerly, using his free hand to fondle them even as Poppy reached down as if to stop him. But her hand paused inches from Dorian's. He stared at her, eyebrow raised in question.

"Argh, *fine,*" Poppy bit out, throwing her head back against the pillow with as much strength as she had left in her, which wasn't much at all.

"Excellent."

There was no more talking for a while after that, the only sound Poppy's hitched breathing until even that was swallowed by Dorian's mouth on hers. And though Dorian was high from her blood, and though he was desperate to shed the rest of his clothes and violate Poppy the way he'd been imagining doing so all summer, he held himself back.

He held himself back even when Poppy wrapped her bloody arms around his neck and urged him closer, and when she curled a foot around the back of his leg, and when she moaned and pushed up against his groin. For Poppy's skin was still a network of crisscrossed cuts and half-healed gashes, and she barely had enough blood in her to survive.

A few days, Dorian thought excitedly. Poppy cried out in pleasure a moment later, Dorian having finally pushed her over the edge. Her fingers tensed up in his hair before relaxing all at once with the rest of her. *In a few days Poppy will be fine, and then I'll fuck her senseless. But not tonight.*

No; tonight was for gentle kisses and cleaning the rest of Poppy's body with warm water and a soft sponge before she curled up against him. Tonight was for watching Poppy slowly fall into a contented and exhausted sleep, for once reaching unconsciousness in front of him neither fearful nor disgusted nor upset.

Dorian nuzzled his face into Poppy's hair. It smelled of tea tree now, not blood. Her silver streak no longer contained a trace of red, either, something which Dorian was amazed by. He'd been sure it would be stained forever.

"Mine," he murmured sleepily, holding onto Poppy as tightly as he dared.

For in a mere month Poppy *would* be his and no-one else's.

PAUL TOBIN

ANDREW

"Andrew? Earth to Andrew? Hello...?"

It took Andrew a few seconds to realise somebody was talking to him. He was so exhausted. He hadn't slept, having spent the small hours of the morning cleaning a literal bloodbath and hauling his former friend and wannabe-murderer back to bed as if nothing had happened.

But something awful *had* happened. And Andrew couldn't process it.

"Please leave me alone, Rachelle," he eventually muttered when he realised who had spoken.

She frowned. "Andrew, are you okay? I can't find Poppy anywhere. And Fred won't come out of his—"

"*Don't talk to me about him!*"

Rachelle took a step back in shock, clearly having never expected an outburst like that from Andrew. She held her hands up in a placating gesture. "I'm sorry, Andrew," she said. "I didn't mean to upset you. I'll leave you alone."

Andrew said nothing. Eventually Rachelle sighed and left, and Andrew clutched his knees to his chest to rock back and forth on the armchair he was sitting in. It was a glorious day outside so most of the club wasn't around to see him this close to a break down. For how could he not break down? What Andrew had seen – what Poppy had gone through—

"How is she alive how is she alive how is she alive how is she—"

"Andrew, buddy, are you okay?"

Andrew nearly screamed. But he held it in; he had to. If he started screaming he'd never stop. When he looked up he saw Paul Tobin, a third year student who very much preferred Poppy's way of teaching to Fred's.

Don't think about him.

"Shit, Andrew, you're not okay," Paul exclaimed quickly when he saw the pained expression on Andrew's face. He ran a hand through his hair. "What is it Poppy does? She said it was – pressure? Andrew, do you want a blanket? Or do you want to go in the pool? Or—"

Andrew just barely had enough mental capacity to realise Paul was genuinely trying to help him. And everything he was suggesting were things *Poppy* had taught him in case he ever needed to help Andrew.

His heart hurt. It ached. He knew exactly what he needed.

He stood up. "I just need Poppy." And then, because it would be rude otherwise, Andrew added, "Thank you, Paul."

He rushed off towards the west wing before Paul could say another word, though Andrew committed to memory his kindness. He'd tell Poppy about it, and Paul would get to go home.

Andrew didn't even bother going to the infirmary. After Poppy's collapse in the caves he knew Dorian likely had her up in his bedroom. That only made Andrew's heart hurt more, but it also filled him with something red-hot that felt like anger but Andrew now understood to be jealousy.

How does he get to be with her even when Poppy isn't speaking to him? Why did she ask for him *to save her?*

Andrew knew that last question wasn't fair, for he'd never have been able to push Fred off of Poppy – let alone been able to help her afterwards. Dorian had been the right call, and Poppy knew it.

It didn't make Andrew hurt any less.

When he knocked on the door it was Dorian who answered, which wasn't surprising. The older man looked worn out, though he smiled politely enough when he realised who was at his door. "Andrew. I should have known. Poppy's awake – do you want to come in?"

He nodded, not trusting his voice. When Dorian let him in Andrew couldn't believe his eyes. For there sat Poppy in Dorian's bed, wearing a navy shirt that was far too large for her with her long hair pulled back in a haphazard ponytail. There was no blood. No gaping wounds. Even the network of cuts that had littered her skin seemed to have all but disappeared, though Poppy was still very pale and her cheeks were sunken.

She grinned when she saw him, all flashing teeth and genuine delight. "Andrew, my saviour! What was with you waiting until afternoon to see—"

Andrew launched himself at her. Forgetting that Poppy was still frail; forgetting that he found most physical contact awkward and uncomfortable; forgetting that he was twenty-two and not ten, Andrew threw himself onto the bed and crushed Poppy in his arms, burying his head against her neck to hide the tears in his eyes.

When he felt Poppy stroking his hair he only hugged her harder.

"Dorian, can you give us some privacy?" Poppy asked of the

other man. Andrew was happy about this because he did not want anybody else to see him act so vulnerable, and he liked the fact Poppy was putting him above Dorian.

"Of course. I'll drop by downstairs and grab some food. You want anything, Andrew?"

Andrew said nothing, but he felt Poppy nod her head on his behalf. Andrew was also happy about this because he was, in fact, starving. He was fairly certain he'd never be able to enter the kitchen in Dorian's facility ever again.

When Dorian's footsteps disappeared down the corridor Poppy dug her fingers into the back of Andrew's head; he stiffened immediately. "Andrew," she murmured, "you have no idea how grateful I am that you saved my life. But we don't have time to sit here and cry about it. Because it's not just *my* life you saved."

He didn't say anything, because he didn't know *what* to say, so eventually Poppy continued, "I'm going to tell you some things, and they're going to sound insane, but you're going to have to believe me anyway. Can you do that?"

Now that Poppy was finally confiding in him Andrew found that he didn't like it. He didn't like it at all. Countless possibilities that explained what had been going on all summer ran through his head – none of them good. But Poppy was telling *him* – not Rachelle or Nate or Casey. She was telling him, Andrew Martin Forbes.

He had to be a man and listen.

Andrew pulled away from Poppy, smeared his palm across his eyes until no tears remained, and nodded. "I'm listening."

"Good. Because after I've told you everything you have to help me do something ridiculous. Something impossible."

"...and what's the impossible thing?"

Poppy smiled grimly, her eyes shining with a determination he hadn't seen in a long time. "We're going to escape the

Highlands Adrenaline Sports Facility."

FRED

When Fred came to he simultaneously felt like he'd woken from a nightmare and jumped straight into a new one. He stared down at his shaking hands, which were dark with dried blood and red as—

"Poppy."

A knock on the door caused Fred to flinch, for how could he let anyone in when he was awash with blood? "Don't come in!" he called out, struggling to reign in the panic in his voice. "I'm not feeling very—"

"You don't get a choice in the matter."

The door opened and closed as Dorian let himself in, his usually genial face twisted into something thunderous and malicious. It turned to disgust when he swept his eyes up and down Fred's bloody appearance.

Fred didn't know what to say. He hadn't even processed what had occurred in the small hours of the morning. But he had accused Poppy and Dorian of planning something over and over again as he plunged a knife into Poppy's body and—

"You will not speak a word of what happened between you and Poppy, Sampson," Dorian said quietly as he took a few steps towards him. "You won't voice any of your suspicions that something's wrong. You will act no differently than you did before."

Fred swallowed. "..and if I don't?"

When the very edges of Dorian's body began to blur and morph into something else Fred was sure he must still be sleeping. But he wasn't, even though he desperately wished he was. For Dorian grew taller – much taller. His hands curled into claws and his teeth grew sharp. His head became encircled in horns, his ears elongated to points, and his legs grew huge, furred and hoofed. Even Dorian's eyes seemed changed somehow; there was something animalistic and entirely inhuman about his dark, barred pupils. And they were too blue. Shining, glimmering, glacial.

When Dorian grabbed Fred's neck and pinned him against the wall Fred was starkly reminded of having done the very same thing to Poppy mere hours before. A low growl began in the back of Dorian's throat. "I'll say the same thing to you that I said to Poppy weeks ago: if you speak a word to anyone, you won't live to see the next day. Understand?"

Numbly, because Fred couldn't speak with Dorian's clawed hand crushing his throat, he nodded. And then the pressure on his neck was gone, and as quickly as Dorian had transformed he reverted to being a human. With one final glare at Fred he turned and left his room.

What have I done? Fred panicked, rushing to his en suite and throwing himself in the shower in his desperation to be rid of the blood caked into his skin. *Poppy is innocent. She's* innocent. *She's abnormal and I hate her and she's innocent.*

And Fred had tried to kill her. Even though he hadn't intended to. Even though he'd never been a violent person before. He'd tried to *murder* someone.

Something told him the act wasn't going to go unpunished.

INTERLUDE VI

GRACE HADN'T BEEN TOUCHED – YET. *By the looks of the rest of the club members in the room that was strange. Even Ciaran, who had only been brought in a day ago, had lost his tongue. But that strangeness was replaced by dread when she finally asked a question about her best friend.*

"Where's Angelica?"

Nobody answered. They didn't have to.

MAX MARSHALL

POPPY

A FULL WEEK HAD PASSED SINCE Andrew and Dorian saved Poppy's life. She'd spent most of that time recovering in Dorian's bed; it hadn't taken much to convince the rest of the club that she had fallen ill. Her health had been all over the place for weeks, after all, and she'd taken the argument with Casey badly. When Poppy finally left Dorian's bedroom she could tell by the looks on everyone's faces that they felt horribly guilty about ignoring her.

Now they were overcompensating, and Poppy found it suffocating.

"Poppy, you really do seem to be working overtime to try and kill yourself these days!"

"Remember it's okay to take a break now and then. Don't overwork yourself."

"Hey, I'm sure if you went to Casey and apologised she'd—"

"*Thank you, everyone,*" Poppy cut in, trying her hardest to keep her irritation and – though she'd never had to deal with it before this summer – anxiety from her face. Out of the corner of her eye she saw Nate smiling nervously as if he was unsure whether it was okay for him to approach Poppy after days of not speaking to her.

Poppy closed the gap between them in answer to his unspoken question. "Hey," she said, "are we okay, Nate? Or are things still weird?"

He laughed in relief, running a hand through his faded silver hair – it was in need of a re-dye. "Of course, Morph. I'm sorry I've been a dick."

"You'd have to *talk* to me to be a dick, you dick."

"Point taken. But even so...Poppy, are *you* okay?" Nate's question was asked very quietly, for Poppy's ears only. From the frown of concern on his face she understood very clearly that the question was about more than merely their relationship.

She sighed. "Rich told you, didn't he? About finding me in the kitchen." Poppy barely suppressed a shudder at the memory of what had directly followed Nate's best friend leaving the kitchen, but to her relief Nate didn't notice.

"He may have...mentioned it, yeah," he replied, eyes on the floor as if he was ashamed of himself. "And I didn't – I really didn't mean to make you feel so bad. And I know Casey didn't, either. Or anyone else in the club for that matter. But—"

"Nate, it's okay," Poppy cut in, feeling wildly uncomfortable by his apology. "None of you did anything wrong. Not even Casey. I mean, she was *right*. She—"

"Poppy, let me finish."

She was taken aback by the seriousness in Nate's voice. He looked her square in the eyes, the deep brown of his irises clouded over by something Poppy couldn't quite understand. But she nodded silently, allowing Nate to finish what he was trying to say unimpeded.

"You don't...you really don't confide in anyone about anything serious, Morph. Not even Rachelle, and she's your best friend. There's been something wrong with you all summer – something really wrong – and it seems like you can't trust any of your friends to help you through it. Except maybe Andrew, but something tells me you aren't being completely honest with him either."

Poppy winced. Until a week ago everything Nate had just said was scarily accurate. But now Andrew *did* know everything. About the monsters, and the human trafficking, and the state of everyone who had gone missing over summer so far. Poppy had laid it all on Andrew's shoulders so quickly she was unsure he had really taken it all in.

But he had to. Poppy *did* need help, and she wasn't afraid to admit it now.

It just...couldn't be Nate that helped her. Or even Rachelle. Poppy couldn't find it in her to drag them into her nightmare. But Andrew had worked things out – Andrew, who was simultaneously the most observant and densest person Poppy had ever met. Andrew, who had saved her life. Come hell or high water he was in this with her.

"Morph...?"

Poppy shook her head sadly. "You're right, Nate. Of course you are. But I'm just...very confused right now. About my life. About where it's going when summer ends. It's not really something you or anyone else can help with."

"That's bullshit!"

"No, it's the truth," she fired back, hackles raised on instinct by the tone of Nate's voice. But the look of hurt he gave her caused Poppy to calm down immediately. "I'm sorry," she mumbled, turning away for her bedroom before she could say anything else to further damage her already doomed relationship with Nate.

Poppy wished the summer could be over already. That everything that was going to happen had happened and she could move on with whatever life she had left once the dust finally settled. But that was impossible. She had too much to do.

When she caught Casey watching her with a torn expression on her face Poppy forced herself to ignore her. She didn't have time to deal with petty apologies over rivalries that didn't matter, even though that very rivalry had been what drove Casey into Patrick's arms in the first place.

No, Poppy told herself. *Casey would have slept with him anyway. And Dorian was never going to deny Patrick's request to have her, either. Casey was a lost cause from the start.*

But that didn't make her friend's fate any easier to bear... nor did it make Poppy's own conflicting feelings for Dorian easier to ignore. She hated herself for the way she felt about him. And yet it was Dorian who had saved her from a man, not the other way around. Fred was as much a monster as Dorian was, and he didn't have the excuse that he needed to eat humans to survive.

Poppy retched simply thinking about Fred; when she reached the corridor containing the board members' bedrooms her heart raced wildly upon spying his door.

When it opened she almost screamed.

"King, please—"

"Get the hell away from me," she mouthed, words silent on her terrified tongue as she wrenched open her own door and slammed it in Fred's pale, despicable face.

"Poppy, open the door! Let me explain! Poppy—"

"Leave her the fuck alone, Fred."

Poppy's eyes darted to her door. The voice was Andrew's, though she'd never heard it sound so harsh. He never, *ever* swore.

"Andrew," Poppy heard Fred protest, his voice almost as manic as it had been when he'd attacked her, "you don't understand. I have to—"

"I understand more than you think. Don't go near her again."

A stretch of awkward, agonised silence fell and then, after another few moments, Poppy heard the angry slamming of a door.

"I won't let him near you," Andrew mumbled just loud enough for Poppy to hear, all the previously sharp edges gone from his voice. "I won't, I swear, Poppy, so just rest, okay?"

A surge of affection hit Poppy like a train. This was the same Andrew who always came running to her whenever he was feeling anxious or confused or bothered by something – who would knock on her door at two in the morning to ask Poppy some ridiculous question that was, of course, not ridiculous to Andrew at all.

And now he was protecting her despite everything she'd told him about her deal with Dorian Kapros.

Poppy stifled a sob.

Resting was the last thing she had time to do.

DONALD BROWN

DORIAN

"Poppy King, get over here."

Dorian watched Poppy hesitate before complying with Nick's request. Nick was standing at the base of the cliffs behind the facility, hand shielding his eyes from the sun as he looked up at them with a calculated expression colouring his features.

Everyone was outside in the meadow enjoying the pleasant weather before the ominous clouds creeping over the horizon ruined it with the inevitable promise of rain. Nate and Rich had strung up a net to play volleyball; Aisling was watching them play from her sprawled position on a blanket, a floppy, oversized hat protecting her pale skin from the sun, whilst Steven was playing cards with Patrick and some of the club members Dorian hadn't much bothered to talk to before.

For the first time that summer Dorian felt deeply uncomfortable knowing that his 'scouts' were interacting with people they fully expected to die. But it was Nick calling Poppy over that concerned Dorian for now: the glint of interest in the man's eye was not something he especially relished.

Dorian knew Nick was interested in buying Poppy. More than interested, going by his comments over the past couple of weeks. Dorian had hoped Poppy's propensity to pass out and become bedridden for several days at a time would have deterred Nick, but no. If anything it had served to fuel his interest in Poppy, which Dorian did not understand in the slightest.

If only she didn't bloody show off, he thought wretchedly, though Dorian knew that – most of the time – Poppy wasn't deliberately showing off at all. She merely thrived when she was climbing and swimming and running and diving and just about anything else physical. Dorian never saw her more alive than when she had a particularly difficult goal in mind that she fully intended to smash.

"What's up, Nick?" Poppy asked carefully when she reached his side. Though Poppy always seemed small next to Dorian – since even in human form he towered over her – next to Nick's height pared with his broad chest and shoulders she looked absolutely tiny. He didn't want to think about how easily Nick's true form could break her in two.

Nick's nodded up at the cliffs. "How high d'you reckon you could make it free-climbing? Without chickening out, I mean."

Oh fuck no.

Despite her knowing exactly why Nick was asking, and innately understanding how foolish and downright dangerous it was to react to his question, Dorian could only watch helplessly as Poppy readjusted her ponytail with a fiery expression that yelled *challenge accepted.*

"Just watch and see," she said, a suicidal smirk on her face, and that was that. She began scaling the side of the cliff without so much as a glance in Dorian's direction.

"For fuck's sake, Poppy!" Dorian howled before he could

stop himself, garnering far more attention than he wanted to bring upon the situation. He bolted towards the base of the cliff where an amused and very impressed Nick stood observing Poppy's daredevil ascent.

Though everyone had now stopped what they were doing to watch what was going on with varied reactions of curiosity, joy, concern and outright terror, Dorian knew that nothing anybody said was going to draw Poppy back down to the meadow.

Which meant he had to go *up* to her.

Shaking his head at how ridiculous the situation had become, Dorian spared half a second to sweep his gaze across Poppy's rapt audience one final time. He spied Fred sitting at a picnic table, his lunch all but forgotten as he stared helplessly at the person he'd so viciously attacked who was, for all intents and purposes, completely fine.

Dorian didn't want to think about Fred, because then he'd murder him in front of everyone for sure, so he located the best place to begin scaling the cliff and promptly started doing so. Poppy was well ahead of him, but it didn't matter.

He wasn't a *mountain goat* for nothing.

"Oh my god – how is Dorian so fast?!" he heard Casey exclaim in wonder far down below him, as Dorian rapidly closed the gap between himself and Poppy. He relished the strain on his muscles as he pushed them to support his reckless climb. The burn of them. The adrenaline urging him higher. It was the closest Dorian's body had felt to being *his* in a long time.

He was satisfied when Poppy paused long enough to turn her head and see what was going on; the grin that spread across her face when she realised Dorian was just five feet below her made him giddy.

"I wondered how stupid I'd have to be for you to actually climb, Dorian," she laughed, clearly full of just as much delirious adrenaline as he was. Her laugh propelled him up the cliff even faster until, in the space of a second, Dorian surpassed her.

"You're so slow!" he teased, soaking up the clamour of the watching audience like a sponge.

Below them Rachelle was shrieking in terror. "Come back, Poppy! Don't you remember what happened last time? *You're going to fall!*"

"As if I'd let that happen again!" Poppy called back between heaving breaths, her body working punishingly hard to keep up with Dorian's breakneck climbing pace.

"If you fall from up there you'll *die.*"

She merely laughed like the somewhat mentally unhinged, invincible being that she was. Now that Dorian was up on the cliff with her instead of down below watching with everyone else, he found he no longer cared that Poppy was showing off and acting dangerously. Dorian had never met anyone so suited to being with him in his entire life. It didn't matter that Nick would undoubtedly push to buy Poppy even harder after this.

He would never have her.

Nobody would, except for Dorian.

POPPY

When Poppy finally reached the top of the cliff, lungs burning for air and muscles twitching, she found Dorian sprawled on the grass laughing like a madman.

"Too...slow," he got out, eyes full of mirth as Poppy

collapsed beside him.

"Fucking goat," she muttered, words barely audible between her gasps for air. Up at the top the two of them could no longer hear what anyone in the meadow was shouting below them; it was bliss. Poppy had learned to enjoy peace and quiet during the week she'd spent recovering in Dorian's room – something which she previously had no patience for.

But the very thought of spending time in Dorian's room caused Poppy's mind to wander and her heart to thump for reasons entirely unrelated to scaling a cliff. For despite what had occurred between Poppy and Dorian after Fred attacked her – Poppy's eyebrow twitched at the memory – Dorian had since then resolutely kept his hands off her. Even though, in reality, Poppy had fully recovered physically from her ordeal after only four days, he'd remained a respectful, gentle distance from her.

I don't understand what game he's playing, Poppy mused, turning her head to stare at Dorian with no shame whatsoever. He stared right back. Nothing but silence passed between them, and then—

"Who are you giving up and saving this week?" Dorian asked, souring the mood immediately.

Poppy scowled. "Why would you...ask such a thing *now*?"

"Because I don't want the question to interfere with what happens next."

Another thump of her heart against her ribcage. "And what would that be?"

When Dorian glanced at the knotted grove of trees some distance behind them Poppy felt her spirits soar. She'd been wanting to explore up here ever since she'd first spied the forest from Dorian's bedroom weeks ago.

"How did you know I wanted to check that forest out?"

Dorian smiled softly. "I didn't. It's where I was born,

though, so I always wanted to show you it."

Oh.

"You were...born in a forest?"

"Let's get the difficult stuff out of the way first. I'd rather like to enjoy the afternoon before – ah, never mind," he murmured just as a drop of rain fell on his face.

"A bit of rain never stopped me before," Poppy said. Then, when it began to fall in earnest, "And it certainly won't now."

"That was the right answer." Dorian flipped gracefully onto his feet before holding out a hand to help Poppy back up. She didn't take it, instead fighting her exhausted muscles to stand up by herself. Dorian merely rolled his eyes. "You're allowed to accept help *sometimes,* you know."

The remark caused Poppy to remember what Nate had told her a few days ago, which Poppy didn't like thinking about at all. "Max Marshall," she said in order to hide her discomfort. "The one with red hair playing cards with Steven. I'm sacrificing him."

"Any particular reason why?"

"I'm running out of good reasons," she admitted. "He doesn't really have any aspirations for his life. I suppose I didn't before we arrived at your damn facility, either, so it's a shitty reason to sacrifice someone. But I guess it'll have to do."

Dorian didn't comment on this. He shook raindrops from his face before asking, "And who are you saving?"

"Donald. That quiet guy who's friends with Paul. Nice guy. Training to be a doctor."

"Definitely a good reason to *save* someone."

Poppy grimaced. "Can we stop talking about this stuff now?"

"Oh, absolutely," Dorian said. "And with that..." He walked over to the edge of the cliff, then looked down and waved like an idiot at the people down below. When a wall of shouting hit him Dorian merely laughed. Poppy couldn't help but join him for a moment, giving Nate the finger when she spied his tiny figure giving her the same gesture.

"Would you agree they can't see past the actual edge of the cliff, Poppy?" Dorian asked when he backed away from the cliff towards the forest.

She eyed him curiously. "I'm fairly certain they'd have to be in your bedroom to get any kind of view of the top. Why?"

"Excellent."

"Dorian, what – *why are you dropping your human form?*"

For no sooner had Poppy answered his question than the very edges of Dorian's body began to ripple and warp right in front of her until, a few seconds later, she was met with all eight feet of his towering, inhuman, true form.

And then Dorian was gone, bounding towards the grove of trees before Poppy could shout a single word in protest. Not knowing what else to do she ran after him through the steadily increasing downpour, legs protesting against doing something so physical after literally scaling a cliff. When she finally reached the edge of the trees Dorian was nowhere to be seen so, with no other option in front of her, Poppy took a slow, careful step into the forest. Then another, and another, and another.

She wound through broad-leaved trees with wide trunks and heavy branches, enjoying the sound the rain made as it hit the canopy above her. After a few minutes shadowy-dark conifers began to creep around her, and all sounds seemed to disappear altogether. Beneath Poppy's feet was a layer of absorbent, spongy moss, making her a silent visitor in a forest that seemed entirely out of a fairy tale.

When she heard the rumbling roar of water Poppy followed it. Before long she came upon a clearing, where a waterfall crashed into a pool as dark as the trees it reflected. Dorian was kneeling by it washing his face and horns.

There was something about seeing Dorian like this outside rather than in the artificial lighting of the facility that set Poppy's heart beating far too quickly. He seemed more realistic in the forest. More substantial, like he wasn't simply a figment of her fearfully enticing imagination.

When he spied Poppy, Dorian scuffed at the ground with a hoof and shook wet hair out of his face, standing up to his full height in the process. His pointed ears twitched when he realised Poppy was unabashedly staring at him.

"What?" he asked. For some reason Dorian seemed nervous.

Poppy cocked her head to the side, regarding him curiously. "What do you mean, 'what'?"

"Why are you looking at me like that?"

"Why am I looking at you like you're an eight-foot satyr who's standing where a man used to be?"

"That wasn't how you were looking at me."

Poppy's stomach twisted. She hesitated before asking, "Then how exactly was I looking at you?"

"Like you were judging me."

"I wasn't *judging* you. How could I even do that? It's not like I know any other satyrs." Poppy paused to take a breath, wondering whether it would be a mistake to be honest with Dorian. But they had come this far together, after all. Being honest *once* wouldn't kill her. "...I was just thinking that you were actually real," she eventually explained. "That I – I hadn't dreamed you up."

"Oh?" Dorian's eyebrows rose infuriatingly when he caught the way Poppy's face burned at her stupid admission. A slow smile slid across his face, and he took a step towards her.

When Poppy took a step back Dorian closed the distance between them in two broad, easy strides that left her trapped between him and a tree.

Poppy averted her eyes from his. "What are you doing, Dorian?" she protested, holding up her hands to stop him from getting too close.

Dorian rested an arm above her head, against the tree, then bent his head low to force Poppy to look at him. His strange eyes were narrowed, as if he was trying hard to work something out, then they widened once he reached a conclusion that Poppy sincerely wished he would never reach. "You prefer me like this, don't you?" he asked, disbelief plain as day on his face. He chuckled softly. "I can see it in your eyes. You actually *like* the look of me as a monster better than my human appearance. I didn't realise you were so kinky, Poppy."

"I'm – shut up, Dorian!" Poppy bit out, sliding out and escaping before Dorian could grab her. She knew it made no sense to prefer Dorian the way he currently looked: on the two occasions she had witnessed him in his true form Dorian had put her through the most traumatic experiences of her life. But it was the very fact it was his *true* form that meant Poppy preferred it. Behind the guise of a human Dorian always felt like he was holding himself back. Hiding parts of himself. Never truly connecting with the world around him – with *her.* A scant handful of weeks ago the last thing Poppy wanted was to learn more about Dorian or for him to open up to her. But now...

Well, things were different now. *Poppy* was different now. Her currently blazing skin, throbbing heart and writhing stomach were all proof of that. She needed to turn her mind to other things.

She needed to cool down.

When Poppy locked eyes on the waterfall she acted before she could think things through properly. Despite her run through the rain her clothes were still reasonably dry, and she didn't much like the idea of walking back to the facility with them soaking, so without looking at Dorian she pulled them off and tossed them onto a low-hanging branch, sliding out of her trainers and diving into the pool as quickly as possible.

Great choice, Poppy, she chided as she swam below the surface of the bracing, refreshingly cold water. *Get called out on your stupid attraction to a giant fucking goat and proceed to take all your clothes off. Genius thought process.*

But the pool was so dark Poppy knew Dorian wouldn't be able to see anything. When she resurfaced by the waterfall she glanced behind her; Dorian was watching with an unreadable expression on his inhuman features. Hating how crestfallen she felt that he hadn't already followed her in – or made no indication that he would do so – Poppy took a deep breath and flung herself beneath the waterfall, revelling in the pressure of it against her skin. It felt like it was removing all of the cuts and wounds and gashes that had been drawn across her very being, leaving her with nothing.

When she resurfaced once more Poppy found herself behind the waterfall, where there was barely enough space for two people between the rushing water and the shelf of rock behind it. There was a very narrow ledge above her, so Poppy sank to the bottom of the pool to gain enough momentum to spring up and reach it. But she had used most of her strength climbing so, after getting her arms, neck and head up, Poppy realised she couldn't push herself up the rest of the way to sit on it.

She contented herself to dangle from it, instead, head resting on her forearms whilst the rest of her from the waist down remained in the pool. The roar of the waterfall filled her ears, masking the sound her unruly heart was making in her chest. Poppy was still too hot. Too unsettled. Every nerve of her body was on edge.

She wanted Dorian to join her. She didn't want Dorian to

join her.

She wanted to throw all her responsibilities to the side and simply *live*. She was terrified of the consequences of doing so.

She wanted...

When the crashing of the waterfall broke for a second Poppy knew her decision had been made. With her dangling out of the water her head was level with Dorian's when he pressed up against her, his mouth against her ear just as hot as she was.

"What are you doing behind here?" he murmured, his irresistible voice melting away all of Poppy's remaining resolve. A clawed hand traced gentle lines down her stomach and thigh. "Hiding?"

She gulped. "I wasn't hiding. I was..."

"Waiting?"

Numbly Poppy nodded, burying her face into her arms out of sheer terror and embarrassment. There was no masking her feelings from Dorian here, not when the two of them were wet and naked and pressed against each other. Poppy was achingly aware of every inch of the monster behind her, whose breathing was as ragged as her own.

Dorian kissed her neck, hands on her waist urging her to turn around and face him. The sheer weight of him against her meant Poppy didn't need the ledge to stay up; when she finally turned she was firmly pinned in place.

Shaking slightly she looked into Dorian's eyes, marvelling at his irises that were a shade of blue no human eyes could ever be. His barred pupils were watching her just as intently as his hands were roaming, all over each and every part of her.

"I can change back, Poppy," he said very quietly, the words a puff of breath against her lips. "I don't want to hurt you. This would be much easier if—"

"Hurt me all you want," she cut in, winding her legs around Dorian's waist as she did so. Poppy realised just how small she was compared to him in the process, but it didn't deter her from her foolish decision. "I don't want easy. I just want to feel it all."

"You'll definitely *feel* it, you tiny idiot."

Despite the furious heat that crossed her face at the comment Poppy remained unfazed. "Are you telling me you don't want to fuck me as you are right now?"

"I absolutely want to fuck you as I am right now. I *always* want to fuck you."

"That's—"

"Just like you've always *wanted* me to."

"No I haven't!" Poppy protested, eyes wide in indignation. "That's not true at—"

Dorian's mouth swallowed the rest of her lie, teeth sharp against her lips and tongue. But they both knew just how hard Dorian would have to dig them in to make her bleed, so Poppy didn't flinch away from their razor-sharp edges. The kiss was different from ones they had shared before. They weren't drunk, for one, and Poppy wasn't teetering on the edge of death. No, she was lucid and in complete control of her actions, and so was Dorian.

The tension between them was unbearable. All Poppy wanted to do was break through it – to finally give in to every dark and dangerous desire she possessed for Dorian. She slid her arms around his neck, pressing herself as closely to him as she possibly could. She squeezed his waist with her legs, body impatient for what was to come next.

"You're killing me, Poppy," Dorian breathed, breaking away from their kiss. He shifted on the spot, making Poppy once more all too aware of how much of *him* there was compared to *her*. "Are you *really* sure about doing this with me like—"

"How many times do I have to say yes? Or will I literally have to push you down and sit on your dick so you get the—"

She let out a cry when Dorian's arms tightened around her and pulled her back through the waterfall, deftly manoeuvring over the rocky base of the pool until he reached the moss-covered bank. He slammed Poppy down upon it, eyes blazing, not caring if the action hurt her. Poppy didn't care, either, instead relishing the way her bones jarred inside her when her back hit rock.

Dorian was enormous and intimidating, looming over Poppy with his crown of terrifying horns that could so easily impale her. And yet there was something ruling Poppy's brain far stronger than fear – the same reckless instinct that made her scale a cliff in front of monsters intent on buying her flesh and blood and bone.

"Last chance, Poppy King," Dorian growled.

"I'm fed up of last chances," she said, running a hand along his horns until she found an ear. All Poppy had to do was graze it with her fingertips and Dorian's self control seemed to evaporate. He pinned Poppy to the ground and, in the space of a moment, he was inside her.

The cry of shock that fell from Poppy's lips only seemed to spur Dorian on harder, and faster, until she was whimpering against his mouth and clinging on for dear life. His claws bit into her flesh as if he couldn't quite get close enough to her, and when Poppy bled his tongue eagerly lapped the stuff up.

When Dorian kissed her again his lips were metallic with the taste of it. It only made Poppy more desperate for him to break her – now that the initial shock had worn off she craved for Dorian to push the limits of her own body as far as possible.

"More," she gasped, pulling Dorian's head down to whisper

into his ear. "I know you can do more than that."

He stared at her incredulously. "What *are* you, Poppy?"

"Yours."

She hadn't meant to say it – Poppy didn't want to be *anyone's* – but the word had the effect she desired. Dorian's mouth was vicious against her own, hands clawing at her thighs and breasts and hair as the entire length of him slammed into her, bringing tears to her eyes.

It was painful.

It was brutal.

It was the greatest pleasure Poppy had ever experienced.

When finally Dorian's entire body tensed and relaxed after one final thrust Poppy was left hardly able to breathe. But then Dorian rolled onto his back and pulled her on top of him, and she realised he was struggling to breathe, too.

The hands that had been so rough before gently stroked down her spine, sending shivers through Poppy's exhausted body. Neither of them said a thing. There *were* no words to explain what had just happened.

They didn't return to the facility for a long, long time.

CHLOE BETTANY

CASEY

THE FACT POPPY KING HAD NOT yet apologised to Casey for slapping her across the face would have, months ago, infuriated her. It likely would have ended their friendship.

Things were different now.

Casey hadn't realised just *how* different immediately after her altercation with Poppy. It was only after spending more and more time with Patrick, and looking at her friend through a furious, hurt lens that Casey finally clocked onto the fact something was up.

And then, when Andrew and Poppy both stopped speaking to Fred altogether despite the fact Fred clearly – and desperately – wished to talk to *them* Casey grew deeply concerned. It wasn't just that something was different or 'up'.

Something was *wrong*.

Poppy and Dorian were different together now, too, insomuch as it felt like they *were* together. But not in a way Casey could strictly understand. There was a distance between

Poppy and Dorian that wouldn't make sense if they were merely sleeping together or dating. It wasn't the same distance Poppy had placed between herself and everyone else, either.

Only Andrew seemed truly close to her now, having become something of a bodyguard for her for reasons Casey could not comprehend. If she'd ever doubted before whether he was in love with Poppy, she didn't now.

It didn't help Casey's uneasiness that, sometimes, when she and Patrick were lying in bed and she was moments away from sleep, Casey thought she could feel...something. The soft, smooth slide of something that wasn't a hand across her leg, creeping up her thigh. Whenever she blinked back into consciousness the sensation was gone, though, and Patrick would shush her back to sleep.

Yes, something was definitely, disturbingly wrong.

Casey needed to figure out what.

She was accidentally given the perfect opportunity when she reached the pool for her usual sunset swim only to find Poppy alone in the water, watching the sun die behind the heather-covered mountains.

"Poppy."

Poppy jumped in surprise. When she realised who had spoken her name she immediately made to exit the pool, but Casey dived into the water and caught her friend's arm before she got very far.

"Don't go, Poppy," Casey begged. "Please. We need to talk."

A frustrated look crossed Poppy's face. She tried to pull her arm out of Casey's grip, but Casey only held on tighter. "Casey, if this is about our stupid fight then I'm *sorry* I slapped you, but—"

"Screw the fight!" she interrupted. "I don't care about that. It was a long time coming, but it's over now."

Poppy hesitated. "So what do you want to talk to me about?"

"What the hell is going on?"

"What the hell is going on with what?"

"With you!" Casey cried, exasperated. "With Fred and Andrew and especially Dorian and Patrick. And don't you dare tell me that nothing's wrong, because I know there is."

When she let go of Poppy's arm her friend leaned against the back of the pool, looking as if she'd rather like to slide down into the water and never resurface. It was a look Poppy had worn often over the summer.

"Why did you bring up Patrick?" she asked, which surprised Casey. "What's happened with him?"

"I – I'm not sure, exactly," Casey replied, leaning against the pool beside Poppy as she did so. "Look, it's going to sound stupid, but sometimes in bed it feels like...I don't know. Like there's something else in bed with me or—"

"Pretend we're talking about something else," Poppy cut in, a bright smile across her face that completely belied the topic of conversation.

"Poppy?"

Beneath the water she kicked Casey's leg, and she looked over to the glass-walled social area. Dorian and Patrick had come in to sit beside Andrew on one of the long sofas; they kept glancing at the girls in the pool with obvious curiosity.

"So something *is* going—"

"Yes, but for the love of god I can't be found to be telling you, so hug me or something like we're making up."

"...aren't we?"

"Of course we are, you dumb bitch. I love you. You know that."

When Casey flung her arms around Poppy it wasn't because of a ruse. She genuinely meant it, though she hated that tears were welling up in her eyes.

"Don't call me a dumb bitch...bitch," she muttered, still clinging onto Poppy as she spoke. Casey was gratified when Poppy's arms wrapped around her and squeezed, hard.

"There's so much to tell you, Casey," she replied, very, very quietly. "But you can't tell anyone. Please."

"Andrew knows, doesn't he?"

"Yes. For a while now."

"...why Andrew?"

"Because he worked some stuff out. And he may have saved my life."

Casey broke out of the hug to stare at Poppy with wide eyes. "What do you mean he saved your life? Poppy, what's *happened* to you all summer?"

Poppy laughed as if Casey had said something silly and hilarious. "Can you keep up this act for ten minutes whilst I give you the most ridiculous, horrific and fucked-up summary of events you've probably ever heard?"

Casey snickered. "You're really asking the girl who can pretend to be interested in what the guys from the rugby team have to say for a solid two hours if she can act happy for ten minutes? Of course I can."

"Then..." Poppy stole an almost imperceptible glance at the social area, "you're never going to guess just how bloody difficult it is for me to die."

When Patrick came by Casey's bedroom that night she had no idea how she was supposed to act normal. After everything Poppy had told her - after she'd lifted her compression bandage and proven that her arm was completely undamaged - Casey was terrified of what to say or do.

"Cass, what's wrong?" Patrick asked, concern colouring his face as he made to pull Casey down onto the bed with him. She hated that she flinched away. "Cass...?"

"You and Dorian," she whispered, silently begging that Poppy would forgive her for not being able to keep a secret. "You're not human. Are you - what do you want from me, Patrick? Are you going to...to eat me or—"

"*Jesus Christ, Cass.* Jesus fucking Christ." Patrick stood up, pacing the room back and forth relentlessly even as Casey began to cry. "Who told you? It was Poppy, wasn't it? I knew something was up when I saw you guys in the pool."

"W-what does it matter if it was Poppy or not? Everything she's told me is true, isn't it? You haven't even denied it."

"Cass—"

"Just tell me the truth, Patrick! Did you *buy* me? Am I an object to you?"

He dragged a hand over his face. "Yes, at first. But—"

"Oh my God."

"Cassandra, let me finish," he said, grabbing hold of her hands before Casey could pull them away. "It was like that at first - and I'm so sorry. But it's not like that now. Cass, I *love* you. It's so stupid. So fucking stupid, but I do. I love how smart and confident and honest you are. I even love your pettiness and how you can charm anyone in a ten foot radius into doing what you want. So if...if you don't want to be with me, then that's okay. I'll let you go."

"You...you will?"

He nodded seriously. "Yes, I will. I hope that you'll stay with me instead, though."

Casey considered this. She *did* care for Patrick, more than any man she'd ever been with. Though she hadn't intended to fall for him at all. Though she didn't *want* to feel anything for him, especially now.

But if Patrick loved her, then...

"Help me and Poppy and Andrew get everyone out of here and I'm yours."

Patrick stared at her blankly. "Help you—"

"Out of here, yes. And tell me what the fuck it is you keep doing to me when you think I'm asleep, or so help me God I'll cut your dick off."

INTERLUDE VII

Lily hadn't meant to cut Chloe's hand open. It was a stupid mistake with a knife in the kitchen. Chloe didn't want to make a scene of the whole thing so she headed to the infirmary by herself, clutching a damp wad of paper towels against the wound. She hoped it wouldn't scar.

When she reached the infirmary, however, nobody was around to help her, and Dorian's office was empty. So Chloe headed up the stairs, though she'd never gone up to the first floor of the west wing before. But Poppy had been up there plenty of times, and so had Andrew and Rachelle and Casey. It was where Dorian's bedroom was, Chloe knew, so her best bet to get help was to knock on his door.

An unsettling sound gave Chloe pause when she began walking down the corridor of the first floor. It sounded... inhuman. She didn't like it at all. She liked it even less when she passed a half-open door and spied what looked like a twisted, scaly—

"Monster," Chloe breathed, barely able to process what her eyes were seeing. She backed away, only to thump heavily against someone's chest. Shivering from head to toe she turned her head: Dorian was looking at her with a forlorn expression.

"I wish you hadn't seen that," he said. "You were one of the good ones."

BETHAN KOT

FRED

FRED THOUGHT FOR SURE HE WAS going insane. He knew he was dead – knew it from the moment Dorian had appeared in front of him as a monster out of a nightmare – but not knowing when and how he was going to die was more terrifying than the act itself. And there was so much else he *needed* to know. There was no getting around it.

He had to speak to Poppy.

She's petrified of me, Fred thought dully as he wound his way through the facility, working out where everyone who might be able to stop him from talking to her was. Casey, who had now inexplicably made up with Poppy, was in the hot tub with Patrick, the two of them sitting so closely together Fred thought it looked as if they were conspiring together. Rachelle and Andrew were with Nate, Robin and Rich, lounging in the social area with far too much food and a few games. Andrew glared at Fred when he spied him looking, though nobody else noticed.

He couldn't find Dorian anywhere in the central wing,

which meant he was likely in the west wing. And he hadn't found Poppy, either, which suggested that either she was in her room or together with Dorian. They'd been different since their suicidal climb up the cliffs, though Fred of course knew better than to believe such a climb was all that dangerous for the two of them.

Not for the first time he was forced to acknowledge exactly why Poppy was the kind of climber that she was – and why she'd never heeded any of Fred's safety warnings. She hadn't been doing it to deliberately get on his nerves. She simply knew the ropes and harnesses were all but useless for her.

I wonder, if she didn't heal the way she did, if we would have been friends, he thought, though considering how many other things the two of them had clashed over Fred somehow doubted it. He laughed bitterly at the notion. Their hatred of each other had been so petty.

Until he turned it into something else.

Until he tried to kill her.

Fred was shaking by the time he reached Poppy's bedroom door. For all he knew she was going to slam the door in his face again or refuse to open it at all. And he didn't know what to say if she *did* let him in. His head was a numb jumble of barely connected words and phrases, sending Fred into a wild panic as he reached out a fist and knocked.

No response.

"...Poppy?" he called out tentatively. "King, I need to talk to you. Please."

Still nothing.

Placing his ear to the door Fred listened carefully. It didn't sound like Poppy was in the shower, nor in her room at all. He turned the handle before he could think better of it, stepping into Poppy's dark and empty room and thus confirming that she wasn't there.

She's with Dorian, then, he concluded. *I wonder how long she'll be. Will she spend the night with him?*

Fred didn't like that idea at all. Dorian had clearly forced Poppy into a horrific situation she didn't want to be in – one which she couldn't speak about to anyone – but nowadays it seemed more and more like the monster pretending to be a man was no longer her enemy.

He looked around her room. Poppy's phone lay abandoned on the bed, all but useless with the non-existent signal in the facility. A sheet of paper was beside it which listed the names of everyone in the club. Some names were scored out: all of the people who had been scouted as well as Ross Bridges, who'd been kicked out, and Poppy herself. Other names were ticked including Nate, Rachelle and Andrew. One girl, Bethan Kot, had her name circled in green with the words 'this week?' scrawled beside it.

Casey and Fred's names were some of the very few still blank.

"G-get out," came a small, uncertain voice from behind Fred.

He straightened up immediately, preparing himself to plead for Poppy to listen to him. When he turned he was relieved to see that Poppy was alone. "Please tell me what's going on," he said, stumbling over the words in his haste to get them out. "You owe me that much at—"

Poppy slammed the door shut behind her in fury, all her previous fear forgotten. "I owe you *nothing,* you sick fuck! You tortured me, tried to kill me – *wanted* to kill me! And for what? Punishment? To get me to own up to something I didn't do? So tell me why the hell I *owe* you anything, Fred!"

"Because I'm going to die and I want to know why that is!"

Poppy cleared her phone and the list of club members away from her bed then took a step towards Fred, though it was clear from her face she wanted to be as far away from him as possible. Her eyes were full of tears.

They unsettled Fred to no end.

"You weren't going to, you know," Poppy told him, which only confused him further. "I was going to save you, though I hated you. I was *always* going to save you. And then you gave me a better reason than literally anyone else in the club to throw you to the wolves. You did that to yourself, Fred. That's not on me."

"Poppy, I didn't want to – I didn't mean to try and kill–"

"Of course you didn't!" she cut in. "Until you *did*. And that's what's wrong with you, Fred: you act all good and caring and proper but, when it came down to it, thinking I was hiding some deep, dark secret from you literally drove you *crazy*. There's something wrong with you. I've always known it."

"Then fine," Fred spat out, hating that Poppy was right. "There's something wrong with me. I hate you, and I obsess about you, and you drive me insane. And now you'll be the reason I die. So put me *out of my misery*. Just...tell me why. I'm begging you. Please."

Poppy stared at him for an agonisingly long time. The tears in her eyes had finally broken to stream down her face, though she didn't seem to have noticed. Finally Poppy looked away, rubbing a palm across her eyes in the process. "Damn it, Sampson. Fucking...damn it."

Fred took a tentative step towards her. "What? Poppy, what's going on? Please—"

"Stop asking me so earnestly! Stop – stop making me want to save you, too. I can't...there's too much to do. There's just too much—"

"Then let me help you! You don't have to do this all on your own. Whatever it is, just *tell* me and I swear I'll do anything."

She glared at him, freezing Fred to the spot just three feet away from her. "Why should I trust you when you didn't trust me?" Poppy demanded. "We might never have agreed on much of anything but at least I *always* trusted you. Why couldn't you afford me the same luxury?"

When Fred reached out to touch Poppy's arm – still wrapped in a useless compression sleeve – she flinched away as if he might run a knife through it like he had done before. It hurt Fred to watch the expression on her face.

He knew he deserved it and so much more.

"Poppy," Fred began, choosing his next words very carefully, "I can never apologise enough for what I did. But when you fell, something...something wasn't right. And my suspicions about that – the ones that drove me mad in the first place – ended up being correct. It got to my head. I couldn't think about anything else. All I wanted to do—"

"Was put me in my place," Poppy finished for him, tone completely flat. "You really are one pathetic son of a bitch, Sampson." She ran a hand through her long, flyaway hair, pulling it away from her face. She took a deep breath. Another. Then she let out all the air as one huge exhalation.

"Poppy...?"

"Fine," she sighed, defeated. "*Fine.* But you have to do absolutely everything I say. You don't question me again – ever. If I explain something to you, that's it. That's all you're getting, and you'll be happy I even told you that much. Do all of this and you'll even look like the hero to the rest of the club when we all escape, and I'll be the villain. I *am* the villain, anyway."

Fred said nothing. He knew Poppy wasn't the villain; Dorian was. But clearly she'd had to do some pretty deplorable things. He couldn't help but wonder if they were worse than what he himself had done to her.

"I'll do everything you say," Fred agreed. "Of course I will. So tell me what the plan is."

She scowled. "It's not like I have everything figured out—"

"Poppy?"

Both of them froze. Dorian was knocking on the door.

Fred's eyes darted from the door to Poppy. "What's he doing here? I thought you were just with him."

"What? No," Poppy bit out anxiously. "I went for a walk. Why did you assume I was with him?"

"Because—"

"Poppy, I can hear you talking to someone. Don't ignore me. I have something important to tell you."

"Don't come in yet, Dorian. I—"

Dorian ignored her anyway, opening the door wide to the sight of Poppy and the person she hated most of all a metre away from her. His face darkened. "What's going on here?"

Fred backed away. "I was apologising. I'm just leaving."

"I told you not to go near her, Sampson. You just couldn't resist, could you?"

"Dorian, let him leave," Poppy insisted, grabbing hold of the man's arm to pull him away from the door. She fired a look at Fred. "Go, Fred. Don't let me find you in here again."

Fred was only too happy to comply; if he lingered for even a second longer he was sure Dorian would kick his skull in. But talking to Poppy had worked...sort of. Fred still had no clue what was going on, but at least now he might not die.

Maybe.

He was itching to find out more about Poppy's blood, and how she planned to get everyone out of the facility and, most importantly, *why* she had to get everyone out of the facility.

Fred never thought he'd look forward to talking to Poppy King, but there was a first time for everything.

MATEUSZ KOWALSKI

DORIAN

"WHY WAS HE IN HERE, POPPY?"

"I told you. To apologise."

"It didn't much look like he was apologising to me."

Poppy winced. "That's because you came in at the wrong time."

"Oh, so there was a *wrong* time to barge in on the conversation?"

"Dorian, why are you making it out like you caught me and Fred screwing on my bed? Ugh, that's disgusting even to say," she said, shuddering.

Dorian slumped onto said bed, indicating for Poppy to come and join him. Though nothing had happened between the two of them since their rainy afternoon in the forest he had only grown more obsessively protective of her.

Clearly that feeling is more than warranted.

When Poppy finally sat beside him Dorian asked, "Why

was he standing so close to you?"

"Because he was trying to see my arm again."

"What, because stabbing you a hundred times wasn't proof enough that you can heal quickly?"

When Poppy's face grew ashen he immediately regretted bringing up the subject. But then she rested her head against his shoulder, which was the most affection she had shown Dorian all week. "Can we please not talk about it?" she begged. "Fred and I...it doesn't matter what he said to me. Nothing has changed."

"You mean that?"

"Of course. Fred's the only attempted murderer in the whole club. He's the one who *deserves* to be sacrificed."

Dorian smiled in satisfaction as he stroked Poppy's hair, then brushed his lips against the top of her head. "Good. But if he bothers you again that's it: I'm killing him then and there."

She snorted. "Deal. You're a couple days late for taking blood, by the way. Are you wanting some now?"

"*You're* asking *me* if I want some?" He laughed incredulously at the notion. "I never thought I'd hear you ask that in my entire life."

"That's a very long life to live without hearing me consensually invite you to drink my blood."

"Well...you were terrified of me and hated me. I didn't have much positive evidence to suggest you'd ever have a good relationship with me."

Poppy raised her eyebrows at him. "And yet you were convinced I wanted to have sex with you all along. That's rather twisted, given I hated and feared you."

He shrugged. "I could have lived with twisted, kinky fuckery...for a while, at least. Then I'd want more."

"You always want more."

Dorian kissed her softly. "And you always give me it, so who's to blame?"

"You. Absolutely you."

Poppy looked surprised when, instead of laughing, Dorian sighed heavily. He pulled away from her and straightened against the wall. "When I came looking for you I really *did* have something important to tell you."

"That's..." she frowned. "What's wrong? What happened?"

Dorian glanced at her out of the corner of his eye. "Chloe Bettany. I don't reckon you were ever planning on giving her up. She was a good person."

"*Was?* Dorian, I don't like the sound of—"

"I caught her in the first floor of the west wing today," Dorian said, talking over her. He knew if he didn't tell Poppy now then he'd never be able to tell her the truth at all. "She must have been looking for someone to help her out – her hand was bleeding. But she saw Franco – Nick's father – through a door. I *told* him to close the door. I always tell him."

"He...wasn't human at the time, I take it," Poppy said, voice barely a whisper. All the blood had drained from her face just as it had done when Dorian forced her to watch Franco dismember Ross Bridges. He couldn't handle the fact that he'd forced that experience on her. It made him feel sick to his stomach.

Dorian shook his head. "Not human. I shouldn't have even let him buy anyone else; Ross was more than enough. But the Richardson's are a powerful family. Filthy rich. I can't turn them away."

Poppy was quiet for a minute. Then she asked a question she clearly didn't want to ask. "So what's happening to Chloe?"

"She's with the others for now. But...I won't lie to you,

Poppy. Someone's already bought her. They'll be here next week."

For a moment it looked like Poppy might cry. Her eyes shone too brightly, and the breath she took was more like a gulp. But then she shook her head and smiled bitterly at her hands. "You'd think I'd be used to all of this by now, but I'm not."

"Poppy, I'm so sorry—"

"Can you leave me for the evening, Dorian? Sorry, I just... I'm tired."

Dorian resisted the urge to push Poppy against the duvet and ignore her request entirely. Instead he contented himself with squeezing her hands – both of hers beneath one of his – before leaving without another word.

When he reached his office Dorian was surprised to find Nick sitting inside, waiting for him. His stomach lurched. "Nick, I wasn't expecting you," he said, forcing a smile to his face. "It's a bit late for you to still be here, isn't it?"

Nick held up a sheaf of paper. "My old man forgot to get your signature earlier. He really should let me take over as family head and be done with it."

Dorian relaxed slightly as he sat down behind his desk, taking the papers from Nick when he proffered them and dutifully signed them. When he handed them back he said, "I'm sure Franco will retire when he feels the need to. And it's not like you're bone idle, Nick. You have plenty to do."

Nick laughed heartily. "I've spent all summer pretending to be one of your sports scouts, Dorian. That's the *definition* of bone idle. Though I suppose if I hadn't taken you up on the offer I never would have met Miss King, so all's well that ends well."

"Nick, I already told you—"

"That Poppy wasn't up for bidding. I know. But I don't

care. I want her, Dorian. Price isn't an issue."

Dorian forced himself not to break away from Nick's hard, imploring stare. The man's sheer bulk made him an intimidating figure, even to Dorian. He knew better than to needlessly rile him up. "Nick," he began carefully, "it's not a question of money—"

"Then what is it? You can't possibly be intending to keep her for yourself. That's hardly fair, Dorian, after you let Patrick have Casey without ever putting her on the market."

"I do believe I can do what I like with my own merchandise, Nick," Dorian said, his hands twitching below the desk.

The other man's eyes grew flinty, and his smile soured into something unpleasant. "A fair point, I'll grant you. But don't forget what the Richardson family has done for you and your father, Dorian. We've never asked for anything in return for our generosity. Consider this the first and only favour I'll ever ask of you. Give me Poppy King."

Nick's reasoning was too solid for Dorian to counter. If it had been any other human up for auction then of course he'd have granted Nick's request. But if he so much as hinted at Poppy being special then Nick wouldn't rest until he found out why, and then Poppy would be doomed.

"She's too good to simply be eaten, Nick," Dorian found himself saying, which was, of course, completely true. "I can't find it in me to sell her off just for—"

"Oh, lord, of course I don't want to eat her!" Nick exclaimed, relief obvious on his face. Clearly he figured Dorian's reluctance to do as he asked was because of this one specific concern. His smile broadened, and this time it was genuine. He leaned heavily on Dorian's desk. "I'll be honest with you here, though I'll kill you if you start spreading this around: my family is dying. We're all getting old. I'm the youngest and I'm already thirty-five. Next youngest after me is my uncle and he's *seventy.*"

Dorian didn't like where this was going in the slightest. "Why has no one in your family had any offspring, then?"

"We've tried. Believe me, we've all tried. But come on, Dorian. You've seen the size of us. It's hard enough finding another *monster* that can handle giving birth to one of us, let alone a human."

"So what makes you think Poppy could *handle* it?" Dorian asked, trying his hardest not to grit his teeth at the question.

"For god's sake, Dorian, you've seen her in action!" Nick said, incredulous. "Girl never stops, even when it might kill her, and then she's out of action for a handful of days before she's right back at it again. Damn near invincible. And at the height of her physical fitness, which we both know is a massive plus. Not to mention how she looks, and damn—"

"Okay, I think I get the picture," Dorian interrupted. He felt physically sick. "Look, let me think on it. The price for a good breeding partner has always been more than livestock. I'll need to work out exactly how much she's worth."

Nick waved a dismissive hand as he got to his feet and made for the door. "I'll pay anything you want, just make sure she's ready to leave by the end of next week. Thanks for doing business with me, Dorian."

And then he was gone, leaving Dorian shaking with anger and disbelief, his human form dangerously close to dissolving around him.

Just one thought passed through his head, so insistent he couldn't help but utter it aloud.

"*Fuck.*"

INTERLUDE VIII

EVERYONE KNEW SOMETHING WAS WRONG. Everyone. But nobody would talk about it, and Mateusz couldn't take it any longer. He couldn't shake the feeling that the entire club – or what remained of it, at least – was in danger. They were penned up in a building nobody could reach or escape from unless they chose to walk the long, dangerous, twisting path around the loch...or swim across the loch itself.

Mateusz decided either option was better than staying another night in Dorian's facility.

When the sun set that night and everyone else had long since drifted off to sleep he packed up his rucksack and walked straight out the front door. For a few moments he wondered whether he should have asked anyone else if they wanted to leave with him, but something told Mateusz that would stop him from being able to leave entirely. Someone would blab about his plan, and that would be it.

He made it to the beginning of the path when a hand on his shoulder stopped him.

"Get off me!" Mateusz roared, turning around to identify who had touched him.

Dorian.

"Why won't you all just stay put?" the man sighed, before punching Mateusz in the face with a strength no human should have ever possessed.

ROBIN FRASER

ANDREW

"Did we really have to do this outside, Poppy? It's starting to get cold now. And the wind is really—"

"I'm sorry, Andrew. But you know we can't talk inside the facility where Dorian can hear us. We won't be too long, I promise."

"But why is *he* here?"

Andrew pointed at Fred without looking at him.

Poppy sidled up a little closer to Andrew to make him feel better, which it did. "Because he has to be. Do you *really* want him to die, Andrew, when we could save him?"

"Yes."

"That was brutal."

"Shut up, Sampson," both Poppy and Andrew said in unison.

Poppy wrinkled her nose in amusement. "You've never called him that before."

"It's better than calling him by his first name."

"I am *right here*, Andrew."

Poppy raised a hand to stop Andrew from saying anything else. "Come on, guys. We have bigger things to think about right now, okay? Once everyone is well away from this hell hole then you *never* need to see Fred again, Andrew. And won't that be great? Sounds fucking great to me."

Andrew smiled at the thought. It really *did* sound great, because despite saying that he thought Fred should die in reality Andrew didn't want anyone to die – but he also wanted to forget Fred existed. When Poppy admitted to him that she'd told Casey what was going on but had omitted Fred's attack on her Andrew had been confused and upset, but it was Poppy's decision to make, not his. If Fred helping out freed them all from Dorian's facility then Andrew would have to respect the choices Poppy made, even if working with his traitorous ex-friend made Andrew want to vomit.

"Fine," he bit out. He held out a hand to Fred, who shook it with a slight smirk on his face that Andrew hated. "But this truce is only temporary."

"I can work with that," Fred replied, wincing when Andrew crushed his hand beneath his own.

"So where the hell is Casey?" Poppy asked nobody in particular, collapsing onto the grassy hilltop which was her and Andrew's favourite place to jog to. Andrew followed suit, and then Fred.

The other man glanced at Poppy. "Why'd you bring Casey in, anyway? Seems like an odd choice."

"She came to me knowing something was wrong."

"Yeah, but Nate and Rachelle and Rich and just about everyone with two brain cells knows that something's wrong with you."

Poppy scowled. "She came to me because of something to

do with her and Patrick."

The meaning of her words was lost on Andrew, but not on Fred, who snorted in laughter despite himself. "What, did he turn into some hulking monster by mistake when they were fucking? What *is* Patrick, anyway?"

Poppy gave him the finger. "That's disgusting. But you're not wrong...I think. Something weird happened, anyway. And I don't know what he is."

"How could you *not* ask Dorian what his best friend is—"

"Fred, shut up."

"Come on!" he protested. "You're telling me all these scouts and facility staff and shit are monsters and you've not once been curious about what they look like?"

Poppy grew quiet then, and Andrew hated Fred even more for his brashness. It also bothered him that, of the three of them, he was the only one who hadn't actually seen a monster yet. It meant Fred had something he shared with Poppy that Andrew didn't, and that made him feel even worse.

"I've seen one other monster besides Dorian," Poppy murmured after a few seconds, "and he was ripping Ross Bridges apart limb from limb. I didn't much want to know what any of the others looked like after that."

What Poppy said was horrific. Stomach-churning, scream-inducing, nightmarish. But Andrew was glad she said it simply for the expression on Fred's face. He looked like he was about to choke on his tongue.

"I've wondered about what Patrick really looks like, of course," Poppy eventually added, as if to lighten the mood she herself had darkened, "but I've never had the guts to ask him."

"How about asking me now?"

All three of them jumped to their feet, immediately on edge when they spied Patrick coming towards them with Casey in tow.

She waved apologetically. "Okay, so I told someone, but you can't be mad, Poppy!"

"How can I *not be mad* that you told Dorian's best monster friend that—"

Patrick laughed. "Calm down, everyone. I'm here to help you, not rat you out."

Fred and Poppy glared at him suspiciously, but Andrew brightened considerably. He liked the idea of Patrick being on their side far more than Fred. In reality he wanted Dorian to be on their side, too, but that was impossible because all of this was his fault to begin with.

"Why would you help us instead of Dorian?" Fred asked, warily sitting back down when Patrick and Casey did so. Poppy was slower to follow suit after which Andrew did, too.

Patrick smiled fondly at Casey. "For her, of course. How could I expect her to ever forgive me if I could help you guys out and didn't?"

"Then you could have helped so much earlier!" Poppy cried, looking as if she might actually pull her hair out. Andrew hoped she wouldn't.

"I'm sorry, Poppy. But you must know how dangerous Dorian's work is. It's not something I would ever dare interfere with, and to be honest even now I'm pretty terrified. So much so that Cass and I fully intend to run off as soon as you guys are over the loch."

"I – what?"

Casey nodded enthusiastically. "I never liked uni anyway. Patrick and I are going to go sailing around the world! How exciting is that?"

Andrew wondered how she could remain so upbeat when her club mates were literally being eaten alive. But, then again, he always felt happy when he was around Poppy. He supposed it must be like that for Casey with Patrick, even if he was actually a monster.

Poppy held a hand to her head the way she always did when a migraine was creeping up on her. "Patrick, please don't tell me in any way, shape or form that you have tentacles, because for the love of all that is good and holy I literally *cannot—*"

"Jesus, he totally does," Fred cut in, delighted. "That makes so much sense! No wonder you always help out with the water sports!"

"Hey," Patrick complained, though he was grinning, "I could be a shark for all you know."

"Except you're not, and now all those Japanese nightmare cartoons Nate showed me are creeping back into my mind to suck my very soul out," Poppy muttered.

Fred laughed uproariously; Andrew had never, in his entire life, heard him genuinely laugh in response to something Poppy had said.

He didn't like it.

"This coming from the woman who fucked a goat," Patrick fired back, causing everyone to stare at Poppy, who promptly cast her gaze to her hands as if they were the most interesting objects in the world.

Casey gasped. "You totally *did* – I can see it on your face. Oh my God, Poppy, what was it like? You have to—"

"I do not have to tell you *anything*," she protested. "I deny it all."

"You really think Dorian didn't tell me about it the second you guys got back from the forest?" Patrick said, chuckling good-naturedly. "We do enjoy gossiping, you know."

Poppy was clearly horrified. Andrew was numb. He didn't like thinking about Poppy with Dorian at all, but Poppy with a *monster* Dorian?

It was even worse than Fred laughing at her jokes.

"How did you even manage it, King?" Fred asked. "Like, how was it physically possible? Surely he must have been close to splitting you in—"

"Shut up shut up shut up *shut up*," Poppy cried, getting to her feet with her hands over her ears, which Andrew very much felt like doing, too. "This is *so* not what we came up here to discuss, or have you all forgotten that?"

Andrew was ashamed to realise that he *had*. Though he didn't like the specific topics of conversation the easy banter of the group was the closest thing to normal he'd experienced in weeks. He knew nothing would ever be normal again, even if they all got away from the facility safely.

"You're right, Poppy," Casey said, wiping a laughter-induced tear from her eye as she forced herself to grow serious. "Sorry. We have a lot to cover."

Fred glanced at Poppy, a grim, determined smile on his face. Poppy held his gaze, reaching for Andrew's hand at the same time in order to squeeze it. He only too eagerly reciprocated.

It didn't matter if she and Fred had reached a truce or if Poppy had slept with a monster Dorian. Andrew was special to her in a way nobody else could ever be. He was the one she'd trusted first. The one she revealed everything to and asked for help from. He was the one who saved her life.

Fred waved a hand in the general direction of Dorian's facility. "So what's the plan, Miss President of the Outdoor Sports Society?"

INTERLUDE IX

TWELVE PEOPLE HAD BEEN LOCKED UP in the room with him, Craig counted, though only ten were left. With Ross and Angelica gone he could only assume he'd be the next to die, so when Dorian entered with two assistants he steeled himself for a fight. Like hell was he going to accept his fate without at least smashing the man's face in.

But they didn't take Craig.

That was the last time he saw Grace Kang and Chloe Bettany.

FREDERICK SAMPSON

POPPY

POPPY WAS TERRIFIED. THERE WAS so much that could go wrong
today – *too* much. But she had no other options.

It was now or never.

When Mateusz was found to be missing, his belongings all
packed and gone, everyone concluded that he simply up and
left. Even though the road around the loch was long and
dangerous, especially in the dark, and swimming through the
loch itself wasn't any easier. But Poppy knew better.

Dorian wouldn't even look her in the eye.

It had been to her benefit that Dorian had been avoiding
Poppy for a few days, though, given what she was planning. It
also meant he hadn't drank her blood in two weeks even when
she gave him Robin Fraser's name to be saved – someone that,
for Rachelle's sake, Poppy should have saved weeks ago.

Poppy needed all the strength she could get so of course
Dorian not drinking her blood was a good thing. And yet it left
Poppy feeling...odd. Like she was too full, or there was too

much pressure inside of her. She needed to let some of it go.

"I don't *want* him to drink my blood," Poppy muttered under her breath as she made her way to the pool, a towel wrapped around her bikini-clad body. If this was to be her final day at the facility she was going to damn well make use of the pool and the hot tub.

"Is that so? Sounds like a lie to me."

Poppy jumped despite herself, scowling to hide her discomfort. "Dorian, don't creep up on me like that."

He smirked, all sharp canines, dishevelled hair and otherworldly blue eyes. "I wasn't creeping up on you. You simply didn't notice me."

"I find that hard to believe."

"Oh?" He raised an eyebrow suggestively.

"Shut up, Dorian."

"I didn't say anything."

"I can tell what you're thinking."

"And what would that be?"

"That you believe I'm always thinking about you, so I must always notice you," Poppy said before turning and making towards the pool. Dorian hooked a finger over the top of her towel and dragged her to a stop.

"You're at least thinking of me eighty percent of the time," he murmured, voice soft and low against her ear. When Poppy held up a hand to swat his face away he kissed it.

"Where do you get all this confidence from?" Poppy asked, all too aware of the uneven beating of her heart. After several days of Dorian being distant with her after their encounter in the forest Poppy found that having him in such close proximity seemed to dissolve her wits far quicker than it usually did.

"It's not really confidence if I know it to be true."

"Semantics."

"Why have you been so cold with me lately?"

Poppy turned her head over her shoulder to look at him; her lips brushed past his in the process. She almost pulled away.

Almost.

Instead she reached up a hand, running it through Dorian's hair as she deepened the kiss, satisfied by the noise of shock emitted from the back of his throat in the process. "Who's being cold?" she remarked when she finally pulled away, biting Dorian's bottom lip as she did so. His hands crawled around Poppy's waist, urging her closer once more. So she turned to face him properly, staring him hard in the face as she said, "You're the one who's been avoiding me, not the other way around. What's going on?"

Dorian's answer was so obviously evasive Poppy almost laughed. "I'm handling it," he said. "It's nothing you need to worry about."

"Which means I do."

"Just sit tight for another two days. That's when everyone is leaving, after all. Everything will be fine by then."

Because we'll all be gone.

Her stomach lurched at the thought. Poppy knew what she had to do – knew that she had to betray and leave Dorian. After everything he'd put her club through it was the very least he deserved. And yet though she found it easy to betray him, *leaving* him was another matter entirely. It was the one part of their deal that Poppy truly didn't want to break, whatever that meant for the way she felt about him.

"Poppy?"

She nodded. "Sorry, I'm just nervous. Understandə' given...everything."

Dorian chuckled darkly. "That's an understatement. But in two days everything will be over and done with, and then we..."

"We what?"

"We figure out what's next. Funny, I've never not had a plan before."

"And I've never *had* one. Guess this is us meeting in the middle."

The smile on Dorian's face was achingly genuine. "I guess you're right. Stay in my room tonight, Poppy."

Of course Poppy knew what that really meant. She'd always intended on spending the night with Dorian, anyway – with entirely unscrupulous, ulterior motives.

She kissed him softly, trying to ignore the way Dorian visibly brightened at the physical display of affection. "I guess I can indulge you this once."

"I can't believe it's taken me fifteen weeks to get you to actually accept an invitation to my room."

"And I still can't quite believe you're an eight-foot-tall monster who traffics human beings, so there's that to take into consideration." Poppy flinched at the words she couldn't help but say, hating that she said them *now* of all times.

Dorian's eyes hardened at the comment. "I know," he sighed, pulling away from her. "But even still: you're going to stay with me tonight, anyway, so I suppose it doesn't matter."

"I suppose it doesn't," Poppy echoed back, watching Dorian walk away whilst knowing that it always *would* matter. For how could it not?

But even still...

When she reached the social area Poppy made a beeline for the loch instead of the pool, where Patrick's boat was docked and, she knew, Casey was holed up inside with the man. And though she was somewhat anxious about what she might see by barging into the bedroom on the lower deck unannounced Poppy still did so, though she half-closed her eyes in preparation.

To her surprise, however, Casey and Patrick were merely watching television. They both eyed Poppy curiously. "What's wrong, Poppy?" Casey asked, a frown of concern creasing her brow. "Has something happened—"

"Before you two run off," Poppy cut in, "after you've helped get everyone away from here. I need you to do one more thing. For Dorian's sake...and for mine."

Patrick stared at her in interest. "I'm listening."

RUTH TOWNSEND

DORIAN

He had two days to sort everything. Tomorrow Steven and Aisling would be responsible for taking away everyone who'd been up for bidding who had not yet been fully consumed and transporting them to their respective clients. The next day Nick was coming to take Poppy.

Dorian was going to make damn sure she was as far away as physically possible before then.

He didn't want to have to run away from the place he was born, even though Dorian knew he'd have to the moment he decided to build an auction site right beside it. People would investigate the sports facility where a group of thirty university students stayed and never returned.

Well, fifteen, he thought, *but that only makes things worse.*

For thirty people mysteriously spirited away with no witnesses to the disappearance was a mystery to be solved; half of them coming back left a damning trail of evidence Dorian could do without. The remaining club members knew something was deeply wrong by now – their fear was hanging in the air, dark and sinister and heavy.

But despite everything that had gone wrong Dorian still couldn't find it in him to regret any decision that had been made. He'd met Poppy, after all, and since Nick's family was growing old and unable to bear any offspring all Dorian had to do was wait them out until they died, and then he could rebuild his life.

Not that Poppy would ever allow him to be a trafficker again, of course, though he couldn't help but wonder if he could convince her to see why such a system was truly beneficial to both humans and monsters. Dorian had always enjoyed his career. He'd taken pride in being good at it. But after spending so much time in the company of the same group of humans he had to consider that he'd quite possibly lost the stomach to give people up for slaughter ever again.

It's not like I can go 'vegetarian', he mused, laughing humourlessly as he paced back and forth in front of the glass wall of his bedroom. Even with his keen, inhuman eyes Dorian could spy very little of the grove of trees where he was born through the glass; the sun had long since set. It left him feeling trapped. *And Poppy's blood is a poor substitute for actual food. I know I need to eat soon.*

Dorian didn't want to think of how he'd manage to do that with Poppy around.

But then he heard a knock on the door and all his worries were easily pushed to the side. "Come in, Poppy," Dorian called out, knowing it could only be her. When the door opened he looked up and saw that Poppy's hair hung long and loose and wavy around her shoulders, and she'd put on just enough make-up to accentuate her cheekbones and fluttering eyelashes. She had on the same button-down, strappy little dress that she'd worn the night everyone got drunk.

Poppy's cheeks flushed self-consciously in response to

Dorian's pointed gaze following her. "...hey," she said, closing the door gently behind her in the process. Dorian wasted no time in eliminating the distance between them, slamming Poppy against the door and kissing her like it was the last time he might ever get to do so.

If Nick got his way, it would be.

FRED

I can't believe Dorian had a room like this all along, Fred thought as his eyes darted from screen to screen. Most every part of the facility was documented through the camera feeds he was watching. The door had been locked, of course, but Poppy had shown him how to get through by swinging up into the ceiling and climbing along the tiles.

"Only King could have worked that out," he muttered, impressed despite himself that it actually worked. But then it occurred to him that creeping into the ceiling to spy on Dorian was what likely got Poppy into all the trouble she was currently in and Fred sobered.

We'd all be dead already if she hadn't, though, he reasoned. When they got out of this mess – *if* they got out of this mess – he wanted to learn every minute detail of what happened to Poppy King over the summer from beginning to end, even if she insisted on never seeing him again. Fred wanted to know exactly what she'd done every second of every day to save their club and never forget it.

It was the least he could do for the woman who was saving his life, despite everything he'd done to her.

Fred glanced at the screen showing Dorian's bedroom.

Poppy had just shown up, meaning Fred had to be careful. As soon as Dorian was out for the count and Poppy crept back out it was time to put their plan into motion. But when he saw Dorian slam Poppy against the door and begin to kiss her like his life depended on it, Fred stilled.

I'm going to see them fucking.

He knew he should look away. He *had* to look away.

He didn't.

DORIAN

"No monster form this time, Poppy," Dorian announced when he carried her over to the bed. He dropped her down without another word then proceeded to straddle her, pinning her in place.

She sighed dramatically. "And why not?"

"Because hooves weren't made for being in bed, and I'd rather like to get a chance to have sex with you like a—"

"Like a normal person?" she cut in, smiling wryly. "Because I'm afraid to tell you, Dorian, but you're not a normal person. You're not even a *person.*"

She watched him with heavy-lidded eyes as he pulled off his top and cast his gaze across the length of her. Even though Poppy liked Dorian's real form better it was clear there was no denying how attracted she was to human Dorian, either.

"I might not be human, no," he said, bending down to begin unbuttoning Poppy's dress. He was gratified – and greatly turned on – to see that she had nothing on beneath it. "But my human form is still a part of me, nonetheless. It's not like I can change it."

Her eyes grew wide in surprise, though Poppy's hands were busy careening down his stomach to slide off his trousers and made no effort to stop. "You can't?" she asked.

"No; I'm stuck like this just as much as you're stuck looking like you."

"I didn't know that."

"That's because you've never asked before."

"Then how do—"

"Shh," Dorian murmured, silencing Poppy's question with his mouth upon hers. "You have your whole life to bother me about such things. I don't want to talk right now."

The air hung heavy between them as Dorian finished unbuttoning Poppy's dress; it was completely unlike the atmosphere the last time they'd been together like this, in the forest. Every time he kissed her Dorian grew more desperate for...something.

A promise.

A proclamation.

Anything.

He didn't know *what* he wanted, but Dorian's fingers were trembling as they glided across Poppy's skin because of it.

Poppy seemed afraid by the way he was acting. She reached up a hand to touch his face. "Dorian, what's—"

"No talking," he insisted, harsher this time, before unceremoniously rolling Poppy onto her front in order to trail kisses down her back. Her breathing accelerated when Dorian's mouth reached the base of her spine, and when he slid a hand between her thighs it wasn't long before she was trembling even worse than he was.

Gradually Dorian's kisses morphed into bites. He moved back up to Poppy's neck, pressing the length of his body against hers until she gasped. When her hands twisted the pillow beneath her head as if to stop herself from speaking out Dorian grabbed both of them with one of his own and pinned them above her.

Poppy turned her head to the side, looking at Dorian with wild, uncertain eyes. "What are you doing?" she asked between laboured breaths.

"I don't know," he replied, disgustingly honest, before crushing his mouth back against hers. And then he shifted Poppy's hips, and it was the easiest thing in the world to slide inside her and connect the two of them together. He was satisfied when she cried out in shock; clearly he didn't need to be a monster to elicit such a reaction.

Yet it wasn't enough. Releasing Poppy's hands he hauled her up onto her knees, pulling her head back by her hair until it was resting on his shoulder and he had full access to her neck. Dorian's teeth grazed the skin there, but he hesitated from moving inside her.

Poppy noticed his hesitation immediately. "Why have you stopped, Dorian?" she asked, eyes glazed over with a desire he felt overwhelmingly sick to witness. This level of cooperation – of consent – didn't sit right with him. It felt wrong somehow, though Dorian couldn't work out why. "Just do it."

"Stop talking," he growled, putting two fingers inside Poppy's mouth to keep her quiet. He was satisfied when she bit down on them, embracing the pain even more when he, in turn, bit down into her neck hard enough to break through to the addictive blood that lay beneath her skin.

Poppy's cry was muffled against Dorian's fingers as he viciously drank from her, and he increased the pace at which he was fucking her in the process. One of Poppy's hands was on his hip, urging him on, even as the other curled into his hair in case she had to pull Dorian away from her neck if he took too much blood.

And he wanted to. He wanted to leave Poppy so drained she'd remain passed out for the next two days and wouldn't wake up until everything was over.

He didn't. Eventually Dorian broke away from Poppy's neck and fell onto his back, pulling out of her just long enough to roughly turn her around to face him. Dorian revelled in the sight of Poppy straddling him, pale and flushed and bloodied all at the same time, rocking on top of him with a frenzy he only too eagerly reciprocated. He imagined the desire displayed so obviously on her face was reflected eagerly on his own.

It wasn't long before Dorian wrenched Poppy's lips back down to his own, keeping them there until, with a desperate cry, he completely and utterly spent himself inside her. "Don't leave me," he mumbled against her ear as he came, exhausted and barely conscious. "Don't leave me, Poppy. Please. Don't leave me."

There was far too long a pause before she quietly replied, "...I won't."

FRED

He wished he hadn't watched. What had been seen could not be unseen, and Fred had seen a lot. Watching Dorian rip into Poppy scared him senseless; watching Poppy *enjoy* it terrified him even more.

But the worst part was that seeing Poppy reckless and naked and completely and utterly herself was making Fred's heart beat madly, and it confused him to no end.

It had to be the adrenaline. It had to be.

Numbly he watched Dorian well and truly pass out. Poppy sat by him for a while, a sad, sad look on her face that Fred didn't like at all. Then, instead of picking up her dress, she padded over to a chest of drawers – stumbling dangerously in the process – and pulled out a pair of denim shorts, a T-shirt and an over-sized jumper. Poppy hauled them on as quickly as possible. With silent fingers she extricated Dorian's master set of keys from his jeans which lay, forgotten, on the floor.

Then she stared dead-eyed at the camera and gave Fred the finger.

I guess it's go-time, he thought, deftly swinging back up into the ceiling and crawling through it until he landed back in the corridor.

It was time to prove to Poppy King that she'd been right to spare his life.

INTERLUDE X

THERE WAS CONFUSION EVERYWHERE.

"You've all got to stay silent," Fred urged in hushed tones, immediately after opening the door and coming face-to-face with the ashen, broken members of the Outdoor Sports Society held behind it. "Silent, got it? We've only got this one shot."

The people in the room stared blankly at each other.

What the hell was going on?

AN ORGANISED ESCAPE

ANDREW

Poppy, Fred and Patrick were in charge of getting the people who had been 'scouted' out of the facility. Those that were still alive, anyway. Andrew and Casey were given the task of herding the rest of the club out, though in truth they'd sent a message around that they were leaving in secret hours earlier.

And so it was that Andrew and Casey were already on Patrick's boat with thirteen very scared, confused Outdoor Sports Society members when Patrick himself showed up carrying two people nobody had seen for weeks: Thomas Pope and Nicolas Frey. The two who had tortured the mountain goat, and confirmed to Andrew that Poppy was well and truly choosing who was staying and who was leaving the facility.

Nic had lost both his legs. Tom had lost one, and a scar on his lower back suggested one of his kidneys had been taken, too. Behind Patrick came Ciaran Radin-Kirkwood, who was missing an arm, and Craig Hunt, who at first glance seemed completely fine. But it became quickly apparent that he'd lost his teeth and his tongue – which even now Andrew struggled to sympathise with, given the way the man had always spoken to him. But then he saw Ciaran had lost his tongue, too, and any sick satisfaction Andrew felt quickly dissipated.

Nobody deserved the fate that had befallen them. Andrew could never have suggested names to Poppy had he truly known what was going on. But then – what had he *thought* was going on? It had been so easy to believe that the people he didn't like had simply disappeared forever, like magic.

But this wasn't magic. This was a nightmare.

When Fred appeared carrying Megan Lo, who had lost her legs just like Nic, followed by Francis Greene and Mateusz Kowalski – who both looked outwardly unhurt – and, lastly, Max Marshall, whose eyes and left arm had been removed and was thus clutching onto Mateusz' sleeve for dear life, Andrew began to grow concerned.

Just where was Poppy?

"She wasn't in any state to carry anyone, Andrew," Fred whispered as soon as Andrew locked eyes with him, his question obvious on his face. "She's just behind us. Patrick, start the engine and get us the hell out of here!"

For a moment it appeared as if Patrick was going to complain about being ordered around. But then he gently laid down the two men he was carrying onto seats in the cabin, wordlessly leaving to start the ferry up. Casey nervously followed him.

Andrew hardly dared to breathe. It didn't help that nobody was speaking; clearly everyone had well and truly grasped the gravity of the situation. In the corner Rachelle was crying against Robin's shoulder, and Rich looked so pale Andrew thought he might pass out.

Only Nate seemed to be okay out of everyone who was still in the dark about what was going on, but Andrew knew it had to be an act in order for him to help the limbless, tortured people Fred and Patrick had carried through.

When Poppy finally showed up the dull roar of the boat's engine had already started. Andrew leapt towards her, flinging his arms around her even as Fred held out a hand to stop him.

"Andrew, don't, she won't be able to—"

When Poppy fell to the floor it was Fred who caught her. Andrew was horrified; her neck was covered in blood.

"P-Poppy, what did Dorian do to—"

"It's okay, Andrew," she said shakily. "It's fine. I'm okay. You know I'm okay."

"*Dorian* did that?" Nate cut in, corralling Poppy out of Fred's arms and onto a seat. "Poppy, what's going on? What's —"

"Let's get across the loch and on the bus before we explain anything," Fred said, quietly but firmly. "Everyone who's able: look after those who are not. I need you all to keep your wits together and stay calm, okay?"

It was clear everyone was looking to him as their *de facto* leader, hanging on his every word. Andrew hated that this was exactly what Poppy had wanted, and that Fred was great at it.

I wish he hadn't tried to kill Poppy, he thought sadly. *I wish none of this had happened at all.*

When someone started passing around bottles of vodka, rum, gin and whisky from Patrick's bar even Andrew took a few swigs of the stuff.

"Not for you, King," Fred reprimanded when she took hold of a bottle of vodka and attempted to put it to her lips.

She glared at him. "Fuck off, Sampson. I need it."

"You don't have enough blood in your—"

"Then it'll do its job faster. I need it to wipe the fact you were totally *watching* out of my brain forever."

"I wasn't...how do you know that?"

"You keep avoiding my eyes. Ugh. I can't believe you watched."

Andrew's gaze darted between the pair of them. "Watched what?"

"Nothing," they said in unison, so quickly that even Nate grew suspicious.

"Tell us what you were watching Poppy do, Fred," he insisted.

"Seriously, Nate, you don't want to—"

"Did you watch as whatever Dorian did to her neck happened?" Nate demanded, his previously calm and cool exterior crumbling by the second. "Did you not think to fucking *stop him doing it*?"

Fred glanced uncomfortably at Poppy, who hung her head in shame. "...I couldn't."

"But why?!"

"Nate, please don't push this further," Poppy said. She kept her gaze locked on her hands, hunched shoulders a clear sign she wanted everyone to stop talking about what happened to her.

Andrew was relieved when Patrick began to dock the ferry a short while later, though he still desperately wanted to know what Fred had seen despite the fact he was beginning to grasp what that was and knew he didn't like it one bit.

It was a struggle getting everyone onto the waiting bus. Casey hired it a few days ago, when Patrick had taken her on a boat trip to the closest town. People were stumbling over their feet to reach it. All around him Andrew could hear people sobbing and barely containing screams, the onset of garbled chatter a clear sign that the alcohol in their systems was beginning to loosen their tongues.

He wanted to hold his hands against his ears and block it all out. But then he felt someone's arms wrap around his back and shoulders, and he knew it could only be Poppy.

"You're okay, Andrew," she murmured between his shoulder blades. "You did so well. I'm so proud of you. You just have to hold on a little bit longer, then everything will be fine. You'll be back home."

"Poppy."

"Yes?"

"Can we still go to New Zealand?" Andrew asked, as everyone but the two of them filtered onto the bus. He could see Fred and Nate and Casey and a sobbing, hysterical Rachelle watching them from the front window.

Poppy chuckled against his back. "I can't believe you still remember that, Andrew. God, it feels like a thousand years ago."

"That sounds like a no."

"Let's call it a maybe. Get on the bus, Andrew."

He froze.

"What does that mean, Poppy? Aren't – aren't you coming with us?"

Poppy said nothing, which spoke volumes.

Andrew broke away from her arms, blinking back furious tears as he turned to face her. "Don't you *dare* go back there!" he screamed, which sounded horrible because Andrew hated shouting. Behind him he heard Rachelle cry out in shock, and then the scrabbling of people coming off the bus.

Poppy's face was completely blank. "I have to, Andrew. I made a deal with him."

"But he was blackmailing you! You have to come back with us."

"What's going on, Poppy?" Rachelle asked, voice trembling and dripping with tears as she embraced her best friend. "What does Andrew mean? Of course you're coming with us. Don't be stupid."

Andrew watched as Poppy's expression broke for just a moment, but after hugging Rachelle for a few seconds she extricated herself from her arms. "I'll explain everything soon. I swear it. But for now I have to go."

"Morph, please," Nate said. Andrew had never heard him sound so vulnerable. He held out a hand to touch Poppy's shoulder, but she moved away.

"Don't do this to me right now," Poppy begged of them. Her eyes moved from Andrew, to Nate, to Rachelle, then back to Andrew once more. "Please, trust me that this is the right thing to do. Get on the bus. *No buts,*" she added on when Nate made to protest. "Get on the bus. I'll speak to you soon. Just...go."

She really isn't coming with us, Andrew realised. He felt sick. This wasn't happening. But he knew Poppy better than almost anyone. *Nothing anyone says will change her mind.*

"How are you getting back there, King?" Fred asked, in as close to an imitation of a classic Fred voice as he could. But it sounded all wrong. Horribly, disgustingly wrong. "You gonna swim in the state you're in? Or do you suddenly know how to operate a ferry?"

Poppy indicated towards the narrow road that wound around the loch and lifted the bottle of vodka Nate was still holding out of his hand. "I'm not smart enough to work a boat," she joked. "I'll do just fine on my own two legs. Lord knows I need the time the walk will take to sort my head out."

Fred took a few steps towards her, and for a moment Andrew thought he would actually hug her. But then he sighed, and shook his head. "Don't die."

Poppy let out a bark of laughter. "Unlikely. Look after our club for me, Sampson."

"You got it."

And with that Poppy ran off without another word, alternately swigging from the bottle of vodka and sprinting away into the darkness.

"She's going to collapse in the middle of nowhere in the state she's in," Nate said, shoulders slumped in defeat as he watched Poppy's silhouette grow smaller and smaller until, between one moment and the next, the darkness engulfed her and she was gone.

"She won't," Andrew said assuredly, though he wished he were wrong. That way Poppy wouldn't reach Dorian, and then Andrew could carry her back to safety to be with her friends. To be with him.

He knew that would never happen. It was a far-off, impossible dream, just like New Zealand had always been.

AFTERMATH

FRED

"SOMEBODY TELL ME WHAT THE *FUCK* is going on!" loud-mouthed John Campbell shouted, when the bus was at least ten miles away from the loch and on its way to the nearest hospital.

"What happened to you guys?!" Lily Johnson cried, stroking Megan's hair as the half-dead girl sobbed in relief at the realisation that she was no longer in Dorian's murder facility.

"M-monsters," she managed to get out, which was echoed by several more of the club members who had been 'scouted'.

"When I tried to leave last week Dorian caught me and threw me in a room with all of them," Mateusz said, the words coming out so quickly they were barely coherent. "I heard some of his assistants say we'd all be taken away soon. I thought I was gonna die. I thought I was gonna die. I thought—"

"At least nothing actually happened to you!" Max called out blindly. "You and Francis are completely unhurt! How did that even happen?"

"Probably getting sold off to be eaten whole," Fred muttered under his breath, but his voice carried across the entire bus. Everyone stared at him.

"How do you know that?" Francis asked, and the mute Craig Hunt nodded his head fervently. "Craig and Megan and I are the only ones who – who saw anything. We saw—"

"Monsters. I know," Fred said. "I had the pleasure of witnessing Dorian as one."

Megan's eyes grew wide. "You saw *Dorian?* As a m-monster? Then why aren't you – how come you weren't in the room with us if you saw—"

"It's a long story, but I have Poppy to thank for that."

"Poppy? Why? What does she have to do with—" Francis stared at Fred, face paling as a sick realisation dawned on him. "After I told you that I knew what Ross Bridges had done – after *Poppy* overheard – I was taken away. And...Grace and Ciaran were taken away after they bad-mouthed her! Was *Poppy* doing this to us?!"

"She didn't have a choice!" Andrew yelled out, speaking for the first time since Poppy ran off.

"Dorian was going to kill us," Casey chimed in, from her position beside Patrick in the driver's seat. "We were *all* supposed to die two weeks in. Poppy found out."

"So why are we not all dead, then?!"

"Because Poppy reached a compromise with Dorian," Fred explained. "She could save half the club. But *she* had to choose who to save and who to...not."

Max laughed bitterly. "And so, what? She gave up people who had a grudge against her? That's awfully nice of her."

"She gave up the worst of us first!" Andrew said, passionate and uncharacteristically eloquent in his desire to defend Poppy. "Ross tried to attack Casey. Angelica was bullying

Jenny. Tom and Nic tortured the goat—"

"Oh my fucking lord," Tom spat out. "You *knew*, even back then, didn't you? That's why you made sure Poppy saw what we were doing!"

"What you were doing was sick," Fred countered, glaring at him. He rounded on the whole bus of muttering, terrified, furious, astounded club members. "Who here could say they'd have done better in Poppy's place? She had to give up half of us – including herself!"

"You want me to tell you the order in which she gave up or saved any of us?" he continued, standing up to ensure everyone was watching him. "Is that what you want to know? Because I have her list, and she told me how she made some of her decisions." Fred looked at Andrew, who was staring right back at him with wide, teary eyes.

"Do you want to know that she begged for Andrew's life first, before even knowing whether she could save any of the rest of us? She didn't think about saving herself: only him." Fred paused for a moment, recalling everything he could remember Poppy reluctantly telling him about her list.

"Or that she saved Gregory, so he could help with his sister's cancer treatment? Or that Max was sacrificed because she was running out of decent reasons to give people up, and he was simply not good *enough* to save? Or that Ruth was last to be saved simply by process of elimination? Is that what you want to know?"

Everyone was silent, except for Andrew, who hugged his knees to his chest and sobbed. "I want Poppy," he moaned. "I want Poppy. I want..." When Paul Tobin moved to sit beside him and murmur reassurances Fred worked out exactly why Paul was still here, too.

"She could have – picked names out of a hat," Tom said eventually, breaking the agonising silence. "To keep things random."

"You really think Poppy could have done that and given up Andrew, Rachelle, Nate and Casey if their names weren't drawn?"

"Actually, she couldn't save me," Casey pointed out. Several heads turned sharply in her direction.

"So how come you were never locked up?" Max asked, tone entirely accusatory.

She glanced uncomfortably at Patrick. "Because Patrick is like Dorian. A monster. He, ah, may have...bought me."

"And you're *okay* with that?!" Rachelle exclaimed, voice cracking as she spoke. "Casey, what's wrong with you? What's wrong with *Poppy*?"

"Look, Patrick and I worked things out."

Nate roared in outrage. "How do you *work things out* with a —"

"Hey, I'm right here," Patrick cut in, annoyed, "and that's us at the hospital. I don't owe any of you an explanation." He looked at Casey. "You ready, Cass?"

"Wait," Nate said, frowning. "What do you mean *is she ready*?"

Casey gave him a falsely bright smile. "We're leaving. Together."

Rachelle looked just about ready to collapse. "No. No, you're not going."

"I'm so sorry, Rachelle. Nate. But I'm going. We need to help Poppy and Dorian, anyway."

"You knew?" Andrew cried. "You knew Poppy was going back to him the whole time, Casey, and you didn't say anything?"

"She only told us this afternoon," Patrick said, not unkindly. "We didn't know before then."

"But why are you helping *him*? Why are you—"

"Because Dorian's my friend, and he was only doing his job. He and I are not the villains you think we are."

Nobody said anything. The entire club could take no more new information – and certainly not anything that suggested they sympathise with the monsters responsible for their entire nightmare.

"Right," Patrick said after a few moments. "Everyone off the bus. Cass and I have some idiots to save."

Fred said nothing as most of the club struggled off the bus. It was only when he was left alone with Andrew, Casey and Patrick that he spoke. "We deserve the full story," he told Patrick. "You and Dorian. You owe it to all of us, even if you don't think you do. You've destroyed our lives, so the least you can do is explain everything."

Patrick frowned. "I thought Poppy had told you two everything?" he asked, indicating towards a despondent Andrew.

"We all know Poppy never tells the whole truth."

Casey laughed despite herself. "Sounds like Poppy."

Patrick sighed. "How about this, then: give us a month. A month to settle and recover. Then Cass and I will be in touch, and we'll make sure to drag Dorian and Poppy along with us. Sound good?"

"I want to see her *now*—"

"Andrew, c'mon," Fred said. "You know you can't. Poppy told you to hold on just a little bit longer. You can do that, can't you? You've always been able to do that for her. So give her some time."

"Don't talk to me about Poppy like that."

Fred sighed. "Fine, I won't. But we're getting off this bus, and we're going to help everyone *together,* and then, in a few weeks, we'll get the answers we want. That's our only option, Andrew."

Andrew said nothing. He knew Fred was right.

Patrick cocked his head towards the door. "Off the bus, guys. Cass and I have lots to do."

When Andrew passed Casey she hugged him, and Fred barely heard her whisper, "Thank you for loving Poppy."

It struck Fred that he'd never really acknowledged that Andrew loved Poppy, because he'd never cared about it. Nate was far more obvious in his affection for Poppy, after all, and in all the time Fred had known her she'd never been serious about having a boyfriend.

But now that he was taking it into account, the way Andrew was reacting made far more sense. He wasn't just upset, or horrified, or in pain. Andrew was experiencing something much, much worse, which Fred knew would make the next month all the more torturous.

Andrew was heartbroken.

DIVINE RETRIBUTION

DORIAN

WHEN DORIAN AWOKE HE KNEW SOMETHING was wrong. A murky, early morning light filtered into his bedroom, informing him that he'd slept for almost ten hours unimpeded. That in and of itself wasn't strange, because he'd been exhausted, but Dorian knew that if Poppy had been with him all night he'd definitely have woken up. He twisted his body round to check the other side of the bed.

She wasn't there.

The realisation crushed the air out of his lungs. Hurriedly Dorian dressed and flung his door open to an unnervingly quiet corridor; taking a moment to check the time he realised it wasn't quite six in the morning. His staff wouldn't be up yet, nor would most of the members of Poppy's club. Hoping that Poppy had simply crept out of his bed in order to spend as much time with her friends as possible before they left for good, Dorian fished out his keys for the observation room.

When he was greeted by screens and screens of empty rooms – including the room where every human up for auction was being held – Dorian banged a fist against the wall and rushed back out to the corridor.

"Jane!" he exclaimed, reaching her door and slamming it open before waiting for a reply. "Everyone is *gone.*"

She gazed up at him, eyes still heavy with sleep. "Everyone?"

"*Everyone*! Tell me you didn't know about this. Tell me—"

"Of course I didn't know anything about it."

"*Then how did it happen at all*?!"

Jane clucked her tongue, unamused. "This was why you should have brought in more staff after you decided to keep everyone here longer than the initial two weeks. You always knew that was foolish. Your father—"

"I'm not my father, though, am I?"

Dorian stalked out of Jane's room without another word, furious with himself. Of course he should have hired more staff to help secure the premises. But everything had been going so well – at least until two or three weeks ago when the sports club began to grow uneasy. Dorian, in his hubris, thought everything was going to be fine. Poppy was on his side, after all, thanks to what Fred had done to her.

But then why was she speaking with him in her bedroom the other week...?

Dorian's blood froze as he realised that Poppy must have been planning to leave for a long, long time – and he'd been completely blind to it. He thundered around the facility, thrusting open doors and checking nobody was behind them on the off-chance his cameras were lying to him.

They weren't.

Nobody was in the kitchen or the social areas or the gym or pool or hot tubs. He could see nobody walking on the nearby hills, nor swimming in the loch, nor sitting in the meadow.

Since it was beginning to pour with rain and was, after all, six in the morning, Dorian felt stupid for checking outside in the first place.

When he reached the east wing he didn't want to open the door to Poppy's bedroom. If he never opened it then she might still be inside, even though Dorian knew from his cameras that she wouldn't be.

He inhaled deeply and opened the door. Of course she was nowhere to be seen.

"*Poppy King!*" Dorian roared, smashing the chair in her room against the bed over and over again until it splintered into sharp, ragged pieces. He could barely breathe: everything was ruined. In a few scant hours Steven and Aisling would arrive to cart away all of the club members who had been bought. Including Frederick Sampson, whom Aisling was eagerly awaiting personally digging her claws into.

Dorian didn't want to think about what would happen once they realised he'd lost each and every one of the members of the Outdoor Sports Society.

It wasn't just the substantial amount of money on the line that was sending Dorian into a frenzy, though that would certainly be one of the main factors for Steven and Aisling. It was the fact that, by failing to provide quality livestock for the monsters in Britain, it was only a matter of time before people started disappearing right off the streets. With no 'sanctioned' food source monsters would begin ripping humans apart in the most gruesome of ways down darkened corridors, empty train stations...and their very beds.

Poppy had destroyed the delicate food chain Dorian, and his father before him, had been so integral in putting in place. She'd destroyed it like it was nothing.

Dorian could never forgive her.

But then he thought of Nick. Nichola Richardson, heir to

the largest, most prominent family of monsters in Europe, who would surely destroy Dorian where he stood tomorrow if Steven and Aisling didn't do so first. Nick would no doubt begin searching for Poppy; it was only a matter of time before he found her. She couldn't have gone that far, after all.

Don't be an idiot and return home, he thought, deathly worried despite the fact he was furious with her. He moved back through the social area, fully intending to pack as quickly as possible and disappear himself. *Don't be that stupid. Go to London. Go abroad. Go literally anywhere that isn't home.*

"Dorian."

Dorian's stomach lurched at the voice. He turned to face the entrance of the facility, closing his eyes for a moment as if doing so would evaporate the person before him into thin air.

But there Poppy stood, soaking wet and shivering, her pale, guilty eyes locked unwaveringly on Dorian. He wanted to kill her for what she'd done. He wanted to kill her for running away. He wanted to kill her for coming back.

He knew he never would.

A BETRAYAL OF THE MOST IRONIC KIND

DORIAN

"You fool. You complete and utter fucking *fool*. Do you know what you've done?!"

Poppy held her ground, still standing outside in the rain. The grey, miserable weather washed her out, as if a particularly strong gust of wind would be enough to simply erase her existence altogether.

"I saved as many people as I could," Poppy said. "It was the *only* thing I could have done."

"You could've done as you were told and let half your club die!"

All of the guilt lingering in Poppy's eyes was gone in a moment. She slammed a hand against the glass door of the facility, the sound it made reverberating dully around them. "You don't get to say that, Dorian. How could I have *ever* done that? I've wanted to save everyone from the beginning!"

"What, so you never intended to stick to our deal at all?"

"What kind of human would?!" she cried. "Of course I was going to try and save my club!"

Dorian shook his head in disbelief. "So what about everything you said after Frederick *fucking* Sampson cut you to ribbons?"

"I was angry! I was hurt! Of course I was going to feel the way I felt back then! But once the anger was gone I knew I could never live with myself if I let everyone die."

"But why did you save *Fred?* Out of everyone he deserved to die!"

"Maybe so," Poppy glowered, "but not by my hands. And it's not like his actions were unwarranted. He knew something horrible was going on. He—"

"Don't you *dare* justify his actions, Poppy."

"Then I won't, but that doesn't change a damn thing! Everyone is gone, Dorian, and you'll just have to deal with that."

Dorian stormed over to her, dragging Poppy back inside by the front of her jumper. He realised she was wearing clothes *he* had bought her, for the life they were supposed to have after summer was over. He almost laughed at that: summer *was* over and the life the two of them had left was most likely going to be frightfully short.

"Let go of me, Dorian!" Poppy exclaimed, clawing at his hand when he ignored her. He threw her unceremoniously onto one of the sofas in the social area, towering over her with his arms crossed over his chest.

"Why did you come back, Poppy?"

"...what?"

"If you were planning to betray me from the beginning – if you were planning to leave with everyone – why come back?

You could have been hundreds of miles away by now."

Poppy didn't look at him, pulling a blanket that lay abandoned on the floor around her shivering shoulders. "I didn't want to break that part of our deal," she muttered under her breath. "It was the only part that was solely on me, not the club."

Dorian slapped her, so viciously he cut through her skin. The thin line of angry red that appeared on her cheek barely had time to bleed before it healed itself over. "You should have stayed away," he seethed, feeling as if he might hyperventilate. "If you were going to steal everyone away then you should have stayed away, too."

For a long moment Poppy stayed silent, rubbing her cheek and eyeing Dorian warily as she continued to shake uncontrollably beneath the blanket. Even now, when he was murderously furious and hurt by her, Dorian badly wanted to stop her shivering.

"What use is it for me to go back with everyone?" Poppy eventually asked, voice very quiet. "My life will be far longer than theirs, won't it? Who else could I be with but you?"

Dorian laughed bitterly. "Your life may be far shorter than you imagined, you unbelievably ignorant girl."

For a second it looked like Poppy was going to fire out a retort. She merely hugged the blanket around her a little tighter, instead, and glared at Dorian. "So, what, you're going to kill me now that I've betrayed you?" she asked.

The question caught Dorian off-guard with how ridiculous it was. He bent down to kneel in front of Poppy. "What. Is. Wrong. With. You?" he asked through gritted teeth, shaking her roughly by the shoulders with every word.

"What's wrong with *me?*" She tried to shrug him off and failed. "Are you really asking me that when you're the reason I'm so messed up in the first place? If it wasn't for *you* I'd never have come back here!"

"How can you so easily betray me and doom me to die and yet still come back to be by my side?!"

"What do you mean, doom you to die? We're leaving this place, are we not? It's not like all your clients could possibly have the resources to constantly look for you wherever you go."

"Are you really that naïve? At the absolute *least* the Richardson family does!"

Poppy hesitated, fear finally flitting across her face. "...I thought they'd already taken all of their *livestock?*" she asked, spitting the final word out like poison.

"Are - are you being serious right now?" Dorian said, torn between incredulity and bubbling, burning anger. "Just how many times have I told you Nick wanted to buy you?"

"I thought you said you were handling that?"

"I could only push him off for so long, you idiot! He's supposed to show up tomorrow to fucking pick you up and—"

"Wait, you were going to let him *eat* me?"

Dorian rolled his eyes. "As if he was going to eat you. He was going to—"

"No. No. Don't say it." *Now* Poppy looked terrified. "Dorian, you weren't really going to let him—"

"Of course I wasn't! I was going to push off everyone who'd been bought onto Steven and Aisling today and then run the hell away with you as far as I possibly could."

"So...if that was your plan, anyway, why does it matter that I saved my club?"

"How am I supposed to protect us from *everyone,* Poppy? I'll be blacklisted and hunted by my entire kind now! And with Steven and Aisling arriving this morning we no longer have a day's head start - we have an hour!"

Poppy stumbled to her feet. "Then what are we waiting for? If you had just *told* me about Nick then I could've—"

"Could have what, Poppy?" Dorian said as he helped steady her despite wishing she would fall and never get back up. "Arranged your escape plan a day earlier? So thoughtful of you."

Poppy shoved him away from her. "Fuck you, Dorian. You don't get to be mad here."

"You're damn right I do. I get to be *furious.* I get to be *this* close," he muttered, holding his thumb and index finger a centimetre apart for emphasis, "from draining you of all but your last drops of blood and flinging you in a locked room in some dark corner of the world where you can't ruin my life any further."

"Then just *kill me*!"

"You know I'll never do that!"

The two of them stood staring at each other, breathing hard and fast and ragged, unsure of what to do next. But then the front door opened and they both froze.

Dorian's heart thumped painfully in his chest. They'd run out of time. "They're here. They're—"

"...sure Dorian won't mind that you came a day early, Nick," they heard Aisling say. "Steven and I are taking away everyone else today, anyway. This probably makes things easier for him."

Poppy started trembling again, eyes darting between the entrance hall and Dorian in fear. "Dorian, what do we—"

"In the ceiling. Get in the ceiling."

"Dorian—"

He didn't let her say anything else. Dorian lifted Poppy up and tossed her though one of the tiles. "Watch from there and look for an opening to escape. Shouldn't be difficult for you.

You're good at that kind of thing."

Poppy lowered her head through the gap in the ceiling, beyond terrified for herself – and for Dorian. "I'm not leaving you alone, Dorian. They'll kill you."

"And they'll do worse to you, so fuck off!"

She hesitated for one agonisingly long second, then put the ceiling tile back in place just as Nick, Steven and Aisling arrived in the social area.

Nick smiled broadly. "Morning, Dorian. I hope it's not a problem I arrived a day early."

"You must be glad to finally get this lot off your hands," Steven said, Aisling nodding along in agreement.

Dorian breathed deeply.

"Well, about that...they already are."

A DISORGANISED ESCAPE

POPPY

"What do you mean, they already are?" Aisling asked, the ceiling tiles somewhat muffling her voice. Poppy didn't dare lift one to watch what was going on.

"Let's talk about this somewhere else," Dorian said.

Poppy heard footsteps heading away from her and she knew then and there what Dorian was doing. He didn't want her to have to witness what was going to happen to him; he wanted her to use Nick, Aisling and Steven's momentary distraction to escape.

She knew she couldn't do that.

Steeling her nerves Poppy began navigating her way through the ceiling, following the fading sounds of footsteps as they headed through to the west wing. But they were walking far faster than Poppy could crawl, and by the time she worked out which room they were in – one of the locked rooms she'd never been in before – Dorian had clearly already told the other three what happened.

A sickening, crunching noise carried through the air, followed by the sound of Dorian screaming in pain. Poppy gasped. She thought of the mountain goat Tom and Nicolas had tortured, crying in agony. Dorian's scream carried more similarities to the goat than any noise she'd ever heard a human emit.

"How do you lose an entire group of humans?" Steven exclaimed. "Six of them were missing limbs, for fuck's sake!" His voice sounded different – transformed somehow. Poppy risked lifting up a ceiling tile half an inch. Just enough to glimpse what was going on.

Below her were four monsters.

Dorian was sprawled on the floor, one of his hoofed legs mangled beyond repair. His eyes were hazy from the pain. Looming above him could only be Nick; memories of Franco Richardson disembowelling Ross Bridges threatened to overwhelm Poppy simply by looking at him.

Nick's head was marginally more human than the ox head his father possessed, though his massive, curling horns were identical to the older man and his entire body – twice the size of his already bulky, human one – was similarly covered in scales. They were yellow and tinged with green where his father's had been pure gold.

Poppy was somehow not at all surprised that Aisling was a harpy, with wicked, razor-sharp talons the inky purple of midnight. Her feathers were a similar colour, too, iridescent in the artificial light of the room. Her skin was a paler tone, almost lilac; only the dark hair tumbling down Aisling's back remained unchanged from her human form. She was disgustingly beautiful and terrifying to behold, her cruel face sneering down at Dorian as if she always knew he was beneath her.

Steven was the only monster who surprised Poppy. Given that he was shorter and slighter than both Nick and Dorian –

and quieter, too – Poppy always assumed he'd be less of a threat. She couldn't have been more wrong. Steven had transformed into something Poppy could only compare to a leopard, golden and lithe and so obviously possessing keener senses than the monsters around him that Poppy held her breath before she could stop herself.

Steven's pointed ears, like Dorian's, flicked back and forth as they listened intently, and his large, feline eyes roved around the room, missing nothing.

One wrong move and Steven would find her.

Nick's long, heavy tail flicked and twitched in anger behind him. "You lost her. You lost *Poppy King*?!" Dorian laughed horribly. Nick kicked him in the face. "Answer me, you son of a bitch!"

"Laughing was the right response," Dorian drawled between coughs and splutters. Nick had broken his nose; it was bleeding profusely. He spat some of it away when it reached his mouth. "Who do you think coordinated the whole escape?"

"But how did she *know* to escape?" Aisling asked, suspicious. "Nobody was supposed to know."

"Clearly she found out."

"And, what? Managed to hide her horror enough to organise a covert escape that you were none-the-wiser to? I think not."

"Well I must be even stupider than you already believed me to be, Ash. Congrats."

When she slashed her talons across Dorian's chest it was all Poppy could do not to cry in pain with him. It was excruciating, watching him being torn to shreds when she could do nothing to stop it. Poppy thought of when Andrew had led Dorian to the kitchen, back when Fred had tried his hardest to drain the very life from her.

Is this how Dorian felt, seeing me so helpless? Poppy

thought, pushing her anger and revulsion at Fred into a box she would probably never open again. *When he saw me ripped open and bleeding, was Dorian ever at a loss for what to do?*

But then Poppy realised that, no, Dorian hadn't been. For all he had to do was storm in, throw Fred off her as if he weighed nothing at all, and carry her away to safety.

Poppy couldn't do that. All she could do was watch, when what she *had* to do was run away.

"Don't play games with us, Dorian," Nick said. "We all know you're not stupid nor oblivious."

"She really did pull the wool over my eyes. I'm not lying about that."

"Oh, but you *are* lying?" Aisling remarked, catching on to Dorian's wording immediately. "About what, though? About none of the humans knowing what was going on? But if that was the case...why didn't you kill King the moment you realised she knew?"

Dorian took too long to reply, but it wasn't his silence that sold him out. It was his wounds.

Or, rather, lack thereof.

For beneath the blood staining his skin and hair Dorian had begun to heal, though it had been almost imperceptible to Poppy from her limited viewpoint in the ceiling. But now she was looking for it Poppy could see that the angle of his broken leg had fixed itself, and his nose was no more twisted than it had been before. Either of these might have gone unnoticed in the heat of the moment.

The rapidly-healing gashes across his chest from Aisling's strike did not.

Steven bent down by Dorian's side immediately, running a clawed finger through his chest even as Dorian yowled in pain. But Steven's attack barely left a mark.

"There's something wrong here – oh. *Oh.*"

Steven licked some of Dorian's blood from his claw; Poppy didn't need to see the look on his face to know it was exactly the way Dorian had looked at *her* the first time he'd tasted her blood. Nick and Aisling caught on quickly, wasting no time in sampling the wounded satyr's blood for themselves. The revelatory looks in their eyes tore Poppy apart, for how was it that something she was born with could have such an effect? But she didn't care about how the others reacted to her blood.

She cared about how Dorian was reacting to them finding out, as if all the life had been drained out of him. Poppy hadn't once thought about how hard he'd actually had to work to keep her secret *secret.* She'd flaunted her physical abilities and shown off. She'd rebelled against Dorian, just because she could.

And now he was paying for that – not her.

"You had a little immortal on your hands and didn't think to share that with your friends, Dorian?" Aisling purred, voice dangerously silky as she prowled around him. "Did you want her for yourself, is that it? I guess I can't say I'm surprised given how you were always watching her."

To Poppy's surprise Nick seemed impressed rather than angry, though considering how monstrous he looked she couldn't be sure. "I have to hand it to you," he said, "you did a fine job of covering it up. And you almost got away with it. Almost."

"Yeah," Dorian laughed, though it came out as a coughing fit full of blood, "if only she was a little *stupider* then I would've been halfway around the world with her by now."

Poppy bristled, though she knew Dorian was saying such a thing to tell her to run away if she hadn't yet done so. Somehow she knew that *Dorian* knew she hadn't, and that she never would.

"But she's not stupid, is she?" Steven murmured, stalking around the room with all senses on high alert, just as Poppy put down the ceiling tile she was watching from. "She's foolish, though, and reckless. And easily emotionally manipulated."

"Don't you dare—" Dorian bit out, but Steven darted towards him and cut his throat, the horrible, gurgling sound he emitted telling Poppy what had happened to him. She held a hand to her mouth and forced down a gulp of air to stop herself from vomiting.

"Come out, come out, Poppy King," Nick called out, voice sickeningly sing-song. "We know you're there. You must know by now that we won't kill you. You're far too *valuable* for that."

Poppy had a split second to think. If she hung around just to listen to Dorian choking on his own blood then he'd die, even if Steven had to cut his throat over and over and over again until it stuck. Poppy didn't want that. Just as she had made the decision to save her club above all else, now she had to save Dorian from horrors she could barely comprehend – nightmares he had thus far shielded her from.

Poppy crept through the ceiling as quickly as she dared until she was certain she reached the kitchen. A month ago she would never have known such a thing; it was all thanks to Andrew and his love of maps that she knew every ceiling tile of the facility.

If I come out of this alive I'll have to thank him a thousand times, Poppy thought, manic as she stumbled against the sink on her way to the massive gas hob that she had entirely ignored all summer. With shaking hands she turned every one of the dials until the sweet sound of whistling hit her ears. Then she grabbed a lighter and as many bottles of alcohol as she could find and ran from the kitchen, being sure to knock open the door as she did.

Poppy was relieved when she saw that nobody had followed her, but that relief was short-lived. For no sooner had she reached the west wing, pouring vodka and rum and gin as she went, than Nick appeared, blocking the corridor with every inch of his monstrous form. Poppy choked on a scream despite herself, legs buckling to the floor in sheer fright.

"Fuck fuck fuck fuck fuck," she stammered, though behind Nick the sounds of screaming and yowling drowned it out.

Nick took a careful, heavy step towards Poppy, the sound echoing across the floor. "I'm sure Dorian will do as much damage as he can in there," he said, tilting his head towards the room he came from, a deeply amused expression on his face. "Hell, it's Steven's fault for getting so close; he's as good as dead. But Dorian can't get through Aisling *and* me, Poppy King, even with your blood in him."

Poppy couldn't take a step back now that she'd collapsed to the floor. For the first time since Dorian wrenched her from the ceiling, shattering her very perception of reality, she was blindly, terribly afraid of what it meant to no longer be a predator.

She was prey.

If this is how a rabbit feels in the face of a hawk then I'm never eating meat again, she thought uselessly as Nick took another heaving step towards her. But then Nick paused and, in the space of a second, shook himself back into his human form.

He smiled disarmingly for Poppy. "Come on, Poppy. If you've known all this time what we are then you can't *really* be that afraid of me, right? And Dorian is no better than me – worse, even. He's a *trafficker,* for fuck's sake. You really want to be with a farmer when you could be part of the family that pays the farmer, instead?"

Poppy had never regretted obstinately feigning disinterest in Dorian's world as much as she did now, when she was frozen in fear and could do nothing but absorb the insults Nick threw her way.

He chuckled softly then knelt in front of her. "Poppy, when have I ever been bad to you?" he crooned. "We've always gotten along well, have we not? No need to change that now."

"Get the *fuck* away from me!" she bit out, though her voice shook and was barely loud enough to hear. "Get away – get away, just—"

Nick held his hands up as if in resignation. "I'm not touching you. I'm not threatening you, Poppy. Do you know how *valuable* you are? Here I was looking for cattle when I should have been searching for a goldmine."

The words finally rebooted Poppy's brain, just as Nick lurched forward to grab her. She kicked his face and jolted away. "I'm not a *thing*!" she cried. Nick swore loudly and lumbered to his feet. "I didn't spend fifteen weeks surviving just for you to fucking buy me!"

Nick burst out laughing, wiping away the dust Poppy left on his face from her kick before stalking down the corridor after her. She knew he was close to reverting to his real form again, but she was beginning to smell propane on the air.

Just a little longer, Poppy thought desperately. *Stall him just a little longer...*

But it was no longer a matter of simply stalling Nick. If he'd been correct and Dorian had successfully dispensed with Steven that still left Aisling for Dorian to contend with. Considering he was concurrently recovering from should-be-fatal injuries Poppy did not have high hopes that he was doing as well as she was.

"You know, I wanted you to be the mother of my children *before* I knew about your blood," Nick drawled, the pace at which he stalked towards Poppy slow in the way only those certain of victory could be. The shadowy, early morning light made him look all the more eerie and sinister, even in human form. And there were times when his shadow broke and bent and flickered in front of Poppy's very eyes, sending her heart into a desperate frenzy.

Just another beat. Two. Three. You can do four, Poppy King. Come on, heart, let's hit five.

"That's such an *honour,*" Poppy spat out, taking a careful step towards the back door out of the facility – the one that led to the meadow at the base of the cliffs, protecting Dorian's facility from the worst of the brutal northern winds that battered the Scottish Highlands.

"You don't sound all that impressed," Nick said, closing the gap between them once more.

"I never really saw myself as a stay-at-home mum, you know? Greatest respect to them, obviously. It's just not for me. Especially when my babies would be *giant lizard oxes* that even Theseus would run from."

"Oh, you know your stuff, don't you? Are you not curious about us, Poppy? About why we exist? About what our existence means for—"

"*I. Don't. Care.*"

Nick could only laugh assuredly. "You will. Trust me, you will. When everyone else is trembling in fear of my family – of the legacy *you* will help me create – then trust me, Poppy King, you will want to know."

When Poppy breathed in deeply through her nostrils and could only smell gas she knew it was time. She had no sign from Dorian that he was okay, but Poppy knew she had to get away – if only to stop somebody like Nick from ever holding her in their grasp. If that meant dying in a ball of flames then so be it.

Poppy glugged down several measures of rum from the remaining bottle in her hand, tossing it to the side before reaching for the lighter she'd stashed in the pocket of her shorts.

Nick was so close. Too close. She hated that she could see

every triumphant line of his face as he reached out and—

Was set alight.

Poppy hadn't even sparked a flame yet.

Dorian had.

"What are you, Poppy King?" he asked, grabbing hold of Poppy and sprinting out of the facility just as the entire building erupted into flames.

An Unwilling
Partnership

DORIAN

WHEN THE TWO OF THEM REACHED the grove of trees in which he
was born Dorian could barely recall how they had reached it.
His body was thrumming with broken bones and shredded
muscles and slashed veins repairing themselves with every step
he took. His throat was in agony; each breath was like
sandpaper against it.

"You should have *run*, you idiot!" Dorian gasped,
collapsing in a barely-conscious heap in the exact spot where
he'd lain with Poppy on his chest two weeks prior, when he'd
been struggling to regain his breath for entirely different
reasons.

Poppy sat beside him, chest heaving. She didn't quite seem
to see – anything. Her pale eyes were made of glass, full of
smoke and rain and everything she had witnessed but hadn't
truly taken in yet.

"You're...welcome," she muttered, so quietly Dorian almost didn't hear her.

But he did, and he had just enough strength left to grab Poppy and slam her to the ground beneath him. "Welcome for what?!" he demanded, even though it hurt to speak. "Welcome for being forced to kill Steven, who was one of my friends? Welcome for having to protect you against others of my kind, though I'm now as good as dead for doing so? Or welcome for allowing you to literally destroy everything I'd been building throughout my career, regardless of what that meant for me?"

Poppy said nothing. She could barely speak after their impossible climb up the rain-soaked cliff; Dorian was still unsure how they'd actually managed it. She looked away from him, though Dorian only tightened his grip on her wrists as a result, claws digging into her flesh despite the way Poppy tensed against the pain.

"Answer me!" Dorian raged, futilely shaking the woman below him until he lost the strength to do so. He collapsed heavily on top of her.

Poppy gasped at the weight of him. "Can't...breathe... Dorian—"

"It would serve you right," he muttered, rolling off her just enough that one of Dorian's long-limbed arms was all that lay across her chest.

"You know I meant *you're welcome for me saving your life,* Dorian," Poppy said once she regained her breath, so conversational that he could have slapped her.

"And who was the one that actually lit the match, huh?"

"You'd never have escaped properly if I hadn't filled the place with gas."

"And now both of us have delayed death for – what, a few hours? Days, if we're lucky. Weeks, if the planets have somehow aligned to grant us all our wishes. If you had simply *left* with your stupid club then you might actually have had a chance at escaping all this!"

Poppy stared at him out of the corner of her eye; Dorian buried his head against the dirt and leaves and moss to avoid looking at her. "If I hadn't come back to help you you'd be dead," she said. "Is that what you wanted? To die?"

"Shut up, Poppy."

"I won't shut up!"

When Dorian felt Poppy move his arm away to clamber on top of him he had to fight every muscle in his aching body from throwing her off. But Poppy nuzzled her way against his neck, sliding her hand through his twisted horns and along his pointed ear until Dorian had no choice but to turn his head to meet her gaze.

"Don't touch my ear," he muttered.

"I'll touch it all I want, if it'll make you talk to me."

"It'll make me do more than talk to you and you know it."

"I'd call that progress, all things considered."

"Poppy—"

"You need to at least drink my blood, Dorian," Poppy cut in, throwing all ridiculous suggestions to one side. "From the looks of things you'd *never* experimented to see how long it takes my blood to affect your system...am I right?"

Dorian shook his head miserably, inhaling the smell of wet, green things as he did so. "I always meant to. I just...didn't."

"Then *drink* from me, and feel better. Then we can talk about what's next."

He didn't want to agree with Poppy – didn't want to do as she said. After everything that had happened it felt altogether like losing.

He turned and sat up anyway.

"You are the singular worst creature I have ever had the displeasure of meeting," Dorian muttered when Poppy sat in his lap, facing him, moving her rain-soaked hair over one shoulder to give him free access to her neck.

"And I thought the same of you, until today," Poppy retorted, just as Dorian dug his teeth into her neck and viciously sucked on it. "Jesus Christ, Dorian!" she exclaimed, clawing at his face in the process. "Not so hard! Not so—"

"I can do what I like," he said, surfacing from her neck just long enough to speak. Dorian's face was covered in blood, though he knew most of that was his own. "I had to have my throat slit *twice* for you. It was agonising sitting there, waiting for it to heal faster than I could die."

"Welcome to the club," she sobbed, though Poppy put up with the pain nonetheless. Eventually Dorian pulled away, yowling in frustration.

"If you just sit there putting up with it I can't fucking—"

"Don't tell me you've grown a conscience *now*, of all times?"

"You act as if I've never had one!"

"That's because you don't!"

Dorian pulled on her hair, dragging Poppy's face up until she was looking directly at him. "I do. Asking me to care about what happens to every member of your stupid club is like asking a human to look after and manually rear every cow they've ever eaten."

He was gratified to see Poppy beginning to grow unsure. "... you're really comparing humans to cattle, Dorian?"

"Are you not?" he replied, unperturbed. "I need to eat you to survive. The more physically fit you are the better it is for me to eat you. Tell me which part is different?"

Poppy reached up to slap him; Dorian caught her wrist in a clawed hand that could so easily snap it in two. Eventually her wrist grew limp. "A better comparison would be if humans ate gorillas, which we don't," she said, unexpectedly resigned.

"You absolutely would if they were your only food source."

"I wouldn't—"

"Don't even go there, Poppy," Dorian glowered, head dipped low over her own. "You and I both know it's an argument you cannot win. My kind needs to eat humans. *I* need to eat humans. Get over it or leave."

"Oh, so now you're telling me to leave?"

He crushed her against his chest with as much strength as he could muster. "Absolutely not. If I'm dying then you're dying with me. If that means stopping Nick or Aisling from stealing you away in the process then so be it."

Poppy froze in his arms. "...are they not dead?"

"What makes you think that – the fire?" Dorian laughed bitterly. "Fuck no. Those scales of Nick's will protect him against most anything, and Aisling escaped through the damn window before I could get a proper hit on her. It was only Steven who died and, trust me, it wasn't the fire that killed him."

A pause. "I'm sorry you had to kill your friend."

"No you're not."

"Are you sorry I had to kill *mine*?"

Another pause. "I guess not. Does that make us even?"

"No," Poppy said resolutely, reaching up and biting the end of Dorian's bloodied, broken-and-rehealed nose. "You've ruined my life. Nothing can ever make us 'even'."

"You've ruined mine!"

Poppy reached up on her knees until her face was level with

Dorian's. She ran her hands along the length and breadth of his intricate network of horns, even as Dorian wished he could tell her not to touch them.

"Then I guess we're just as stupidly matched as you always hoped we were," she said, the words sounding more like a curse than anything else.

Dorian wanted to push her away because of it – to vehemently reject everything that Poppy King had done to him. Everything he was going to *let* her get away with doing. Instead he ran a hand through her hair, enjoying the way Poppy winced at the sharp edges of his claws grazing her scalp.

"Where to next, then?" he asked, watching in suspicion when Poppy fidgeted and looked away. He frowned. "...what have you done?"

"I haven't done anything, *per se*," she mumbled, still not looking at him. "Though I may have swung Patrick over to the human side of my escape plan by way of Casey, and they *may* be waiting for us half a mile or so along the south-west shore of the loch."

Dorian felt like strangling her. He felt like strangling *himself.* For what did it say about him, that his best friend from childhood could be convinced to betray him for a human girl? But all Dorian had to do was look at Poppy – infuriating, damnable, deadly Poppy King – and his question was answered.

"Fine," he sighed, knowing that he'd hate every second of the next few days of his life – if he even lived that long. "Fine. Lead the way."

Poppy raised her eyebrows. "Are you sure?"

"No, but I have no other choice."

"You could stay here and die."

"Do you want that?"

"No."

"Then it's not a choice for me."

Poppy chewed on his words like they were particularly tough to digest though, in truth, they weren't. She simply didn't want to acknowledge the depth of Dorian's feelings for her – something which he had long since made peace with.

And so, in true Poppy King style, she ignored those feelings, just as Dorian allowed her to get away with ignoring them...for now. They both had a lot they had to answer for, but neither could do so if they were dead. But one thing was certain as Poppy crept out of the forest, Dorian following closely behind as if he didn't know each and every one of the trees surrounding them like the back of his own hand.

Whether today or a hundred years from now, Poppy King would be the death of him.

EPILOGUE: FRIENDS ON BOTH SIDES

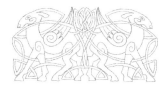

POPPY

IF ANYONE WAS TO EVER ASK Poppy King what her idea of hell was, it would be the exact scene unfolding in front of her very eyes.

She, Dorian, Casey and Patrick sat on one side of a gloomy café booth, whilst Andrew, Nate, Rachelle and Fred sat on the opposite side. Poppy couldn't believe Casey had signed her up to such a meeting against her will.

"So...you're not *dead*, which is always a good place to start," Fred murmured, grimacing as he took a sip of his murky, discoloured cappuccino. Beneath the table Poppy kicked him, even though he was sitting as far away as possible from her.

"Why are you here, Sampson?" Dorian outright demanded, in lieu of asking how anybody had been coping since escaping from his murder camp masquerading as a sports retreat.

"Because he wants answers, just like us!" Rachelle said, which was the most confrontational thing Poppy had ever heard her say to Dorian.

He stared at Poppy, agape, pointing at Fred as he did so. "You can't be serious, Poppy. You *can't* be serious."

Rachelle's brow furrowed. "What do you mean?"

"What do you mean 'what do I mean'? Do *none* of you know what Sampson did, aside from Andrew?"

"Dorian, don't do this right—"

"Shut up, Poppy."

"Don't talk to her like that!" Nate exclaimed, immediately furious. Poppy avoided his eyes. She had to.

"I'll talk to her however I want, all things considered," Dorian replied, icily calm. "Isn't that right, Poppy?"

A single glance at Dorian's right hand, shaking slightly around the cup of coffee he'd never drink, was indication enough that she shouldn't push him right now.

"Nate, lay off," she said, waving him down when it seemed like he might protest. "A lot has happened that justifies the *shitty way* Dorian is treating me right now."

It was Dorian who kicked her leg beneath the table this time.

"Which brings me back to my original question," Dorian said smoothly, as if Nate and Poppy had never interrupted him. "Why is it that, out of everyone at this table, *I'm* the villain, when Fred is sitting right there?"

Out of the corner of her eye Poppy saw Andrew and Dorian exchange a look of understanding, which was precisely one more look than Andrew had given Poppy since they'd entered the café.

It was Casey who spoke next, reaching over to take Poppy's trembling hand before Poppy herself knew she was shaking.

"Dorian, what the hell are you talking about? Fred, what is he talking about?"

"I don't want them to know!" Poppy blurted out.

Just as Fred exclaimed, "I tried to kill her!"

Poppy aimed for his knee this time when she kicked him; Fred recoiled just in time. "You fucking *fool,*" she muttered, so angry she felt inclined to throw Fred's coffee in his face.

But Fred held her gaze as if he had done nothing wrong. "They all deserve to know," he said. "The fact they didn't know before now is insane."

"Trying to kill her makes it sound like Sampson made *one* attempt and failed," Dorian spat out bitterly. Beside him Patrick dug into his arms with short, stubby nails, but Poppy knew it was enough to keep him grounded. "Andrew, care to tell your oblivious friends what it was you found in the kitchen, when you came crying to me for help?"

Poppy slapped Dorian on reflex. "Don't you *dare* drag Andrew into this, you sick son of a—"

"You're calling me sick when Sampson is literally sitting *right there* and—"

"Stop it stop it stop it stop it stop it!"

It was Andrew who spoke. Of course it was Andrew who spoke. Poppy ached at the sound of his voice, and how much she wished it was only the two of them talking right now. Not for the first time she acknowledged that, though Rachelle had been her best friend all throughout university, and Casey was the one who could empathise best with what Poppy was going through right now, it was Andrew who was truly Poppy's closest friend. Even that didn't seem enough to describe their relationship properly.

Poppy wasn't sure anything ever would.

"Andrew, I'm sorry—" Poppy began, but Andrew spoke over

her, addressing nobody in particular.

"I went looking for Poppy at four in the morning because I couldn't sleep and she didn't respond when I knocked on her door so I went to look for her and when I reached the kitchen the light was on and Fred had stabbed her with a knife so many times all I could see was red and *I had to clean it up.*"

The fact Andrew had missed out arguably the most important section of the story would have made Poppy laugh if not for the looks of horror spreading on most everybody's faces, even Patrick. Clearly Dorian had never divulged what happened to his best friend, though Poppy knew for a fact he'd immediately told him about having slept with her in the forest.

Interesting choice of subjects to spill and keep secret from your best friend, she mused, though Poppy supposed she could hardly judge Dorian when she caught sight of Rachelle's ashen, desolate face. She was looking at Fred as if he were a stranger.

"How could you?" she whispered. "How many times did I talk to you about leaving Poppy alone? *How many times* did I —"

"It wouldn't have mattered how many times you told me, Rachelle," Fred said. Poppy hated how genuinely sad he sounded. "I'd have done it anyway."

"What's wrong with you? What's wrong with *all* of you?!" Nate demanded, standing up from the booth as if he couldn't bear to sit with them any more. He turned to Poppy. "Morph, I'm so sorry you had to deal with all of this. I'm so, so sorry. I can't believe I stopped talking to you just 'cause I was hurt you didn't like me back. It was so fucking childish of me, when the whole time you were dealing with – this!" He waved a hand towards everyone but Rachelle.

"And you!" he continued, rounding on Dorian despite the audience they were quickly gathering. "How could you do this to her? Even if you didn't give a damn about the rest of us, how could you spend so much time with Poppy and *still* put her through what you did? Do you have no feelings at all?"

"No," Dorian said dourly. Poppy elbowed him in the ribs; Dorian gently whacked her round the head and deftly moved away from the booth to avoid her fist when she aimed it at his shoulder.

He walked right into Nate's.

"Oh for fuck's *sake!*" he complained, holding a hand against his nose as he glared at Nate. "That was it. That was your one shot. I hope it was worth it."

"You massacred our club, you son of a bitch. It'll never be —"

"Nate, Dorian, sit down and stop arguing for five minutes!"

"Why should we?!"

"*Fine;* argue like children until you fucking die for all I care!" Poppy screamed, storming out of the café with what felt like a million pairs of eyes following her but was, in fact, more like twenty. She didn't have to look behind her to know that Andrew was following closely behind, only stopping when Poppy herself dropped onto a bench overlooking the turbulent waves of the Firth of Clyde.

"You didn't bring your jacket," Andrew said simply as he sat beside her, taking off his own jacket and proffering it to Poppy. She shook her head, but when Andrew placed the jacket over both of them Poppy edged closer to him.

They sat in silence, but it wasn't awkward. It was almost like old times.

Almost.

"I'm sorry, Andrew," Poppy said after a while. Her words were barely audible over the wind and waves. "I'm sorry for all of them in there, acting the way they're acting. For leaving you. For letting you get on the damn boat to Dorian's facility in the first place. Everything."

"You're only responsible for one of those things."

"Yeah, and that's the worst one."

"So why did you do it?"

Poppy turned her head; Andrew's face was furious and confused. All she wanted to do was cry. "Why did you leave, Poppy?" he asked once more. "Why did you leave when—"

"I wish I could tell you why," she said, leaning towards Andrew until their foreheads were touching. "I really do. But I don't exactly know why I did it...only that I had to."

Andrew's earnest eyes were so close Poppy could see flecks of gold in his brown irises. She didn't like that she could see herself reflected in them, so she tried to look away.

Andrew's hands came up to stop Poppy's head from turning.

"Do you love Dorian?"

"Andrew—"

"Don't *Andrew* me, Poppy. I'm not a child. I'm not your brother. Do you love him?"

"Andrew, please—"

"Do you?!"

"No!" Poppy bit out, too loudly considering how close the two of them were. "I don't love him, Andrew. How could I?"

He frowned. "But then why—"

"I already told you I don't understand why I went back. Don't you trust me?"

"I did! I do! I just...I thought you might be lying to me."

Poppy raised a hand and gently placed it over one of Andrew's. When she squeezed it he returned the pressure.

"When have I ever lied to you, Andrew?" Poppy asked,

very softly.

"Never. You've never lied to me."

"So why would I start now?"

"Poppy, we need to go."

"Fuck off, Dorian," Poppy replied immediately in response to the man's clearly deliberate interruption.

"Poppy—"

"I heard you, so give me a minute!"

Andrew flung his arms around Poppy's neck before she could move away. "Don't go, Poppy," he begged. "Don't go with him. You'll never be safe if you go with him."

"And *you'll* never be safe if I stay with you," Poppy said, pulling away from Andrew in order to stand up.

"I don't care about that," he replied. Poppy hated that it was the truth. "I don't care that—"

"She can't stay with you, Andrew, so stop making this harder on her than it already is," Dorian said, talking over Andrew as loudly as possible. Poppy glared at him. Dorian merely glared right back, arms crossed tightly against the cold. "We *do* have to go, Poppy. You know as well as I do that—"

"I know, I know!" She glanced back at Andrew. "I'll get in touch as soon as I can, okay? I can't promise when that'll be - I just promise that I *will*. Can you live with that?"

Andrew nodded miserably. "I'm going to have to, won't I?"

Poppy squeezed his hand once more, then fled down the street with Dorian towards the ferry that would take them back to the mainland. She swore loudly when a wave crashed onto the pavement, soaking her up to her knees.

"Serves you right for feeding Andrew so much false hope," Dorian muttered.

"What do you mean, *false hope*? I really will be in contact as soon as I can!"

He merely shook his head, laughing incredulously. "The more I get to know you – really, truly know you – the stupider you seem. How can you not see how much Andrew loves you?"

Poppy paused on the spot long enough for another wave to hit her; she didn't care. The salt water that filled her mouth only seemed appropriate given what Dorian was saying. "Don't joke about things like that!" she complained, a beat too late, though somewhere deep inside Poppy knew he wasn't lying.

"Fine. If you want to remain wilfully ignorant and forever run from your problems then be my guest. It's not like I have to be around to witness you doing so or anything."

"You could *leave.*"

"And yet I won't and you know I won't."

Poppy felt like banging her head repeatedly upon the beaten metal railings surrounding the ferry's upper deck after they boarded. "You can't complain all the time if you're staying with me."

"I can, and I will."

"Why are you so obstinate?!"

"And why are you so self-absorbed you literally cannot see how people feel about you when it's staring you right in the face?!"

Poppy opened her mouth to reply. She thought about what to say – about everything she *could* say, especially after her conversation with Andrew.

Instead she said nothing.

"I never thought I'd be happy to see the back of Scotland," Dorian finally sighed, when it became apparent he'd won the argument by virtue of Poppy not replying. She knew it was his least favourite kind of victory.

"Where to next?" Poppy asked. She looked at him standing by her side, tall, windswept, infuriatingly handsome and maddeningly Dorian.

He shrugged.

"Wherever you'd like to go."

COMING SOON

INSATIABLE MONSTERS

FRED

A WEEK HAD PASSED SINCE FRED and everyone else met up with Poppy and Dorian. A week. Seven days. One hundred and sixty-eight hours.

It felt like a lifetime.

The month following the Outdoor Sports Society's escape from Dorian's facility had, conversely, passed by in a blur. There had been so much to deal with: police reports, interviews, hospital check-ups, teary family reunions and, above all else, the shock of their entire terrifying summer to wrap their heads around.

But now the worst of that was over, and most of Fred's questions had now been answered thanks to Dorian and Patrick. Which left...nothing.

Fred had no idea what to do next with his life. It felt like a distant, ridiculously banal dream that he'd ever tortured himself with what came next after university regarding his career. For all Fred cared now he could happily *never* have a career. A steady income and a secure place to live were insignificant goals in the grand scheme of things.

For how could he worry about a job where there were monsters lurking in the dark, waiting to tear him limb-from-limb whilst he screamed for his life to be spared? He shuddered simply thinking about it. And yet that fear was nothing compared to the terror Fred's memories of ripping Poppy apart instilled.

He had done that. Not a monster.

Not for the first time Fred wondered if that qualified him as one.

Yet there was no physical sign Poppy had ever been hurt by Fred, thanks to her blood. Dorian had called it immortal. The idea still baffled him, all things considered, for how did Poppy King of all people end up with such a wonderful, tragic, dangerous ability?

He was desperate to fully understand how it worked. Perhaps that desperation was a result of Fred's well-honed instinct to research all things unusual – an instinct shared with Poppy, given their six years of forcibly studying for identical biology degrees together.

He wondered how much Poppy actually knew about it herself. How did it feel, to have such a substance coursing through her veins? Did it feel different than regular blood? Could Poppy even feel a difference between the two?

But it was too late to find out now. Poppy and Dorian – as well as Casey and Patrick – made no mention of when Fred and Andrew and Rachelle and Nate would see them again. For all Fred knew he'd forever be left in the dark about the subject of immortal blood.

"Frederick Sampson."

He froze. Fred recognised the sultry, low, feminine voice that spoke. But it was out of place: a voice from another, nightmarish time. Reluctantly he turned to face the woman who had spoken.

Aisling smiled broadly, her perfect teeth gleaming.

"You here to eat me or something?" Fred asked, his voice flat and dispassionate despite the throbbing of his heart and the adrenaline coursing through his body.

"Maybe later. I have a job for you first, though."

Interest piqued despite himself, Fred muttered, "What kind of job?"

Aisling's dangerous smile grew wider. "A manhunt, if you will. Help me find Dorian Kapros and Poppy King."

Acknowledgements

Hey everyone, and thanks for making it to the end of this bizarre, genre-hopping book of madness. I don't actually really know what to say.

The inspiration for this came in the form of a very lucid dream back in August 2018, which I promptly noted down as soon as I woke up. When I finally got round to looking at the notes properly I realised at least half of what I wrote made zero sense.

Anyway...

After some careful planning and character development I came up with *Invisible Monsters*. It was supposed to be a one-off book but I very quickly grew far too attached to the characters, and there was so much story left to be explored. Hence it became a series! Books two and three have a bit more of a dark urban fantasy vibe mainly because they're not limited to one singular location.

Invisible Monsters is set in Scotland, in case that wasn't obvious. I know broadly where I *imagine* Dorian's facility is, though it's unlikely something could ever get built there. I guess that's what fiction is for. I really like setting my stories in places I know, so when the characters start moving about in book two they'll be going to places I've been to *laughs*. Barcelona, anyone?

I don't really know who is *supposed* to be the protagonist in the story. At first glance it's Poppy, and I suppose she is. But if you look at it from Dorian's perspective *he's* the protagonist, and if you look at it from Andrew's perspective he's...okay, you get it. Actually, Andrew will always be the protagonist, or certainly at least the 'hero' of the story (and my heart). If anything happened to Andrew I'd kill everyone in the room and then myself, even if I was responsible for killing him and therefore the only person in the room, because Andrew doesn't exist.

What a sad thought, though in reality it's a reassuring one, since I'd rather there weren't monsters lurking our streets even if it also means Andrew doesn't exist. However, as the ever insightful Clopin in Disney's *Hunchback of Notre Dame* asks us, "What makes the monster and what makes the man?"

I really hope *Invisible Monsters* explored that dichotomy appropriately, or at least started to. I shall continue doing so in the second book, so please bear with me as I muddle through scary things like themes and character arcs and, you know, story in general.

I'd of course like to thank (because this is, in fact, an acknowledgements section) my partner Jake, our wonderful pets, and each and every one of you out there who decided to pick up this book and read it to the end. But most of all I'd like to thank Kirsty, because this book is for her. What a bizarre token of my platonic affection: fictional, ravenous, murderous monsters.

Oh well.

Until the next one!

P.S. This book is littered with awful references to various books, films and television shows. Let me know if you spotted any!

ABOUT THE AUTHOR

Hayley Louise Macfarlane hails from the very tiny hamlet of Balmaha on the shores of Loch Lomond in Scotland. After graduating with a PhD in molecular genetics she did a complete 180 and moved into writing fiction. Though she loves writing multiple genres (fantasy, romance, sci-fi, psychological fiction and horror so far!) she is most widely known for her Gothic, Scottish fairy tale, Prince of Foxes – book one of the Bright Spear trilogy.

You can follow her on Twitter at @HLMacfarlane.

Also by H. L. Macfarlane

Fairy Tale Shared Universe:
Bright Spear Trilogy
Prince of Foxes
Lord of Horses
King of Forever

Dark Spear Duology
Son of Silver (Coming 2023)
Heir of Gold (Coming 2023)

All I Want for Christmas is a Faerie Assassin?!

Chronicles of Curses
Big, Bad Mister Wolfe
Snowstorm King
The Tower Without a Door

Other books:
Gold and Silver Duology
Intended
Revival (release date TBC)

Monsters Trilogy
Invisible Monsters
Insatiable Monsters (Coming October 2022)

INVINCIBLE MONSTERS (COMING 2023)

THRILLERS
THE BOY FROM THE SEA

ROM-COMS
THE UNBALANCED EQUATION
COURTNEY CAN'T DECIDE (RELEASE DATE TBC)

SHORT STORIES
THE SNOWDROP (PART OF ONCE UPON A WINTER: A FOLK AND
FAIRY TALE ANTHOLOGY)
THE GOAT
THE BOY WHO DID NOT FIT

Printed in Great Britain
by Amazon